"ARIANNA AND RAINE ARE TWO
IMPASSIONED LOVERS WHO WILL MAKE
YOU LAUGH AND CRY AND KEEP YOU
READING AND GUESSING UNTIL THE
LAST PAGE. KEEPER OF THE DREAM IS A
GRIPPING NOVEL, DON'T MISS IT."
—CATHERINE COULTER

THE FATEFUL VISION

The bard's bowl, when she touched it, felt warm against her palms. For a moment she thought it glowed with a strange, pulsating light. . . . Not wanting to, still she lifted the bowl and looked . . . and knew this time the vision would come.

She made one final, desperate effort to resist. But the force of the vision, so ancient and so powerful, was too strong for her. She looked down, down into the bowl's glimmering depths—and the water swirled and eddied, darkening into a pool of blood.

The bloody pool whirled faster, sucking her in. She clenched the bowl with a white-knuckled grip. A blinding mist rose up from the vortex of the spinning liquid, searing her eyes with its brightness. A final mewl of protest pushed through her lips as the clang of sword against sword battered her ears . . . and death screams carried on the howling wind. She smelled the tang of hot metal, the acrid sweat of fear. . . .

A mailed knight burst out of the swirling mists. His horse reared, pawing the air, and for a moment he was silhouetted, large and menacing, against a slate sky. He raised his mighty lance and a gust of wind snapped at the pennon, unfurling it against leaden clouds—a black dragon on a bloodred field. With a cry of triumph he whirled and charged. . . .

Penelope Williamson

Keeper of the Dream

A DELL BOOK

Published by
Dell Publishing
a division of
Bantam Doubleday Dell Publishing Group, Inc.
666 Fifth Avenue
New York, New York 10103

The trademark Dell® is registered in the U.S. Patent and Trademark Office.

ISBN: 0-440-21107-7

Printed in the United States of America

Published simultaneously in Canada

May 1992

10 9 8 7 6 5 4 3 2 1

RAD

For Derek,
Keeper of my dreams . . . and of my heart.

Their Lord they shall praise,
Their language they shall keep,
Their land they shall lose,
Except Wild Wales.

> —Prophecy attributed to the great Welsh
> bard Taliesin, who lived in the sixth
> century . . . and perhaps
> in other times as well.

1

Wales, 1157

The wind carried with it the stench of burning thatch and the anguished wail of a woman's scream.

A knight on horseback rode through the sacked town. The wind sent an ell of bright ruby silk floating toward him down the muddy road. The cloth snagged a moment on a broken cartwheel before a gust whipped it free, and it was trampled unnoticed beneath his charger's hooves. But when a pack of squealing rats darted into the road from a smoldering hayrick, the horse reared in alarm. The knight controlled the enormous black beast easily and without thought.

He passed a wall of burning timber, and the flames flickered in the sheen of sweat on his face, flaring in his flint-gray eyes. A spearman darted in front of him, waving a pitch-soaked brand. Laughing, the man called out the knight's name as he put the torch to a hovel roof and the straw ignited into a fountain of fire. A hail of cinders and shrieks of terror swirled up from inside. But the knight rode on.

The door of a nearby cottage burst open and an archer reeled across the threshold. He stumbled into the knight's path to sprawl facedown in a puddle, a ploughman's sickle buried in his back. Rivulets of blood, like spilled wine, ran from his outstretched hands. A sobbing girl crawled after him. Her tunic was ripped down the front, baring small, blue-veined breasts. Yet the knight passed her by without sparing a glance—just as he failed to see the discarded loot of dented pots and burst sacks of grain that littered the way before him.

On he rode with single-minded purpose out the town's battered gate, where he pulled up within the shadow of the wall.

His brooding gaze followed the rutted road where it wound along the river toward a castle. In the gray twilight the castle's sandstone walls took on the black-red color of dried blood. It loomed thick and heavy against the rain-sodden clouds, but in the tower, light glowed from a solitary window.

"Rhuddlan . . ."

The knight spoke the castle's name aloud, but there was no inflection in his voice. Just as his face—though streaked with marks from his helm and splattered with another man's blood—bore no expression. It could have belonged to an effigy on a tomb.

He stared a long time at the keep with its frail speck of light. When at last he turned away, it was with a savage, parting promise. . . .

Rhuddlan, you will be mine.

Behind the shuttered window where a light still burned, a young woman cradled a bowl in her palms. It was fashioned of gold and rimmed with a band of pearls, and for a moment, as she held it, the vessel seemed to glow softly and pulse in her hands. But though she calmed her mind and peered into the bowl's luminescent depths, she beheld only water and a shimmering reflection of the cresset lamps swinging on the wall above her head.

A rough voice barked in her ear. "Do you see anything yet?"

Arianna jerked, slopping water onto her rose silk bliaut. She set the bowl down onto a nearby chest with a clatter, and wiped at the growing wet stain on her skirt. Tossing a fat brown braid over her shoulder, she glared at her brother.

"God's death. Nothing is likely to happen with you peering at me like a nervous priest in an alchemist's shop. As if you expected to see brimstone come curling out my ears at any moment."

"What I expect is for you to tell me what I need to know." He spun away from her, then turned back, flinging out his arm and pointing a stiff finger in her face. "You wear the seer's torque around your neck, yet you are next to useless when it comes to *seeing* anything."

Unconsciously, Arianna touched the ancient collar that encircled her throat. It was of bronze—two twisted snakes, their heads meeting in the center with flicking tongues and staring emerald eyes—and in that moment it felt as if they were strangling her. But she tilted up her chin and matched her brother's anger with her own. "And what of you, Ceidro? You wear a man's sword around your waist, yet I don't see you acting the part of a man on this night."

A dark flush spread over Ceidro's cheeks. Hunching his shoulders, he turned away from her, and Arianna regretted her hasty words. She went to him and laid her palm against his rigid back. "I tried, Ceidro. But you know it doesn't work that way. The visions never come on command."

Ceidro said nothing. Nor did he turn around. Arianna fought back another urge to shout at him. She didn't want to argue with her brother. It was frustration that caused them to snap at one another. Frustration and fear. Ceidro knew well the visions had never once come when summoned. And when they did appear, rare and unexpected, they often left her feeling ill and terrified, having revealed things she'd sooner not know. But her brother, too, was afraid. He wanted her to look into the future and tell him whether he would prevail in the battle he had to fight on the morrow.

She forced him to turn and meet her eyes. She tried a smile. "It's the cursed Gwynedd temper. But we shouldn't be fighting one another. Not now."

Ceidro retrieved the bowl and thrust it at her. "Then try again."

Arianna looked down at the golden vessel, but she didn't touch it. It was a mazer, a drinking bowl, and centuries old. One day two years ago a mysterious bard had arrived at her father's court, saying that he'd heard of the Prince of Gwynedd's daughter, how she wore the seer's torque and possessed the *filid*'s gift of prophecy. He had given Arianna the bowl and told her it had once belonged to Myrddin, the greatest magician and seer who had ever lived. But though she kept it with her always and though the visions continued to appear, sporadic and unbidden, in every mundane medium of water imaginable, from a bathing tub to a rain puddle, Arianna had never been able to call forth a single glimpse of the future in the bard's so-called magic mazer.

So now Arianna lifted her head to tell her brother that it was no use, but the sight of him stilled her words. In the soft light his thin, beardless face looked pathetically young. Like her, he possessed the Gwynedd features of pointed chin, sharp cheekbones, and wide-spaced, seafoam eyes. Tonight, fear showed in those eyes. And lingering traces of a bitter grief. Only a month ago his young wife had died in childbed, and he'd barely had time to mourn before he found himself defending this border *cantref* and castle against an enemy force twice as large and more powerful than his. And he was but twenty, only a year older than she.

Ceidro pushed the curved edge of the mazer against her chest. "Are you going to cooperate with me, or no?"

Arianna swallowed hard, forcing a smile. "I'll try again. But mind, you quit hovering over me like an anxious midwife."

She was reaching for the bowl when a gust of wind ripped through the thin parchment windowpane, loosening a shutter. It slammed against the wall with a loud bang and Ceidro whirled, his hand flying to his sword.

He flashed Arianna a sheepish smile as he returned the mazer to the chest and strode across the rush-covered floor to refasten the latch. But he stiffened when he reached the window and his hand wrapped around the wooden shutter in a crushing grip. "God . . ."

"What? What is happening?" That morning the scouts had reported the enemy was on the march, but miles away. Yet through the rent in the window Arianna suddenly smelled smoke and heard an hysterical clanging of church bells from the village that lay between the castle and the sea. "Ceidro?"

"Christ Jesus save us," Ceidro said on an intake of breath.

Arianna's mouth went dry and her knees trembled as she joined her brother at the window. The town below was ablaze, gilding the lowering clouds and the distant sea with an iridescent glow. Flaming brands were reflected in the blades of countless weapons, flickering like hundreds of fireflies against a night sky. As they watched, a woman fled up the road toward the castle, a knight on a white charger pounding after her. Arianna held her breath, expecting the man to cut the woman down with a slash of his sword, but instead he leaned over and jerked the woman up by her arm, throwing her facedown across his saddlebows.

"God curse the English and their Norman masters," she whispered, almost choking over the fury that squeezed her chest.

Ceidro stirred beside her and Arianna heard an answering tremor of hatred in his voice. "Aye . . . God curse them all." Then he added fervently the oft-repeated prayer: "And God grant the Cymry victory."

Though outsiders called their land Wales, the people who dwelled within its dark forests and misty mountains called it Cymru. They called themselves the Cymry, and they could not remember a time when there hadn't been war. All their lives and the lives of their fathers and grandfathers had been spent in a desperate struggle for their freedom against first the Saxons and then the Norman invaders. Still they believed and they dreamed of liberty, and the bards sang of a time when the great King Arthur would arise from the Isle of Avalon, where he slept, to lead their people in one final and victorious battle against their enemies.

The bards sang, too, of Arianna's family. Of the House of Cunedda, lords of Gwynedd, direct descendents of the great heroes of Britain. The sons and daughters of Gwynedd were the embodiment of the past and the caretakers of the future. They ruled over a quarter of Wales and their duty was to keep the dream of freedom alive.

But it was at times like these, Arianna thought as she watched the town burn, that it was easy to despair.

Behind them, the door crashed open beneath a heavy fist. Their cousin, Madog, stood beneath the arched entrance, his peaked helmet brushing against the curved stones, his big hand curled around a longbow. He looked huge in his quilted leather gambeson with its thick layers of rag padding.

"The high-and-mighty bastards have sent a messenger demanding our surrender," he reported, a sneer curling the thick lips beneath his drooping mustache. "They've promised the villeins and cotters will be released—unharmed they say, though we know how the maggots do lie." He snorted. "All freemen are to be ransomed, of course. And they want an answer within the hour."

Ceidro's face grew even paler, but he said nothing. Madog waited, the tense flexing of the hand that gripped his longbow his only movement. *Of course we will never surrender,* Arianna thought. But it was Ceidro's place to answer the insulting challenge.

Above the moans of the rising wind, Arianna could hear the blare of trumpets and the shouts and pounding feet of the men being summoned to defend the battlements. "Tell the Norman cur we will never surrender," she prompted her brother. "Not as long as there is a man or woman in this castle left alive to draw breath. Am I not right, Ceidro?"

Ceidro started as if awakening from a trance. "Aye . . ." His lips thinned into a tense grimace. "Tell him we'd rather burn in hell. Or better yet, simply cut off his messenger's head and toss it back to him over the ramparts."

Madog showed his teeth in a wide grin and turned to go. But Ceidro stopped him. "Wait, there's something else. I . . ." He flicked his tongue across his upper lip. "How do you reckon they got to us so fast? I thought Father's army was supposed to be between here and the English border."

Madog shrugged his hulking shoulders. "They came up the coast by boat. And they've brought a lot of equipment with 'em—catapults, sappers, scaling ladders, and the like. 'Tis my thought they aim to put us under siege." He flashed another white-toothed grin. "But we'll be all right, if we hold them off long enough for your da an' your brothers to whip King Henry's puny army."

Ceidro's head jerked in a nod and Arianna suddenly felt safe here, deep within the keep. The freestanding tower was made of stone and mortar and around it wrapped a tall shell wall. The whole of this keep stood within the heart of the bailey atop a motte—an enormous and steeply-sided man-made mound. And all of *this* was surrounded by a wide stone curtain wall that fairly bristled with battlements of arrow loops, merlons, crenels, and hoardings.

Surely, Arianna told herself, the only way such a fortress could be taken would be through guile or starvation. And there was a six-month supply of salt beef, wheat, and ale in the storerooms below.

"Aye, we'll be all right," Ceidro said, echoing her thoughts. "As long as we hang on."

Once more Madog turned to go, but then he hesitated. "Did ye happen to catch sight of the banner yon Normans are flyin'?"

Ceidro's glance flicked back to the open window. "It's dark and I—"

" 'Tis a black dragon on a red field."

"Black dragon . . ." Arianna repeated in a harsh whisper.

The Black Dragon . . . Sir Raine the Bastard . . . from the Holy Land to Ireland, mothers invoked his image to frighten their children into obedience and young squires spoke his name with awe. He was the base-born result of a union between the powerful Earl of Chester and a castle whore. A knight-errant, without land, he supported himself by ransoming prisoners taken in tournaments and wars, and sold himself and his army to the highest bidder. Ruthless in battle and merciless in victory, he was said to have sold his soul to the devil in exchange for a supernatural prowess with the sword and the lance.

He was said to be invincible.

Ceidro stared at the thick iron-banded door long after it had closed behind Madog's broad back. In the lengthening silence Arianna could hear the hiss of the coals in the brazier and the persistent groan of the wind. She hoped it would storm tonight. She hoped a summer gale would whip in from the sea and the skies would dump rain so that the Black Dragon—whose body at least must be human, even if his soul was the devil's—would be wet and miserable.

Arianna watched her brother pace the room, from the great curtained lord's bed to the glowing bronze brazier and back again. His shadow loomed then receded on the blue and gold-spangled walls. Of all her madly brave and reckless brothers, Ceidro was the gentle one. His temperament wasn't suited to war; he couldn't even bring himself to slit the throat of a wounded stag. He would be no match for the Black Dragon and he knew it. She pitied him for the uncertainty and fear he must be feeling.

"Cross of Christ!" Ceidro exploded. He kicked a stool, sending it skidding across the floor to bang against the footboard of the great bed. "How am I supposed to keep this castle with only a handful of men?"

Arianna spoke his name softly. "Father wouldn't have put Rhuddlan in your hands if he didn't have faith in you."

He paused before her, stroking her cheek. "Poor little sister. You should be safe at home, not caught up in this mess with me. I shouldn't have asked you to come . . ." His voice trailed off. They were both remembering that she had come to help with the lying-in for his first child, and that she had stayed to comfort him after the birth had gone so horribly and tragically wrong.

"You know how I relish a chance to fight the cursed Normans." Wrapping her arms around his waist, she held him tight, knowing she received more comfort than she gave. "The Black Dragon has never taken on the House of Gwynedd before. Come the morrow, he'll be sorry for it. He'll be feeling like a honey thief caught in a swarm of bees."

Ceidro emitted a shaky laugh. "Aye, you're right." He pulled away from her. "And now I had better go see to my defenses, such as they are. Arianna . . ." He hesitated. "If the castle should fall—"

"It won't fall."

"But if it does, I might be too busy to look after you.

Or I might . . ." He didn't finish, but Arianna knew what he meant. He might be dead.

"I can take care of myself," she said, though in truth she could already taste fear in her mouth, like the aftermath of a bitter draught.

Ceidro's eyes crinkled with genuine amusement. "Aye, that you can. In a close fight you're probably more lethal than I am." They shared a smile, both remembering all the trouble Arianna had brought on herself while growing up by trying to mimic the daring feats and athletic skills of her nine brothers.

Then Arianna's face grew serious. "I know what my duty is, Ceidro. I will never forget my duty." She was Prince Owain of Gwynedd's daughter. She would not beggar her family by allowing herself to be captured and ransomed. She would not shame them by letting herself be raped.

Brother and sister stared at one another a moment longer, each lost in thought. Then Arianna flashed a sudden grin and punched her brother on the arm hard enough to make him wince. "Now go see to your army, my lord. Before the battle is won without you."

Though she kept her smile in place until her brother was out the door, Arianna didn't feel nearly so brave now that she was alone. She found herself going again and again to the window, but except for sputtering and intermittent flames swirling up against the black sky, it had grown too dark to see anything. In between trips to the window, her gaze kept falling on the golden mazer. She told herself it was only tension and fear that made her feel as if the useless bowl was beckoning her. She didn't want to know the future anyway, not if it was going to be bad. She didn't want to know, didn't want to . . .

The bowl, when she touched it, felt warm against her palms. For a moment she thought it glowed with a strange, pulsating light, but in the next instant she decided it must be an illusion—a draft causing the flames of the torches in the brackets on the wall to sputter and flicker, bouncing off the bowl's shiny surface. And yet not wanting to, she lifted the bowl and looked . . . and knew this time the vision would come.

She made one final, desperate effort to resist, turning her head aside. But the force of the vision, so ancient and so powerful, was too strong for her. She looked down, down into the bowl's glimmering depths . . .

And the water swirled and eddied, darkening into a pool of blood.

The bloody pool whirled faster, sucking her in. She clenched the bowl with a white-knuckled grip. A blinding mist rose up from the vortex of the spinning liquid, searing her eyes with its brightness. A final mewl of protest pushed through her lips, as the clang of sword against sword battered her ears . . . and death screams carried on a howling wind. She smelled the tang of hot metal, the acrid sweat of fear. . . .

A mailed knight burst out of the swirling mists. His horse reared, pawing the air, and for a moment he was silhouetted, large and menacing, against a slate sky. He raised his mighty lance and a gust of wind snapped at the pennon, unfurling it against leaden clouds—a black dragon on a bloodred field. With a cry of triumph he whirled and charged.

The hooves of his black steed shook the ground. Closer he came, close enough for her to see the fury in his flint-gray eyes, the set of ruthless determination on his hard mouth. He lowered his lance, pointing it at her heart, and her mouth opened on a silent scream, as if she could already feel the sharp tip piercing her.

Thunder cracked in her ears. A lightning bolt slashed across the lowering clouds, striking the burnished spearpoint, and in the second before the steel tip impaled her, shattering the vision into a thousand shards of light. . . .

The smell of sweet rosemary filled her nose and something tickled her cheek. She opened her eyes and saw straw and the three bronze clawed feet of the brazier. For a moment she felt drugged and bemused, and she pushed herself to her knees, swaying dizzily. She waited for the room to stop spinning, then groped for a stool, dragging herself to her feet. White-hot flashes of pain sizzled across her eyes and vomit rose in her throat. She barely made it into the garderobe before she was violently sick.

She retched and heaved until she thought she would pass out again. She had always felt slightly dizzy and nauseated after one of her visions, but it had never been this bad. The image of the charging knight kept flashing across her mind in staccato bursts, like sparks from a blacksmith's anvil. Groaning, she pressed her fingers against her throbbing temples and stumbled to the bed.

The painted walls with their floral motif spun and whirled. Vines, petals, tendrils curled and undulated, reaching out for her. She shut her eyes on a moan, then immediately opened them again to stare at the blue sendal canopy overhead. The marten-fur coverlet felt cool against her fevered skin. Her stomach clenched and for a moment she thought she would be sick again.

Slowly the nausea receded, but the fierce hammering in her head remained. After a moment, when she was sure she could stand without fainting, she arose on quaking legs to prepare a quick poultice of peony root mixed with rose oil. She soaked a linen rag in the mixture and pressed it against her head. The pounding subsided to a dull ache.

She lay back on the bed. Below in the bailey the watchman's horn was answered by the trumpeter of the guard. All was well, or as well as things could be with an enemy army camped outside the gate. Yet she was afraid to shut her eyes, afraid the image of the knight would return.

That vision . . . it had been unlike any that had come before. The others had been of distant, shadowy figures reflected in pools of water, some so vague she had been unable afterward to interpret what she had seen. But this one . . . she had been *in* this one. She had smelled the hot metal, heard the pounding hooves, and felt the lance tip piercing . . . oh God, but it had seemed so real. She had *been* there.

Turning her head, she stared at the tall wax candle beside the bed. It was supposed to burn all night, to keep away evil spirits. She almost laughed at the irony. Imagine the Black Dragon, that limb of hell, being kept at bay by the light of a solitary candle. Still, though the candle's flame stabbed at her eyes, she did not draw the curtains around the bed.

The wind, which had been buffeting the keep all night, suddenly ceased. The promised storm had blown itself out, which was a pity, for the God-cursed Normans would not get wet after all. She wondered if she should tell her brother about the vision, but it would avail him nothing and only add to his anxiety. Besides, the threat presented by the charging knight was to her, not Ceidro. She pressed her hand to her heart, as if she could feel the lance point piercing her.

Her legs jerked and she twisted onto her side, burying her face in the bolster. But behind her clenched lids she saw a knight in black armor charging with lowered lance. And a long time later, after she finally slept, she dreamt of a black dragon with gray eyes.

Arianna awoke to the sickly light of a cloudy dawn and the wail of a bagpipe. The mournful notes drifted from the great hall below, where the men broke their fast and sang of past glories.

For a moment she couldn't think where she was, and she sat up with a start, making herself dizzy. She pressed her fingertips against her closed lids, and then realized it was not a headache that caused the dull throbbing echo within her skull. It came from outside the keep, an incessant rumble like distant thunder. The enemy had started the siege. They were pounding the curtain wall with rocks and boulders hurled from their war machines.

Arianna had slept fully dressed on top of the bedcovers, but she hurried now to change out of her rich noblewoman's clothes. She had borrowed a tunic and boots from a dairy maid yesterday, for if by some ill fate the Normans did manage to storm the castle, she would do better to pass as a villein girl. As the Prince of Gwynedd's daughter she was worth triple her weight in silver pennies as ransom.

She kept on her fine, pleated linen chainse, but over that she donned the loose, rough tunic, and on her feet she pulled a pair of gray felt boots. She laced the dun-colored tunic tightly around her neck to hide her torque, then cinched it around the waist with a plain leather belt. Using her fingers, she unplaited her dark brown hair and combed it loose about her face.

Through a loop in her belt she attached a small scabbard for a quillon dagger. She pondered the dagger a moment before sheathing it. This was no peasant's clumsy weapon, but it was important that she be well armed. It was long, shaped like a miniature sword, made of the finest metal. She ran her thumb along the edge of the honed blade. She would use it if she must, to defend her honor, for no man would pay a *cowyll,* the virgin-price, for a tainted bride. No, the loss of her virginity would bring shame not only on herself but on all her kindred.

"My honor . . ." she whispered, and her fist tightened around the dagger's embossed silver hilt.

The knight.

His image haunted her mind just as she had seen him in the vision—his black horse rearing, his eyes and mouth so hard and so ruthless. And his lance . . . pointed at her heart.

She stared for a long time at the golden mazer. The thing seemed dully ordinary in the day's light, yet still it frightened her. She would leave it behind; it would only hamper her flight if she had to make a quick escape. No, she was lying to herself. She feared the awful power of the visions that came from the bowl, but she could never give it up. She couldn't bear to think of it falling into Norman hands. Not if it truly had belonged to the great magician Myrddin.

She touched the mazer and was relieved to feel the metal cool against her fingertips. She attached it by one of its handles to her belt, then covered her whole drab ensemble with a mantle trimmed in cheap, spotted-yellow civet fur.

Arianna sucked in a breath through her mouth, wrinkling her nose. These clothes she had borrowed were none too clean, but then their barnyard-like odor would only enhance her disguise. For good measure she took some ashes from the brazier and dirtied her face.

The tower stairway was dark, for the rushlights had burned down, and she groped her way, running her palms along the rough stones. A guard on the battlements called out as she left the tower and dashed through the gate of the keep. Ignoring him, she descended the steep timber stairs that led down the side of the motte. Her boots were slightly too big for her feet and their thick leather soles slapped against the wood, sounding like sheets flapping in the wind. She crossed the drawbridge that spanned a dry, narrow ditch and entered the bailey.

The morning air was still and humid. Leaden clouds the color of slate pressed down and the air felt thick and damp against her face. In spite of the wet rawhides that had been draped over all the bailey's wooden roofs, a flaming pitch arrow had managed to set the hay grange alight. Now a raging fire crackled and choking gray smoke blanketed the yard. The burning hides stank so vilely that Arianna's stomach heaved.

A pair of ravens swooped down low over her head and Arianna swiftly made the sign of the cross. They were called corpse-geese, these scavengers of the battlefield, and she hated them. They were harbingers of death.

The ravens wheeled across the gray sky, their caws mixing with the coos coming from the dovecote and the shrill screeches from the hawks in the mews. The bailey was a tumult of sounds—the lowing of the cows in the byre, crying out to be milked; the clang of the blacksmith's hammer as he banged out one last spear; the baying of the excited dogs in the kennels. And the steady, pounding thud of the missiles from the catapults as they struck the outer wall.

She found her brother on the eastern parapet, standing with Madog behind the square, toothlike protection of a merlon. The men dissected the enemy's next move, for the Normans had abandoned the town and marched to the edge of the great forest that lay to the east of the castle. Arianna's step disturbed a roosting pigeon into flight, and both men whirled.

Ceidro's face registered instant anger. "What in hellfire are you doing out here? You should be back within the keep where it's—" His brows came together and he sniffed loudly. "God's bones. What have you done to yourself? You stink worse than a butcher's midden."

Arianna started to open her mouth.

"Never mind about that," her brother snapped, waving an imperious hand in her face. "Just get yourself back to the keep this instant."

Arianna decided to ignore him. The men in her family were always ordering her about, and she was always ignoring them. Ceidro must have come to terms with his fear sometime during the night. A light of excitement blazed in his eyes. It was a light she had seen often in the eyes of her father and brothers before they set out on a fight or a raid. He wore his gambeson, and at his thigh hung his sword and a buckler.

"Arianna . . ." Ceidro growled.

Arianna stepped around her brother, intending to

sneak a look at the besieging army through a crenel in the parapet. Ceidro seized her arm, yanking her away from the wall.

"Curse you, girl! Are you trying to get yourself—" He stopped abruptly, as if someone had clamped a hand over his mouth. It took Arianna a moment to realize what had happened. The barrage from the catapults had ceased.

Ceidro dropped her arm and looked cautiously over the parapet. Arianna moved in beside him, standing up on tiptoe to peer over his shoulder.

Rows of knights and arbalesters were lined up at the edge of the woods, just out of bowshot. They stood in a splendid, colorful array: gaudy pennons fluttering from blue-painted lances, kite-shaped shields decorated in all the hues of a peacock's tail, helms and mail polished to a shine. Against the backdrop of black forest and gray clouds soggy with rain, it was a sight to dazzle the eyes.

"Pretty, are they not?" Ceidro said with a scornful twist of his mouth. The Welsh thought it cowardly to fight, as the Normans did, in chain-mail armor.

After the constant pounding the silence was unnerving. Even the castle dogs had stopped their yapping. It was so quiet, Arianna could hear a frog croaking in the algae-covered moat below. A pall of smoke drifted over them from the burning hay grange, and behind her Madog coughed. They were the only sounds to shatter the silence.

"Do they mean to attack?" Arianna asked in a hoarse whisper.

"Splendor of God," Madog exclaimed softly. "I think they're withdrawing." And, indeed, as they watched, first the men-at-arms and then the knights turned about and disappeared up the high road, toward England. The war machines were left behind, abandoned and silent.

The Welsh burst into loud jeers and a hail of javelins and arrows flew from the battlements. A few of the enemy shouted a return barrage of insults, but they didn't fire back. Like a patch of ice on a sunny winter morning, the Norman army melted away. . . .

Until only one knight remained.

He stood within the shadow of a tall pine. The tree was black and withered, with a lightning scar down its side, and it seemed a part of the knight somehow, for his armor was burnished to a dull black and he was mounted on an enormous soot-colored war-horse. Then slowly, man and horse separated from the tree, coming forward until they stopped fully exposed in the middle of the cleared field below the castle walls.

Lightning flared across the sky, followed almost immediately by a crack of thunder. The black horse reared. A sudden gust flattened the pennon on the knight's lance—a black dragon on a bloodred field.

Fear knocked Arianna in the chest, as fierce as the sudden wind. "Oh, God, no . . ." Her hand fluttered up to her heart.

But unlike in her vision, the knight didn't charge. Instead he regained control of his skittish mount and stood there as the wind whipped around him, and the first drops of rain began to fall. Stood there as if waiting for something.

"Don't move, ye bastard. Don't move," Madog muttered, snatching up his longbow. He took an arrow from the quiver at his feet, knocking it over in his haste. Arrows spilled from the leather case with a clatter and rolled across the uneven paving stones.

In one swift movement Madog nocked the arrow, lifted the bow, and pushed it forward, stretching the taut string. His eyes narrowed and his arm tensed, the muscles bulging around his leather arm-guard. . . .

"*No!*" Arianna cried.

Ceidro whipped around, his mouth agape. But Madog kept his sight on the knight, the bow steady. He released the string, the arrow hissed, cleaving the air . . . to bury itself in the rough marsh grass inches from the destrier's hooves.

For one poised second more the knight stood motionless, then he whirled his horse around and cantered off into the forest.

"Damn it, Arianna!" Ceidro raged. "What in Christ's name possessed you to bleat like a poked sheep? You spoiled his aim."

Arianna could only stare at the place where the knight had been, bewildered by herself, over what had made her do such a thing. She had wanted the man dead. She did.

"I thought—" Her voice cracked. She tried again. "He was out of range." But he wasn't. Not for a Welsh longbow. And not for an expert shot like Madog.

"It wasn't milady's fault," Madog said. "I missed, that's all. Ye're forgetting the bastard's got the devil for a guardian angel."

"Sound the horn!" Ceidro cried. "We're going after him. We'll make the man swallow his own blood before this day is through!" He brushed past Arianna, his sword knocking against the parapet.

"Wait, lad, it could be a trap," Madog called after him.

But Ceidro's back was already vanishing down the battlement stairs. "Hurry, Madog. Else the whoresons will be halfway to England ere we can catch them."

Madog hesitated a moment longer, then, cursing, he scooped up his longbow and arrows and lumbered after the younger man. "Ceidro, for the love of Christ, let's think on this minute. I don't like the looks of this . . ."

Arianna looked across the field at the silent and empty forest. Another bolt of lightning flashed, thunder rumbled. A raven circled, black wings against a black sky.

She whipped around, crying her brother's name, but in that moment the shrill blast of a trysting horn rent the air. The rain, which had started with scattered drops, suddenly pattered down hard on the walls and packed dirt of the bailey. The wind shrieked, seizing Arianna's mantle and swirling it around her head.

Ceidro's small war-band poured out the sally-port with a bloodcurdling cacophony of battle cries, and still the field and forest were empty.

Once, their ancestors had fought naked except for a helmet and a torque. Today the men of Gwynedd rode forth wearing leather gambesons and carrying longbows and war clubs. But many still painted their faces blue in the old way and went to battle laughing and bellowing the ancient songs. They were brave and valiant and strong, these men of Cymru, and Arianna's heart beat hard with a fierce pride at the sight of them.

And then her pride turned to horror.

The enemy erupted from the forest, as if trees and brush had suddenly metamorphosed into men and horses. Within seconds they enveloped Ceidro's pitiful band. Suddenly thunder crackled and rain spewed down as if pouring from the mouths of a thousand gargoyles. Arianna clung to the parapet, squinting through the curtain of water, her hands pressing so hard into the rough stone that the skin tore, leaving smears of blood. Lightning flared, giving her a brief glimpse of flashing blades and flying hooves. Then she saw nothing again, though the air quivered with the sound of clashing swords, whinnying horses and the wails of the dying, and a sharp metallic smell floated to her on the wind.

She heard the hoarse blast of the olifant sounding the retreat.

She ran along the wall-walk, slipping and sliding on the wet stones. She hurled herself down the stairs and into the bailey just as the huge iron-bound gate screeched open and the drawbridge crashed down with a clatter of its mighty chains.

There was no time for her brother and his men to enter the castle back through the sally-port. Their only chance was to make it through the gate and close it behind them before the enemy could get through. The blinding rain-storm, which had first been on the side of the Normans, would help them now.

But no sooner did the thought form in Arianna's mind than the downpour stopped, as suddenly as it had begun.

Through the open gate Arianna saw her brother and what was left of his men race across the field. A group of mailed knights rode in hard pursuit, cutting down the stragglers like a woodcutter felling trees. In the forefront of those knights was a man in dull black armor on a soot-black steed.

And yet, yet . . . there was a chance that they would make it.

"Virgin Mary, Mother of God, save them," Arianna prayed as the first of the Welshmen reached the draw-bridge. Their horses' hooves pounded on the old wood. Hundreds of crossbow bolts rained down, striking the wall and the gate and the bridge, clattering like hail. Ceidro pulled up beside the bridge, letting his men go first, and Arianna thought how their father would be proud.

Then Ceidro was across the drawbridge and through the gate. The doors started to swing shut behind him as he turned to face the charging enemy. A high-pitched squeal echoed throughout the bailey as the guard in the gate-house began to wind the windlass, hauling up the chains to the bridge.

"Ceidro!" Arianna's shout turned into a scream as the knight in black armor easily leapt the growing span be-tween the ground and the bridge. His iron-shod lance caught Ceidro square in the chest, lifting him from the saddle, hurling him to the ground.

Horses thundered past Arianna where she stood among the fighting men, frozen with horror. Then, heedless of the slashing blades and flying hooves, she ran to where her brother sprawled in dreadful stillness beside the gate.

He lay on his back, his eyes staring sightless at the sky.

She threw herself across his blood-soaked gambeson, cradling his cheeks between her palms. "Ceidro, please . . ." Her hands slid down his face to clutch his shoulders and she shook him roughly. "Ceidro, please don't be dead."

She wanted to scream, to wail, but it felt as if some great beast had ripped open her chest, tearing out her heart and lungs. She opened her mouth, tried to breathe, and thought she was dying. She wanted to cry, but she couldn't.

She didn't notice the horn that trumpeted the Norman victory, or hear, in the heavy silence that followed, the groans of the dead and the dying. Nor did she see the horses milling around her, trampling blood-soaked pennons into the mud, or the shattered shields and broken stubs of lances. But when a raven landed nearby, she screamed at it to go away, that it had no business being here.

A pair of boots came up beside her, splattering mud on Ceidro's face. She took the sleeve of her tunic and gently wiped off his cheek. "Be careful," she said. "You're getting him dirty."

The boots were trimmed with metal and mounted with pointed spurs. Her gaze moved up long legs encased in mail, to the edge of a hauberk slick with rainwater and the tip of a sword that dripped blood into the mud. Slowly she lifted her eyes.

She saw a dark face framed in metal. The nasal on his helmet curved down over his nose, giving him the look of a predatory bird. All that she could see of his features was his mouth, and it looked ruthless and cruel. He moved and Arianna flinched, but he was only loosening the straps of his helm. He pulled it off, then pushed back the mailed hood of his hauberk.

The wind lifted his sweat-dampened hair, hair that was as black as the ravens that wheeled overhead. She looked into his eyes, but they didn't see her. They were focused on the distance, and they were gray and cold. And as hard as his dull black armor.

They were the eyes of the man in the vision.

2

The knight stared hard at the bloodred walls of Rhuddlan keep. The rain had stopped, the wind had died, and a gray mist roiled in off the river, enshrouding the motte and bailey with an air of mystery and gloom.

The castle was his now. His. He felt the old fires of ambition flaring within him. Once, when he had been young and full of faith and hope, he had sworn that someday he would wrest for himself a title and land. Someday, he, the earl's bastard, would forge for himself a dynasty to rival that of his father's. It seemed only fitting now that the dynasty would be built here, at Rhuddlan. The scene of his father's betrayal.

Title, land, and power.

His. At last, at last these things would be his.

Sheathing his sword, Raine had started to turn his back on the keep, when he felt someone's eyes on him. He looked down, startled to see a girl staring up at him with a look of rage on her face. She knelt beside the body of a young man.

Wet, tangled dark hair framed a pointed, sharp-boned face filled with eyes the dusky green color of the sea on a wintry day. Those eyes held him, and he thought of dark, misty mountains, hidden forests, and fairies dwelling beside deep, forgotten lakes. For a moment he felt a childish compulsion to make the sign of the horns to ward off the evil eye.

He shook his head over his own foolishness. He had taken a step away from her, when a raven landed on the bloody chest of the slain boy. The girl screamed and rose up, and Raine froze, expecting her to leap at him like a cat, all teeth and bared claws. But she flung her fury at the raven instead. The bird flew off with a flap of black wings just as Raine heard a familiar voice shout his name.

A knight approached the open gate at a canter. His silvered coat of mail sparkled like newly minted coins even under the gray skies. He rode a cream-white palfrey accoutred with a gilded saddle and a breastplate decorated with jingling bells. In his wake followed a squire mounted on a dappled rouncy with a hawk on his fist. Another twenty knights in full panoply galloped in a pack behind them.

Raine's eyes narrowed. This dazzling knight was his younger and so-very-legitimate half brother, Hugh, Earl of Chester, ruler of a good part of England. And the man who had everything Raine wanted.

He turned his head and spat the taste of envy from his mouth—

And caught the flash of a blade out of the corner of his eye. He whirled, throwing up his arm. A quillon dagger grazed the mail sleeve of his hauberk with a grating of sparks. All Raine saw were muddy tangles of dark hair and blazing green eyes. The girl pulled back the dagger and came at him again. But this time he was better prepared. He grabbed her wrist, squeezing hard. She made not a sound, though he was almost crushing it enough to break the bone. When the weapon dropped from her outstretched fingers, Raine let go of her.

And knew an instant later that he had made a mistake. She flung herself at him, her clawed fingers going for his eyes. He jerked his head aside and her nails raked his neck. She rained blows on the front of his hauberk, heedless of the fact that she was cutting the hell out of her hands on the sharp metal links. She did it all in a silence that was more unnerving than her crazed fury.

She went for his eyes again. This time he grasped both her wrists, twisting her arms behind her back. She tried kicking him instead, and she seemed to have as many legs as a spider. There were thirty knights and over a hundred and fifty men-at-arms in Raine's army, and he wondered what in hell had them all so busy that they couldn't come take this cursed madwoman off his hands.

"Will"—he grunted as her head flew up, connecting with his chin, and nearly causing him to bite off half his tongue—"somebody get her off me, for God's sake!"

He spotted his second-in-command standing in front of him, a grin like a drunken jester's all over his gnarled and pitted face. Raine thrust the squirming, clawing, kicking, and scratching female into a startled Sir Odo's arms. The big knight automatically wrapped her up in a bearlike embrace. She struggled a moment longer, then stilled. But her eyes, glowing like a pair of firebrands, remained fixed on Raine's face.

"Murderer!"

It was the first sound she had made.

Raine daubed at the blood that trickled down his neck. He spoke to her in Welsh, the language she had used. "What hell spawned you, woman?" When she said nothing, he snapped, "Answer me. Who are you?"

The girl's full lower lip curled into one of the finest sneers Raine had ever seen. "I, you Norman piece of filth, am the woman who's going to kill you."

Her vehemence startled him a moment, but then he laughed. "The road to hell is littered with the corpses of those who've tried to kill me."

"Doubtless they were all cowards. Surely none was Welsh, else you'd be roasting in hell yourself by now."

Raine laughed again. But then he glanced down at the discarded quillon knife and his face sobered. The day he had seen a five-year-old child slice through a man's tendon, he had stopped thinking of anyone, no matter what their age or sex, as harmless. He wouldn't put it past the wench to have a dozen such daggers hidden about her.

"Strip her," he said to Sir Odo in a clipped voice. The girl sucked in a sharp breath.

Sir Odo grinned, flexing his arms. "No reason to get her naked, sire. The wench is all bones. If you want to swive her, why not just toss up her skirts?"

The girl's eyes opened wide. Then she exploded like a bung out of a fermenting cask, rearing, flinging back her head, smacking it into the knight's jaw so hard, Raine heard the bones crack together. "Christ Jesus!" Odo bellowed. She jammed an elbow into his midriff. Snarling another curse, the big knight shook her until her neck snapped.

"I said strip the wench, not kill her," Raine called out, though he made no move to take the girl off Odo's hands.

"I don't guess the wench is in the mood for a tupping, sire," Sir Odo said around grunting breaths.

At his words the girl stiffened, then she made a strangled, whimpering noise, sagging back into the big knight's arms. "Please, don't . . ."

Sir Odo looked down at her lolling head and a look of tenderness came over his gnarled face. "Ah, the poor dearling . . . sire, will you just look at the poor dearling?"

Raine looked. The girl's eyes, glazed now and filled with terror, had focused on the body sprawled before the gate and a dry sob tore from her throat. Raine saw a wretched, pathetic whore. But Sir Odo, Raine knew, had suddenly seen a broken sparrow that needed mending. The big knight was always swallowing some wench's sad tale, and though Raine kept expecting these rescued waifs

to strip the man down to his braies and leave him with the
pox, they never did.

Sir Odo stared at his liege lord with big, sorrowful
brown eyes that often reminded Raine of a milk cow's. "If
you're still feeling randy, sire, let me find you another
girl."

Raine stared at her a moment longer, at her pale, mud-
streaked face. "Christ's bones . . . just get her out of
here."

Rich laughter floated over his head, and Raine turned.
His younger brother sat atop his palfrey, one leg hooked
negligently around the saddlebow, amusement brightening his splendidly handsome features. "Can this be the
Black Dragon's legendary way with women that I have
heard so much about?"

An answering humor glinted in Raine's eyes as he
heaved a mock sigh. "As you can see, I have but to look
at them and the poor, besotted creatures fling themselves
right into my arms."

Earl Hugh tossed back his head and emitted another
hearty laugh. His gaze fell on the girl, and Raine was
surprised to see his brother's cornflower-blue eyes darken
with lust.

"In truth, she doesn't appear to be overly fond of you,
big brother," Hugh drawled. "Do you mind if I relieve
you of this particular bit of the spoils? Or we could even
share the plowing of her, if you like. Such hot passion as
hers could help to pass an interesting hour or two."

"Hell, Hugh, show the child some mercy. She's just lost
her man," Raine said, then wondered what in God's eyes
had possessed him. He was becoming as soft and addle-
pated as Sir Odo. The "child" had almost buried her dagger in the back of his neck. Even now she was looking
death at him and muttering something that sounded like a
Latin prayer but was probably a witch's incantation.

Raine felt a shudder curl up his spine, and he whipped

around to growl at Sir Odo. "I thought I told you to take her away."

Sir Odo nodded his big, shaggy head. "Aye, that ye did. But then where now, by all that's holy, am I supposed to put her?"

Raine gave the big knight a look that said he didn't want to be bothered with details. "Use your initiative. It's what I pay you for."

Hugh nudged his horse forward for a better look at the girl. "I trow, Raine," came that drawling, sardonic voice. "Sometimes you are as squeamish as a maid. She's a whore, not a child. And she'll be wanting a new protector soon enough."

Raine said nothing. But he looked again at the girl to see if he had missed something the first time.

His gaze roamed the length of her, starting with the worn, dung-splattered felt boots and moving up the shapeless, drab gray tunic and cheap, civet-fur mantle. The tunic and mantle were splotched with mud and blood, and her hair fell in tangled, wet clumps over her shoulders. What he could see of her face was . . . well, striking—he would grant Hugh that. But she was likely one of the castle whores, and as whores always swarmed around an army more plentiful than corpse-geese, Raine couldn't see what the fuss was about.

Odo had hesitated a moment longer, but now he began to drag the girl toward the keep. She bucked violently, trying to break away, and she almost succeeded. The knight wrapped his big arms around her again in a crushing embrace, squeezing her so tightly that her feet came off the ground. For a moment longer Raine and the girl faced each other. Her eyes pierced the distance between them, and a look of the purest hatred blazed from those smoky green depths.

"Murdering Norman bastard," she said on a hiss of breath.

Raine's face remained as blank as fresh parchment. He

didn't care that she wanted him dead, or why. He had spoken the truth when he'd told the girl there were many who had tried and failed to kill him. By the time he had turned and stepped forward to greet his brother, he had already forgotten her.

Earl Hugh of Chester sprang from the saddle with a jingling of bells. He clasped Raine on the shoulders, giving him the kiss of peace. "Well met, brother."

"Hugh." Raine nodded stiffly and moved out of his brother's embrace. Beside the young knight's splendor, Raine suddenly became aware that he was covered with the grime of battle.

Hugh flashed a knowing grin and used the sleeve of his bliaut to rub off the black smudge on Raine's nose left by the nasal of his helm. His eyes fell on the oozing bloody scratches and the grin widened. "You look about as pretty as a horse's ass, dear brother."

Raine couldn't help smiling back at him. "Thank you."

Hugh doffed his helm and ran his fingers through thick curls the color of burnished gold. He looked around, his mouth pursed with exaggerated awe. "Well, well . . . I see you've dispatched many a man to hell this day. And with your usual thoroughness."

Raine looked around him as well. He saw a field littered with riven shields, broken lances, and corpses. He felt no satisfaction over his victory. The Welsh had been sorely outnumbered and no match against his crossbows and mailed knights. Their leader had been a fool. "At least they died on the field of honor," he said to Hugh. "And not a cow's death in their own beds."

He saw Hugh's frown and allowed a lazy smile to curl his own lips. He had said it just to goad his brother, who thought himself a coward because he rode terrified into every battle. Hugh hadn't yet learned that every other man out there was also scared enough to piss in his braies. In truth, Raine thought, he would sell his own soul for the chance to die an easy death in a bed. But he wanted it to be *his* bed. Not in some lice-ridden tavern or among the rushes of another man's hall. At the thought, his gaze shifted up to the mist-veiled keep.

Hugh stepped in front of him. His brother's expressive mouth bore a bright smile, but his voice held a honeyed malice. "I believe I owe you my thanks, Raine, for winning me this castle from the accursed Welsh. But then my gratitude is hardly enough for you, now is it? I forget you fight for profit, not honor."

The shock Raine felt didn't show on his face, but Hugh's words had been like a mailed fist in his gut. He'd never expected that his brother would put in a claim of Rhuddlan. It was such a paltry bit of land compared to the hundreds of commotes Hugh already ruled. *And it is mine, damn it*, Raine thought. He had taken it, and now it was *his*.

"Name your reward," Hugh was saying. "A new destrier? But how about a white one this time—black is *so* unfashionable. Or what say you to a new coat of mail?" He flicked his fingers against Raine's hauberk. "This one is beginning to get that battered look."

Raine said nothing; he didn't even blink. He knew why Hugh was doing this. His brother had always had the knack for discovering the things Raine wanted most and then ensuring that they were denied to him. Hugh would go after the Honor of Rhuddlan for no other reason than to keep Raine from having it.

Hugh's smile had faltered. "Didn't you hear me, Raine? I said I was going to claim Rhuddlan of the king."

"I heard you. I was just wondering what you would do with it," Raine said, imbuing his voice with boredom. "I thought you found Wales dreary."

Either he failed, or perhaps his brother simply knew him too well. Hugh's eyes opened wide with exaggerated surprise. "Oh, Raine . . . surely you didn't think *you* would be allowed to keep such a valuable fief as Rhuddlan for yourself?"

Raine continued to stare blankly at his brother until Hugh's eyes were the first to shift away. But he couldn't help saying, "Why don't we let the king decide," though he knew well that whatever Hugh asked for, the king would feel compelled to grant to him. The Earl of Chester was too powerful a baron for Henry to offend.

Hugh knew it too. His smile was dazzling. "Oh, by all means, we shall let the king decide. He has summoned you, by the way. That's why I'm here. Our good King Henry is about to engage that wicked Welsh chieftain in a rather nasty battle, and he has asked for the presence of his best and bravest knight. That's what you're best at, isn't it—being brave? You needn't worry though. I shall take good care of Rhuddlan in your place."

A bowman suddenly lurched between them, waving a burning firebrand in Hugh's face. The earl recoiled violently, stumbling backward and nearly falling on his butt in the mud. He put a hand to his forehead and to Raine's amusement a horrified look crossed his brother's face as he realized his hair had been singed.

"Get out of my way, you pricklouse!" Hugh roared.

The bowman giggled drunkenly. "My lord earl. Do we burn down the hall, or no?"

Hugh looked as if he were about to choke on his fury. "Christ, man, use your head. Where will I sleep tonight if you fire the hall?"

Laughing openly now, Raine turned and bellowed for his squire. "Taliesin!"

A youth of about seventeen with russet-colored hair ran up, leading Raine's sweating destrier. "Sound the trysting horn," Raine told him. "We're joining the king." He fixed Hugh with a hard look. "But tell Sir Odo he's to stay behind with a contingent of men. To help Earl Hugh secure the castle." *And look after my interests* were the added words, unspoken yet understood by all.

The squire glanced from one brother to the other. He had skin as fair as a girl's and his smile was beautiful. " 'Tis done, my liege," he said, somehow making the mundane words sound as melodic as a song. But he did not scurry to obey Raine's command. "Sire? What happened to the girl?"

Raine was thinking about whether to send a messenger to tell Henry he was on his way. His attention focused on Taliesin's face. The boy wore an odd look, a sort of worried smile. "What girl?"

"The one that, uh . . . attacked you."

First Sir Odo, then Hugh, and now the boy. . . . *Women,* Raine thought with a shake of his head. They could wreak more havoc than a Saracen ambush. He struggled to keep a smile off his face. "You stay away from her, Taliesin. You're too young for that sort of trouble."

Taliesin's brow furrowed. "But, sire, it's not I—"

But Raine had turned abruptly away as the sound of an agonized wail suddenly penetrated his consciousness. It had been going on for quite some time now, but he'd paid it no heed. He'd heard it so often in his life—the scream of a wounded man who knew that he was dying. Yet now Raine was suddenly possessed with a terrifying certainty that someday very soon, if he didn't stop the fighting and the killing, that screaming man would be him.

He gritted his teeth around an oath. Hugh was right, he was turning squeamish as a maid. "Tell Sir Odo to find the bloody priest and castle leech," he said to his squire. "And either get that man healed, or get him shriven and buried."

"Aye. But, sire, about the girl—"

"Taliesin," Raine said in a calm, flat voice. "I gave you an order."

No one dared to disobey the Black Dragon when he used that tone. The squire dashed off, calling for Sir Odo. Hugh grasped the charger's bridle, holding it steady for

Raine to mount. Raine swung himself into the saddle and
Hugh stepped back quickly as the spirited war-horse
reared.

Hugh laughed up at him. "Do try not to get yourself
killed, big brother."

Now it was Raine's turn to smile. "I won't, *little* brother
. . . and you can wager Rhuddlan on it."

Raine brought his horse under control and started for
the gate. But as he crossed the drawbridge, he turned
back for one last look at Rhuddlan. He had taken this
castle. It was *his*, by God, a part of his past and all of his
future. And it would remain his. No matter what he had
to do to keep it.

He felt an odd exhilaration. For the first time in a very
long while, he had something to fight for.

Arianna leaned against the rough wooden staves of a
beer keg and rested her chin on her drawn-up knees. That
big, ugly knight had disposed of her by locking her in the
castle's wine vault. It was part of the tower cellars, built
deep underground within the motte. But the Norman had,
with a kindness surely uncharacteristic for a man of his
race, left with her the stub of a tallow candle.

The small flame flickered forlornly, casting looming
shadows on the stone walls. The room was stacked with
barrels of wine and ale. The smell of yeast mixed with the
tart tang of vinegar into a fumy aroma that made her head
reel. She could hear the sounds of revelry from the great
hall above. Drunken songs, trumpets and laughter, the
wail of a pipe. Occasionally she heard a scream.

Arianna's throat worked as she struggled to swallow.
She blinked, and her lids grated as if they had been
coated with sand. Her eyes ached as though she had been
weeping for hours, yet she hadn't shed a single tear. She
hurt beyond tears.

Ceidro was dead. Her brother was dead and she had
failed. Failed to take revenge on his murderer.

Even worse, she had allowed herself to be captured. She remembered the sight of the village woman running up the road, the knight on the white charger pounding after her, and Arianna shuddered, feeling a primal terror she only dimly understood. She hadn't seen what happened to the woman afterward, but she knew. . . . Rape. Arianna would have no value to her family after that was done to her, though duty and honor would still compel her poor father to pay handsomely for her return.

She rubbed her forehead across the hard bones of her knees, squeezing her eyes shut. But that was a mistake, for immediately the image of the black knight appeared. Even after all that had happened, she knew the vision had yet to be fulfilled. He waited for her still, somewhere in her future, and never had she known such fear.

"No!" She thrust herself to her feet, her hands balled into fists. She couldn't afford to be afraid, else she would fail in her duty.

She paced the dimensions of her prison. The floor was packed earth, not covered with rushes, and dampness seeped through the soles of her felt boots. Water trickled in a stream down one corner of the cellar's stone wall. She had already tried the stout oak door a dozen times, but she lifted the latch once more. It was still bolted from the outside.

A particularly raucous bellow of laughter echoed from above and Arianna jumped, backing quickly away from the door. They would drink up all the wine and ale in the buttery soon, and then they would descend into the cellars for more. And they would find her.

For a moment Arianna's control slipped and she shuddered. But she refused to give in to her fear, telling herself she must concentrate on escape. She dug the toe of her boot into the dirt. It was packed solid, she had no pick, and even if she did she would be a withered, toothless crone by the time she had dug her way through the motte. She frowned at the barrels of ale and wine. Her brother Cynan had once sliced his hand open on his sword while drunk and hadn't even felt it. Perhaps she should drink her way into oblivion, then she wouldn't feel or care what was done to her. Oddly, in one corner of the room, she suddenly noticed, were several sacks of flour stacked among the kegs. Tucked beneath an empty bag was a small stone quern, a hand mill used for grinding grain. Someone within the castle had obviously been grinding grain illegally and hiding his nefarious activity here deep within the wine vault.

She picked up the quern, hefting its weight in her hands. She looked at the door. Its hinges were old and rusted. Perhaps she could use the quern like a chisel to . . .

The door flew open, banging against the wall like a clap of thunder. Arianna reared back, a scream bursting from her throat before she could stop it. A man stood before her, resplendent in a bliaut of sky-blue satin, a pelisse trimmed in ermine, and a mantle the red-orange color of a sunset. He wore a gold chaplet on his head that was no brighter than his hair.

Arianna scuttled backward until her hips struck the wall.

He didn't come after her. He leaned his shoulder negligently against the jamb, crossed his arms, and grinned at her. She recognized this Norman lord, though he had removed his splendid coat of silvered mail. He had sat on his white palfrey and laughed with the black knight while the big one had held her in his bearish grip. They had discussed her in mocking words she couldn't understand, because, though her father had made her and her brothers learn that impossible Norman tongue, she had never been able to follow it when spoken rapidly.

He spoke to her now though, drawling the words. He told her what he wanted to do to her and she understood him very well. "Keep away from me, you Norman cur!"

she cried, and was not surprised when he laughed. She had sounded ridiculous even to herself.

He pushed off the doorjamb and took a step into the vault. Arianna flung the quern at his head. It sailed two feet through the air and landed on the packed dirt with a dull thud.

He stopped and eyed the hand mill with a quirk of one blond brow. Then he laughed again. "You've got spirit. I like that in a woman. My bitch of a wife is as timid as a hedge hen."

He took another step. Arianna pressed back against the wall and swallowed the terror that rose in her throat.

He stopped when he was a hand's breadth away from her. This close she could smell him—sweet wine, sweat, and a spicy perfume. Fine lines radiated around his eyes and the skin below his cheekbones looked sallow and slack.

She eyed the distance to the door. But he barred the way to escape. She shifted the tiniest bit to her left. When he didn't appear to notice, she shifted a bit more. If she could distract him but a moment . . .

"You should not be doing this if you are married," she said. " 'Twould be a grievous sin."

His eyes glittered with mockery. "Ah, but sinning is such fun."

He lifted his hand. Arianna froze, but he didn't touch her. Instead he reached up to his neck and unclasped the gem-studded crescent brooch that fastened his mantle. He pulled off the heavy silk-lined cape and let it slither to the floor, then held the brooch out to her. "I always pay my women first. I find it makes them much more generous in turn."

A fury engulfed Arianna, freeing her from her paralyzing fear. "Norman swine! I'd kill myself first!" she cried, knocking his hand aside.

His gaze left her momentarily, to follow the brooch as it

rolled, glittering in the dim candlelight, and Arianna ran for the door.

He snagged the trailing edge of her mantle, swinging her around and slamming her back against the wall, pressing the length of his body against hers. His breath washed over her face. "So you like to play the ravished virgin, do you?"

He kissed her hard. She tried to twist aside, but he clasped the sides of her head, holding her in place. His tongue slid between her lips and she gagged. She arched against him and he laughed into her mouth, pushing his thigh between her legs. She felt his erection and terror filled her. She fought harder, and he pressed harder, banging against the golden mazer that dangled from her waist.

"What the hell?" Grasping the bowl by one of its handles, he wrenched it off her belt. He threw it across the vault and it struck the stone wall with a loud clatter.

But he had given her the space she needed. Arianna had nine brothers and they had taught her how to fight dirty. She slammed her knee up hard into his crotch.

He gasped and fell to his knees, cupping himself. Arianna sprinted for the door.

His hand snaked out, grabbing her ankle, and she crashed to the floor. She struck her head against the metal band of an ale keg and a jagged bolt of pain streaked across her eyes. For a second they both lay there, while his wheezing breaths filled the vault, and Arianna struggled to keep from passing out. She tried to jerk her ankle free of his grip, but his fingers only tightened. Black dots danced before her. She shook her head and the black dots bled one into the other, her vision dimmed. She saw the smooth, rounded edge of the stone quern and she stretched out her hand, her fingertips not quite touching. . . .

A pulsating, glowing light suddenly filled the open

doorway in front of her. A lambent mist rose from the ground, swirling upward.

"No . . ." Arianna shook her head hard, trying to clear it of the swirling mists. God help her, she couldn't be having a vision now. There wasn't even a pool of water.

But the glowing mist remained and within it a slender figure began to take form, a wraith, floating in the air on a sea of luminescence. Light shot up in rays around its head, like the halos of the saints painted on the chapel walls.

The Norman lord didn't see the flickering wraith in the doorway. He had pushed himself to his knees, his hand groping up her leg. Hysterical laughter bubbled in Arianna's throat. Of course he didn't see it. It was her vision, her dream. She inched forward, stretching out her arm, and her fingers curled around the mill. . . .

The mist swirled and eddied and darkened to the color of blood. But the sea of light around the wraith glimmered, brightened. He lifted his arm and pointed . . . pointed right at the knight.

The light pulsed, throbbed. It was so intense now, it burned Arianna's eyes; all she saw was a piercing whiteness. She felt the knight's hand close around her breast, and with the last visages of her conscious control, she swung the quern, aiming for the place where she hoped his head would be, though she could see nothing but the cold, white light.

The quern thudded into something soft and she heard a grunt and a curse. "You'll pay for that, you bitch."

Fingers tore at her clothes, kneading her breasts. The light shimmered, flared, she saw the figure of the vision so clearly she thought he must surely be real. A blue-white flame shot from the end of his pointing finger, a bolt of fire that leapt across the room to strike the knight, engulfing him in a sudden flash like lightning.

In the second before darkness swallowed her, Arianna thought she heard the knight scream.

3

It was the closest he had been to home in six years.

If he could call it home. It was, at least, the place where he had been born, where he had lived the first fifteen years of his life. They had been years spent in the Earl of Chester's stables, shoveling dung and dodging the marshal's fists.

He had been back only once since he had left. And on that day, that single day out of all the days of his life, he had been full of such hope that anything, even love and happily-ever-after, could come true if only you believed. It had been the same month as this, July. The sun had risen in a sky that was the exact lavender-blue of her eyes and the air had smelled of primroses and the sea, and . . .

But, no, it was wiser, safer, not to remember at all.

The man they called the Black Dragon rode with half his company of knights, moving at the fast pace of a good war-horse and well ahead of the main body of his army. Henry's summons had not sounded urgent, but it was never politic to keep a king waiting.

They traveled through the thick of the Coed Euloe, a forest of mountain ash, pine, and tangled oak thickets.

The storm had blown away and the sun was out, but the world beneath the dense leafy bower was the dim gray of twilight. The air smelled of the damp earth, and their chargers' hooves made no sound as they padded across a ground mulchy with leaves and rotting cones. The trill of a blackbird was the only thing to break the soft silence. Amid this quiet and peace, the knight tried not to think, because on the other side of these wooded hills lay the English border, and just across the border was Chester . . . and home.

He could go there now. Now that his father was dead.

If he went home now, Sybil would be there. She would greet him at the gate of the castle, and her face would light with joy, for it had been so very long. "Oh, Raine . . ." she would say. Just that. *Raine.* But the sound of his name falling from those lips would be sweeter than the song of an angel.

She would send servants for food and drink, and she would lead him into the great hall. There, she would play and sing for him, just as she had when they were children. He would feast his eyes upon her—but only on her pale blond head as she bent over her psaltery, for then she couldn't catch him looking at her and see the pain in his eyes. She would ask him what he had done, the sights he had witnessed these last six years. She would laugh in all the right places, and tears would form in those lavender-blue eyes when he spoke of the sad times.

But eventually the evening would end. Then he would watch as the girl he had once loved climbed the stairs without him, to enter her bedchamber. The chamber where she had spent every night of the last six years . . . sharing his brother's bed.

Raine cursed savagely beneath his breath. He should have had the sense to stay away from this corner of England. Maybe he shouldn't ask the king for the Honor of Rhuddlan. It was a marcher lordship, true enough, and like the other borderland fiefs it could be parlayed, if its lord was ambitious enough, into one of the more powerful baronies in England. It was all he wanted now, all he needed, but for one thing—it was too damned close to Chester.

The silence was suddenly shattered by the sound of a large animal in panic crashing through the trees, and Raine pulled up just as a riderless war-horse burst through the underbrush in front of him. Blood spurted from a wound in the charger's neck. It wheeled, rearing, tossing back a head that was all flaring nostrils and red, burning eyes. Close on its heels followed another horse, this one with a man in chain mail on its back.

The knight thundered by Raine and his men. "Ambush!" he shouted over his shoulder. "The Welsh have attacked and the king is down!"

Raine spun around to take his shield and lance from his squire. "Taliesin, ride back—" The order stopped midway out Raine's mouth as he stared into the frightened fawn eyes and thin, freckled face of Sir Odo's ten-year-old page. "What in hellfire are you doing here, and where is my squire?"

The boy quailed beneath Raine's fury. "B-back at Rhuddlan where you l-left him, sire. He said there was something there you w-wanted to keep from falling into the earl's hands."

There was nothing at Rhuddlan that Raine wanted to keep from Hugh, beyond the castle itself. More likely Taliesin had spotted that green-eyed wench he fancied. Women would be the death of that boy. *He* would be the death of the boy, when next he got his hands on him.

Raine sent one of the other squires back to alert the rest of his army. He had started to touch his spurs to his destrier, when he spotted Sir Odo's page hunched over his cob, trying to blend inconspicuously into the middle of the pack of knights. He glared and pointed at the boy. "And you, lad . . . you keep away from the fighting. If I

catch you trying to be a hero, I'll blister your backside
with my sword belt afterward. Is that clear?"

They rapidly pressed single file along the path created
by the fleeing horses. Before long they could hear muted
sounds of fighting—neighing horses, screams and curses,
the hysterical bleat of a trumpet. They emerged into a
clearing atop a small rise, and Raine took in the flux of
the battle at a glance.

Below them King Henry and a small band of knights
were trapped in a narrow wooded defile. The way ahead
was blocked by felled trees, their retreat cut off by the
enemy, who sniped at them from the protection of the
forest. The knights in their cumbersome armor were no
match for the fleet-footed Welsh and the deadly, mail-
piercing arrows of their longbows. Already the narrow
path and stream were clogged with the bodies of men and
horses.

"The king is dead!" someone screamed, and at that
moment the king's men broke, running for the dubious
safety of the forest. Raine saw the royal standard fall. *"A
moi, le Raine!"* He shouted his battle cry and spurred his
horse down the rise.

Bellowing like a man possessed, Raine rallied the fleeing royal troop. He paid no attention to the arrows that
came at him from all sides, fighting his way toward the
place where he had last seen the king. He found Henry on
one knee trying to fend off a battle-ax with a shattered
shield. Raine leaned from his horse and slashed backhanded with his long sword, striking the attacking Welshman in the chest with a blow that rattled Raine's teeth
and nearly cut the man in half.

Raine leapt from his horse and hauled the dazed king
to his feet with one hand, while with the other he
snatched up the royal standard from where it lay, trampled in the mud. He waved the banner with its distinctive
fox device high over his head and his voice carried clearly
over the tumult of battle.

"À Henri, le roi!"

Within moments it was over. A Welsh olifant blared a retreat as the enemy melted back into the thickly wooded hills.

Raine blinked the battle fog from his eyes. Wiping his bloody sword on the hem of his bliaut, he turned to his king. The young monarch's freckles stood out like ink marks above his red beard. His protruding gray eyes were wide with fear. Raine realized it was the first time Henry had ever truly been close to death.

"You look in fine fettle, sire," Raine said with a lazy smile, "for a man who's supposed to be dead. Owain of Gwynedd will be sorely disappointed."

"Aye, he will." Henry's voice cracked, and he had to clear his throat. Then he threw back his head and barked a laugh. "He will at that!"

The king's normally ruddy color started to come back into his face. His large, coarse hands clasped Raine's shoulders. "You saved my life." He fixed Raine with his eyes and his voice grew rough with genuine emotion. "Be thinking what you want most, my dear friend and bravest knight, for if it is in my power, be sure that I will grant it."

"Your Grace. I ask only that I might serve you."

The king's fingers tightened and he shook Raine gently. "It was more than a man's life you saved on this day. You saved a kingdom."

Aye, I did. Raine lowered the lids over his eyes to hide the surge of hope he felt. *And you, my lord king, are going to give me Rhuddlan for it.*

"Now is no time to be taking a nap, my lady."

Arianna opened her eyes and looked at the face of a boy. He had the palest skin she had ever seen, which made the dark red brows on his forehead look like cuts. The brows arched above sloe-black eyes that glinted with a strange, shimmering light. He blinked and the light

faded. His mouth quirked into a mischievous smile that
was all boy.

Arianna tried to sit up and the world reeled. The boy
slipped a firm hand beneath her arm, steadying her.
"Whoa, careful," he said. "Don't sit up too fast."

When the earth stopped tilting she looked around her.
She was still inside the wine vault. The blond Norman
who had tried to rape her lay sprawled among split sacks
of the illegal flour. His head was laid open with a bloody
gash, and she thought he was dead until a drunken snore
puffed out his lips.

Her temples throbbed and nausea cramped her stomach. She closed her eyes for a moment. "What happened?"

"You must have struck your head and passed out for a
minute," the boy said. He had a strange voice. The words
he spoke were ordinary Welsh, but he almost sang them.

Arianna's eyes opened and her glance flickered back to
the knight. The boy flashed a knowing grin, pointing to
the stone quern that lay beside the snoring Norman. "He
seems to have struck his head, as well."

"I didn't . . ." She faltered. She remembered swinging
the quern at the Norman's head, but she had landed only
a glancing blow, for he had cursed her afterward, and
pawed at her breasts. There had been something else . . .
a figure in a vision that had seemed real living, breathing
flesh. And a flash of blue fire . . .

The stone walls of the vault suddenly tipped again and
Arianna groaned. She thought she might have to vomit.
She took several deep breaths and touched the swelling
lump on her forehead.

The boy rose to his feet with a smooth, athletic grace.
He was dressed as a Norman squire, but he wore on his
head a battered helmet gilded gold, a relic from the time
of the ancient ones. Arianna had seen such a helmet only
once before—in the hands of the bard who had given her
the magic mazer. But the bard had been an old man, and

the face below this helmet belonged to a youth who couldn't have been older than seventeen.

He held out his hand to her. "I don't mean to rush you, my Lady Arianna, but we really should be getting the hell out of here."

She stared up at him; she did not take the proffered hand. "You know who I am?"

"Know you, my lady? How could I not know you, when your beauty, your wit, and your charm are so legendary. There isn't a red-blooded man in all of Wales who would fail to recognize you."

He gave her such a delightful, teasing smile that Arianna couldn't help smiling back. "What nonsense," she said.

"Aye, isn't it." He held out his hand again. "Now, if you will, my lady . . ."

She waited for him to enlighten her with his identity, but he did not.

"I'm not leaving with you until I know who you are."

He cocked his head at the blond knight snoring among the flour sacks. "You'd rather stay here with him?"

Arianna's pointed chin took on a stubborn tilt her brothers would have recognized.

The boy sighed. "I am called Taliesin, but if you must have my pedigree it would take me all day and night to list it. Would it suffice you to know that the first sight my eyes saw upon my birth was the snow-capped peak of Yr Wyddfa Fawr? I am," he added with obvious pride, "a bard."

Arianna was impressed in spite of herself, for Welsh bards were of a chosen few and almost always of noble blood. But she was also suspicious. "Then why do you dress as a Norman squire?"

"Why are you dressed like a kitchen wench?"

Arianna acceded his point. She took his hand and let him help her to her feet. She was only a little dizzy now, and she was relieved to discover she would not have to throw up after all. "You are a child of Gwynedd then?"

"Did I not just say so?" he snapped irritably. "Now are you coming, or no?"

"Do you know my father? Are you taking me to him? Where are you taking me?"

He rolled his eyes heavenward, muttering something that sounded oddly like *"Goddess, preserve me."* Then he sighed. "I'm leading you to safety, my lady."

But at the door he paused, snapped his fingers and muttered a curse before turning back. When he emerged again from the recesses of the vault, he carried the golden mazer. He had the bowl cradled in his hands and for a moment Arianna was sure it pulsed and glowed. But when he pressed it into her hands and she touched the metal it felt cool and ordinary. There was a new dent in the rim, where it had struck the wall.

She glanced at his face. His jet eyes shimmered brightly, then dulled.

"Are you quite ready to leave now, my lady?" he asked, irritated, impatient, as if she had been the one to send him back for the bowl.

He led her up the narrow mural stairs and behind the passage screen that opened into the great hall. She looked with trepidation within, where a great fire burned, and men crowded around the trestle tables, drinking and eating. A jongleur, wearing a gaudily striped tunic, moved among the raucous warriors, strumming a gittern and singing a raunchy song. Arianna was sure the man looked right at them as they passed, but he sounded no alarm and his voice didn't miss a single note.

They passed through the heavy iron-banded door of the tower. The gate to the shell keep was wedged partly open by a stone, though it was guarded by a pair of spearmen. The men leaned against the wall and passed a cannikin of wine back and forth as they shared a naughty tale about a monk tupping a burgess's wife. Arianna and the boy walked practically beneath their noses, but the guards appeared not to see them.

It's as if they *can't* see us, Arianna thought, and felt an awe tinged with fear.

A second later, she was smiling over her foolishness when a knight, who climbed toward them up the motte steps, casually nodded his head and called a greeting to the boy. No one had sounded the alarm simply because they all knew Taliesin and trusted that he had the authority to be taking her . . . wherever he was taking her.

Arianna followed the golden helmet as it descended the timber stairs. She debated the wisdom of placing her own trust in this strange boy. But as promised, he was leading her safely out of the keep. Once free of the castle she could always break away from him; for, in truth, she was more than a little afraid of him. The image of that wraith in the doorway haunted her. He had been like an angel of vengeance, blue fire leaping from his finger to . . .

But, no, *she* had been the one to knock out the knight, she had struck the man down with the stone quern. The rest had all been only a dream, brought on by the blow to her head.

She studied the slender back that moved in front of her, the thin waist, narrow hips, and lanky legs. He was all too real, a mere boy, and an irritating, cocky one at that. He wasn't an angel. He was too much like one of her brothers.

They crossed the drawbridge and entered the bailey, and walked into an enshrouding whiteness. Never had Arianna seen mist so thick. It was as if she were looking at the world through a winding sheet. The mist had a strange density to it, but it wasn't damp. Rather it glimmered and glinted like millions of ice crystals, though it wasn't cold either, and it glowed as if lit from within. She could hardly see two inches in front of her, yet the boy forged ahead, his long legs covering so much ground that she had to run to keep up with him.

Though Arianna saw no one else, she heard others moving about within the bailey. Sounds echoed around her—the whinny of horses, the curses of men, someone whistling a drinking song. Occasionally she caught the glimpse of a shadow. Yet she had the strangest impression that she and the boy were the only ones enclosed within the impenetrable mist, that just beyond them the sun shone warmly in a blue sky.

They passed through the gatehouse, again without challenge. The mist was less thick here, though tendrils of it curled up from the river bank. The boy picked up his pace after they crossed the drawbridge. Arianna cast a quick glance over her shoulder at the castle. A low-lying, foggy cloud hugged the keep and tower, explaining the origin of the mysterious mist. God's eyes, but she was starting to let her imagination run away with her.

Taliesin led her at a quick trot down the rutted road toward the town. The gate swung, moaning, on its battered hinges. Within the walls the streets were deserted, for those still left alive had long since fled into the forest. But though empty of people, the way before them was littered with water-logged loaves of bread, ripped tunics, stoved-in buckets, and other things the Normans had thought too useless to steal.

The stink of wet, burnt timber hung in the air. But as they neared the market square, Arianna saw that the narrow wooden shops and houses belonging to the well-to-do burgesses had been spared. The Black Dragon was no fool; the new Lord of Rhuddlan would need the tax revenue produced by the draper, the miller, the saddler, and their ilk.

A squealing pig darted out of an alley, trailing saliva from its snout, and startling Arianna into an embarrassing scream by nearly colliding with her legs. She tried to side-step out of its way and tripped over a scattered pile of faggots. She would have gone sprawling, except that the boy was suddenly there to catch her. Though he was slen-

der of build, there was a strength to his grip that was
oddly comforting.

"Mind your step," he said in his mellifluous voice. They
were the first words he had spoken since leaving the wine
vault.

"Shouldn't we have set off through the forest?" Arianna asked, her voice betraying her uncertainty.

"Nay. We'd do better to go by boat."

Arianna nodded. They could sail out the river estuary
and up the straits. Within hours they would make landfall
in Gwynedd—a trip that would take days traveling overland on foot.

They walked in tense silence the rest of the way to the
river wharfs. A grainy powder dusted the gray weathered
boards of the dock, flour from the looted mill house
nearby. It was eerily silent but for the slap of water
against the pilings. Taliesin went immediately to a skiff
and began untying the mooring lines. He helped Arianna
into the small boat, settling her down in the bow, then
climbed in after her. He expertly hoisted the single sail.

Arianna felt a sudden surge as wind filled the canvas.
He flashed her a bright smile as he pulled off his beautiful
helmet, carelessly tossing it toward the stern. As he ad-
justed the tiller to allow for the current, the wind caught
his long hair, billowing it around his head. It was a bright,
orange-red color, like the fur of a fox.

They sailed up the long tidal estuary of the river Clwyd.
The land here was flat, sandy beaches and wild marsh
grass, stretching to the variegated green sea. Arianna
breathed deeply of the heavy, salty air. Shore birds
dipped and soared, riding the wind currents, and in spite
of all that had happened on this day, she felt suddenly
carefree, as if she flew with them.

They slid out the mouth of the estuary and into the
open sea. The storm had left the water frothed with white
caps. Arianna stood at the bow, looking toward home,
enjoying the feel of the sea spray on her face as the skiff

cleaved the waves. Then she heard the sail flap behind her, and the boat heeled suddenly as it took on a new tack. She whipped around, gripped by fury, and fear. . . .

For they sailed now not toward Gwynedd, but England.

The boy was not at the tiller. He was right before her, staring at her with those shimmering jet-black eyes. *Where are you taking me?* she asked, except that she had used no words, for they had only just formed in her mind. But he, it seemed, answered with a thought as well.

Forgive me, my lady, he said. He pressed a dripping sponge to her lips and nose. Panicked, suffocating, she opened her mouth and sucked in the reeking fumes of the narcotic henbane plant.

It was the last thing she remembered before darkness overwhelmed her.

She smelled bean potage cooking over an open fire, heard laughter and the cheerful lilt of a reed pipe. Arianna opened her eyes. The flame of a brass oil lamp winked back at her.

She stirred, and pain shot up her legs. She lay, she discovered, on a densely packed straw pallet that would have been comfortable if her feet had not been bound to her hands with leather thongs that cut into her flesh. Her mouth felt dry and cottony, as if it were stuffed with a rag. It *was* stuffed with a rag, she realized an instant later; there was a gag across her mouth. She swallowed, and almost retched over a bitter metallic taste, as if she had just bitten down on a sword.

She lifted her head, trying to see her surroundings. She was in a campaign tent sparsely furnished with an iron-studded war chest, a leather coffer, a brazier filled with cold ashes, a padded stool . . . and something odd—a treelike object made of woven straw and shaped like a man's upper torso. She stared at it, trying to puzzle out what it was, and then it came to her. It was what a knight would hang his coat of mail on, when he wasn't armored.

She was trussed up and lying in a knight's tent. A Norman knight's tent by the look of it. And as if in confirmation she heard footsteps passing by and the clipped, nasal intonations of French.

Arianna squeezed her eyes shut. She had trusted that wretched, hateful boy, and he had betrayed her by delivering her into the hands of her enemies. Tears trickled out from beneath clenched lids to run down her cheeks, soaking into the gag. She didn't know why, but the pain of this betrayal made her weep when Ceidro's death and all that had followed afterward had not.

After a long time she opened her eyes onto the conical canvas roof. Gold-tinted clouds scudded across the smoke hole above her. It felt too early to still be today, so it must already be tomorrow, and she must have slept unconscious through the night. The boy must have bathed her, too, for she was no longer covered with mud. Even her hair had been cleaned and she'd been dressed in a new tunic that didn't stink of the stables. He had kept her magic mazer for himself though, for it wasn't with her and she didn't see it lying about.

Her duty now was to plan an escape, but the task of getting loose from her bindings and making her way through an enemy camp bristling with knights and men-at-arms seemed insurmountable. Besides, she had no idea where she was, for all she knew she could be in the black heart of England itself.

She jerked at the sudden sound of laughter that came from right outside the tent. She caught snatches of words: *king, battle,* and something that sounded like *accursed Welsh bastards.* But then the voices dwindled. Far in the distance a trumpet sounded.

The wind came up, rippling the canvas. The flaps that covered the entrance were tied shut, but there was a gap that let in a welcome breath of fresh air. A lance had been stuck into the ground beside the entrance, its bright iron point buried deep into the soft earth. The pennon that hung from the shaft stirred in the sudden draft, and Arianna gasped.

It was a black dragon on a bloodred field.

4

I'm getting too old for this, Raine thought, wincing at the stiffness in his legs as he walked along the banks of the river Dee, searching for his tent.

Deep in his bones, he felt the hours of a night spent in the saddle. But it was more than that, he knew. He had wasted his youth in tournaments and war, hunting and carousing, drinking and wenching, and he was tired of it all.

Tired unto death.

Gaudily colored tents and pavilions were spread in a rainbow array over rolling meadows and among groves of sycamore. They had ridden through the night and most of that morning to arrive here at the main encampment of Henry's army near Basingwerk Abbey.

The war-horses and pack animals corralled by the river had churned the ground into mud, and Raine had to side-step around a particularly noisome puddle. The camp sprawled before him. Sergeants and squires bustled to and fro. Strolling minstrels sang love songs, followed by strolling strumpets ready to satisfy the itch inspired by those same songs. Mountebanks and peddlers relieved new recruits of their hard-earned coppers. Shouts of dismay and triumph mingled with the aroma of simmering soups and potages carried by the breeze from the cooking fires, where men had gathered to drink and gamble at nine-men's morris and dice.

Yet for all the tumult of activity around him Raine felt alone.

Word of the Black Dragon's feat had spread and men called out their praise, but few approached him. He'd always intimidated most men, and he had few close friends. He had stopped making friends long ago, when he started losing them to sword thrusts, crossbow bolts, and the bloody flux.

Contrary to yesterday's storm, today the sun beat down with a vengeance. Rivulets of sweat soaked into the quilted bliaut Raine wore beneath his mail. A fellow knight hailed him as he passed, holding out a wineskin. Suddenly made aware of his thirst, Raine reached for the skin with a smile of gratitude.

He took a swallow, rinsed out his mouth, spat into the dirt, then drank deeply. They spoke of the Welsh ambush; the knight sounded disappointed to have missed the fight. Raine listened with half an ear, mumbling monosyllabic replies. A pair of whores strolled by, arms linked, laughing. One had striking cinnamon-colored hair.

She turned her head and her gaze locked with Raine's. She had dark, velvety eyes. Raine gave her a slow smile. She pouted and tossed her head. But a second later her eyes, full of invitation, were back on Raine's face. His sex thickened and hardened with a fierce and instant response. He felt a sudden need to bury himself in this woman and just forget, forget everything.

Raine jerked his head in the direction of the river. She mouthed the word *later* and passed by on a cloud of laughter and cinnamon hair. Raine thanked the knight for the wine and moved on.

He finally spotted his black dragon standard flying from the center pole of a red tent twenty yards beyond, where a group of squires and foot soldiers had gathered around a fire. He heard the lilting notes of a crwth, accompanying a clear, sweet, and very familiar voice.

"Taliesin!" he roared.

The song halted in midchord. The crowd around the fire dispersed like leaves before the wind. Taliesin emerged with his instrument—a Welsh version of a viol— its bow tucked beneath his arm. He walked toward Raine with his lazy, lanky stride, hair flashing coppery in the sun. He smiled; Raine did not smile back.

"I ought to beat you to a blood pudding. Where the hell have you been?"

Taliesin lowered his eyes meekly to his boots, an act that didn't fool Raine for a minute. "I've been sort of busy."

Raine felt a stirring of alarm. "Busy doing what?"

Taliesin lifted his head and fastened wide, coal-black eyes onto Raine's face. He looked as innocent as a virgin in church. "Why, taking care of your interests, sire. Of course."

"Oh, of course. And did it possibly occur to you that my interests might lie in the general area of riding into battle with my squire at my side, not with some wet-behind-the-ears page who probably still sucks his thumb at night!"

Taliesin shrugged. "He was the best I could do on short notice." His mouth quirked into a grin. "Besides, I understand you managed just fine without me. You even saved the king's life. I've already composed an ode about it. Would you like to hear it?"

"Christ." Raine shuddered at the very idea.

He started for his tent and the youth fell into step beside him. For the hundredth time Raine wondered what possessed him to put up with Taliesin as his squire. The boy made a better poet than he ever would a belted knight, and the last thing Raine needed in his life was a cursed poet, for the love of Christ. He wasn't even sure where Taliesin had come from. One day the boy who had been serving as Raine's squire for five years had been killed by a stray crossbow bolt, and the next day Taliesin was there. And was still there two years later, though it seemed a week didn't go by when Raine wasn't threatening to have the boy flogged within an inch of his life.

A pot of bean potage simmered over the fire in front of his tent. Raine scooped up a ladleful and tipped it into his mouth. While he ate he worked one-handed to unbuckle the baldric that supported his scabbard and sword. Taliesin helped him off with his cumbersome, heavy coat of mail. It jingled softly as the squire laid it down on a nearby patch of grass. Later it would be cleaned by soaking it in a tub of vinegar and then polished to prevent rust.

Raine rubbed at the raw, red marks the mail had left on his neck and wrists. The bliaut he wore beneath his armor was smudged black, stained with sweat, and flecked with mud and dried blood. He thought about a hot bath and sighed because he would have to wash off in the cold river instead.

He had picked up his sword and scabbard and started toward the tent when he felt Taliesin's eyes on him. "What?"

The boy cleared his throat and a guilty flush stained his pale cheeks. "Sire, there's something you should—"

Raine held up his hand. "Whatever it is you've done this time, I don't want to hear about it. All I want right now is wine to get drunk on and a wench in my bed."

Raine missed seeing his squire's eyes widen with alarm. He was imagining running his hands through that cinnamon hair, watching it flow over his thighs as she lowered her head, took him in her mouth. . . . He reached for the tent flap.

"Wait!" Taliesin lunged in front of him, spreading his arms across the entrance like a crucified martyr. "Wait. Don't go in there . . . yet."

Raine lifted one brow in a mild inquiry.

"It's just . . . you could be in a better mood, sire. A *different* mood. If you don't mind my saying it."

Raine wondered if a knight could be hanged for justifiably murdering his squire. "There's nothing wrong with my mood that wine, a woman, and some sleep won't cure." He waited for the boy to move; the boy did not.

Raine's patience was formidable, cultivated after years of bitter experience. But his temper, when he lost it, was awesome. And he was about to lose it. His voice turned deceptively calm and his eyes took on a lazy, hooded look. "Now . . . you have precisely three seconds to get out of my way."

Taliesin jumped aside as if he'd just been prodded with a hot iron. But when the tent flap had closed behind Raine's broad back, the squire's teeth bit down hard on his lower lip and worry lines furrowed his high, pale brow.

Raine blinked, letting his eyes adjust to the dim light. He grasped the hilt of his sword, thinking to take it out of the scabbard to oil it down. It was still stained with blood and would rust if . . .

His grip tightened suddenly at the rustling sound that came from his bed at the rear of the tent. He whipped the sword from the scabbard and lunged forward, to point the blade right between a pair of terrified green eyes.

"You!" he said on a hiss of breath as the tension left him. "What in Christ's name—" He spun around and in three strides was at the entrance. He jerked the flap aside. "Taliesin!" he bellowed. The boy, naturally, was nowhere in sight.

He kept the sword in his hand as he walked back to the bed.

She lay there, staring wide-eyed up at him, tied hand and foot, a gag disfiguring her mouth. A throbbing pulse beat in her throat. Her hair spread across his pillow like a mantle of sable. He had heard tales of wild women who dwelled within forgotten forests, all flowing hair and rent robes. The Welsh called them Furies, and if their eyes were like hers, so filled with damning anger, then they were aptly named.

Her tunic wasn't rent. But it was twisted and pulled tautly across her chest and stomach, outlining her breasts. They were small and uptilted, rising and falling with each labored breath. He caressed those breasts with his gaze and when a rosy flush spread across her high cheekbones, he bared his teeth in a wolfish smile. Her eyes widened further, her breasts rose and fell faster.

Her tunic had also worked its way up above her knees. Her legs were long and bare, and folded up behind her where they were tied to the thongs that fastened her wrists. Very deliberately, with the tip of his sword, he worked her tunic and underlying chainse up until they were as high as the parting between her thighs. There was an intriguing shadow, the hint of dark hair. The inner skin of her thighs was white, like frothed cream, and it rippled beneath his gaze like a lake suddenly stirred by a gust of wind.

He didn't see any hidden daggers.

He raised the sword until it pointed at her throat. Her throat constricted as she swallowed. He pressed the blade closer until it just nicked the skin. And kept it there until her eyes began to glaze and he saw one bead of sweat and then another trickle down from her brow.

Only then did he lower the sword, tossing it behind him on top of his war chest. His eyes never left her face.

Her lids closed and he saw the muscles of her mouth, stretched wide around the gag, sag with relief. Her nostrils flared and her breasts heaved once more, then stilled.

"I'll take that rag out your mouth if you promise not to shout curses at me," he said in Welsh.

She jerked her head up, and the fury was back in her eyes.

"In that case . . ." Raine started to turn away. She

made a strangled sound behind the gag. He looked back; she was nodding her head vigorously.

He eased down onto the folding wooden frame that supported his straw pallet. She'd cleaned herself up some since last he'd seen her—instead of reeking of the stables, she smelled of the sea. Though her disposition didn't appear to have improved any. Using his dagger he sliced through the strip of linen that bound the gag in place.

He watched as she worked her jaws, dredging the saliva back into her mouth. It was a wide, expressive mouth with very full, almost puffy, lips. He counted off the seconds, and got as far as three.

"You filthy, murdering, bitch's whelp—"

He stuffed the gag back in her mouth.

"You left off liar," Raine said.

Color crept up her neck to flood her face. She turned her head aside and he caught the glint of tears. His lips curved into a cynical smile as he said, "Shall I give you a second chance?"

She nodded, very slowly, keeping her head averted, her face buried in the straw ticking. But when he didn't remove the gag right away, she twisted her head back around to look at him.

He had been mistaken about the tears; her eyes were dry.

He took the gag out her mouth. He could practically see her thoughts churning behind her eyes. She wanted to curse him so badly, she was turning purple with the effort to hold it all in. "That's better," he said. " 'Tis a most grievous sin, to break an oath like that."

She had been rubbing her swollen lips against her shoulder bone, but at his words, her head snapped up. "We have a saying in Wales. 'An oath sworn to an enemy is made to be broken.' "

She was quick, he had to grant her that, not that it mattered a whit. He didn't care if his whores had straw between their ears, as long as they were fair and buxom and at least pretended willingness. This wench was none of those things. He wondered what misbegotten maggot had gotten into his squire's brain, that the boy had thought to stow the wretched girl in his tent.

"If you've come to ply your trade for England now," he said, "then I should warn you that we prefer our whores with more honey and less spice—"

She sucked in a sharp breath. "I'm not a whore!"

"Aye? Then you will explain to me how you came to be here." He paused, then added, "In my bed."

Her eyes opened wide and she blinked. "God's death. Do I look like I arrived here willingly?"

He laughed, not about to be taken in by her air of outraged innocence. The wench was after something—doubtless a new protector, or a second chance to bury a knife in his back. But Raine had no intention of becoming either her next *pimpreneau* or her next victim.

He stood up to search through his coffer for a costrel of wine. He hooked a stool around with the toe of his boot and rested his foot on it, one arm draped over his bent knee. He pulled the flask's leather stopper out with his teeth, and tilting back his head, drank deeply. Then he offered it to her with a lift of his brows.

"I can't very well drink with my hands tied behind my back."

"No, you can't." He wasn't going to untie her until she asked him to do it. And all nice and humbly too. "Why did you have my squire truss you up like that in the first place? If you thought to gain my pity, it hasn't worked. And I like my sex in the more conventional ways."

"He's your squire? That wretched, God-cursed, traitorous boy—the liar told me he was a bard! When next I get my hands on him I'm going to gut him with a sword and feed his innards to the dogs." She thought a moment, then added, "He must have lied about his birth as well. No true Cymro could stomach serving the likes of you."

"Isn't that rather too fine a sentiment to be coming

from a wench who serves any man for the price of a sop of
ale?"

She had a strong jaw for a girl, and she was clenching it
so hard he could see the muscle throb. "I am . . . not
. . . a whore."

Raine took another drink, regarding her in silence. He
wasn't surprised to feel his sex stir, lengthening, swelling.
He had been a while without a woman and fighting always
made him randy. He considered taking her after all,
though he'd likely have to leave her bound, and stuff the
gag back in her mouth.

While he studied her, she hadn't moved, nor did her
expression give anything away. Finally, she took a deep
breath. "Would you . . . the ropes are tied so
tightly . . ." Her mouth pressed into a long, tight line.

He waited, but that was the most he was going to get
out of her. "I might consider untying you, if I weren't
convinced you'd come after my eyes again with your
claws."

"I won't. I give you my word."

Raine read the lie in her eyes. He knew well the Welsh.
They would die before breaking their word if given to
friend or kin, but they didn't consider binding an oath
given to an enemy. They reckoned that God, being on the
side of Wales, would forgive such perfidy. In truth, in their
perverted way, the Welsh considered it honorable to
cheat and trick a foe.

" 'Twould be a waste of your breath," he said. "We
Normans have a saying as well . . . 'A Welshman's
honor isn't worth a leper's piss.' "

She reacted as if stung by a wasp. Her whole body
jerked and her head snapped back. "How dare you, of all
people, impugn my honor. I'll have you know that I
am—"

"You are?" he prompted.

"Nobody."

Suddenly weary of the game, Raine turned away.

"Wait! Please . . ." He turned back. "I swear to you on the blood of Christ I will not harm you." Raine snorted, and her voice grew desperate. "I'll even take an oath on the relic in your sword if you like."

Every knight's sword had a holy relic encased in the hilt. Raine's happened to be the eyetooth of Saint Peter, or so he had been told. He thought it more likely, considering the size of the thing, that the tooth had belonged to a wolfhound with a penchant for gnawing on tough bones. But whether the relic was of saint or beast, he wasn't letting her within a spitting distance of his sword.

Still, he restoppered the costrel and tossed it back into the coffer, then strolled over to the bed. He sat down beside her again and she struggled awkwardly over onto her side so that he could get at the bindings. Her tunic was now rucked up practically around her waist, revealing just the barest hint of firm, rounded buttocks. He ran his finger beneath the curved edge of one soft cheek.

She sucked in a sharp breath and her head whipped around. "You b—"

He held up the gag. "Don't say it."

She snapped her jaws together. But if looks could kill, he would have been dancing a carole with the devil in hell.

Her flesh had been softer than the down of a newborn chick. He wanted to run his hands along the length of her calves, up the inside of her thighs, between them. . . .

He sliced quickly through the thongs and pushed to his feet, backing away from her. He did not at all like the way his body was reacting to her, not when his mind insisted on leaving her the bloody hell alone.

The first thing she did was jerk her tunic down over her legs. She straightened, moving slowly, a grimace twisting her face. She chafed at the marks on her wrists. Though the blood rushing back into her cramped muscles must have been agony, she didn't make a sound.

Raine had backed up until he was propped against the

tent's center pole. He crossed his legs at the ankles and folded his arms across his chest. She lifted her head to meet his eyes and he saw her throat work as she swallowed hard. "What . . . what do you mean to do with me?"

"Nothing. Let you go."

Her eyes grew wide. "But why? Aren't you going to—" She cut herself off, and he was amused in spite of himself at the color that flooded her face. As if she didn't know a dozen such words for what she was offering.

He supplied a few. "Plow you? Swive you? Lay you? Tup you? Nay, wench, I think not." He let his gaze roam over her, pretending to consider her charms and to find them lacking. And ignoring all the while the growing heat and pressure in his loins that made him out to be a liar. "You're not to my liking."

Her face had gone from bright red to pale to red again. "Damn you, how often must I say it? I am not a whore!"

Raine stared at her a moment longer. It was as if they played at hoodman's bluff; he couldn't catch her in the truth. Suddenly weary of the game, he jerked his head toward the tent flap. "Ah, Christ. Go on. Get out of here."

She wet her lips, as if seeking the words to change his mind. But in the end she said nothing. She swung her legs around, easing off the bed. Giving him a wide berth, she hugged the side of the tent where his coffer and war chest lay. He saw the intent in her eyes the split second before she acted upon it.

She seized up his sword, slashing sideways in a wide arc. He ducked and the blade bit into the pole with a *chunk* sound, like an ax cutting into kindling. She'd come so close to taking off his head, he'd felt the blade lift his hair.

Her breath came in sobbing gasps as she jerked at the sword, trying to work it free from the tough ash wood. He tackled her around the hips, dragging her down to the

ground and rolling on top of her, trapping her arms behind her back. He pinned her beneath the weight of his
chest and brought his face close to hers. He felt the frantic
pumping of her heart.

She arched her back once, desperately trying to buck
him off, then subsided. For the first time he saw fear in
her eyes.

"Murderer! I hate you! You killed my—"

He smothered the rest of it with his mouth.

He made the kiss brutal and punishing. She tried to
twist her head aside, so he grasped her cheeks between
his hands. His pressed his mouth down harder, bruising
her lips, forcing them open, and he plunged his tongue
inside, burying it deep. She went rigid a moment, then her
pelvis arched, rubbing across his stiff arousal. He tore his
mouth away to watch her face as he pushed his bulging
sex up hard between the cleft in her legs.

Her mouth was wet and open, and her pale face bore
the marks of his fingers. Her neck muscles were pulled
taut and rigid, and her eyes stared up at him, so dark a
green they looked almost black.

He hooked his fingers into the top of her tunic, ripping
it partway open, and the words spilled out of her on a
gasp of breath, tight and raw. "Oh, God, please,
don't . . ."

Raine's mouth twisted into a hard smile. "It seems,
wench, that you are to my liking after all."

"Sire! I'd never thought you'd do such a thing!" Sunlight spilled over them. Taliesin stood just inside the tent,
his face ashen with shock.

Raine's head snapped up and around. "Damn you, boy,
can't you see I'm busy?"

"Oh, goddess . . . This is not at all working the way I
had planned it. Sire, if you but could try to contain your
lust—"

"Taliesin . . . go away."

The boy took a step into the tent. "Nay, sire. Please

don't make me do something we'll both later regret. Only I can't let you dishonor her."

Raine's head sagged. He squeezed his eyes shut, struggling for breath. Slowly, he lifted his head to look at his squire. "Then what in hellfire did you give her to me for?"

"You were supposed to . . . to like her, not bed her."

"Well, as it happens, I don't like her at all. But if I had liked her the end result would be the same, with me on top and her . . ." *Beneath me.* In truth, he rather liked the feel of her beneath him. She was slim-hipped and long-legged and he'd never kissed a softer mouth. He stared at her mouth. Her lips, red and swollen, trembled as she drew in deep, panting breaths, and her eyes were wet and dark. As he watched, a single tear rolled sideways across her cheek and into her hair.

"Sire, please," Taliesin said, sounding almost frantic with worry. "You are not behaving as you ought. You were supposed to have wooed her first."

Raine cursed himself, for that single damn tear had somehow managed to cool his lust. "Wenches like her aren't wooed, they're taken." He lunged to his feet, roughly jerking her up with him. He thrust her so hard at Taliesin that their heads collided. "Next time you think to supply me with a whore, try to ascertain if she's sane first."

He didn't see it coming. Even if he had he would never have believed it.

She drew back her fist and punched him in square in the nose.

A jagged pain blew out the top of his head like a bolt from a catapult. Blood splattered down the front of his bliaut. It poured over the hand he had put up to the throbbing, burning hurt in the middle of his face. Through a red haze he heard her screaming at him.

"God rot your tongue, you loathsome, puffed-up toad. I'm not a whore!"

Raine was a man who prided himself on his self-control. Emotions brought you pain and trouble; they often got you killed. Not giving a blessed damn about anything was the creed he lived by. In his twenty-five years he had been sliced and stabbed, and once he'd even been set on fire. But no one, absolutely no one, had ever succeeded in bloodying his nose, and he was furious. He was going to strangle the wretched bitch.

The squire held her by the arm in a tight grip. Raine advanced on them, heedless of the blood that poured into his mouth and down his chin.

Taliesin thrust the girl protectively behind him and seized Raine's rigid arm. "Sire, you can't kill a woman."

"Yes, I can," Raine said viciously. But the red haze that blurred his vision was beginning to recede.

Blood was splattering everywhere. Raine tilted back his head; blood ran down the back of his throat into his mouth. He tried to wipe the blood off his face with the sleeve of his bliaut. He pressed the soft linen against his nostrils; blood soaked through the material and dripped in a steady stream, as if from a lavabo spigot, onto his chest.

"Get rid of her," he said to Taliesin, his voice deadly. "Permanently this time. And don't ask me what to do with her," he added as Taliesin's mouth opened. "Put her in a grist sack with some rocks and drown her like a cat. Sell her to a Saracen brothel."

Taliesin gasped. "Sire! You can't mean it!"

"No, you're right. Even infidels don't deserve such hell. Bury her in a hole somewhere. Or, better yet, put her in a rotting vessel and send her out to sea. Whatever you do with her, just make cursed certain there isn't a thief's chance in hell our paths ever cross again in this lifetime." He lowered his head. "Christ, where is all this blood coming from?"

She laughed. "I hope you're bleeding to death."

He tilted his head back again. He spoke very calmly, very precisely. "Taliesin, why is she still here?"

"My liege, there is something you should know. She's—"

"I don't want to hear it."

"Prince Owain of Gwynedd's daughter."

"Christ Jesus . . ."

Slowly, he lowered his head again. The bleeding, thank God, had at last stopped. He looked at her with new eyes, seeing things he hadn't noticed before—the breeding in the elegant bones of her face, the delicate white hands that had never toiled in the hot sun, the arrogant tilt of head and chin that came from a lifetime of ruling instead of being ruled. He had thought her uncommonly attractive for a whore; now he saw that she was beautiful. But then anything looked beautiful when it was worth its weight in gold. "Owain's daughter . . ."

She lifted a proud chin. "I told you I was no whore."

Raine ignored her. His gaze jerked over to Taliesin, then back to the girl. "Are you sure . . . ?"

"Aye. But sire, I don't think I like what you're thinking."

"God in heaven . . . This cursed wench is worth a fortune in ransom," Raine said as the full import of her presence in his tent, in his hands, sunk in.

Her chin came up another notch. "Now that you know who I am, you Norman son of a poxed whore, you will accord me the proper respect."

He laughed in her face. "How much do you reckon I can get for her?"

"Goddess preserve me," Taliesin muttered at the avaricious light that blazed in his master's eyes, but Raine wasn't listening.

He was always short of money. He'd won fortunes in wars and tournaments, but the chivalric code he lived by demanded extravagance—in alms and gift giving, in entertaining, in dress and daily living. Money trickled through Raine's fingers like water. If the king gave him Rhuddlan . . . if the king gave him Rhuddlan, he could well use the gold this highborn wench was going to bring him.

An excited voice jerked Raine's attention off the girl. Sir Odo's page appeared at the entrance to the tent. "Forgive me, sire. The King's Grace commands that you attend him. He's bathing at the abbey, sire, in the holy well."

Raine spun around, pulling the bloodied bliaut over his head. He kicked his coffer onto its side, dumping out the contents to find a clean overtunic. "Don't let her out of your sight," he said to his squire over his shoulder.

"But—"

"I swear by the cross, if you lose her on me, Taliesin, I will string you up by your thumbs."

"A moment ago, sire, you wanted me to put her in a leaky boat and send her out to sea."

"A moment ago she was a useless whore. Now she's the highborn wench who's going to make me rich. If you lose her on me, boy, I will tie you up with your own guts and toss you in the river to drown."

Taliesin heaved a huge sigh. "I won't lose her, sire. But if you'd only think a moment beyond this ransom business you would see that—" But Raine had disappeared.

Taliesin looked down into Arianna's stunned face. His grip around her arm tightened and he gave her a little shake. "What is wrong with you two?" he demanded with childish petulance. "This isn't at all turning out the way it is supposed to."

5

Raine tossed a coin into the toll keeper's basket, then pushed his way through the band of pilgrims that clogged the abbey's gate. They had a bagpiper with them, and they sang a rousing crusader's song, swinging their palm branches back and forth in time to the beat.

One of the fronds slapped Raine in the face. He brushed it aside irritably, almost tripping over a beggar's staff thrust across his path. He whirled around, his hand on his sword . . . and looked into puckered, black and empty sockets.

"Alms, messire, alms!" The beggar held out a scabrous hand. Raine fished in his alms purse for some coins, but he was careful to keep his eyes averted from the mutilated face.

The abbey was packed with people. Besides the usual pilgrims and penitents seeking salvation, and the diseased and deformed seeking a cure, there had been added the stewards, pages, and sycophants who everywhere followed in the wake of the king. In a grove of sycamore before the abbey church, a geyser spewed up from a spring to fall into a rock-lined pool. Droplets of water clung to the leaves and sparkled in the sun like diamond chips.

The king bathed alone, but at least twenty fawning nobles stood around him, bearing towels and clothes, food and drink. Their shouts and laughter almost drowned out the abbey's bell as it rang for sext. Disdaining assistance, Henry pulled himself out of the pool by the strength of his long, muscular arms. An earl handed him a linen towel edged with lace. He rubbed it briskly over his deep chest and a belly that was already showing a slight tendency to swell with fat.

Raine had been to the abbey well once before. When he was six he had been forced to make a pilgrimage here, along with the other Chester stableboys. The castle chaplain had told them a story about the well, about a Welsh girl by the name of Winifred who had been a beautiful virgin dedicated to her chastity. As Raine remembered it, one day a horn-mad prince had come along and decided, naturally, that he wanted to tup her. When she denied him, he struck off her head in a fit of temper. Winifred's head had rolled down a hill and where it came to rest a spring gushed forth, the holy well now known for its miraculous cures.

As a boy, Raine had pictured the lady's head bouncing down the hill like an inflated pig's bladder, and he'd laughed out loud. The priest had given him a clout on the ear for it, but he still thought it funny.

"Do you find something amusing, big brother?"

Raine turned at the sound of his brother's voice. His smile widened when he saw that Hugh's flushed face was topped by an overly large gold-tissued cap that didn't quite hide the purple crust of clotted blood along his temple. He wondered how his brother, who hated fighting, had acquired the wound. "What happened to you? Did you run into a Welsh ambush too?"

"At least *I* didn't lead my king into one."

"Neither did I," Raine said, but his voice was cut across by King Henry's roar.

"You will cease this childish bickering at once, the pair of you!" The king stood before them with his bandy legs spread wide, his fists on his hips. "For God, I will banish you both if you insist on disturbing my peace!"

Hugh flushed and mumbled an apology. Raine met the king's fiery gaze with a blank expression, though he knew that if Henry decided one of them must go, it would not be Hugh.

But King Henry's temper had always sputtered and flared like a guttering candle. Now he was smiling at Raine, drawing him to his side. Draping his arm around Raine's shoulder, he led him around the well toward the open doors of the abbey church. Water lapped over the edge of the pool. The air smelled sickly sweet from the queer reddish grass that grew on the stones that lined the basin.

Henry gestured to the bottom of the well. "They say 'tis Saint Winifred's hair and blood that we see."

"It looks like moss to me, Your Grace."

Henry barked a laugh and his arm squeezed Raine's shoulder in a rough embrace. "God's eyes, you're a cynical bastard. Don't you believe in anything?"

"Precious little," Raine said truthfully.

Henry stopped and turned Raine to face him, his big hands resting heavily on the knight's shoulders. "I'd like to think you believe in me. For you're a damn fine man to have guarding one's back."

"I am your liege man, sire," Raine said, but there was an edge to his voice. The code of a knight, the code he lived by, was the only thing in this world he still believed in. But he was afraid, so very afraid, that he had even stopped believing in that years ago. And if that were true, then he would have nothing.

Henry said nothing, but his pale eyes misted and he punched Raine lightly on the neck. It was a gentler version of the buffet given to a man on the day he was first knighted and swore allegiance to his liege lord. "Come with me, for I would seek your advice on what to do about these accursed Welsh," he said, then turned and strode briskly into the church, leaving Raine to follow in his wake. "I trow, there is no honor among the Welsh," he tossed over his shoulder.

Raine said nothing. It was his experience that there was no honor anywhere.

The king was using the church as his headquarters. Bedding and cooking fires littered the nave. Horses, tied to the columns, fed from oat bags and staled into the rushes. Armed men lounged along the aisles, playing at draughts and dice, while varlets scurried about, bearing baskets of bread loaves and jacks of ale.

A trestle table draped with white cloths had been set up for the king's repast, but Henry hated the idea of sitting down for anything. Now he paced the aisle of the nave, chewing on a capon leg. Raine wondered if he dared to bring up the subject of Rhuddlan again. He'd already spoken to the king about it once, on that long overnight ride. But he'd been given no definite promise.

Raine mouthed a silent curse. To hell with it—he would come right out and ask Henry for the fief and accept the decision, be it aye or nay. But then the sight of Hugh strolling toward them down the nave stilled his tongue. The earl's lips bore a satisfied smirk, but Raine detected the small tick at the corner of his right eye that meant Hugh was nervous. Raine began to hope again.

Until Henry turned to him and said, "Your brother the earl has put in a claim for Rhuddlan. I regret to say this, for I know how you've set your heart upon it, but he does have a measure of right on his side." The king, who had a fascination with the law, went on to explain with some exuberance the legal precedence for the Earl of Chester's claim.

Raine wanted to put a fist through his brother's gloating face. He told himself that it didn't matter, it didn't matter, there would be other castles, other chances, but he was twenty-five . . . twenty-five and all he had to his name was a sword.

A procession of chanting, white-cowled monks entered the transept, drowning out the king's words. A squire genuflected before Henry, presenting a wine cup. Raine's gaze fell on the top of the squire's bright coppery curls.

The squire started to back away and Raine's hand lashed out, jerking the boy to his side. "What in Christ's name are you doing here?" he growled beneath his breath. "Where's the Gwynedd wench?"

"She's safe, sire. Never fear."

"Safe? What is that supposed to—" But Taliesin wriggled free, slithering like an eel in and out among the columns to disappear into the crowd.

"Goddamn it!" The monks suddenly ceased their chanting and Raine's curse echoed against the soaring ceiling like the clap of a bell.

"Raine?"

Raine jerked his eyes from the last place Taliesin had been and onto his king's perplexed face. "I'm sorry, Your Grace. I wasn't listening."

"I said that it is impossible to wage a proper war against a people who refuse to stand and fight in the open. What say you to the notion of making inquiries of this petty prince? To see if he is whipped enough to sue for peace."

"I say we don't stand a piss-pot's chance of conquering the Welsh." Raine saw Hugh roll his eyes, but he knew King Henry preferred plain speaking and he went on. "But then neither can Gwynedd defeat us. It's a stalemate and Owain knows it. He might agree to talk peace. The best you can hope for out of it all is to compel him to do homage to you for Wales, then let him rule his country as he wills, declare yourself the winner and leave."

Henry nodded reluctantly. He might not like his alternatives, but he was no fool. "And if he doesn't agree to my terms?"

"He will." Raine allowed a slow smile to curve his lips. "Particularly when you inform him that we have his daughter."

Henry's protruding eyes bulged even further with his surprise. "We do?" He tossed the naked capon bone into the rushes and slapped his greasy hands together. "Ah, Raine, Raine, my best and bravest knight, *do* we?"

"How on earth did you ever acquire Gwynedd's daughter?" Hugh asked, a worried frown on his face.

Taliesin came toward the king bearing a tray of nuts and wafers.

"Aye, Your Grace, I have her," Raine said, silently praying that was still the case and trying to catch his squire's eyes.

"Then we shall send a messenger to Owain immediately," Henry exclaimed as he paced. "By God's eyes, but I would barter my immortal soul to see the fellow's face—"

"If I might make a humble suggestion, Your Grace," said a clear, young voice.

Henry stiffened and whirled, to gape at the kneeling servant who had suddenly spoken without permission. "Who are you to dare interrupt your king?" he roared.

Raine sighed. "Forgive him, Your Grace. The lad is my—"

"Bard," Taliesin supplied, with a bright smile.

"Squire," Raine ground out between clenched jaws.

"Your bard!" Hugh hooted. "You have no land, no castles, yet you have yourself a bard." His laughter boomed throughout the nave. "I suppose no self-respecting knight-errant should be without one."

Henry quelled Hugh with a single look. His big hand fell on Taliesin's shoulder, propelling the boy to his feet. "You are Welsh, lad, are you not? I detect a certain accent in your speech." Raine had detected it as well. The wretched boy had spoken flawless French for two years and now he had suddenly acquired a Welsh burr on his tongue.

"I have heard that yours is a race of people that believes in the freedom to speak one's mind, even in front of a prince," Henry was saying with a hard-edged smile. "So I will listen to what you have to say, and afterward Sir Raine will have you flogged for your impertinence."

"Aye, well . . ." Taliesin cast an apprehensive glance at Raine, then focused all his attention onto the king, flashing a smile so dazzling that Henry blinked. "Your Grace, do not ransom the Lady Arianna back to her father. Rather, keep her as hostage, as surety against the prince's future aggression."

He paused, and when this elicited no response from the three men he plunged on. "As your hostage she becomes your ward and you can dispose of her as you will, either to convent or marriage. I say give her as bride to the new Lord of Rhuddlan. For the prince will not likely attack the man and castle that harbors his only and most cherished daughter." A stunned silence followed this speech. Taliesin kept his gaze carefully fixed on the king.

"But I'm already married," Hugh finally said.

Raine said nothing, merely stared at his squire with an utterly appalled look on his normally impassive face.

The king stroked his beard. "There is merit to what you suggest . . ."

Taliesin's head bobbed with his enthusiasm. "Aye, aye, much merit, milord. And think, too, since Your Grace is torn over the disposition of Rhuddlan, perhaps Your Grace might want to hold a tourney to decide who wins the honor. A trial by mock combat. A tourney would also be a grand celebration to mark your victory in Wales, milord."

A slow smile broke over Henry's face. "Aye . . . Aye . . ."

"But . . . but . . ." Hugh sputtered.

Taliesin turned the full power of his beautiful smile onto Hugh. "Should you win the tourney, my lord earl, you could always reward a most deserving and loyal vassal with the fief and the bride." His gaze passed on to Raine's frozen face. "You, sire, are of course free to take the Lady Arianna to wife."

"Fight a tourney for Rhuddlan!" Hugh exploded. "That is the most ridiculous—"

"By God's eyes!" Henry roared. "But I do like the way this lad thinks. He has a brain like mine."

"He's a God-cursed fool," Raine said, completely unmindful of the fact that he'd just insulted his king. He rather liked the idea of settling the issue of Rhuddlan in a tournament, for he had no doubt that he would win. But to have to take Owain's daughter to wife . . . For this I will kill the boy, Raine thought. This time, for certes, I will kill him.

But to his horror Raine heard the king's bullish voice exclaiming, as if it had been his idea all along, "You, Sir Raine . . . and you, my lord Earl of Chester, will meet man-to-man in a joust with blunted lances. And the winner will get Rhuddlan and Owain's daughter as the prize!"

"Up, up, up, milady!" The bed curtains snapped apart with a rustle of embroidered damask and a cloud of dust. Bright sunlight pierced through the closed lids of Arianna's eyes.

Groaning, she rolled onto her stomach and pulled the pillow over her head. "Go away, Edith. Leave me alone."

There was no reason why she should get up. Not when this day promised to be another like yesterday. A day spent spinning out the hours shut up in this bedchamber within Rhuddlan's great hall, while the King of England met with her father. And used her as a whip to bring Gwynedd to heel. Even now they were probably setting the price of her ransom. She dreaded finding out what her life would cost her father, and Wales.

The maidservant had not gone away. She pulled back the bedcovers, exposing Arianna's naked flesh to the sting of the cold morning air.

"God's death!" Arianna leapt up, snatching at the fur-lined robe Edith held out. But the woman's bovine smile didn't waver. She had a round, poxed face, with small, squinty eyes like squash seeds and wren-brown hair that hung in strings over her bony shoulders, like a hank of flax. She had yet, in four days, to say anything to Arianna beyond the commonest banalities.

"It's too fine a day to be a slug-a-bed, milady," Edith said, and smiled again.

Arianna gritted her teeth around another blasphemous curse. Couldn't the fool woman see that she was a prisoner? She could spend the day abed or up and pacing the floor and it would make little difference.

Nevertheless Arianna did get up, going over to the laver by the window. As she washed, the ringing of the chapel bell drifted in on the breeze, calling the faithful to worship. But she wouldn't be able to attend Mass until after the nooning. It was the only time she was allowed out of the bedchamber, and even then she was accompanied by guards—two thick, knotty fellows, each big enough to carry off the prize ram at a wrestling match.

On a stool beside the empty brazier, Edith had set a tray of manchet bread glazed with honey and a pot of ale, and Arianna sat down to break her fast. " 'Tis wash day, milady," Edith said, as she stripped the bed. "You'll be having nice fresh, clean sheets this night."

"Thank you, Edith," Arianna said, giving the woman the warmest smile she could muster. It was hardly Edith's fault that she was a prisoner of the Normans, and Arianna felt guilty for having taken her temper out on the hapless servant.

Her arms loaded with linen, Edith bustled from the

room. Arianna wandered over to the window. It was indeed a beautiful morning, though it had poured rain throughout the night, turning the yard into a sea of mud. At least she hadn't been shut up within the keep's stone vault this time. Her prison was a comfortable chamber in the long, two-storied timbered hall within the bailey.

The yard below her window was alive with activity. A cook, lugging a steaming cauldron, emerged from the kitchen, almost colliding with a baker who performed a fancy two-step while balancing a tray of loaves on his head. Now that the chapel bell had ceased its pealing, she could hear the smack of the laundresses' wooden paddles beating sheets in the wash trough. A cart piled high with new rushes for the floors rattled by beneath her window.

Just then the watchman blew his horn and the gate swung wide. A dozen men on horseback clattered at a fast trot across the drawbridge, the man in the lead bearing the standard that had haunted her dreams—a black dragon on a bloodred field.

Rache and lyam-hounds dashed among the flying hooves. The pack bayed in a fever of excitement, red tongues lolling. A man bore a slaughtered boar's head on the point of a spear, while another blew on the hunting horn, announcing the kill. The black knight reined up before the hall. He must have been out hunting since dawn. His horse's sides were flecked with foam from the gallop of the chase, but still the spirited charger danced about, so a squire had to run up and hold the stirrup for the knight to dismount. The squire, she saw by the flash of his red hair, was that wretched, traitorous boy.

The knight had on spurred boots that were higher than was fashionable, reaching to his knees. His plain leather tunic was slit up the side for riding. It revealed thighs encased in tight chausses that hugged every sinew of lean, hard muscles built from hours spent in the tilting yard. His head was bare and the wind stirred his raven-black hair. His chainse showed white beneath the open neck of his tunic, contrasting with the sun-browned skin of his hard and ruthless face. His incredible arrogance was evident in the very way he walked, in his purposeful, long-legged stride and the sauntering sway of his lean hips.

He stopped just below her window. Close enough to spit on. He stood in profile to her and the sun highlighted the sharp bones of his predatory nose and high cheekbones. He was close enough that if he tilted back his head he would see her. But he was in deep conversation with his squire.

Though she was his prisoner, the only time they had been face-to-face since that day in his tent was last afternoon, when their paths had crossed in the bailey while she was on her way to Mass. She had made certain he knew just what she thought of him by allowing all the hatred she felt to show in her face, and he . . . he had looked right through her with those opaque gray eyes.

She was of no importance to him beyond the ransom she could bring. In truth, she thanked God nightly that he had no desire to lie with her, for she would be returned to her father a virgin still. But for some reason she couldn't begin to understand, his lack of interest stung her pride. Dozens of men had begged for her hand in marriage, but none had been deemed good enough for her. Yet this Norman knight, who was a drab's by-blow without title or land, looked at her—when he bothered to look at all—as if she weren't good enough to wipe his boots.

Arianna started to push away from the window when her gaze fell on the laver nearby. The basin was filled with water covered by a soapy scum left over from her wash.

Before she could lose her nerve, she picked up the basin and flung the contents out the window, shifting her aim at the last minute so that the water landed not on his head, as she'd originally intended, but at his feet. The water splattered on the wet ground, splashing mud onto his boots.

The knight's dark head snapped up and around. Arianna looked right through him, then she shifted her gaze over to the squire, who was also staring up at her, surprise on his face, and she smiled at the boy.

"Oh dear, forgive me, Taliesin," she said in her sweetest voice. "I didn't see you there. I hope I didn't muddy you."

The squire had been standing well apart from his master and had not been touched by the flying mud. A big grin stretched his mobile face. "Nay, and good morrow to you, milady."

"Good morrow, Taliesin," she said, flashing a brilliant smile in return.

Arianna turned from the window, pleased with herself. That had certainly shown the Norman that if she meant little to him, he meant even less to her.

A few moments later the sound of footsteps on the stairs caused Arianna to regret her rash impulse to put the man in his place. But when the door swung open it was Taliesin who entered.

"Sir Raine summons you to the bailey, milady," he said, his face blank, though she thought she caught a twinkle of gleeful anticipation in his eyes.

Arianna's mouth went dry. She nodded and, her spine rigid, her head held high, she followed the squire out the chamber. But it was the two burly guards, and not Taliesin, who brought her outside and into the bailey.

The knight stood next to the hitching post beside the hall's front stairs. She stopped before him and met his hard, gray eyes. "You wished to speak with me, Norman?"

He braced one muddy boot against the rail. "Clean them."

Arianna's chin jerked up. "Summon a servant."

"You dirtied them, wench. Now you will clean them."

There wasn't a trace of inflection in his voice, and his eyes remained flat, inscrutable. They could have been discussing the weather.

She gave him a freezing smile and cooed in a sing-song, "Clean your boots, sir bastard knight? Why, I would sooner eat them."

He bared his teeth back at her. "Shall I summon the cook?"

He wouldn't dare, would he? Of course he wouldn't dare. "You wouldn't dare."

He shrugged. "Nay, you are right. It would be a waste of a perfectly good pair of boots." His face hardened, and his eyes took on a lazy, dangerous cast. "Clean them, wench. Or feel the flat of my sword across your backside."

She heard a snickering coming from the two guards behind her, which was abruptly cut off at a look from their master. The laundresses had stopped their beating, and an expectant silence had fallen over a bailey, which seemed suddenly filled with people. Even the mews and kennels were quiet. She thought of how humiliating it would be to be beaten like a disobedient child in front of all these strangers, and she knew she didn't have the courage to test his resolve.

His eyes had fastened onto her mouth, as if he waited for her to speak. Her lips felt suddenly dry, and she wet them with her tongue. "I . . . I don't have anything to wipe them with."

His hand lashed out and Arianna flinched, thinking he meant to hit her. Instead he grabbed a fistful of her bliaut and yanked. The material gave way with a loud rip and Arianna flinched again. He jerked at the thin silk cloth twice more until a piece of it came free in his hands. He held it out to her.

"Now you do," he said.

Beneath her bliaut, Arianna wore a pelisse, and beneath that a chainse. He hadn't exactly stripped her naked, and her cheeks burned more from anger than embarrassment. She snatched the piece of ripped cloth out of his hand, but in the next instant she was possessed with a desire to laugh. It seemed he thought her good enough to wipe his boots after all.

Leaning over, she brushed off the drying flecks of mud. The boot was made of the finest Cordovan goatskin, but it had long since seen better days. The leather had almost worn through at the inside of his calf, from rubbing against his horse's flanks. Her father would have thrown such a pair of boots out long ago. The knight obviously needed the money she would bring him. It angered her to think that his lot in life would now improve because of her.

Finished, she glanced up, expecting him to be watching her and gloating over her humiliation. But his eyes were focused instead on the keep at the far end of the bailey, and she saw to her surprise a look of naked hunger on his face.

"I've finished, Norman."

His head jerked around, and he looked at her a moment, and she thought he might really be seeing her this time, though his face had regained its usual closed expression. He studied the boot, pointing to the heel. "You missed a spot."

Arianna's jaws clenched. She bent over, rubbing so hard her hand slipped and she cut her knuckles on the sharp edge of his spur. Tears of pain stung her eyes and she cursed beneath her breath.

"Did you say something, wench?"

She straightened with a snap. "I said give me the other boot and damn you to hell."

His lips moved slightly, and she thought he might be about to smile. Instead, he dropped the spotless boot to the ground and supplanted it with a muddy one. Arianna finished the task in silence.

He examined her work. "Passable, but just barely." His head came up and she saw in his eyes the glint of some unnamed emotion that came and then vanished. "I wouldn't hire myself out as a servant though, if I were you. You haven't the talent for it."

In spite of herself Arianna almost smiled. But before she could think of a snappy retort he had started to turn, and she realized he was about to walk away. She had found out nothing about what he intended to do with her.

"Wait!" she cried out, louder than she'd meant to. He paused, black brows raised in a mild enquiry. "Have . . . have you spoken with my father? Is the ransom arranged?"

"The matter has been concluded to my king's satisfaction," was all he said.

Arianna wanted to scream with frustration. She wanted to slap that impassive face. She wanted to pound her fists against his indifferent chest. She wanted to make him *feel* something. "Well, it has not been concluded to my satisfaction! You owe Gwynedd a blood debt, Norman. The day will come, and soon I pray, when that debt will be paid with your life."

"What blood debt?"

He looked genuinely surprised. She realized suddenly that he truly didn't know the identity of the youth he had struck down before the gates of Rhuddlan. "The man you took this castle from, the man you killed with your lance . . . he was my brother."

His eyes widened slightly. "Ah, I see . . . So that explains why you've been trying to stick something lethal in me since first we met." He shrugged, shaking his head. "I owe you no blood debt, girl. The blame for your brother's death lands on your father's and King Henry's heads for starting this fool war in the first place. And on the boy's own head for being stupid enough to fall for a trick the veriest babe shouldn't have fallen for."

He hesitated, and though his voice remained flat and cold, she thought his face softened a little. "It was war, my lady. If it was in truth my lance that killed your brother, it wasn't personal. God willing his soul found salvation."

Tears burned her eyes, but she would be damned first before she would weep before this man. It made it worse somehow, knowing that he was right. She drew in a deep breath to alleviate some of the crushing ache in her chest, and to her horror a sob burst from her throat. Humiliated, she whirled, stumbling away from him, but he snagged her arm, hauling her up against his chest. His fist closed around her hair, pulling her head back and he brought his mouth down over hers.

She went still as all the breath left her body. His lips moved over hers, hard at first, then gentling. She brought her hands up between them, to push him away. Instead her fingers curled around the edges of his leather tunic and she clung to him as the blood rushed from her head. She didn't know she kissed him back, she didn't hear him groan. Her senses reeled, focused only on the strange, sweet, and painful feel of his lips on hers.

He released her mouth. She looked up at him, dazed, confused by the sensations that coursed through her body. She was dissolving, melting, burning up inside. Her lips parted open.

His head dipped, but then his fist tightened in her hair and he pulled her away from him. He stepped back, staring at her with eyes that were wide open and filled with the same bewildered shock she knew were in her own.

That afternoon Arianna sat on a stool before the empty brazier, listlessly picking at a bowl of veal piquant, when behind her the door flung open, slamming against the wall. She whirled in alarm, her fist pressed to her breast, just as a boy came hurtling into the chamber, shoved in by one of the guards.

"Rhodri!" Arianna jumped up to fling her arms around the boy. But her joy turned immediately to horror as it occurred to her what her younger brother's presence must mean. "Oh, Rhodri, is Father dead? Has he been captured?"

"Leave off, Arianna, for the love of Christ. You're smothering me." Rhodri wriggled out of her hug. At fourteen he considered himself too old for such displays of affection. He smoothed the front of his ruffled tunic. "Nay, Father is well. He's just agreed to a truce with that devil's spawn, King Henry."

"A truce? Have I been ransomed then? Are you here to escort me home?"

"Well, not exactly." Rhodri's eyes shifted away from hers.

"What exactly?"

He ignored her, prowling the room. Like all of Owain's children, he bore the Gwynedd features. His eyes were several shades paler than Arianna's, the color of baby ferns. His hair was a lighter brown, tipped golden by the sun. Though it had only been a little over a month since she had last seen him, he seemed to have sprouted a foot. He was all skinny arms and legs.

He stopped his prowling when he discovered her dinner. He tore off a piece of bread, stuffing it in his mouth.

Arianna heaved an impatient sigh. "Rhodri, will you tell me—"

"Aye, aye." He spoke around the food in his mouth. "As I said, Father signed a truce with England. He paid homage to King Henry, but England has agreed to withdraw and respect in future our right to rule ourselves. In return he had to give up Rhuddlan, along with the whole of the *cantref* of Tegeingl, and two hostages as surety for future peace." He took a swig of the ale to wash down the bread. "Us."

Arianna's mouth quirked into a funny smile. "Us? We . . . we're to be the hostages?" The thought of being condemned to a life in England was so horrible she could scarce imagine it.

"Aye." Rhodri's chin began to tremble and he clenched

his jaw to stop it. "At least we won't be locked up." He shuddered. "I don't think I could bear that. It won't be so bad, you'll see," he said, sounding as if he tried to convince himself. "I'm to be made a squire in some Norman's household."

"And what of me?" Arianna asked, though she hardly needed to. Women hostages were invariably entombed in some convent. She told herself such a life would be for the greater glory of God, but that didn't make her feel any better. "Oh, Rhodri. I don't think I will make a particularly good nun."

"Huh? Who says you're going to be a nun? You're being married off to the new Lord of Rhuddlan. Whoever he's to be." He tilted back his head and started to drink again from the ale pot.

Arianna seized his arm. "Married! Married to *whom?*"

"Jesu. Look what you've done." The ale had splattered over the front of Rhodri's tunic. He wiped at the wet spot, then picked up another piece of bread and began to gnaw on it. "King Henry is to hold a tournament to find out who it's to be—a joust between two contenders. One is the Earl of Chester—'course, he already has a wife and plenty of castles, too, so he'll no doubt bestow the honor onto one of his vassals and that'll be the man you have to marry."

"And the other one?" She snatched the bread from his hand. "Damn you, Rhodri! Will you leave off eating for a moment?"

Rhodri gave her a wounded look. "I've been trying to tell you, if you'd only let me get a word in. The other knight to joust will be the Black Dragon."

Though she had expected, dreaded, as much, Arianna didn't want to believe him. She shook her head wildly back and forth. "Nay, you lie, Rhodri. Father wouldn't do this to me. He wouldn't marry me to such a man."

Rhodri's eyes filled with pity. "Father explained it all. 'Tis for Gwynedd that he does this. Once the truce is signed and your, uh . . . marriage takes place, King Henry will withdraw and leave us in peace to rule ourselves." He lifted one shoulder in a tiny, hopeless shrug. "Mayhap the Black Dragon won't win the joust."

Arianna spun around, clutching at her hair, her scoffing laughter hoarsened by the sobs that threatened to burst from her chest. She wanted to rage at how unfair it all was, but then she'd always known that when she married it would be for the good of Gwynedd, and to a man she'd likely never met before. It was just that a secret part of her, the romantic part of her, had always believed that she would take but one look at her betrothed's handsome face, gaze once into his adoring eyes, and fall wildly in love. As he would fall passionately, irrevocably in love with her.

But it hadn't happened that way.

Her eyes clenched shut and she saw a man's face—hard and remote, with a ruthless mouth and cold, flint-gray eyes filled with nothing at all.

The face of the man who would be her husband.

6

"I'll marry the wench if I must, to get Rhuddlan. But I sure in hellfire don't have to like it."

"Goddess, preserve me," Taliesin muttered beneath his breath. He blew on the pointed bronze boss of Raine's shield, then gave it a vigorous polish with a linen rag. "She doesn't appear to think much of you either, my liege."

Raine stopped pacing the narrow confines of his tent to point a finger at his squire. "And don't think I've forgotten who's responsible for this entire mess. I still intend to punish you for it too. Once I decide on a method painful enough. At the moment I'm torn between putting you blindfolded into a pit with a wild boar, or dropping you from the top of the keep into a cauldron of boiling oil."

Raine's threats as usual had no effect on his squire. Taliesin grinned as he rested the shield against the side of a war chest to admire his handiwork. He had varnished it red, then painted Raine's black dragon device on the vaulted surface.

Bright sunlight streamed through the open flap of the tent, causing the red canvas walls to glow like the inside of a brazier. Outside, a loud fanfare from a brace of horns competed with the incessant clatter of squires nailing on spear heads and heralds crying out knightly challenges, for within the hour the tournament would begin.

Taliesin placed a stool in the center of the tent, along with Raine's boots. Raine's brooding gaze had fallen on the raw gouge in the pole left when the Lady Arianna had attempted to take off his head with his own sword. He traced the mark with his finger and the squire, watching him, flashed a teasing smile. "Mayhap, sire, you should wear your armor when you go to bed her."

In spite of his sour mood Raine had to laugh at the picture conjured by his squire's words. In truth, the thought of bedding the wench was the only thing that pleased him about the marriage. He wanted her naked and beneath him. He wanted to ravish her mouth with his tongue. He wanted to thrust himself so hard and deeply inside her, she'd well and truly know who mastered her.

Raine's sex swelled, thrusting against his tight braies. The reaction, unbidden and instantaneous, surprised and annoyed him. After the vigorous romping he had indulged in this past week with a cinnamon-haired wench by the name of Maud, a whole bevy of women strolling naked past his tent shouldn't have been able to raise more than his eyebrow. Always before, no matter how long the abstinence, he could still maintain an iron control over his sexual appetite, but he'd never felt lust like this. He could almost taste it in his mouth, like blood.

With reverent care, Taliesin had lifted the burnished mailed hosen that lay across the bed and brought them to Raine. "The Lady Arianna will make good bedsport, don't you think so, sire? The bards of Gwynedd all sing of her beauty."

"Doubtless they'd better, since she's old Owain's daughter. They'd be singing her praises if she had a face shaped like a battle-ax and warts on her nose." Raine eased down onto the stool, stretching out his legs so that

Taliesin could pull on the hosen and trying to ignore the throbbing heat in his groin.

Taliesin knelt and began to fasten the buckles that ran up the back of the leg armor. "The two of you will get along much better once you're wed," he said. His brow furrowed, and he sighed as he pushed on Raine's boots. "At least I hope so."

Raine stood, stamping down his heels. "It is her place to learn to get along with me."

"And if she does not, you can always pack her off to a convent once she produces your heirs." The boy was laughing as he climbed onto the stool, bearing Raine's coat of mail. "Shall I pray that she conceives quickly and often?"

Raine shook his head, unable to keep from smiling at his squire's antics. Turning, he grunted as the hauberk settled onto his shoulders. The mailed coat, varnished a dull black, was made of a double thickness of tiny, finely tempered steel links and weighed close to thirty pounds.

In spite of what Taliesin implied, it was not Raine's intention to treat the girl cruelly once they wed. Nor would he set her aside once she produced his heir. As long as she performed her duties as his wife, bred him sons, and obeyed his commands, he would treat her well. If she rebelled, however, she would suffer for it.

"Sire, I really do think you misjudge the Lady Arianna. Is your dislike of her because you've heard those ridiculous rumors that she's a witch?"

Raine hadn't heard, but he wasn't surprised. Half the women in Wales claimed some sort of talent for bringing lovers together, casting spells, and predicting the future.

"Well, they're all terrible lies, sire. The Lady Arianna is a true *filid*, a seer in the manner of the ancient ones, and much revered by our people."

"Aye? Well, she can't be very good at it and more's the pity. Otherwise she'd have seen her own future soon enough to have avoided it, and we'd both have been spared a marriage neither of us wants."

Taliesin heaved a loud sigh as he buckled the leather baldric at Raine's waist. Raine unsheathed the sword, flexing and loosening his wrist with a few practice parries. It was not the sword he normally fought with, but rather an arm of courtesy used only in tournaments, its blade dulled, the point blunted. His lance would be dulled, too, and made of brittle wood to shatter on impact, for the Holy Church preached that a man who died in a tournament was automatically condemned to the fires of hell. A destination, Raine thought with a mental shrug, most knights were bound for in any event. Still, they normally tried not to kill each other in the course of a tournament, although it frequently happened.

Raine became aware that Taliesin was watching him intently, and he wondered what new mischief the boy was up to. "What have you done now?"

Taliesin's eyes went blank and round. "Who me? Why nothing, sire. It's just . . ." He licked his lips and cleared his throat. He scuffed the dirt with his shoe. "It's about you and the Lady Arianna and, well . . . it seems you haven't exactly taken to one another. I didn't want to mention this to you before, but the Lady Arianna is your destiny, sire, and you've bungled things so badly I fear you are now going to have to go on a most arduous quest to win her love." A baffled expression crossed the boy's face. "I can't understand why this is happening, but the whole thing is not going at all as smoothly as I had once thought it would . . ."

Raine stared at Taliesin as if the boy had suddenly started gnashing his teeth and foaming at the mouth. He'd never noticed it about the Welsh before, but he was beginning to suspect they were all a little mad.

He was sure of it an instant later when Taliesin said, "So I was thinking . . . there's still time before the tournament starts, my liege. Time enough to pay your respects to the Lady Arianna. Ask her, mayhap, if you might wear her favor. Woo her a little."

"No."

"Why not? Do you fear she'll attack you again? If she does, all you needs must do is kiss her. That seemed to work well the last time."

Raine stared at Taliesin in stunned silence, then he threw back his head and laughed. It was either that, he thought, or go mad along with everyone else.

He was still smiling moments later as he left the tent and Taliesin called after him. "You're going to speak to the Lady Arianna then?"

"No, I am not," he said. He meant it too. At the time.

Raine strolled the avenue of gem-colored tents and pavilions that hugged the banks of the river Clwyd, sheltering within the shadow of Rhuddlan's walls. A smoky haze drifted on the air from great fire pits where boar and stag roasted for that afternoon's feast. But the gold-and-blue banners that lined the way still snapped in a breeze that took the edge off the heat of the summer sun.

The road to the castle was crowded with knights on destriers and ladies on white mules; boys playing football and squires airing their masters' hawks; and everywhere people selling things, from horse dealers to pasty hawkers to armorers pulling carts piled high with weapons. A jongleur wearing a rainbow-striped mantle strolled past, strumming a gittern and crooning a love song. But he could barely be heard above the blare of trumpets, the clang of timbrels, and the beat of tabors, all clamoring for attention.

King Henry had sent out criers over a twenty-league radius announcing the tournament. Knights and nobles and their ladies had come from as far away as Shrewsbury for the event. For the past week hundreds of peasants had been drafted to build the lists and loges on the grassy plain that stretched beyond the castle moat. The lists—the

long narrow field where the jousting would take place—
was fenced off by a wooden palisade. Behind the lists rose
the loges, the wooden grandstands where the king and
other noble spectators would sit.

Raine always walked the length of the lists before a
tournament. But today he had a hard time focusing his
attention on the condition of the ground he would soon
be galloping across at breakneck speed. Rather, his gaze
was drawn again and again to the crowded loges.

The tiered benches were shaded by a red-and-white
striped canopy and festooned with gay pennons. Everyone had dressed in their finest. The bright sunlight sparkled off gold and silver embroidery and added a glistening sheen to scarlet velvet, indigo samite, and jade silk. It
twinkled in the precious stones that adorned brooches
and chaplets, belts and girdles.

In all of this gaudy and dizzying spectacle, Raine
searched for a single face that had been seared forever on
his soul, for the flash of pale gold hair, the color of the
hottest sun. Then he saw her, walking toward him across
the field, and in spite of his rigid control, he felt his heartbeat quicken and his face break into a smile.

"Raine!" she cried.

She began to walk faster, and then she was running,
running toward him, and he thought that at any moment
she would be in his arms.

Sybil stopped running before she got to him, aware suddenly that she couldn't throw herself into his arms no
matter how badly she wanted to. She covered the last few
feet in a more sedate fashion, though her legs shook so
badly she wondered how they supported her.

She drank in the sight of him. He had been nineteen
when last she saw him, and had not yet attained his full
growth as a man. He was taller now, his chest deeper, his
shoulders broader. The prettiness had been stamped out
of his face, along with the gentleness.

"Oh, Raine . . ."

His gaze moved over her and his pale eyes warmed and darkened. "You haven't changed."

She laughed softly, her hand fluttering up to her hot face. "Oh, aye, I have. I've grown older and fatter. This morning I found yet another gray hair. I plucked it out, but I can't keep doing that else soon I'll have a bald spot, like a monk's tonsure . . ." Her voice trailed off as she realized that she was babbling.

He smiled, and in that smile she saw the barest trace of the boy that he had been. "I was hoping you'd come," he said.

She almost reached up and caressed his cheek. Instead, she dug her nails into her palm. "Oh, Raine, you know I would never miss this. Your triumph."

His gaze shifted beyond her, to the castle's dark-red walls, and a taut, hard look came over his face. In that way he hadn't changed at all. The fires of ambition that had consumed him as a boy burned brighter than ever. At times, the fierce intensity that drove him had frightened her. She had known that he would sacrifice anything to get what he wanted, anything. Even her.

"Aye, my triumph," he said.

"You will have everything you ever wanted. Land, a title . . . everything."

His eyes focused back onto her face and she could read nothing in them now, neither pain, nor joy, not even satisfaction. It hurt her that he felt the need to hide his feelings from her. When had he learned to do it so well?

"Aye," he said. "I will have everything I ever wanted."

Except you. She waited for him to say those words, but he did not. She realized then, looking into his hard, inscrutable face, that he never would. She had forfeited his love the day she married his brother, and she would never get it back.

But she had done it to save him. No, she had done it to save herself.

To entertain the crowd while it waited for the tourney to start, a bearbaiting was being enacted in front of the stands. In that moment the bear's claws caught in the throat of a mangy gray wolfhound, ripping it open. The dog screamed and the spectators roared their approval.

Sybil and Raine both turned to see what the excitement was about. Sybil's attention was caught immediately by the girl who sat in the front row, next to the canopied high-backed chair, or faldstool, that the king would soon occupy. Unlike the Norman ladies around her, whose heads were covered by coifs and veils, she wore her hair loose and flowing down her back with only a wreath of yellow woodbine to keep it in place. The sunlight glinted off strands of gold and red that were threaded through the darker sable-brown. She was dressed simply in a pleated bliaut the color of bluebells and her only other ornament, besides the flowers in her hair, was a pagan-looking neckband. From this distance the circlet gave the illusion that a pair of snakes were wrapped around her throat.

For a moment Sybil pitied the Welsh girl. She knew how it felt to have one's life directed by the whims of nations and kings, with no more will than a piece of straw blown about by the wind. Sybil turned her head, and she saw that Raine, too, looked at the girl and the expression in his sooty eyes filled her with a hot, sick jealousy. The hard, taut look was back on his face. The look he wore when he wanted something.

"I have yet to meet this Welsh princess you are to marry. What is she like?"

For a moment she didn't think he would answer her. But then his gaze left the girl and came back to her, and a strange smile twisted his lips, though his face was set with anger. "That wench is either the bravest I have ever encountered or the most witless."

Sybil knew that above all else Raine admired courage in a woman, courage and a sense of honor, and so her smile was strained. "And I suppose you have already tried your manly best to terrorize the poor little thing."

Raine made a noise that was closer to a grunt than a laugh. "Quite the contrary. The poor little thing has done her best to terrorize me." A strange, baffled look came over his face, before it tautened again. "The first time I saw the wench, she tried to stab me in the back with a dagger. The second time she near took off my head with my own sword. She has spat at me and clawed me and damned me to hell and back. She even had the audacity to muddy my boots."

Sybil's laughter sounded harsh as it came out her constricted throat. "Oh, Raine. It seems as if you have truly met your match."

He didn't laugh with her, and his gaze went to the girl who was to be his wife. "Nay. But the Lady Arianna has met hers."

Arianna knew they watched her, these fine Norman lords and ladies. They watched her with the same avid and bloodthirsty enjoyment with which they watched the bearbaiting. It was all an enormous jest to them, that the daughter of a Welsh prince would be given away as a trophy in a joust, like the prize ram at a village fair.

Her shoulders began to bow beneath the weight of the watching eyes and she stiffened her spine. *They are nothing to me,* she told herself. *I am the Prince of Gwynedd's daughter.*

The king's faldstool waited empty beside her. On the other side of her sat a willowy girl with butter-yellow hair and contrasting doe-brown eyes. She looked vaguely familiar, and after a few distracted moments, Arianna finally placed her. She had met the girl at Rhuddlan's weekly market day during the month she had spent here with Ceidro. She couldn't recall the girl's name, but Arianna remembered now that she was the only child of the town draper, who had died over a year ago.

Arianna had been impressed at the time—and, in truth, a bit envious—to learn that the girl had inherited and was running her dead father's business all on her own. As she thought back to the conversation they had had, Arianna remembered something else about her as well. The draper's daughter was of pure Saxon blood, and she hated the Normans almost as much as the Welsh did.

Arianna cast another glance in the girl's direction and was surprised by the offer of a warm, encouraging smile. But then Arianna's attention was caught by the sight of the black knight. He stood within the lists, deep in conversation with a woman with hair so blond, it was more silver than gold. A woman who was everything Arianna was not, fair and pale and so very dainty, the epitome of the feminine ideal. As she watched them the knight threw back his dark head and laughed.

A strange tightness squeezed Arianna's chest. She felt swamped with an overwhelming sadness and a sense of failure, and she couldn't understand where it was coming from.

Then, over the pounding of the blood in her ears, she became aware of a loud, three-way conversation going on behind her. She caught an echo of her name and the words *Black Dragon* and *wife*. The women spoke French, but slowly, for they intended her to hear every word.

"I knew it wouldn't take long for Lady Sybil to seek him out," one said. She had a grating, strident voice, like a fishmonger's.

"I myself do wonder why she came," a pleasant, lilting voice chimed in. "How can she bear to watch the Black Dragon wed another? And do you think they're lovers still?" She *tsk*ed. "The shame of it. His brother's wife."

"*Half* brother," said a third. Her voice, soft as cream, was laced with a poisonous malice. "Nay, I doubt they're lovers now, if ever they were, for he hasn't been back to Chester for at least six years. Since the wedding. Though 'tis said she loves him and always has, even though she wed his brother, and if such is true . . . Poor Sybil, she won't enjoy having to share Raine's ardent favors with another, even if that other is only his wife."

"But surely she doesn't fear Raine will grow to love his new bride? Jesu, the girl is Welsh!"

"Aye. But Welsh or no, she'll share Raine's bed. Something the Lady Sybil would most dearly love to do."

" 'Tis my thought she's done so already. It's why she's been barren these six years of her marriage to Earl Hugh. 'Tis God's just punishment for her sin."

"I, for one, pity this poor Welsh girl who must marry Sir Raine. If she's like the others of her race, then she's plain and dark and hairy. Such a one could never turn a man's eyes away from Sybil's dainty fairness."

"Aye, the poor girl. She'll have the Black Dragon in her bed but long enough to beget an heir. Then she'll see little of him, I trow. Not with Chester and Sybil but a day's ride away."

The women burst into peels of laughter, and Arianna's fists clenched to control her trembling. But she hadn't once taken her eyes off the black knight, who smiled and laughed still with the small, blond woman. As she watched, he lifted his hand and tucked a wisp of sun-gilt hair back into her coif.

His brother's wife . . . 'tis said she loves him and always has. . . .

A swift, fierce anger seized her, replacing the taut ache that had filled her chest. She didn't expect him to care for her, yet he could at least have respected her enough not to flaunt his indifference before all of England. She wished there was some way to show those cackling hens behind her just how little it mattered to her that the man she was about to wed loved another. Then it occurred to her that she could play their own game.

She turned and addressed the girl beside her, pitching her voice loud enough for the women in back to hear. She regretted not having been more diligent in her French lessons as she searched for the unfamiliar words.

"You are the draper's daughter, are you not?" she asked the girl.

"Aye . . . I am called Christina, milady."

"Christina." Arianna gave her a brilliant smile. "And you are English, too, are you not?" She heaved a melodramatic sigh. "It seems I have been doomed by fate and my father to share your pitiable existence of living among the Normans." Arianna leaned closer to the girl, but her voice rose higher. "Have you noticed how they all have such rapacious eyes? Tell me, is what they say true, are the Normans so greedy they would steal the last crust of bread out a widow's mouth?"

Christina's lips twitched with a repressed smile. Arianna felt a rush of affection for the draper's daughter, for the girl had quickly caught on to the game. "Well, I know they do often try to cheat me, milady. By not offering fair price for my cloth."

Arianna nodded wisely, aware of the rigid silence behind her. "It's as I suspected. And their manners are most foul, have you not remarked it? The way they clean their teeth with the point of a knife and spit bones into the rushes."

"Perhaps they know no better, milady."

"Perhaps . . ." Arianna sighed again. "It is particularly sad though, how the men must all feel the need to wrap themselves up like snails in their coats of mail before they go off to fight." She shrugged. "Perhaps it is a weakness in their constitution, this lack of courage."

"Now that you do mention it, milady, I believe I knew of a Norman gentleman once, who swooned at the sight of blood."

Arianna shook her head sadly, then went on, her voice growing even louder. "But it's their womenfolk I truly pity the most. For they say a Norman's privy member is much like a willow switch . . . too limp and skinny to satisfy a woman properly."

Perhaps I've gone too far, Arianna thought, for Christina's face seemed suddenly to drain of all color. She swallowed so hard her throat clicked, and her eyes grew huge, shifting to focus on something over Arianna's shoulder. Slowly, Arianna turned . . .

To be pinned by a pair of flint-gray eyes.

7

He loomed above her, a knight in black armor. His gaze moved over her insolently, and there was such a look of utter disdain etched on his long, hard mouth she was in no doubt that he had heard every single one of her damning words.

Arianna felt the heat of blood rushing to her face and knew that it had turned wine-red. She thrust out her chin. "We were just discussing the trials and tribulations of living among the Normans," she said, in a voice that to her dismay betrayed a slight quiver.

"So I heard."

He flicked a glance at Christina, and Arianna felt the girl shudder. She could almost envy the man's ability to slay a person with one look. But just then a squire approached the English girl, bearing a gift on behalf of a shy but amorous knight, and Christina turned aside with obvious relief, leaving Arianna at the Black Dragon's mercy. Not that Arianna blamed her; she longed to flee that cold, disdainful presence herself.

His gaze moved back to her, and his lips curled into a smile of such scathing mockery she wanted to tear it off his face. "I particularly found your opinion of Norman manhood most interesting," he said. "Do you speak from personal experience?"

He'd as much as called her a whore again, and Arianna was getting tired of it. "Take care, sir bastard knight. For your manners are betraying the base origins of your birth."

Something dangerous flickered in his eyes. He stepped forward until his thighs brushed her knees, and leaned into her until she could feel their hardness. And their heat.

"And your tongue, my lady Arianna, is betraying a regrettable lack of discipline," he said in a silky voice. "Obviously your father should long ago have thrown you across his lap, tossed up your skirts and flogged your naked backside until you learned differently. Fortunately it is an oversight that I, as your husband, shall soon be able to rectify . . ." He leaned closer still and his voice deepened into a soft growl. "With *my* willow switch, perhaps?"

The hair on Arianna's arms rose up as if from a sudden chill, though she knew her face was damp and flushed. His eyes smoldered at her now with a fire that seemed to scorch the very air she was trying to breathe.

It was too hot to bear. Her gaze fell to the hands she had clenched in her lap. Her cheeks burned and her throat constricted tightly. She wanted to run away, except there was no where to run to.

She lifted her head. That burning intensity had left his eyes; they were cold and flat again. She felt her courage return.

A silence settled between them, charged with tension. She wondered why he had approached her in the first place. Out of the corner of her eye she saw Christina unravel a silk ribbon from her sleeve and give it to the squire to take back to his shy master, and a thought occurred to her. Perhaps the knight had come to pay court to her because he thought it was expected of him.

She gave him a condescending smile. "Surely you don't harbor a hope that I will give you a token of my favor to carry into battle on the end of your lance? For if I pray for anything, sir knight, it is that your brother the earl will knock you flat on your arrogant face."

His laughter was sudden and harsh. "I don't want your favor, madam. Or your prayers. I'd rather take the castle without the bride."

"And I'd rather suffer the torments of hell than wed a Norman bastard!"

"Then you, my *lady*, are about to discover that hell and a Norman bastard are one and the same."

With that parting remark, he pivoted on his heel and left her. She stared after him, so furious she wanted to burst into tears. "God's death! He is the most insufferably arrogant, despicable, hateful, vile, contemptible—"

"Poor Raine . . . he seems to have misplaced his charm somewhere."

Startled, Arianna's head whipped around, and she looked up into a fair and startlingly handsome face. A spasm of fear twisted her stomach, for this was the man who had tried to rape her in Rhuddlan's cellars. She sucked in a deep breath, telling herself he could do nothing to her here among all these people, not with her under the protection of his king.

Sunlight shimmered off his dazzling silver hauberk. The helm he had tucked beneath his arm sported a panache of white egret feathers on its crown. His hair shone almost as brightly as his armor, and she wondered if he had curled the locks in a press, to get them to coil so precisely over his shoulders. He looked the epitome of a brave and glorious knight.

His gaze, blue as a mountain lake, moved over her with obvious appreciation. "I fear we have yet to be formally introduced. You behold before you Hugh, Earl of Chester." He flashed a smile full of charm and teeth. "Your other champion."

Arianna stared up at him, so stunned that she forgot to breathe. *This* was the Earl of Chester, this man who had tried to rape her. If the black knight lost the joust it would be this man to whom she would go as the prize.

"I couldn't help remarking," he drawled, "that you do not seem overly fond of my brother. Come now, is he really all that terrible?"

She found her voice. "Aye. And you, my lord earl, are not much better."

He did not appear to be insulted. Instead his smile deepened. "You refer to that little incident in the wine vault." He spread his hands in a supplicating gesture. "You must acquit me, my lady. I thought you naught but a villein girl."

"And thus fair game for your lechery?"

He laughed, tossing back his golden curls. "Something like that. Can you imagine then my dismay, my utter horror, when I discovered who you really were?" His smile faded and his voice turned earnest and imploring, though shadows lurked beneath the placid surface of his lake-blue eyes. "Can you ever forgive me?"

"I think not."

He sighed deeply. "You behold before you then a man in abject misery, a man despairing that he will ever be restored to grace in his fair lady's heart."

"Since you were never in my heart in the first place, my lord earl, you can hardly be restored there."

"But surely I've been punished enough for my dreadful misdeed. You gave me a frightful blow to the head, and I shall bear the scar for the rest of my life. Fortunately for us both, you were not so successful with your other assault upon my person. Though I confess for a moment there I feared you had truly unmanned me."

"Pity then I did not succeed, and thus spared the women of Wales future assaults from your *person*." She bared her teeth in a false smile. "My lord."

There was a lull in the noise from the crowd, and the

earl's laughter carried across the field. "Damn me, but I
like your spirit. It's a pity my brother is so skilled with the
lance. For though I cannot marry you myself, if I won
you, my Lady Arianna, you would find me a most kind
and generous liege lord. I would settle you on a gentle
husband, one that would make you happy."

And who would look the other way when you crawled
into my bed, Arianna thought, though for once she held
her tongue.

A blast from a host of trumpets cut across Earl Hugh's
next words, drowning them out. The King of England
came striding toward them, an entourage of nobles and
servants trailing in his wake. A sudden silence fell over
the loges, followed by a lot of crackling and rustling as
everyone came swiftly to their feet.

The king slapped Hugh on the back with such hearty
force the earl staggered. "What are you doing still dan-
gling after the ladies, my lord earl? The tourney is about
to start."

Hugh gave his sovereign a self-deprecating shrug.
"Since everyone assumes I am going to lose, I'm beginning to wonder why I should bother competing at all. The
only thing I'm likely to get out of it is a collection of
bruises."

"Nonsense!" the king admonished in his gruff voice.
"It will be good sport."

Hugh inclined his head. "Then by your leave, Your
Grace . . ."

He backed away and Arianna was left face-to-face with
the king.

She had met Henry of England once before, but it had
been shortly after that episode in the tent, and she had
been so distraught she scarcely noticed the man. He had
barked at her, demanding to know if she was Gwynedd's
daughter, and she hadn't even had the sense to try to
deny it. The black knight had been standing next to him,
looking right through her, and all she could do was stare

at that hard, tight mouth and feel still the searing heat left by his brutal, punishing kiss. The King of England might as well have been invisible.

"I had no idea you Welsh lasses were so comely," the king was now saying. His eyes flashed over her and his grin had a touch of the leer in it. Though married to a woman who was considered to be one of the most beautiful in all Christendom, Henry had a reputation for straying from the queenly bedchamber.

He threw himself down onto the faldstool. "Sit," he commanded, seizing Arianna's hand and dragging her down onto the bench beside him. He motioned to a hovering varlet, who handed him a jewel-encrusted chalice of wine.

She studied the man from beneath downcast lashes. Though his clothes were rich, as befitted his royal status, he wore them carelessly. He had on a short tunic of blue samite trimmed with ermine. His tawny hair was cropped close to his head and covered with a chaplet of gold studded with rubies. There was the stamp of power on his square, freckled face. She suspected he was a man much like her father, confident in his ability to rule and conscious always of the motives and actions of those around him—from his fellow princes to the servant who emptied his chamber pot.

The king fixed Arianna with his protruding eyes. "And who do you favor to win the joust?"

"If you must know, Your Grace, I abhor the idea of wedding any Norman."

"Nevertheless, it is your father's command that you marry the new Lord of Rhuddlan."

"I know my duty, Your Grace."

He stroked his beard, studying her a moment. Then he smiled and patted her hand. "I shall offer you some fatherly advice, my dear, and I suggest you heed it well. For the Black Dragon is likely to win this contest, and so he will take you to wive. Tread softly with him then, my girl.

He is a man who has been tempered in hell and you challenge him at your peril."

Arianna's hands clenched together in her lap, but she lifted her head. "I have been raised properly, Your Grace. I will serve and submit to my husband, whomever he's to be."

Yet even as the words came out her mouth, Arianna wondered if she spoke the truth. She had been raised to please, to serve a husband's needs, to be chatelaine of his castles and ultimately to submit to his will in all things. But a part of her must always have expected someday to have the same loving marriage her parents had, a marriage wherein the man would respect and cherish her, so she would be not so much his servant as his partner in life. Such a thing seemed impossible now, and she didn't know how she could be obedient and submissive. Not when she wanted to rage and rebel against fate and the Norman knight who would own her.

Just then the tournament marshal approached, wearing a scarlet bliaut and bearing a white baton. At a nod from the king he rose the baton high in the air and shouted, "Bring on the jousters!"

Trumpets blared. Four heralds, arrayed in purple silk, led the procession on foot, followed by a jongleur on horseback who twirled a sword, tossing it high in the air to catch it by the hilt on its way down. Then up rode the knights, singing to the accompaniment of tabors and drums. Their burnished armor glittered in the sun, their gaudily painted shields and lances looking like a meadow of wildflowers dancing in the wind.

Without conscious thought, Arianna searched for the black knight, and found him. He and the Earl of Chester rode side by side and last, for theirs would be the final contest.

The knights paraded by the loges, their chargers prancing and sidestepping. Ribbons, sleeves, and garters rained down from the stands. Most were tossed the Black

Dragon's way. He managed to snag a green-and-yellow striped stocking out of the air, and its twittering owner let out a shriek of delight. Laughing, he spurred his horse into a fancy curvet and the crowd roared its approval.

The knights filed by, splitting in half and cantering to the end of the lists. Two trumpets challenged each other and the first contest was on.

Arianna sat rigid beside the king, saying nothing, careful to show no emotion. Two knights were carried off the field on their shields, one with a broken leg, another with blood pouring from his nose and mouth. It occurred to Arianna that the black knight made his living in this way —when he wasn't risking his life in a real war. Hurling his body and his horse at reckless speed, again and again, to shatter his lance against another's shield, and with a jarring blow that must strain and tear at every muscle, pound and bruise every bone.

It was long past noon before only two knights remained left to joust, and an expectant hush fell on the crowd. At that moment all eyes turned on Arianna. She kept her back stiff and her face impassive, but when she felt a cramping pain in her arms she realized she had her fists clenched so tightly she was cutting off the blood. From opposite ends of the lists Earl Hugh of Chester and the Black Dragon emerged on their huge war-horses, led by their squires. Unlike the other matches, this contest would not stop with three broken lances, but would go on until one man was defeated or cried out for mercy.

The two men faced each other. They lowered their long and heavy lances and clasped their shields to their chests. The squires stepped aside and the marshal raised his white baton.

"In the name of God and Saint Maurice, patron of knights, do your battle!"

Simultaneously, the two chargers lunged forward. The ground trembled with their pounding hooves, clods of dirt and sod flew through the air. The black knight seemed a part of his enormous black charger, man and horse fused into one flying weapon. His lance struck Hugh's shield dead center, shivering and splintering with a loud crashing sound that silenced the crowd. His blow struck with such force that the earl's horse was thrown back on its haunches. Hugh's lance had slid harmlessly off Raine's shield, though it left a raw, jagged scar on the paint.

"Fairly broken! Fairly broken!" the crowd roared, and Arianna sucked in air, realizing suddenly that she had been holding her breath. Raine wheeled his charger and cantered back to the end of the lists. He tossed the broken butt aside, and Taliesin ran up with a fresh lance.

Again the two men charged each other, but this time Raine feinted with his body and the earl's lance missed entirely, sailing out of his hands like a javelin and eliciting hoots from the stands. At the same time, Raine's lance smacked hard in the center of the earl's shield, flinging Hugh out the saddle with a ringing clatter of chain mail. A pair of heralds started to dash forward, but Hugh struggled to his feet, drawing his sword.

Raine wheeled his rearing charger, vaulting from the saddle while its hooves still pawed the air. He whipped his sword from the scabbard and sunlight leapt along the blade like a stream of fire. He caught Hugh's first cut with the brunt of his shield. Hide and wood split with a loud, ripping groan.

Arianna leaned forward, her hands clenching the edge of the bench, her breath caught in her chest, her eyes riveted on Raine. She had never seen a man fight with such grace and power, with such controlled and flawlessly executed violence. The earl hacked with his sword, while Raine's weapon seemed to dance through the air. He toyed with his brother but a moment, then with a blurring series of strokes and thrusts, Hugh was disarmed, lying on his back in the dirt with Raine's blade pointed at his throat.

The roar of the crowd crashed against Arianna's ears.

Beside her the king leapt to his feet, bellowing his approval. Raine walked toward them, his sword curving from his fist like a natural extension of his arm.

He stopped before his king. Arianna looked up into his face. The protective nasal of his helm emphasized the harsh handsomeness of his features by drawing attention to the angular bones of his cheeks and nose. The metal brim shielded his eyes, but she could feel their life and their fire.

He sheathed his sword with a snap of his wrist and doffed his helm, tossing it onto the ground. He knelt and placed his hands between those of his liege lord's, King Henry of England. His deep, strong voice spoke the oath of homage in return for the Lordship of Rhuddlan and all its dependencies, and for the Lady Arianna, daughter of Gwynedd of Wales, whom he would take as his wife.

He rose to his feet and received the king's kiss of peace. Then his eyes lifted to the bloodred walls of Rhuddlan Castle, and a faint smile touched his taut mouth. Arianna sat beside the king, her heart thundering heavily, her chest feeling as if it would crack in two. She waited for him to look at her.

But he never did.

8

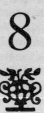

The golden mazer pulsed and glowed, beckoning. . . .

"God's death!" Arianna swore at herself for being such a witless nit. Of course the bowl would glow, for bright morning sunlight streamed on it through the open window. The pulsing was only an illusion, too, caused by the floating clouds reflected in the mazer's shiny surface. She had no need anyway of magic bowls to reveal her destiny. She knew her future—today was her wedding day.

The mazer sat beneath the window, on the padded lid of a clothes chest. She hadn't dared get close enough yet to see if it held water, but somehow she was sure it did. The thing had suddenly appeared in her bedchamber this morning. Either that God-cursed, traitorous squire had returned it while she slept, or it had magically appeared on its own. It was after all Myrddin's bowl, she thought, at the same time sneering at herself for her susceptibility.

Arianna fingered the torque at her neck, then resolutely she turned her back on the mazer. As she paced the floor, her feet crushed the sprigs of mint scattered through the rushes, releasing a sharp clean scent into the hot summer air. On the great canopied bed lay the clothes she was to wear for her wedding, a gift from her betrothed.

She smoothed her palm over the chainse of filmy saffron-tinted linen. In spite of her fear and uncertainty, she smiled as she thought of how the soft undergarment would feel caressing her skin. The pelisse itself was of the sheerest sendal, the color of spring poppies, and trimmed at the wrists and hem with ermine. Over the pelisse would go an elegant sapphire silk bliaut embroidered with gold, and with sleeves so long they swept the ground. Any woman would feel beautiful gowned in such splendor, she thought. Any man's eyes would glow with love at the sight of such a bride.

But not the Norman's eyes.

A tightness squeezed her chest as she thought of the joy she should feel on this, her wedding day. Dreams from her girlhood . . . She would try to do her duty as her father would wish it, but the thought of marrying the Norman filled her with fear and despair. He was such a hard man, ruthless and cruel, and he despised her because she was Welsh. How could there ever grow between them the kind of love that she had dreamed of for so long?

The cursed bowl . . .

Arianna could feel its power drawing her, beckoning. Slowly, she turned her head . . . The mazer glowed red now, like a clot of fresh blood, and throbbed as if it breathed. The knowledge trapped within the ancient drinking cup both enticed and repelled her. Afraid . . . She was so afraid. Her palm drifted up, pressing against her thudding heart.

She had no conscious memory of crossing from the bed to the chest, but suddenly she was before the window with the mazer in her hands. The smooth metal seared her palms and a torrent of heat, like the fire of a dragon's breath, flooded through her body.

"Please, no . . ." she whispered. But the power pulled,

drew her. Down she looked, down into the bowl's luminescent, whirling depths.

The water, red as a bleeding wound, spun and swirled,
sucking her in. Fingers of a silver mist spiraled upward,
wrapping softly around her mind. A blue-white flame
flared before her eyes, then faded to a gentle radiance.
She floated, floated on a sea of light . . . smelled hyacinth and marigolds, and wet earth steaming under a summer sun. A hot, moist wind caressed her face. . . .

*She stood on top a windswept hill, a bouquet of wild-
flowers cradled in her arms. Above her a golden sun hung
suspended in a sky of so vivid a blue it made her eyes ache.
Yet within her there dwelled a choking grief, suffocating
her heart. She had lost him, lost him, oh God, she had lost
him.*

*In the distance, something moved . . . a knight on
horseback, riding toward her. Hope flared within her,
sharp and hot and brilliant, like a spark off flint.*

*The fiery wind blew harder, searing the skin on her face.
The perfume of the flowers tickled her nose. Closer he
came, at a slow and easy canter. Tears blurred her eyes and
she stretched out her arms. The wind snatched at the flowers, blowing them away in a swirl of purple and yellow
petals.*

*He reined in halfway up the hill, dismounting. He
looked up at her, tense and hesitant as if afraid to come
farther, as if unsure of her, of her love, and the thought
made her smile, for he was her man and her love for him
was indelible and eternal. He took a step toward her. Sunlight flared off his golden head, like a beacon on a black
and storm-tossed night.*

*She was laughing, hysterical with joy, running down the
hill, running to her one true love. His arms wrapped
around her, hard and strong, and she settled into his embrace as if coming home after a long, long time away. His
voice flowed over her, warm like the wind. I love you,
Arianna, love you, love you . . .*

She tilted back her head to see his face, the face of her beloved, but the hot ball of the sun blazed behind his golden head, setting it afire . . . melting the vision into red mist and swirling water and nothingness. . . .

"No . . ." Arianna clutched at the mazer, trying to will the vision back into life. But the water within the bowl was flat, motionless. Dizziness overwhelmed her and she swayed on her feet. A bout of nausea cramped her stomach, but quickly passed.

She rubbed at her cheeks, surprised somehow to find them wet, though tears still streamed from her burning eyes. She felt a tightness in her chest, a sweet ache. Love . . . she hadn't known what the emotion truly meant until now. Oh, she loved her parents and her brothers, loved them deeply. But not with the fierce possessiveness, the consuming hunger, that she had felt for the man in the vision. Her lips lifted in a trembling smile . . . *My golden knight.*

Laughing out loud, she hugged herself and twirled around on her toes. Love. There was love in her future. Love and a golden-haired knight . . .

And marriage to a man with raven-black hair and hard, gray eyes, a man who despised and rejected her. A man who had said, *I'd rather take the castle without the bride.*

Disappointment, like the sudden swift thrust of a sword, stabbed at her chest. For a single, panicked moment she thought of running away; she even half-turned toward the door. But duty was as much a part of Arianna as her dark hair and green eyes. Her father had pledged her for Gwynedd's honor. If the marriage failed to take place the truce would end, King Henry would invade Wales again, and this time he might succeed. Her land would be lost to the greedy Norman conquerors; her people enslaved. Weighed against that, her own happiness was worth nothing.

But still, still . . . the fierce, incredible love she had felt while held fast within her golden knight's embrace, as his voice washed over her, saying the words, those wondrous words. *I love you.* . . . It would be worth almost anything to live that single moment out of time, that moment when she ran down a windswept hill and into the arms of the man she loved.

The door swung open with a creak of its hide hinges. Edith marched in bearing an armful of towels, followed by a pair of varlets struggling under the weight of a tub filled with steaming, lemon-scented water.

"Milady, there is much to do, much to do, indeed," the maidservant said. "Here 'tis almost terce. We've only a little over an hour left to prepare you for your wedding."

Arianna turned her head aside, blinking hard, as she fought back tears, for she would not disgrace herself by weeping in front of a servant. She looked out the window. The bailey below was already filling with cotters and villeins, herdsmen and burgesses—all the people of Rhuddlan and the *cantref* of Tegeingl who had come to witness their new lord's wedding.

It occurred to her that the people within the bailey had divided themselves according to how they lived. The Welshery—sheep tenders and herdsmen who dwelled up in the hills—had grouped together on one side of the yard. On the other congregated the Englishry, who lived in the towns and farmed the fertile lowlands. By law, all these people owed their allegiance and their service to the Lord of Rhuddlan, whoever he might be. But from the Welsh side of the bailey animosity, suspicion, and hatred crackled in the air like summer lightning.

The Welsh were a poor people, as evidenced by their dress—drab-colored tow-cloth leggings and tunics of coarse wool. So it was not surprising that the two men in gem-bright samite bliauts would catch Arianna's eye. They stood apart within the shadow cast by the malting house, talking together, but with their eyes constantly shifting, their hands on their sword hilts. One was tall and whip lean, with skin bronzed by the sun and tawny hair docked in the front like a priest's. The other was much older, middle-aged, with meaty shoulders and thick thighs corded like barrels, and long metal-gray hair that hung lankly about his shoulders.

Arianna knew these men. They were her cousins Kilydd ap Dafydd and Ivor ap Gruffydd, castellans of the neighboring *cantrefi* of Rhos and Rhufoniog. These *cantrefi* were part of the dower lands Arianna would bring with her upon her marriage. Her cousins would be allowed to remain as castellans of her lands, but only if they swore allegiance to her husband as their liege lord. Thus, they were here today not only to witness her wedding but to offer homage to the new Lord of Rhuddlan. But Arianna could tell by the way they held themselves stiff and aloof, dark scowls marring their faces, that to them a session on the rack would be preferable to giving homage to a Norman.

Just then, as if she had willed them to, both men turned and looked up toward the hall. She was sure they saw her at the window, but when she lifted her hand in a greeting, they remained unmoving. She could almost feel their fury, scorching across the yard like a grass fire. It was if they blamed her for the state of affairs that had brought them here to Rhuddlan on this day, to kneel before its Norman lord.

Slowly she let her hand fall, fighting off fresh tears as a tight, burning ache filled her chest. Suddenly she felt so alone, so very alone.

"Milady, your bath is ready."

Arianna was about to turn from the window when she noticed something odd. A pale had been erected on the lists where the tournament had taken place the week before. As the peasants streamed toward the castle from the countryside, many herded cows, bulls, steers, and oxen into pens, which were already filled to near capacity with the bawling, lowing beasts. Around the pale stood a dozen knights in full armor, doing nothing but watching.

"Why do you suppose they bring their cattle to Rhuddlan?" she mused aloud.

" 'Tis the fine they be paying, milady," Edith said. At Arianna's confused look, she added, "The fine Lord Raine has imposed upon every Welsh household, be they villein or free, because of the raid. They are to make up for the cattle what was stolen from him."

Three days before, the restless King Henry and his conquering army had left, taking the high road back to England. No sooner had the dust of their passing settled than a mysterious group of horsemen, wearing black hoods over their faces, had raided Rhuddlan's cattle. Within an hour there hadn't been a bawl to be heard or a tail hair to be found on the lord's demesne. At the time, Arianna hadn't been able to hide her pleasure at seeing the Norman usurpers made to look such fools. She also had a suspicion as to whom had been responsible for the raid. It was just the sort of trick her roguish, risk-taking cousin Kilydd would play. He was perfectly capable of swearing homage to the Norman usurper with one hand while raiding the man's cattle with the other.

Except the trick would turn out not to be so amusing to the herdsmen of Tegeingl if this were true, if they were the ones being made to pay the price. "But I thought no one knows who did the raiding," she said.

Edith shrugged. "It was Welshmen who raided, so it is Welshmen who must pay the fine, so my lord says. All Welshery be one and the same. Milady, please . . . your bath water cools."

But Arianna continued to stare at the growing herd, at the peasants driving their cattle into the pens and then turning away with heads bowed and shoulders slumped. Rage filled her at the unfairness of it. That this man, this Norman knight who could only rule with a mailed fist, would punish a whole people for what one man had done. Her hands, lying on the sill, curled into fists as she remembered how she had tried to convince herself that she could be an obedient and submissive wife to such a man. Well, she could *not*. She refused to accept injustice such as this.

But her resolution faltered when she realized that, aside from calling the man a tyrant to his face, there was little she could do. Her cousin had flaunted his contempt for the man who was to be his liege lord by raiding his cattle. Even the peasants gathering now within the bailey evinced defiance with their stiff backs and sullen faces. If only there was some way that she, Arianna of Gwynedd, could show the black knight how much she despised him for what he had done. And show her people, too, that though she be forced to wed one of the accursed Norman race, she was still a Cymraes, a woman of Wales, and one of them.

By the time Arianna had finished bathing she knew exactly what she would do. When the maidservant brought the beautiful poppy-red pelisse to her, she waved it away. "Nay, Edith, such clothes are inappropriate."

"Inappropriate, milady?"

"Aye, such a gown is for celebration. Whereas I . . . I am in a mourning mood."

The sun beat down on the open bailey. Heat waves shimmered up from the earth, adding to the blasts of hot air coming from the cooking fires, where great copper cauldrons bubbled with stews and sauces. Scullions, naked because of the heat, turned the spits on which huge carcasses of stag and boar roasted for that afternoon's feast.

The wedding procession, trying not to sweat in their silk bliauts and fur-trimmed pelisses, gathered before the great hall. The chapel bell began to peal, competing with the music made by the minstrels' pipes and tabors.

The Lady Arianna was to be carried to her fate on a white mule, another gift from her betrothed. The mule was expensively equipped with a saddle enameled with small blue flowers, a saddle-cloth of scarlet samite and a breast-plate of silver hung with bells that tinkled with each breath the beast took. Custom dictated that the bride's mount should be led to the church by her father, but in this case her younger brother Rhodri was to act in the Prince of Gwynedd's stead.

The boy stood now beside the mule, running the reins through nervous fingers as he shifted his weight from foot to foot and glanced repeatedly at the entrance to the great hall. The bride was late.

The groom, sweltering in a bliaut of violet silk, could feel the rigid control he held over his temper begin to slip. He knew his bride's tardiness was due to no last-minute primping. This was her not-so-subtle way of underscoring how much she abhorred the idea of marriage to the Earl of Chester's bastard.

Raine caught his squire's eye; he would send Taliesin up to drag his tardy bride out of the hall by the hair if need be. But just as he opened his mouth to issue the order, the minstrels broke into the bridal song. Raine saw Taliesin's face sag with shock. Then the singers' voices sputtered and died. A pall of silence descended over the bailey as the new Lord of Rhuddlan slowly turned.

She stood at the foot of the stairs. She wore not the fine silk and fur-trimmed, and ruinously expensive, bridal gown that he had given her, but a coarse, knee-length tunic made of sacking. She was barefoot and black ashes streaked her face. Her hair flowed over her shoulders in wild and matted tangles.

Sackcloth and ashes.

He stared at her, not able for a moment to believe what he saw. He heard the beginnings of the crowd's tittering laughter. And from the Welsh, building slowly at first, then crescendoing to a roar—her name, they cheered her name.

Ten yards separated them. Raine started toward her, and the laughter and cheering cut off, as if everyone had simultaneously clapped a hand to his mouth. Taliesin tried to step in front of him, but he shoved the boy roughly aside. He saw nothing, he was aware of nothing, but her.

He stopped when only a hand's space separated them, but he didn't touch her. If he touched her, he thought, he would surely kill her. Their eyes clashed, and hers widened and darkened. But she didn't look away.

"People of the Tegeingl!" she shouted. "I mourn with you the loss of your cattle—"

"Shut up."

His words, dry and searing like the coldest ice, stopped her. Her gaze started to waver, then held firm, and she said to him alone with scorn in her voice, "It is a poor lord who steals from his own peasants and calls it justice—"

"Don't . . . Don't say another word."

Blood roared in Raine's ears, harsh and loud as ocean breakers. He took a deep breath, then another. The roaring receded. Slowly, he reached up and wrapped his fists in the sackcloth at her neck. She shuddered, once, and he saw the muscles in her throat work as she tried to swallow. His forearms bunched and she tensed. Still she didn't look away.

He ripped the sackcloth clean in two.

The tearing sound made by the rough material reverberated in the stunned silence. His eyes, hot and hard with anger, moved over her. Her hands jerked and started up to cover her breasts, and then with a visible effort she forced them back down to her sides. She clenched her fists, holding them rigid.

He raised his eyes to her face. His voice was rough with the effort it took to control his rage. "You shame yourself, woman. You will return now to the hall. And when you descend once again, you will be clothed as befitting a bride to the Lord of Rhuddlan."

For a moment she did nothing, simply stood before him, her whole body still, her eyes bright and unblinking.

Slowly, she turned and started up the steps into the great hall.

Arianna shut the door and leaned against its iron-banded panels. But a moment later the door thrust hard against her back and sent her stumbling into the middle of the room.

Taliesin strode across the threshold and stopped, his hands on his hips. Arianna opened her mouth to berate the boy for his impudence in barging into her chamber unbidden, and instead backed up a step at the sight of him. The air around him seemed to quiver with a force both ancient and frightening, as if he were some great dragon stirred to wrathful life. His jet eyes glittered unnaturally bright, shooting off sparks like metal against flint, his red hair crackled and sizzled around his head like a burning bush. He opened his mouth and Arianna half-expected him to breathe fire.

"You stupid female. If I didn't know better I would swear the goddess had given you feathers for wits."

The words, delivered in the whine of a pouting boy, snapped Arianna back to reality. A dragon? God's eyes, the lad was but a mere squire and an insolent one at that. "Who are you to talk of wits when—"

"It passes my understanding why two reasonably intelligent people like you and my lord turn into such fools when in each other's company. Goddess spare me, but this whole affair has been nothing but one bungle after another." He paced the floor, throwing his hands up in the air to punctuate his points. "First you try to stab him, then he tries to bed you, so you bloody his nose, and he refuses to woo you, so you decide to make a bleating ass of yourself by—"

"Bleating ass! If *you* would stop bleating long enough to listen—"

He spun around to shake his finger in her face. "What possessed you to do such an addle-pated thing?"

She slapped his finger aside. "Your insolence is astonishing, boy. And who are you to talk? How can you, a Cymro, serve such a lord? A lord who would deprive his own peasants of their cattle. What is he going to do come winter when they starve—laugh at their suffering?"

Taliesin cast his eyes heavenward. "There you see . . . addle-pated."

"I could hardly allow such an injustice to be done to my people without a protest. They are your people, too, do you not care? And you call *me* a bleating ass."

"Aye, an ass who bleats instead of thinks. An ass who doesn't take the time to learn of the facts before she acts. An ass who has bungled things so badly, I'll likely be talking myself hoarse and ruin my singing voice trying to put my lord back into his good humor. Which, if you knew my lord as well as you should be getting to know him, then you would know such is not going to be an easy thing. Goddess have mercy . . ."

"Facts?" Arianna's belly tensed with a horrible premonition. "What facts?"

"He was going to give the cattle back, my lady. As part of the wedding largesse."

"The wedding largesse . . ." It was the custom to give out large quantities of gifts at a nobleman's wedding. Everyone received something, even the lowliest villein. "But I don't understand. If he never meant to keep the cattle, why collect the fine in the first place?"

Taliesin gave her a withering look, as if he couldn't believe anyone could be so dense. "Whoever raided Rhuddlan had help from the Welshery of this *cantref* and my lord knew this. He wanted his people to understand that those who rob him, rob from them as well. And to show that while he will deal ruthlessly with disobedience and rebellion, he can also be a merciful lord. The whip and the carrot. 'Twas meant to be but a lesson. A lesson in just how sorely he can hurt them should they ever dare to challenge him again." The squire smirked at her stunned expression. "Well, my lady, have you suddenly nothing to say? Swallowed your tongue, have you?"

Indeed there seemed to be something caught in Arianna's throat, and she had to clear it before she could speak. "Perhaps I might have acted a bit hastily . . ."

Taliesin's lips curled up at one end, like a viol bow. "A bit hastily, she says . . . and this from the girl known throughout all of Gwynedd for slipping a pair of mating hedgehogs into the bishop's bed when he came to visit. Only this time it won't be just yourself who'll suffer for your impulsive behavior, my lady. It's time you understood, that because of who you are, your actions can have repercussions. Much like the ripples, when a stone is dropped into a lake, reach distant shores you cannot even see."

Arianna felt guilt as a biting pain in her chest. "He won't give the cattle back now, will he?"

"Aye, you've truly bungled things." The squire wiped at the tears that had somehow appeared on her cheeks without her knowing it. "Here now, don't cry. Your face is getting all red and blotchy. You're spoiling those pretty looks my lord likes so well."

Arianna rubbed her face with the scratchy sleeve of her sackcloth tunic. "I'm not crying, you fool boy. I never cry."

Again that strange light flared in Taliesin's eyes, and again, just as quickly, it was gone. "Hurry and dress yourself, my lady. Don't keep him waiting long, else you rouse his ire further."

Arianna was already running a wooden comb through her hair. "Aye, aye . . . Taliesin? What form do you think his punishment will take?"

"Oh, my lord is very imaginative in his punishments," the squire said in gleeful tones. "Why, I remember the time a mountebank fleeced all his men of their pay and my lord . . ." His voice trailed off and his cheeks turned rosy, like a girl's. "Mayhap I shouldn't be telling you that particular story. In truth, I doubt Lord Raine would wish to mar your beauty with any permanent scars . . ."

"You are of immense comfort, boy," Arianna said. "Perhaps you should think of becoming a priest." Though, in truth, she did not like the ominous sound of the squire's tale. But whatever the black knight would do to her she would have to bear it with dignity, as befitted a daughter of Gwynedd. Somehow she would try to ensure that she, and she alone, would suffer the brunt of his anger.

She put on the gown that he had given her and went back down to the bailey. She stood before him, her head held high. His gaze was impassive as his eyes flickered over her. She could read nothing in them, neither satisfaction, nor lingering anger.

"My lord, I do ask forgiveness for my behavior," she said.

"Louder."

She lifted her head even higher and shouted. "My lord, I do most humbly ask forgiveness for the shame I have brought upon myself and upon Gwynedd."

A long silence greeted her speech, followed by a restless stirring from the Welsh side of the bailey. Raine's hand closed around her elbow as he steered her to where her brother Rhodri stood, clutching the lead of a white mule. She lowered her voice for Raine's ears alone. "My lord, punish me. Don't force my people to suffer for what I have done."

His fingers tightened until she had to set her teeth against the pain. "Their suffering will be your punishment."

"But, my lord, I would beg of you—"

"Don't beg. It ill becomes you."

The knight propelled her forward and Rhodri stepped up to help her mount. As he hefted her up into the saddle, the youth grinned and winked at her. "You were magnificent," he whispered, and Arianna squeezed her eyes shut in shame as again the enormity of her mistake struck her. For not only had she encouraged her people in a rebellion that would only bring them further suffering, but she had probably spurred her brother, who shared her exile among the Normans, on to God knows what foolishness.

They rode through the castle gate. The minstrèls danced ahead of the procession, singing love songs and playing on gitterns and tabors. The town church bells joined in, clanging with faint disharmony. More villeins, cotters, and shopkeepers lined the road and cheered as they rode by.

They dismounted in the town square and walked to the small stone church on a path strewn with straw and roses. She walked alongside Raine, not touching, almost having to run to keep up with his long strides. He is a conqueror, she thought. He has conquered Rhuddlan and now he will try to conquer me.

She stumbled over the stone-flagged step and Raine steadied her by grasping her elbow. This time his grip was not punishing, but fleeting.

A figure robed in embroidery-encrusted vestments stepped out from beneath the portal shadows and Arianna was surprised to see, not the round and ruddy face of the town curé, but the gray, wizened visage of the Bishop of St. Asaph. But then this marriage was to solidify the truce between England and Wales, and it would take no less a personage than a bishop to solemnize the vows.

The gold fringe on the bishop's miter swayed as he dipped his head. He cleared his throat and began to speak, but Arianna made no sense of his words, for just then Raine took her hand. His palm was rough and callused and seemed to swallow hers up, and she was aware of nothing beyond the man who stood beside her. She dared a sideways glance up at him. For a brief moment their eyes met, but his were as blank as the stony church walls.

Afterward, she couldn't remember repeating the marriage vows, though she must have, for the next thing she knew the bishop was blessing the ring. Raine took the gold band and slipped it in turn on the first two fingers of her left hand, but when he went to put it on the third finger, the ring stuck on her knuckle. Arianna was possessed with an hysterical desire to laugh, for folklore said that how goes on the ring so would go the marriage—easily and the wife would be docile; with difficulty and she would be a shrew.

She looked up at him. His eyes glittered at her now with an enigmatic promise.

"With this ring, I thee wed," he said, as he thrust the ring onto her finger, hard enough to scrape the skin.

"And with my body I thee worship. . . ."

9

A fanfare of trumpets smacked against the hot summer air and bounced off the flowing waters of the river Clwyd. Arianna jumped at the harsh blast of sound, but the man beside her didn't even blink. He sprawled in the chair, one arm hooked over the back, his long legs stretched out beneath the table. He looked relaxed, but she could feel the tension in him, like a banked fire.

They had yet to exchange a word since their marriage vows.

The wedding feast was taking place beside the river, within the shadows of the castle walls, for it was cooler there beneath the shade of the sycamores. Trestle tables, covered with gleaming white cloths, spread over the grassy banks. A canopy of yellow silk sheltered the bridal dais.

As the shrill notes of the trumpets faded away, the marshal of the hall marched toward the dais, holding aloft a white staff. He was followed by a procession of servants bearing ewers and basins and towels for the ritual washing.

Taliesin dumped an enameled bronze basin onto the table with a clatter. The boy looked miffed, as if such servitude was beneath his dignity. He gave his liege lord an impatient nudge. "Sire, if you will . . ."

Arianna watched the water pour over her husband's hands. Though marred by calluses and scars and browned by the sun, they were the hands of a nobleman. Long and fine-boned, and strangely graceful.

"My lady . . ." Taliesin waited, the ewer poised to pour. She held her hands over the basin. The water was warm and smelled of roses.

The squire handed her a fresh towel. For a moment she was sure his jet eyes glittered at her with the same strange light she had seen earlier. But he blinked and the light faded. "My lady, do you wish to dry your hands, or no? Otherwise you'll be dripping rosewater into the cook's splendid ginger-sauced lampreys."

Arianna snatched at the proffered towel, and he answered her with an impish smile. "You make a beautiful bride, my lady," he said. "Is she not beautiful, my lord?"

The knight turned his head. He looked at her in a weighing manner, the way a man would judge horseflesh for sale at a fair, and in spite of herself, Arianna felt the blood rush to her face. But whatever his opinion of her, he didn't voice it.

"She is a quest worthy of a brave knight," Taliesin persisted. "Do you not think so, my lord?"

Raine shot his squire a hard look. "Give it up, Taliesin."

The boy heaved a beleaguered sigh. "Aye, my lord . . ."

He picked up the basin, then slammed it down again, spilling oily water onto the cloth. "But I ought to point out that the trials you must suffer to be worthy of the Lady Arianna's love grow more arduous by the moment. I fear the goddess is now so wrathful over your stubbornness that you'll be stripped of your pride completely ere your destiny is concluded to her satisfaction." The boy put his hands on his hips, his head snapping like a scolding alewife's. "And I can only do so much for you, after all, so don't go saying later that I didn't warn you."

Throughout his squire's odd speech Raine looked at her, and Arianna watched, fascinated, as his eyes changed color from pale ice to the dark gray of thunderheads just before a storm. "And do you love me even a bit, little wife?"

Arianna was so startled that the arm she had resting on the table jerked, sending a spoon spinning across the white cloth. Raine's hand lashed out, trapping the spoon. He held it out to her, handle first. The action reminded Arianna in the strangest way of a defeated knight surrendering his sword to the victor. Their gazes held and the silence stretched between them.

"You haven't answered my question," he finally said.

Arianna couldn't understand why she found it so hard to speak. It was as if the devil had snatched away her breath. Her hand trembled as she reached for the spoon. "Nay, I love you not at all."

"You heard her, boy. She loves me not at all, so this quest you keep prattling about is pointless. Now, bring me some wine."

Taliesin's fiery brows met in a straight line over the bridge of his nose as he shot Arianna a look of aggravation before he whisked away the ewer and basin. Raine went back to staring with shadowed eyes at the walls and keep of his castle. Another blast of trumpets announced the serving of the first course.

Arianna wanted to ask him about the boy who was his squire, this Taliesin who had strange, moonlit eyes and claimed to be a bard, and spoke of a goddess as if he truly believed in such nonsense.

Her father's *bardd teulu* had often sung prose tales about a race of beautiful goddesses who once dwelled in a city of gold beneath the ocean waves. It was said that when the tides and the mist were just right, a bridge would rise up from the watery depths connecting their magical city to the land, and in those times the goddesses often crossed the bridge to take mortal lovers. Through the love of a goddess, these men, brave and handsome knights all, were given the gift of eternal life—though only after they had overcome the most difficult of quests. Of course, these were only stories, passed down from the time of the ancient ones. Such pagan beliefs had died out long ago. Arianna had heard of no one who still swore by the goddesses . . .

Except, she remembered suddenly, for the old bard who had given her the golden mazer. But then he had been such a very old man, all yellow-skinned with the barest wisps of white hair on his wizened skull, so old in truth that his mind had seemed to wander when he spoke. Oddly, his name, too, had been Taliesin.

"Eat, eat, my lady."

The boy named Taliesin appeared suddenly at her side, bearing a swan with an almond-silvered body that swam in a green-gravy pond. He dumped the gilded tray beside Arianna, and the bird rocked in its pea-colored lake. "You must eat, my lady, for you'll need all your strength later . . ." He paused, then added with a wicked grin, "For the dancing."

Arianna gave him her haughtiest, mistress-of-the-castle look. Though a bit strange, he was still a boy. No different from her brothers at that age.

Raine wasn't eating either. In truth he was supposed to be feeding her. They shared a bread trencher and goblet and he was supposed to be picking out the choicest morsels from the bowls and platters and putting them to her dainty lips.

He must have felt her eyes on him, for just then he lifted the wine goblet. It was of bronze and fashioned into a fanciful shape—a dragon with its scaly tail forming one handle, its curved neck and fanged head the other. He took a long drink. Then he held out the goblet, turning it so that she could place her lips where his had touched.

Arianna took the cup, and deliberately turned it to drink out the other side. The wine was warm and heavily spiced. As she passed the goblet back to him she glanced up from beneath her lowered lids.

He dipped his head toward hers. His breath was warm and smelled of the wine. "You don't surrender easily, do you, wench? It is going to be a pleasure to tame you to the bit."

"There is not a Norman alive man enough to tame me."

He leaned into her, so close she felt the heat of him. Their shoulders touched, and his thigh brushed hers. "But even the most finely bred mare is always the better mount when she is under the hand of a firm master."

"As is a stallion," Arianna shot back. She raised her head until their eyes met. She could feel the blood beating in her neck. "Perhaps it will be the other way about. Perhaps I will be the one to master you."

He moved and she almost flinched. He drew his fingers along her cheek and down her neck and a tenseness began to coil inside her, seeping into her flesh like smoke. He stopped when he touched her throbbing pulse. "Perhaps I will let you . . ."

He looked as if he would say more, but instead he let his hand fall, and he turned away from her again. Arianna felt a strange disappointment, as if she had been on the verge of discovering the answer to a riddle that had been eluding her her entire life.

"For shame, big brother. Married scarce hours and already you ignore your lovely bride."

Startled, Arianna jerked around as the splendidly attired Earl of Chester eased onto the bench beside her. His lake-blue gaze roamed over her with blatant appreciation. "By my troth, there isn't a woman in England to match you, sweet Arianna. And the pity of it is you are utterly wasted on my brother."

Raine didn't move, but his voice went flat and cold.

"Nevertheless, she is mine, Hugh. And if you even think of swiving her, I will kill you."

Arianna stared straight ahead, her hands clenched into fists in her lap. He had spoken of her, her own husband had spoken of her as if she were a whore, a thing with no honor who would lie with any man. But this was a matter that must be settled between them in private, not before their wedding guests.

If the earl was moved by his brother's threats he didn't show it. Instead he laughed and reached across her for the flagon of wine, brushing her breasts with his arm. He filled the empty cup he carried in a hand laden with jeweled rings. Unlike his brother's, the earl's hand was white and smooth. But his nails had been chewed to the quick.

Hugh's eyes were focused on his brother. He raised the cup, tilting it in Raine's direction, and some of the wine slopped over to stain the cloth. "Such a brave and glorious knight . . . is our Raine. It's hard to believe he had to follow along behind me when we were lads, sweeping up my pony's droppings."

"If you hope to cut at my esteem in the lady's eyes, then you might as well save your breath, Hugh. For I can hardly sink much lower. . . . Can I, little wife?"

She looked up at him in surprise, to be fixed by a pair of opaque gray eyes that told her nothing. Yet she thought she had heard something in his voice. A challenge, perhaps.

His gaze fell to her mouth and she saw his eyes darken. His face hardened, as if the skin across his sharp cheekbones had somehow drawn tauter.

What she saw in his face frightened her. She sucked in a deep breath, and she didn't need to follow his gaze to know her breasts had lifted, straining against the thin silk of her bliaut. The air suddenly pressed down, moist and heavy.

She pushed up from the table, nearly upsetting the wine goblet in her haste to get away. "I—I believe I will seek out my cousin Kilydd. It's been months since we've seen each other. . . ."

Her chair rocked on its legs, nearly tipping over. They reached for it at the same time and his hand closed down over hers. For a moment she stood frozen, staring at that long, brown hand. She could feel the strength of his grip, the rough calluses earned by hard work with a sword, and she thought that he now had the right to put that hand on her body. Anywhere on her body.

She snatched her hand from beneath his and took off, practically running, for the river. "For shame, Raine," she heard Hugh drawl. "You've frightened the poor girl away with all your black scowls."

It was sultry down by the river, and smelled of rotting fish. Her chest heaved as she fought for breath. She closed her eyes, trying to call forth the image of the golden knight as she had seen him in the vision that morning. She smelled the hyacinth and felt the hot wind on her cheeks as she ran down the hill and into her golden knight's strong arms, and heard the words, *I love you, Arianna, I love you, love you* . . .

Tears burned the backs of her eyes. *He* should be her future, her golden knight. Not the Norman upstart she had married. But tonight . . . tonight it would be the Norman who would put those rough, brown hands on her body. . . .

"Arianna, *geneth* . . ."

Arianna spun around to confront two men, one tall and lean and tawny-haired, and the other gray and scowling and shaped like a squat ale keg. A smile started to break across her face, but she stopped it when she remembered how her cousins had both scorned her earlier.

"I am *geneth* no longer," she said. A girl no longer, but a wife. God help her, a wife . . .

The older man, Ivor, looked her over from head to toe with unblinking eyes that were tiny and dark, like olive pits. "What did you want to go and marry the Norman bastard for, Arianna? I'd have never thought you'd stoop so low."

"God's death, you think I did it willingly! I did it for Gwynedd, for you—"

"Bah!" Ivor hawked and spat in the dirt.

Kilydd laughed. "Ivor has never understood the whys and wherefores of politics. He thinks the only thing to do with a Norman is to kill him—"

"Aye, dead and they can go to hell and be bothering the devil instead."

Kilydd laughed again, and then he fastened earnest eyes on Arianna's face. She had always liked his eyes. They were a warm gold to match his hair, the color of summer honey. "Arianna. Are you all right? No one's hurt you, have they?"

Arianna shook her head, a smile peeping out and then blazing across her face. She hugged them both in turn, kissing their beard-roughened cheeks, allowing their drooping Welsh mustaches to tickle her nose. "Oh, but it's so good to see you two."

"We've come to speak to you, girl. About tonight," Ivor said.

"Tonight?" She turned to the younger man. "Oh, Kilydd, please don't be up to any mischief tonight. That raid of yours has already caused far too much trouble than it was worth."

Kilydd's mouth jerked into a grin. "What raid is this you speak of?" Then he stroked her cheek. "Nay, sweetling, 'tis you we fear for. You know the tales of how the Normans do abuse women, especially those not of their accursed race. We came to tell you—we'll be waiting in the hall below the lord's chamber tonight, should you have need of us."

"What . . . what is it you think he'll do to me?"

The two men exchanged looks, Ivor's face darkening to the color of blackberries. Kilydd met her frightened eyes, then his gaze shifted away from hers, and he cleared his throat.

"There is a decent way to bed a virgin bride, and then there are those God-cursed foreign ways. You'll be remembering whose daughter you are, and you'll not let him be shaming you with any disgusting French perversions."

"Aye, and if he hurts you," Ivor put in, "even if it's only a belting he gives you, we promise we'll kill him for it, aye, and to hell with Owain and King Henry and their god-be-damned truce."

The knot of fear in Arianna's stomach tightened. But it wasn't until Kilydd brushed the damp curls from her face that she realized she was sweating. "You understand what we speak of, Arianna?"

"Aye, French perversions . . ." she said, though in truth she was not sure she did. She only knew that the hazy fear that had been like a mist in her mind all day suddenly became sharply focused on the wedding night to come. But in spite of their chivalrous offer, she couldn't call on her cousins to save her from whatever vile things the Norman bastard chose to do to her, for here in his castle, surrounded by his men-at-arms, whoever dared to attack the Black Dragon would be cut down as soon as he drew sword.

When Arianna returned to the bridal dais, she discovered to her relief that her husband was no longer there. A group of minstrels played a high-stepping carole and several couples were dancing next to the tables, spinning so fast they blended together into whirls of color, like streams of spilled paint, and their joyful singing nearly drowned out the viols and tabors.

Taliesin popped up suddenly beside her, causing her to jump. He had a silver tray of blancmange balanced in his hand and as he leaned over, the jellied pudding sailed off the tray to land with a soggy plop onto the table. It quivered a moment, then stilled.

"God's death, boy. You are the most inept squire it has ever been my misfortune to meet."

The boy's lower lip pouched out. "Well, it's playing my harp I should be doing anyway, not serving blancmange, and I told my lord as much. But he threatened to string me up by my thumbs if I didn't start better fulfilling my duties as his squire." The pouting mouth suddenly lifted into a grin. "In truth, I think he feared I would sing the ode I've composed in his honor."

Arianna started to laugh, but when she looked up at him, the light in his eyes was so bright it was as if twin candle flames flared in the sockets. "Who are you really?" she said, but he was already gone, disappearing among the flow of varlets and pages bearing platters of food and ewers of wine and ale.

The carole had finished with resounding shouts of laughter from the dancers. To her surprise, Arianna spotted her husband in the circle, though unlike the others he was neither laughing nor smiling. He held out his hand and a woman took it. It was Sybil, his brother's wife. Earl Hugh, who sat alone at the end of the dais, had seen them as well. He reached for his wine cup, nearly knocking it over, and he had the strangest look on his face—like a starving child being forced to watch while others feasted.

He loves her, Arianna thought with sudden shock. The jaded and profane Earl of Chester loved his wife. And for a moment she pitied him.

But then her thoughts turned inward, to the wedding night to come, and her belly fluttered with panic as she thought of her cousins' warning. She wondered how she would survive the coming hours and have still at the end of it her honor and her dignity.

I will not beg, she promised herself. *No matter what he does to me, I will not beg, or cry, or shame myself in any way.*

* * *

Sybil fought to regain her breath, her breasts heaving. Her skin was flushed, glistening with a light film of sweat. Raine bowed over her hand, preparing to lead her back to her seat.

"Wait, Raine . . . I've a stone in my slipper."

Her fingers closed around his, dragging him away from the new dance that was forming. She slipped her arm around his waist and leaned into him, balancing on one leg as she pulled up her skirt, well beyond the pink garter that held up her stocking. Her ankle was small enough to span with his thumb and forefinger; but then he had already made that discovery years ago. The skin above the garter was still the pure white of a fresh snowfall.

She removed her dainty satin soler, turning it upside down. No stone fell out, not even a pebble. The slipper was embroidered with fine gold and silver wires and studded with sapphires and pearls, and Raine estimated its cost to be equal to a good suit of Damascus armor.

He looked down at her coifed head. He wished he could see her hair. When she was a girl she had worn it loose and it had fallen like a mantle of gold down her back, brushing the swell of her hips when she walked.

The slipper was back on her foot, but she had not removed her arm from around his waist. "Raine, do you remember that day we danced by the river?"

"I remember." She had supplied the music, trilling in her sweet soprano, and they had twirled around and around until they became dizzy and had to lie down in the sun-bleached grass. He had been fifteen, but he had already known for two years what to do with a girl on a bed of grass.

"You spent most of your time . . ." Her voice trailed off, as two pink roses bloomed in her cheeks.

"Trying to put my hands all over your breasts," he finished for her.

She had tiny pleats at the corners of her mouth that turned into dimples when she smiled. At last she removed her arm, though she did it slowly, trailing her fingers across his back. She still had that dusting of freckles across her cheekbones and nose. Once they had played a game where he had tried to kiss every single one individually.

"This is a splendid wedding, Raine."

"Is it? I wouldn't know. The last one I went to was yours."

Her head whipped around, and her lavender-blue eyes filled with tears. "I thought you had forgiven me. That we could be friends again. But you hate me still, don't you? You hate me for marrying Hugh."

He watched as a single tear trembled on the end of her pale lashes, then fell to roll down her cheek. "I don't hate you. I learned long ago that life is divided into a few grand tragedies and a lot of little disappointments. You, sweet Sybil, were one of my little disappointments."

Her eyes squeezed shut and her mouth twisted, deepening the pleats and making her look older. "And this marriage of yours. Would you call it a grand tragedy or a little disappointment?"

His gaze found his wife sitting by herself on the bridal dais. The diffused sunlight filtering through the yellow silk canopy made her sable hair gleam as if sprinkled with gold dust and highlighted the spare bones of her face. She looked like the princess that she was, and she was his, and he wanted her.

"She brings me Rhuddlan and a title," he said to the woman he had once loved, though his eyes remained on his wife, and the ache in his loins was for his wife as well. "And she will breed me sons with noble blood in their veins. I call that damned good fortune."

"You've changed, Raine. I don't think I like the man you've become." And pressing her hand to her mouth, Sybil whirled and ran away from him.

Raine followed after her, but all his attention was still

on his wife. And she was staring with avid fascination at his brother.

"Take your eyes off my brother."

Arianna's head jerked up, and she almost recoiled at the look of raw fury on Raine's hard, dark face, especially because it was unexpected, and so undeserved.

Raine sat, straddling the chair. His knee pressed into her thigh and stayed there. Arianna's pulse tripped, and she clenched her jaw to control the shudder that coursed through her. She was afraid of him but a part of her knew, too, that if she didn't begin now to stand up to his powerful personality, he would grind her down until there would be nothing of Arianna left but the chaff.

"You are truly a bastard," she said, her voice a choking whisper.

"Aye, I truly am. And you are now a bastard's wife, so take care you don't forget it. Stay out of my brother's bed."

"How dare you imply that I am so lacking in honor that I would betray a vow? Even one given to you, sir bastard knight—"

"Enough!" He slammed the flat of his hand down onto the table. "My name is Raine, and from now on when you speak to me you will use it."

"Go to hell."

"I mean this, Arianna. Don't push me too far."

"I intend to push you, Norman *bastard*. I will push you back into the English bog from which you crawled."

She hadn't been aware her fist had wrapped around the eating knife, until his hand lashed out, pinning her wrist in place.

"Do you know who wins a joust? It is the knight who smites the hardest, cruelest blow. The man who shows no mercy." He plucked the knife from her nerveless fingers. "I have never lost a joust, Arianna. Remember that."

The people at the tables around them had long ago

gone silent, watching this first marital spat with unconcealed amusement. Raine still had hold of her wrist. He wasn't hurting her. Yet she had no doubt that he could snap the bone in two simply by flexing those long, brown fingers.

"Our guests are getting the wrong impression, wife. Smile at me." He applied the barest pressure. Enough to draw her rebellious gaze back up to his face. "Smile at me, Arianna. And look as if you mean it."

She bared her teeth at him.

Taliesin elbowed his way between them, throwing a heaping platter of sugared pancakes onto the table. One slid off the platter, bouncing off Raine's lap on its way to the ground. "A fine performance, my lord," the squire scolded. "Everyone is now convinced that you two adore one another."

A muscle jumped in Raine's cheek as he swung his icy gaze onto the boy. "I have had enough from you as well."

"Aye, my lord. But you are bungling things again and—"

"Taliesin . . ."

The squire's pale face went a little paler. He left without another word, but he was soon back—to carve a haunch of stag—and wearing a sulky look.

Food and drink continued to be piled onto the table in ever greater quantities: boar's head larded with herb sauce, godale spiced with juniper, roast pike in aspic. As the guests became satiated, the marshal of the hall sent forth entertainers—a juggler who could catch balls in a cup on his forehead, acrobats and conjurers, a man with marmosets that turned somersaults.

Lastly came the morris dancers with their blackened faces. The bells on their legs jangled as they whirled to the accompaniment of a pipe and tabor and twirled long streamers of brightly colored cloths. One dancer carried a stick high in the air, and on it, bouncing in the hot summer breeze, was a bladder blown up and graphically painted to resemble a giant phallus.

The guests burst into loud laughter, pointing at this enormous, bobbing, throbbing symbol of masculine power. Loud and bawdy jests about the night to come flew around the tables. Arianna sat stiff as a lance, fighting down the queasiness in her stomach. She had been to weddings before, so it wasn't the first time that she had seen the raunchy spectacle. But she'd never been forced to witness it while sitting beside the man who would be instructing her in the marriage duty as soon as the sun set.

The man beside her inclined his head in the direction of the dancer who bore the graphic bladder. "Now *that,* little wife, is more the sort of willow switch you'll find beneath a Norman's tunic."

God's death . . . He'd meant it as a jest, surely he was only teasing her. But now Arianna began to fear the Normans not only engaged in unnatural acts but were built unnaturally as well.

Earl Hugh of Chester banged his fist on the table, demanding quiet. Picking up a wine chalice he stood, lifting it high in the air. "Gentle ladies and noble men . . . I drink to my brother Raine, Lord of Rhuddlan, and his lady."

The guests all stood, lifting their wine and ale in the toast, while the local populace, hanging about beyond the lists and waiting for the wedding largesse, tossed their caps into the air and cheered. Again Earl Hugh banged for silence. "I drink to England and King Henry. May they reign supreme."

The wedding guests all drank to England, except for a scowling Ivor and Kilydd. There was less cheering from the ranks of peasants this time, and some rather loud grumbling in Welsh. Raine raised the dragon chalice to his lips, and then he held it out to Arianna.

"Drink, wife."

Arianna's hands curled into fists in her lap. "I would

choke ere I swallowed one drop in a toast to England. It's all I can do to sit here and watch you and your friends gloat after having tried to carve up my country as if it were a meat pie."

His pale eyes narrowed, his mouth hardened, and for a moment she fully expected him to force the wine down her throat, but instead he lifted his shoulder in a lazy shrug. "That's the price you pay for losing."

"At least I find solace in the knowledge that it is not forever. One day King Arthur will arise from his golden bed on the Isle of Avalon and take up his magic sword, and you will be driven from this island. The day will come when Arthur will once again sit on his throne in London. The great seer Myrddin has so prophesied our ultimate victory."

"Ah, yes . . ." His long fingers toyed with the wine goblet's dragon tail. "Taliesin tells me you're something of a seer yourself. Be sure to let me know when Arthur is about to come so that I can begin to worry."

"That is a fault of you Normans—one of your *many* faults. You have no imagination."

"On the contrary. I know well the stench of a man after he's been dead but a few hours, so I can easily imagine how your King Arthur must reek after lying on that golden bed and rotting for six hundred years. If he came back to sit on the throne in London, the inhabitants would expire from the stink."

Goaded now beyond fear, Arianna hurled at him the worst insult she could think of. "You, sir, are no true knight!"

He startled her by throwing back his head and laughing. Sunlight glinted off his strong, tanned throat. For a moment she lost herself in looking at him. At his finely cut mouth, his flaring cheekbones. God help her, but he affected her in ways she didn't understand, and didn't like.

"You may scoff, but the day will come," she said,

though her voice shook, "when you Normans and all your name will know defeat."

His face still bore traces of laughter and his eyes had changed color, from flint to soft smoke. His smoldering gaze fastened onto her mouth. "My name will include your son, Arianna. For you will have a son by me."

Arianna was convinced her heart had stopped. When it started up again, it beat in unsteady lurches. "No . . . I won't . . ."

"You will. I will plant him in your belly tonight."

10

Raine knelt among sweet-smelling rushes, his brooding gaze focused on the bed. The gray fur coverlet had been folded back, the fine camlet sheets strewn with violets.

The bishop swung a censer, sending clouds of incense wreathing around the embroidered canopy. The bronze lamps overhead swayed on their chains, causing shadows to undulate against the gilt-painted walls. The old man's dry voice crackled like dead leaves as he chanted, *"Dominus vobiscum . . ."*

If ever a marriage bed needed blessing, Raine thought, it was this one.

God's truth, he would rather have her willing. But willing or no, he would take her virginity. Their marriage had to be consummated this night, in case Owain showed up outside Rhuddlan's walls tomorrow demanding back his daughter and his land. More than the truce, more even than his possession of the castle, Raine's claim to Rhuddlan rested on his marriage to Arianna.

The bishop shook the aspergillum and holy water flew out the holes of the perforated silver vessel, splattering the bed. The droplets spread, darkening the satin like tears of blood. He needed her virgin's blood on the sheets come morning. He wanted a son growing in her belly before the end of summer.

The bishop withdrew on a fanfare of horns. Raine stood and looked down at the bent head of his wife. He was struck by how white was her scalp where it showed in the part of her dark brown hair. He reached down for her, offering his hand. A moment later she put her palm in his. He felt a shudder pass through her body as he pulled her to her feet. When she lifted her eyes to his, he saw that they were filled with a stark kind of fear.

Then a laughing, chattering group of women surrounded them, pulling her away from him.

In the great hall below, his brother and the other guests had already made heavy inroads into a tun of malmsey wine. Raine endured in silence their ribald jests while he drank and waited for the women to put her to bed. He suddenly felt so tired that he just wanted to get it over with.

His mood had turned so grim that when it came time for him to rejoin his bride in their chamber, the men took one look at his face and decided to forego their part in the bedding revels. Raine mounted the stairs alone.

The door's hide hinges squealed as he swung it open and Arianna jerked, snatching the sheet up under her chin. The cresset lamps had been doused, the room lit now only by the fire in the brazier and the single flame of the tall, filigreed candlestick beside the bed. The dim, flickering light threw the bones of her face into shadowy relief.

He searched for something to say to her, but could think of nothing. He pushed the door shut and leaned his shoulders against the worn, iron-banded wood. She stared back at him, her eyes black in her pale face.

"Arianna . . ." he began, his voice slurred, husky with fatigue. He struggled for a way to reassure her without promising not to hurt her, for he knew that he would.

But the words wouldn't come. The tense silence

dragged out between them. Her chin lifted and her lips curled into that beautiful sneer—the one that made him want to master her and make love to her, both at the same time. "Well met, Norman. Have you come to plant your babe in my belly?"

His jaw hardened. He pushed himself off the door and started toward her. "Aye, wench," he growled between his teeth.

Her hands clutched the bedcovers tighter to her chest and she pressed back into the pillows.

"Drop the sheet," he said.

"You could at least be chivalrous enough to—"

"I *said* . . . drop the sheet."

Her hands fell to her sides, and the sheet slithered to her waist. His fist shot out, grabbing a handful of the satiny material and ripping it completely off her.

Her palms pressed so hard into the mattress that the tendons stood out on her wrists. Her chest shuddered with the effort she made to contain her breathing. The smell of violets hung heavy in the air around the bed, but it was the sight of her naked body that caused the sweet ache of his sex to swell and harden with need.

She wore still the bronze torque of twisted snakes around her neck; they seemed to curl and writhe with her heaving breaths. The skin of her breasts was so pale he could see the blue tracery of veins. He cupped one in his palm and felt her heartbeat quicken.

He turned away, pulling off his tunic and chainse. The air felt cool on his bare chest. He sat on a leather coffer at the end to the bed to pull off his boots. Standing up again, he fumbled with the cords that fastened his braies to his chausses, cursing when one snarled into a knot. He peeled the undergarments down over his buttocks, kicking them aside.

Her breath sucked in on a gasp.

He turned his head and saw that her eyes had fastened on his blood-engorged sex. Her wide gaze moved up his stomach, over his chest, and he actually thought he could feel it caressing his flesh like hot, moist breath.

He lay down onto the bed beside her, not touching her yet. The leather springs groaned beneath his weight and she shrank back as if she could pull the pillows around her like a shell.

"Arianna, look at me."

She wouldn't look at him, but lay instead staring straight up at the canopy overhead, as pale and stiff as the painted statue of the Virgin in the chapel. God's mercy, but this was going to be impossible.

He traced the bronze circlet where it followed the contours of her collarbone. The metal was hot, scorching hot, and it seemed to throb and pulse beneath his fingertips. For a brief moment a strange, curling silver mist blurred the edges of his vision and a roaring rose in his ears, like the surf crashing against rocks. He shuddered and the mist dissipated, the crashing, sucking sounds receded. The metal collar was cool against his fingers and he was sure then that he had imagined it all.

He pushed himself up onto his elbows and looked into his bride's still face. She blinked and then at last her eyes focused onto him. Again he touched the circlet at her throat. "Why do you wear this?"

"You wouldn't understand."

He wrapped his hands around her neck, pressing his thumbs into the hollows just above the twisted metal collar, and felt the drumming of her blood. "When I ask you a question, wife, I want an answer."

Her pulse plunged and dipped. Her eyes were dark and haunted, like a Welsh mountain forest. He felt her swallow. "It is a seer's torque. Only one with the true sight is allowed to wear it."

"And what things have you seen?"

He watched, fascinated, as she ran her tongue along her full lower lip and then sucked the lip hard into her mouth. "You. I saw you."

That mouth . . . he had to taste that mouth. He lowered his head, but she flinched, turning her face away, and so he stroked her hair where it pooled, thick and dark like spilled wine, over the violet-strewn pillows. He twisted a hank of it around his fist and brought it up to his face, breathing deeply.

"It smells like a lemon," he said, and cupping her cheeks in his hands, he forced her face around and kissed her.

She jerked her head violently aside.

He spanned her jaw with his long fingers, holding her in place as he lowered his head to recapture her lips. But she twisted beneath him, panting against his open mouth. "Stop. Please stop . . ."

He grasped the sides of her head and gave her a little shake. "You are my wife, damn your thick head. You are supposed to submit to me."

"No, I don't want—"

His grip tightened, shaking her again, harder. "You will submit, Arianna. You will feel my seed spilling inside of you and then I will know that Rhuddlan is well and truly mine."

"Rhuddlan! That is all you care about. I am nothing but a name to you, a means to buy legitimacy, when all I ever wanted . . . all I want . . ." Her eyes brimmed with sudden tears and her chest heaved as she fought off a sob. "You can't have me, not the part of me that matters."

He drew in a deep breath as he struggled with his temper. "You are making this into much more of an ordeal than it need be." He slid his finger across the fullness of her lower lip. "If you would quit fighting me, you might even take pleasure from it." He moved his finger along her jaw and down her neck, stroking, stroking. . . . "But I will have your virginity this night, Arianna. Easy or hard, I will have it."

She arched back against the pillows, thrusting her arms

down rigid at her sides. "Oh God, take it then and be done with it!"

He moved his head to kiss her again, but she jerked her mouth away from his. So he brushed his lips across the elegant hollow beneath her cheekbone. Her skin was as smooth as melted wax. Her hands came up to his chest and she tried to push him away. He trapped her fingers, pressing them against his flesh.

She pulled her hand from his, and her palm brushed through his chest hair, rubbing his nipples, and he groaned deep in his throat. He slanted his lips onto hers and her whole body shuddered and tensed. He ran his tongue along her lower lip, felt it tremble.

"Open your mouth."

She opened her mouth, to breathe, to protest. Whatever the reason, he didn't hesitate. He broached it with his tongue, slowly and carefully, the way he intended to broach her below. Her mouth was hot and he filled it.

She went absolutely still. But when he met her tongue, stroking the length of it with his, she reared against him, breaking the kiss.

He reached between them and caressed one breast, his callused-roughened palm grating against her soft skin. She shuddered, her nails digging into his arms as she tried to push him away from her.

He tensed his muscles, resisting her. He cupped one breast, lifting it, and she gasped arching against him as his lips closed tightly around her nipple. She made a little mewling cry of protest as he sucked the nipple deep into his mouth, and it budded up hard against his tongue.

She was almost frantic now, bucking against him like an unbroken colt. "Don't do this to me," she pleaded, her breaths grating harshly in her throat. "I will hate you all the rest of my life if you do this."

He lifted his head. Her eyes were stained black. She shivered although her skin felt hot, and everywhere he touched her, it rippled. He drew her closer against him and his stiff rod brushed against her belly. He shuddered at the feel of her softness against him. She cried out, squeezing her legs tightly together.

He covered her, moving so that his chest hair rubbed across her nipples, while he pushed her thighs apart with his knee. She tried to shield herself with her hand, but he pried it away.

"I hate you," she said on a sobbing breath.

"Yes, I know. Hate me, Arianna. Hate me all you want. But open your legs for me."

He stroked her heaving stomach, and followed his hands with his mouth. He palmed her mound, his fingers stretching her open. He lowered his head and thrust his tongue inside.

A blade flashed by the corner of his eye, and pain exploded in his arm. "Christ!" he hissed, on an intake of breath.

She tried to stab him again, and he reacted instinctively, grabbing for the weapon. She flung up her head just as his arm moved forward to block the fall of the blade, and his wrist bone slammed hard into her eye. The blow stunned her so that he was able to twist the knife from her fingers. He flung it across the room.

He held her hands above her head, pinning her down with his weight. He lay between her spread thighs, and the blood dripped from the cut on his arm onto her breasts. Their harsh breaths grated together into a sobbing sound that filled the still night air. He looked into her eyes . . . eyes that damned him with her hatred and her scorn.

He thrust into her, trapping her scream with his mouth. He finished it quickly. While he still could.

The slash on his arm was long but not very deep.

There was a stack of linen cloths by the laver. Raine wadded one up and pressed it to the cut to stop the bleeding. He looked over at the bed. She lay on her back, her arms rigid at her sides, her face turned away from him. She wasn't making a sound, and he didn't think she was crying.

Enough blood stained the sheets to prove he had ravished ten virgins, and it was all his. Or mostly his.

God . . . he could still taste her scream on his mouth.

He wet another cloth in the water basin and brought it back to the bed. He eased down beside her. There was blood on her thighs, her blood, along with his seed. Wet red smears were all over her breasts, belly, and arms. His blood.

Leaning over her, he started to wipe off her stomach. She jerked upright, snatching at the cloth. "Don't touch me anymore." The face she turned to him was blanched of all color, but for the eye he'd accidentally struck. It was purple and nearly swollen shut, and would be black and blue by morning.

She began rubbing almost frantically between her thighs with trembling hands. "That was the most vile, disgusting thing that has ever been done to me."

He swung off the bed. "You'd better resign yourself to getting used to it," he said, in the flat, cold voice he used to mask all emotion. "Because it will happen again. Most likely as soon as tomorrow morning."

He jerked the pillows off the bed, where she'd hidden the first knife, and found two more. He went over the room, searching for weapons. They made a growing pile on the floor: three swords, a half dozen daggers and knives, a battle-ax, even a mace—a particularly gruesome-looking, heavy wooden truncheon covered with iron spikes. He was both amused and astonished at the size of the arsenal his wife had hidden in their bedchamber.

When he was sure he'd gathered everything that appeared even remotely lethal, he went over to the window and lifted the bar off the shutters.

"What are you doing? You're letting in the evil night air, you dolt."

She had spoken with such indignation that Raine stopped to stare at her in utter bewilderment. She sat cross-legged on the bed, naked, with blood still smeared on her thighs, her hair in bird's-nest tangles around her face, yet as calm and composed as a queen holding court. She baffled him, this wife of his, for he'd never known another woman like her. She had more courage than most men, and she spoke of duty and honor as if she truly believed they were more than just words.

Courage, honor, duty—he had believed in all those things once. When he was young.

"I have this peculiar fondness for my life," he finally said, surprised at the tightness in his throat. "And I intend to hang on to it at least through the night." He pitched the mace out the window. A startled bellow echoed up from below. Belatedly he called out a warning, before tossing out the battle-ax.

"I won't try to kill you in your sleep."

He lifted his brows, gesturing at the weapons scattered among the rushes. "Then what were you planning to do with these—beseige the Tower of London?"

She waved a hand through the air, the way a lady would dismiss a servant. "I never meant to kill you. For, whether I like it or no, you are my husband before God. But I had to make you stop . . . stop . . ." Her voice cracked as a breath hitched in her throat.

"Doing that vile, disgusting thing?" He came back to the bed and stood over her. "We've been through this before. The Holy Church calls it the marriage *duty,* Arianna. You are supposed to submit to it."

"I know." She looked him full in the face, her eyes wide and clear, the color of sea foam. "But the marriage duty is one thing, and your unnatural French perversions are another. I had my honor to defend."

He sucked in a surprised breath, then pushed it out in a

noiseless sigh. "Mother of God . . ." He sat down next
to her, ignoring the way she flinched from him. "Arianna,
it often hurts at first and it's no dishonor nor is it unnatural for a wife to open her body to her husband so that he
might plant his seed within her."

"I know that. But what you did was a perversion."

He studied her averted face, trying to understand her.
He thought back to what he had been doing to her before
she stabbed him and he emitted a crack of laughter.
"God's love . . . Don't Welshmen kiss and suck their
women's—between their women's legs?"

Her head swung around. "Nay, of course not!"

"I pity the women of your country then, aye, and the
men, too, for they don't know the pleasure they are missing."

Doubt flickered in her eyes, but then she shook her
head. "I don't think they would like it. 'Tis unnatural."

He cradled her chin in his hand, lifting her face. He
stroked the strong line of her jaw with his thumb. "There
is nothing unnatural in what I will do to you, Arianna.
When I touch you like this . . ." He brushed the backs of
his knuckles across her breasts, oh so very lightly. Her
nipples rose and tightened and she caught a groan deep in
her throat. "And when I kiss your sweet mouth . . ." He
slid his hand around the back of her neck, hooking her
head toward his. His tongue stroked her lips, coaxing
them to part.

She pulled away from him, twisting her head aside.
"You have done it once this night, husband. I don't see
the need to do it again."

For a moment he was damn well tempted to do it to her
again just to prove that he could, that it was his right.
Instead, he threw himself down on the bed, cradling his
head in his clasped palms. His arm throbbed and a thundering pain had developed behind his eyes. He was tired,
so very, very tired.

He eyed her now with weary indifference. She sat up

still, looking down on him. Her face held more confusion than fear. He supposed it was an improvement, but at the moment he no longer cared. "Go to sleep," he said.

The musky smell of sex hung heavy in the air, and the cloying odor of crushed violets. They lay side by side, not touching, and though the bed was wide, it was not so wide that he couldn't feel her warmth. After a while he felt the down-filled mattress move. He turned his head and saw her shoulders shake, though she had her face pressed hard into the pillow to stifle any sound. He brought his hand up, but in the end he pulled it back without touching her.

She cried for a long time. When at last she slept, he lay awake still, his eyes staring sightless at the canopy over-head.

The feeble morning sunlight wakened her, for she was used to sleeping with the bed curtains drawn and the window shutters bolted. But when she tried to open her eyes she found one lid wouldn't work properly. The eye throbbed. She touched it with tentative fingers; it was puffy and very sore.

Slowly, she pushed herself upright. Her knee brushed against hard and hairy flesh. Snatching the sheet up under her chin, she looked to see if she had awakened him.

He lay sprawled on his stomach across the bed, his face turned away from her. He had kicked the sheet off during the night and it was twisted around his legs. He has the body of a warrior, she thought. Brown and battered and brawny from years of fighting in wars and tournaments. His flesh bore the scars of those years. There was a grue-some, puckered one on his shoulder, and an angry red welt wrapped around his waist. Unconsciously, she reached out to touch it—

He was on her before she could draw breath to scream.

He pinned her to the bed, his chest flattening her breasts. His pale gaze swept over her. Then his eyes darkened, and his mouth softened. He lowered his head until she could feel the heat of his breath on her lips. "What were you doing?"

"Nothing." She stared up into his face. His cheeks were darkened by a stubble of beard. She hadn't noticed it before, but there were tiny specks of black in his gray eyes. They merged with the deep, dark centers, and it was what gave his eyes that sooty color when he laughed or when he was about to . . .

To kiss her. His mouth lowered another inch. He was about to kiss her. "I was looking at your scars," she said quickly.

"Do they disgust you?"

"Nay," she said, surprised that he would think so. "They are the proud trophies of a warrior's life."

He smiled . . . and her breath caught. She had never seen him smile, really smile, before. The lines that bracketed his mouth deepened into crescents and his eyes took on a sleepy, lazy cast. It was a boyish smile, and oddly tender.

"They are trophies, it's true," he said. "But I'm not proud of them, because every one resulted from a mistake I made. Something stupid that almost cost me my life." He ran his finger along her cheekbone, just below her bruised eye, and the breath she hadn't realized she'd been holding eased out of her on a soft sigh. "Shall I admire your trophy? You look like a spotted cow."

Arianna lowered her lids, biting her lip to hold back a laugh, for she suspected that he had just accused her of having done something stupid. She noticed the sheet had fallen and she yanked it back up.

He slipped his hand behind her neck, his thumb tilting her chin until their gazes met. Her lips parted open as his mouth came slowly toward hers.

The door opened with a bang and Taliesin entered, bearing a tray piled high with honeyed manchet loaves and jacks of ale in one hand and carrying a copper bucket of steaming water in the other. "Your brother the earl and his lady wife are leaving immediately this morning, my lord," he called out cheerfully. "And they ask that you ride with them as far as Offa's Dyke—"

Taliesin froze and his face blanched as his wide gaze first took in the dark brown splotches of dried blood smeared on the sheets, and then Arianna's startled and bruised face. He took a stumbling step forward, dropping the bucket. "Oh, milady! Goddess save you . . ."

The tray started to slide from his hands, but Raine was on his feet to catch it. Taliesin turned horrified eyes onto his master. "My lord, what have you? . . . Oh, but this is terrible. Truly you have done worse than bungle it this time. . . ."

Raine's mouth kinked into a half-smile. "The blood is mine, not hers. You warned me, after all, that I might need my armor to bed her."

"Huh?" Taliesin's gaze went from Arianna's black eye to Raine, narrowing at the gash on his liege lord's arm. "You hit her and so she stabbed you."

Arianna almost laughed. "Nay, boy, 'twasn't like that at all," she said. "I stabbed him and so he hit me . . . sort of."

Taliesin's lips tightened into a thin line. "This isn't at all the way these things are done. You, my lady, are not supposed to try to kill your husband. And you, my lord, are not—"

Raine whipped around, pointing a stiff finger in his squire's face. "Taliesin, if you don't start minding your own affairs, I will give you a black eye to match hers."

Arianna did start to laugh then, but the laughter died in her throat as her attention was caught by the sight of her husband standing naked in bright sunlight at the foot of the bed. She studied him with an unconscious curiosity.

The English called it a *prick* and the Welsh a *bonllost*. It thrust up from the dense black hair between his thighs, thick and raw-red and heavily veined, and even as she looked it seemed to swell some more.

"Do you like what you see, little wife?"

Arianna's gaze flew up to his face; she didn't look away from him though she could feel a heat begin to spread up her neck. For a long, dragging minute, they stared at one another, while she tried to pretend that she wasn't afraid of him. *My duty,* she thought, *I must do my duty.* But the fear grew worse as she remembered the pain when he had taken her last night and later, his saying in that cold, flat voice, *You'd better resign yourself to getting used to it. Because it will happen again. Most likely as soon as tomorrow morning . . .*

She had almost forgotten, because of a smile, just what she was to him, what he saw when he looked at her— Rhuddlan, and a noble brood mare for his heirs.

She heard the sound of splashing water as Taliesin retrieved what was left in the pail, and Raine turned aside, going to the laver. The squire stomped around the room, pretending to be busy and casting dark looks in his master's direction.

Arianna's muscles slackened with relief that Raine was not going to exercise his husbandly rights on her, but soon she became increasingly uncomfortable when she realized she was going to have to wait in bed until he left or get up and dress in front of him. After he washed, he crossed back into her line of sight, naked still, and her discomfort increased when she realized he was headed for the garderobe. He kept his back to her, but he left the door open and she could hear plainly what he was doing. She felt a sudden urge to use the privy closet herself. But she could not even begin to imagine doing such a thing with him in the same chamber, even with the door closed.

Finished with relieving himself, Raine headed back toward the washstand. Arianna whipped her head around, focusing her fascinated gaze on the wall.

"Is my horse saddled yet?" Raine asked around the hazel twig he was using to clean his teeth.

"No, my lord," Taliesin replied. "Milady, you ought to bathe that eye in rosewater. I could fetch you up—"

"Never mind her. She'll live. Go see to my horse."

The door slammed behind the squire and the room fell expectantly silent.

"Come here."

Arianna looked at her husband. He had put on his braies, but that was all. He stood with his feet spread wide, pelvis tipped slightly forward, his hands on his hips. The pose was intimidating and Arianna didn't like it.

"Come here," he said again.

She pulled the sheet up tighter beneath her chin. "You haven't finished dressing."

He sucked in a deep breath, expanding his chest. "You have a lot of things to learn, Arianna. And the first lesson is obedience. Come here."

"Go to hell, Norman."

He took a step toward her, and she was out of the bed, taking the sheet with her. She discovered two things immediately—the first was that she couldn't run and clutch the sheet to her chest at the same time. The second was that she'd jumped off the wrong side of the bed. All that faced her was a blank wall.

She whirled to meet him, the sheet as her shield, backing up until her bare bottom hit the cool, gilded wood.

He reached her in two strides and jerked the sheet from her grasp.

"You bastard—"

His hand smothered her mouth and her head would have slammed against the wall if he hadn't cushioned it with his other palm. "You are overly fond of that word, little wife. And I don't like the sound of it coming from your sweet lips."

Arianna wanted to tell him that she didn't give a leper's damn for his likes and dislikes, but she couldn't speak with his hand pressing so hard against her mouth, and she was cutting the soft underside of her lips on her teeth.

"Now you will apologize," he said, slowly and distinctly, "and you will address me as 'my lord husband' when you do it."

She stared up into his ruthless face, telling him with her eyes where he could go, and what he could do with himself and his title once he got there. But he'd had more practice at this sort of jousting, and she was the first to blink and look away.

He released her mouth. "I will have your apology, Arianna," he said in that soft, flat voice.

He would have it, too, she knew that. She lifted her chin and attempted to stare at him down the length of her nose.

"Forgive me for bringing up the shameful circumstances of your birth, my *lord* husband. I shall endeavor not to do so in the future . . . no matter what lengths you go to remind me of them."

A startled look came over his face. "Jesus Christ . . . only you could manage to apologize and insult a man all in the same breath."

He stared at her a moment longer, and his brows drew together while his lips twitched, as if he couldn't decide whether to frown or to laugh. Then, muttering an oath, he hauled her up against his chest and slammed his mouth over hers. His hands moved down to clasp her shoulders, lifting her up on her toes so that he could kiss her deeper, his tongue thrusting between her teeth.

Balling up her fists, she pushed against his chest, breaking the lock his mouth had on hers. His head flung up and his fingers tightened their grip. A muscle jumped in his cheek and she could see little tremors coursing through his body as he fought for control.

His hands fell away, and he stepped back, though he kept her pinned to the wall with his flinty gaze. "I was patient with you last night because it was your first time,

KEEPER OF THE DREAM

but you are my *wife,* Arianna, and I need an heir. And, by God, if I have to swive you day and night I will do so until I get one."

Arianna wanted to scoff at the man's idea of patience. She lifted her head. "I will do my duty, for Gwynedd's sake, but don't expect me to take any pleasure from it."

"I don't give a damn whether you take pleasure from it or not. As long as you take it."

Their eyes stayed locked in silent combat a moment longer, then he turned away from her. She snatched up the sheet, wrapping it around her like a shield.

He finished dressing in silence, pulling on a quilted chainse and the leather coat lightly armored with horn plates that the Normans called a *broigne.* Arianna remained where she was, armored in the sheet and following his every move.

He paused at the door and turned to point at the bed. "You will be here, in that bed, waiting for me when I return tonight. Do I make myself clear?"

"Perfectly . . ." She paused a beat, then added, "My *lord* husband."

11

From the window of their bedchamber, Arianna watched Raine ride across the open marsh with his brother at his side. Their horses' hooves sent up sprays of water behind them. Both men bore hawks on their gauntleted wrists and the shore birds, sensing danger, took flight.

But before Raine left he had pulled his black charger around at the gateway to his castle and looked back toward the great hall. He took his lance from his squire, lifting it high in the air. The hot summer wind caught his black dragon pennon, unfurling it against a shell-colored sky.

As if she needed reminding of who ruled her now.

She washed and dressed quickly, for she had decided that she would begin right away to assume her duties as chatelaine of her husband's castle. She had prepared all her life for this mantle of responsibility, and she looked forward to feeling the weight of it. Raine might think himself to be master of Rhuddlan, but she was his lady, and she knew from watching her mother over the years that a woman could acquire much power beyond supervising the spinning and seeing that the rushes were changed once a week. In truth, a capable wife could make herself indispensable to her lord and his demesne.

The hall downstairs was in shambles from the revels of the day before, and that was the task she would set about first. She required a horde of servants to clean it out, but she decided to take a quick tour of the other buildings and bailey first and make a complete list of everything that needed to be done.

Though barely past matins it was already brutally hot outside. There wasn't a cloud in sight to mar the deep blue of the sky. The bailey was a beehive of activity, for the new Lord of Rhuddlan was wasting no time in improving his castle. A group of men pitched new thatch onto the roof of the granary. The smith hammered on a plowshare at the forge. A pair of villein boys whitewashed the walls of the kitchen with long-handled brushes.

Arianna was crossing the yard when she spotted her cousins Ivor and Kilydd at the mounting blocks, preparing to leave. She opened her mouth to call out to them, only stopping herself just in time. One look at her black eye and they would jump to the wrong conclusion and start a war. To avoid them she ducked into the open door of one of the rambling, thatch-roofed stables.

It was dim inside but only a little cooler. The scent of freshly strewn hay lay thick in the air. The horses were busy chomping their morning fodder, but the squires and stable boys appeared to be occupied elsewhere. She heard an adolescent, off-key voice singing a Welsh drinking song about a warrior who preferred quaffing his mead to tupping a woman.

She followed the music to a small tack room. She paused at the threshold, smiling, as she watched her brother sing to himself while he straddled a sawhorse and rubbed goose grease into the seat of a saddle.

At the sound of his name his head jerked up. "Oh, Arianna, 'tis you . . ." He started to grin, and then his pale green eyes opened wide. "He beat you! The Norman bastard beat you!"

Arianna's hand flew up to her eye, and she winced at its soreness. "Nay, he did not," she said. Rhodri had been made a second squire to the Lord of Rhuddlan, but he was a hostage nonetheless. She could not have him charging to the defense of her honor. "It was an accident. You remember the time you and Dafydd were wrestling and he accidentally broke your arm? Well, it was like that."

"You were wrestling with Lord Raine?"

"Don't be a witless nit," she snapped at him to cover a sudden and unexpected blush. "Is this my lord husband's saddle?"

Rhodri scowled at the rag in his hand. "Aye, that wretched Taliesin has put me to this task." He gestured at a tangled pile of bits and bridles that rested in one corner. "He said he'd string me up by my thumbs if I didn't have all this tack cleaned and polished ere nightfall. God's eyes, you'd think the little sot was King Henry himself, the talent he has for ordering a body about."

Sensitive of her brother's fourteen-year-old dignity, Arianna struggled not to laugh. "Nevertheless, Lord Raine will be pleased when he sees how his saddle now shines."

Rhodri shrugged and his mouth turned down. "Aye, but I'm only biding my time." He leaned into her, lowering his voice. "The guard on me is lax, Arianna. I could have escaped long since, but I knew you'd want to come with me. Mayhap we could try tonight?"

Arianna seized her brother's shoulders, giving him a rough shake. "God's death, use your wits. Have you forgotten that we're hostages for Gwynedd's honor? Do you want to give King Henry an excuse for invading our lands again with his accursed army?"

Rhodri stared at the packed dirt of the stable floor. "Nay . . ."

"A hostage is not supposed to escape, 'tis not the thing.

Besides, did you not swear an oath of homage to Lord Raine when you became his squire?"

Rhodri's mouth was set in a mutinous line. "That oath doesn't count. 'Twas given to a Norman." He picked at a splinter on the sawhorse. "I hate Lord Raine near as much as I hate that wretched Taliesin." His gaze fastened onto her face and he frowned at her bruised eye. "Arianna? Do you remember the tale of that Norman earl who married a daughter of Powys and then killed her when he later found himself at war with her father?"

Arianna knew well the story, what child of Wales did not, for it was such a splendid example of Norman perfidy and cruelty. The earl had arranged an ambush for the Lord of Powys, and his wife, upon getting wind of it, had warned her father off. The earl, enraged over what he perceived as his wife's treachery, had cut off her head and impaled it on a stake atop his castle wall.

Arianna ruffled her brother's thatch of light brown hair, then laid her arm across his shoulders. "Don't worry about me, for I don't intend to give Lord Raine reason for putting my head on a spike," she said. She could well imagine what the Black Dragon would do to her should she ever, for the sake of her father or her people, be forced to betray him.

Rhodri squirmed out of her embrace. "God's death, leave off, Arianna! Don't be hanging around my neck like a wet mantle. If that wretched Taliesin had seen this I'd have never lived it down."

Arianna refrained from teasing her brother about "that wretched" Taliesin, who was assuming all the proportions of the plague in Rhodri's eyes. She left him to his polishing, only warning him to have a care for his thumbs, and then set about her own work. She decided she ought to approach Sir Odo, who had been made bailiff of Raine's demesne, and inform him that she would take on all responsibility for what fell within the bailey walls.

She found the big knight out by the pale that had been

constructed on the lists to hold the confiscated cattle. But except for a cow with a bald patch on her rump and a bow-legged calf, the pens were empty.

"He gave them back," Arianna said.

Sir Odo turned. Sweat gleamed in the pits and seams of his cheeks and he scrubbed a hand over his face. "Milady?"

"Lord Raine has given the cattle back."

Odo's mouth cracked open in a smile. A gap showed black between his two front teeth. "Did you think he would not?"

"But Taliesin said—"

"Taliesin!" The knight drew in a snort that flared his nostrils wide. "When that boy dies the last thing to quit working is going to be his tongue. And as for your husband, milady, the last thing to go will be his pride. Never apologizes and doesn't explain. It can get annoying, especially if you're the one who's got to follow around after him and do all the apologizing and explaining."

Arianna stared, frowning a moment longer at the empty pens, and when she turned she found that Sir Odo studied her bruised eye with a look of disgust on his face. "But for that"—he pointed his chin at her eye—"the boy will have to do his own apologizing."

The eye suddenly throbbed and Arianna had to resist an urge to touch it. "It was an accident," she said, and wondered why she felt the need to excuse her husband in front of his own man.

Sir Odo grunted, rubbing a big paw across his chin until his beard rasped. "I would tell you a story, milady. Though by the Cross, he would have my guts strung on a Maypole if he knew I was flapping my jaws like this."

"I would keep faith with you, Sir Odo," she said solemnly.

He rolled his thick shoulders like a horse with an itch. "Aye . . . well, it happened a few years back when Lord Henry did battle with the French king over Aquitaine.

Henry made this certain knight his bailiff over the castles we'd taken, while he went off to spend the winter at his court. But the land had been savaged by the fighting and the winter was a bad one. By Candlemas the serfs were eating boiled grass and the bark off the trees. That was when the bishop sent out his minions to collect the tithing."

"But if the people were starving, how could they collect a tenth of nothing?"

"There's always something, milady, even during a famine. But they didn't get so much as a kernel of corn, because this knight we speak of chased the devil's spawn away—even hanged one who was being stubborn. Then he went to the bishop, fat as a Martinmas hog in his palace, and informed his excellency there'd be no tithing that year, and he held a sword to the man's throat as he said it." Sir Odo's eyes took on a gleam at the memory, then he turned his head aside and spat between the gap in his teeth. "'Course, the bishop put him under the ban for it."

A chill crawled over Arianna, lifting the hair on her arms. If a man died while under pain of excommunication his soul would be cast down into the pit of hell for all eternity. And a woman who married a man under the ban damned her own soul as well. "And did Ra—did this knight we speak of stand up to the ban?"

"Aye. Balls of iron, he's got—" Sir Odo's pitted face flushed red as a holly berry. "Forgive me, Lady Arianna. I've been too long with naught but other knights and my horse for company."

Arianna dismissed his apology with a wave of her hand. "With nine brothers I've heard words foul enough to curdle the devil's blood. But what happened? Surely the knight is no longer an excommunicate."

"Nay, Henry used his influence to get the ban lifted and thought it a right good jest too. Until he found out none of the lord's tithing had been collected either. The knight we speak of had to sell everything he owned then, down to his sword, to pay Henry back, not only for what he never took in as bailiff, but for what he gave out to the serfs that winter from the castles' own stores . . ." His large brown eyes fastened onto her face. "Leastways, that's how the story goes."

Arianna looked back at the empty pens. She felt strangely light and gay. She hadn't danced at her wedding yesterday; she felt like dancing now.

Smiling, she turned to the big knight. "Thank you for telling it to me, Sir Odo. And I would ask a favor of you." She informed him of her plan to become, in effect, steward of her husband's dominion within the bailey walls.

"I would welcome it, milady," he answered readily. "What with worrying about harrows and hedges and pigs and fodder, my head's near splitting as 'tis." He kneaded his brow with thick, knotty fingers. "'Struth, I'd rather be fighting a war somewhere."

Arianna brought Sir Odo a tonic of peony root for his headache, which earned her a hearty kiss on the cheek that nearly knocked her over. For the rest of the morning she threw herself into the considerable task of setting Rhuddlan Castle to rights.

The stores of wine and ale in the butteries of both the keep and the great hall had been sorely depleted by the wedding feast, and Arianna decided to spend the hour after dinner taking inventory of the stocks in the cellar.

She threw herself into the task of counting the tuns of wine. She had just rolled aside a keg of ale when she saw something that made her pause. A name had been etched into the wall of the vault. She tried to make out the letters, but the carving must have been done years ago for it was begrimed with dirt. Taking up the torch she had stuck into a bracket near the door, she leaned over to spell aloud the crude letters.

"R . . . A . . . I . . . N . . . E."

She leapt back, so startled that she dropped the torch, and she spent a few anxious moments coaxing the flame back into life. With the torch wavering in her hands, she bent over to read the name again. She touched the first letter.

A tide of raw terror washed over her—*his* terror. She was locked in this cellar and waiting, waiting for . . .

Eyes.

A pain stabbed behind her eyes, so fierce that she clenched them shut. *They're going to put out my eyes.* "No . . ." she sobbed. But the sound came not from her throat, but his.

For the flash of a second she saw him—a dark-haired boy huddled in the corner of the vault, tears streaming unheeded down his dirty cheeks. She felt his terror and his pain as surely as if they had sprung from within her own breast. He threw back his head and screamed. *"I am your son, damn you! Your son! How could you do this to me, your own son?"*

"Oh, please, don't," she cried, and reached for him. . . .

She was falling into a whirling vortex of howling wind and white, pulsating light. She smelled wood smoke and rain. She heard the croaking of ravens and harsh laughter and a man's voice, thick with excitement . . . *"After this morning's work, Chester's bastard will be making no bastards of his own."*

The sea of light swirled, darkened to the color of blood. The blood flowed, flared, turned into tongues of flame, became a fire in a stone forge in a castle yard, a yard she knew, cast in shadow by a hulking shell keep, and . . .

A raven wheeled overhead, black wings flashing against the dim light of a stormy dawn. The air was cool and smelled of rain, but sweet, so sweet after so many weeks shut up in the dank cellar. Then he saw it . . . a forge glowing ruddy, the fire hissing as it was splattered with the first drops of rain.

Fear walloped into his chest like a battering ram, and his legs almost gave out beneath him. He stumbled, but didn't fall. They dragged him toward the forge and he set his teeth on begging words. They might take by force his sight and his manhood, but only he could give away his pride.

A man in a black leather hood turned then . . . a long iron staff, burning red, red, pointed at his eyes. He would have begged then if he could have, if he could have gotten the words out past the choking fear. Eyes. Oh, God, how could a man live without eyes?

A knight in scarlet stepped in front of him. "No, cut off his balls first. Make that be the last thing he sees. . . ."

Rough hands tore at his braies. A gust of wind and nervous laughter. Ravens screeched, already smelling blood. The flash of a knife pressed, cold against his shrinking flesh. God, God, don't do this to me, he prayed. But he didn't believe in God, and he'd never known mercy, so he had no hope. He thought of the girl he loved and felt sick to think of what they were taking away from him.

The knight in scarlet pushed his face against his, snarling, "Tell your father, the earl—this is what we do to the sons of traitors." My father doesn't care, *he wanted to scream. The Earl of Chester doesn't care what you do to me. The knight waited, waiting for him to break. And he was breaking, inside, where it didn't show. "Christ, boy. Are you made of stone?"*

Not stone. Blood. And flesh. Flesh of his flesh. He couldn't believe that his own father had abandoned him to such a fate . . . could love him so little . . .

He found the words he sought, and somewhere the courage to speak them. "Afterward . . . will you give me a knife?"

Surprise showed on the knight's face. Triumph. "So that you may kill yourself?"

I am your son, damn you! Your son! How could you have condemned me to this, your own son? *"Nay . . . So that I can kill him . . . my father."*

Hate ate at his guts. Hate and a sick despair. He felt unwanted, unworthy . . . unloved. A raven croaked, the wind blew. Rain fell on his face. He lifted his gaze toward the bloodred walls of Rhuddlan keep and waited for the pain. . . .

Rain splashed on her face. The ravens croaked her name as she fought through luminescent mists that clung to her mind like silver webs. She brushed the sticky strands aside and touched smooth skin instead, and the ravens' cries changed, became a boy's voice. "My lady . . ."

She felt hard dirt beneath her back and dampness seeping into her clothes. She looked into two eyes, black as bruises. A white hand flashed across her face and water flicked onto her cheeks. "Taliesin?"

She tried to sit up, but the world spun around and darkened. Nausea rose in her throat. She clutched at the front of his leather tunic and struggled not to gag.

"Now, don't you be spewing up all over me, my lady," he said. "This is a new tunic I've got on and it cost me all my winnings at dice."

Arianna started to laugh and choked instead. Eventually the dizziness subsided, along with the nausea. She leaned back. Taliesin was wearing his golden helmet and it seemed to glow within the darkness, lighting his face so that his eyes shone like twin stars.

She released her grip on his tunic. "What are you doing here? Has Lord Raine returned?"

"Nay, not till nightfall. Milady, you are trembling." His head dipped forward until his face was only inches from hers. He had the strangest eyes she had ever seen. It was almost as if they were lit from within, but with a cold light, like moonshine. "You saw," he said. "You saw what happened to my lord here."

His eyes drew the truth from her. "I saw . . ." she whispered, "but I don't understand." Suddenly the memory of the vision was so fresh that she could taste it, salty and rusty, like blood. She hadn't just witnessed what had happened in Rhuddlan's bailey that day, she had *been*

Raine. "Eyes . . . oh God, Taliesin, they were going to
put out his *eyes.*"

Somehow she was pressed against his chest and he was
stroking her back. He no longer seemed like a such a boy.
Perhaps it was the strength of the arm that held her, or
the deep musical tones of his voice. "Hush now. It didn't
happen, for you know how my lord grew to manhood
whole and hearty."

She shuddered again, pulling away from him. "But it
almost happened, didn't it? Taliesin, do you know why?
What was he doing here?"

Wisps of hair had come loose from her braids. He
brushed them back from her face. "It was before your
father took back Rhuddlan Castle from the Normans,
back when the old Earl of Chester was overlord of this
part of the marcher lands."

"Raine's father?"

"Aye, back when Stephen and Matilda were fighting
over England's throne and all the barons were forced to
take one side or the other. The old earl seemed to have a
knack for knowing which side would emerge the victor at
any given time and he switched his allegiance often. But
one day he outguessed himself, jumping over to Stephen
when he should have stuck with Matilda. The mistake
cost him several castles, one of which was Rhuddlan.

"The castle was taken over by one of Matilda's favorite
barons, Roger de Bessin. The Earl of Chester also agreed
to give up his son to this new Lord of Rhuddlan, as a
hostage to ensure his future neutrality. But the earl had
the last laugh because the son he delivered was not Hugh,
as everyone expected, but his bastard. Who was and is, as
you know, my liege lord, Raine."

"So they kept him locked up here in the cellars." Arianna's heart ached as she thought of the letters painstak-
ingly carved into the stone. It would have taken weeks,
months . . .

"For the whole of that summer and autumn," Taliesin

said, as if he had read her thoughts. "And Roger de Bessin vowed that if the old earl broke his neutrality, he would pluck out Raine's eyes and . . . well, do worse in retaliation."

Terror filled her mouth, acrid and hot. She was in the bailey, waiting, waiting for them to cut him, to put out her eyes—no, *his* eyes.

"But it didn't happen," she said. Her head throbbed. He had been so hurt, so bitterly hurt to think that his father had abandoned and betrayed him. The pain, *his* pain, was so still raw and fresh it was as if she had a gaping hole in her heart. She pressed her hand to her chest. "He was wrong, you see," she said to Taliesin, desperate to set this one point straight, for it seemed important. Important to that boy in the cellar. "It never happened, so his father must have loved him after all."

Taliesin shook his head, and Arianna saw within his moonstruck eyes a wisdom that was old and battered and worn like the earth itself. "Roger de Bessin was so awed by my lord's courage that he couldn't bring himself to carry out the deed. 'Tis that simple, milady. And that difficult."

The pain grew worse. She ground her fist into her breast. "And his father—"

"Laughed. When he was told what they would do to his son, the Earl of Chester laughed. They vowed to blind the boy, to cut out his manhood, and all he did was laugh and laugh."

Arianna was at the window, waiting, when the trumpeter of the guard sounded the lord's approach.

The sky was a deep indigo blue, with only a thread of light on the horizon. A new moon, thin and sharp as a sickle, hung above the gatehouse. At the bottom of the stairs to the hall, a varlet was just lighting the torches. The flames flapped like banners in a gusty wind.

Two horses trotted into the pool of light. Arianna saw a

flash of fox-red hair. Somehow she was not surprised to find Taliesin at his master's side, as if he had never left there. That afternoon he had vanished from the wine vault when her back was turned, like a wraith fading back into a crypt. Already she wondered if she had imagined him, a codicil to her vision.

She watched from the window as Raine dismounted. He glanced up as soon as his foot touched the ground. She almost backed away, but then she didn't. Torchlight glimmered off the sharp bones of his face; the wind ruffled his hair, causing it to stand up like devil's horns.

Someone hailed him from the door of the hall. With one last look at her, he mounted the stairs. Fear and excitement unfurled deep within her belly, like coils of hot smoke that became entwined until she couldn't tell one from the other.

She looked around the bedchamber while she waited for him to come. A fire burned in the brazier and nearby stood a bathing tub, perfumed steam coiling into the air. A carpeted dormant table had been laid out with simnel and oat cakes, fruit and cheese, and ewers of wine and ale. Dried herbs smoldered in a bowl to sweeten the air. The rushes had been changed. Even the bed curtains had been taken down and had the dust beaten out of them.

He was a long time in coming. She was pacing by the time she heard the clink of spurs and scuffling sound of boots coming up the stairs. She noticed that her hands were clasped together like a penitent nun's and she forced them down to her sides. Her palms were sweating; she wiped them on her skirt.

The door swung open on newly tallowed hinges and he entered, bringing with him the coolness of the night and the smell of the sea.

He was not alone. Sir Odo came with him, followed by three other men, all speaking at once, vying for his attention. She poured a jack of ale and put it into his hand, but he was talking at the time and acknowledged her with only a nod. She felt in the way, but when she started for the door, he said, "Stay, Arianna."

When he spoke to his men there was a tone of quiet command in his voice, and they made their respect, their admiration, of him obvious. As she watched him she thought of how, with a title and lands even half the size of Chester's, a man of his talents could have made himself powerful enough to rival the king. Yet he had been given nothing from his father. Nothing but betrayal. No wonder he wore his base blood like a shirt of pitch, when it had brought him nothing but pain.

The men left and at last they were alone.

He turned from shutting the door, and his gaze roamed the length of her. His eyes grew dark and heavy lidded, and a tautness came over his face. Within her the strange tension coiled, warm and moist like the steam from his bath.

She wished he would speak first, but when he didn't she said, "There is a bath prepared for you, my lord. And food."

He looked around the room. "I think I could easily come to like having a wife," he said, and a smile blazed across his face, bright and dazzling like hot sunshine.

Arianna's heartbeat skittered. Surely it was against the laws of God for a man to look like that when he smiled. It wasn't until she opened her mouth to speak that she realized that smile had stolen her breath. "But I doubt I shall come to like having a husband," she finally managed.

His gaze fastened onto her mouth, and she felt it as if he had touched her there with his fingertips. Or his lips.

"Help me to undress, wife," he said, his voice rough.

She obeyed, coming up to help him off with his *broigne,* as she had done so often for her brothers after a raid or a day's hunting. But his hands closed over her arms and he pulled her up against him. He dipped his head and for a poised moment they stood almost nose to nose. She had time to think that his eyes really did darken to warm soot just before he kissed her.

He kissed her hard, bruising her lips. Her hands slid around his waist and she arched against his chest, flattening her breasts against the horn plates in his *broigne*. His hand slid down her back, cupping her bottom, bringing her up against the hard ridge of his sex. When at last he raised his head, her lips throbbed and she touched them with her tongue, tasting ale, and him.

He seized her wrist and thrust her hand up beneath his chainse. "And what about that, Arianna? Will you come to like that?"

His member was alive beneath her palm—stiff, thick, hot. Her breathing was so loud, her heart hammering so wildly, she thought he wouldn't have been able to hear her answer even if she could have found the words. She waited until he let her go before she backed away from him. Her hand felt on fire.

He shrugged out of his *broigne* and she took it from him. Its weight dragged against her arms as she hung it on a wall perch. When she turned around he was pulling his quilted chainse over his head. He winced as the abrupt movement tugged at the cut she'd made on his arm. He had bandaged it with a rag and the cloth was stained brown with dried blood. She wondered how he would punish her for cutting him. And for the sackcloth and ashes.

He stretched, flexing a back strapped with muscle. He walked over to the table and poured more ale into the leather jack. As he brought the jack to his mouth, the veins and tendons in his forearm pushed out against the skin. She thought of how one blow from that arm with all his strength could kill her. She knew him better now but not well enough, and she was still afraid of him.

"Will you beat me, husband?"

He turned to face her, his brows raised slightly in a look of surprise. Foam laced his upper lip and he licked it off.

"I don't normally beat my women just to get in the practice. Have you done something today that deserves punishment?"

She clasped her hands behind her back and held herself tall. "So you would beat me if you determined I deserved it," she said.

He set the jack back on the table, though his gaze remained fixed on her face. His lips parted slightly on an expulsion of breath. "What have you done?"

"You misunderstand. It's simply that I am not used to your Norman ways and I only wished to know where . . . where I stand with you." *If I need to be afraid of you,* was what she meant, though her pride would not let her ask that. "In Wales, the law states a husband may beat his wife for three reasons only—if she lies with another, if she gambles away his goods, or if she insults his manhood. If he strikes her for any other reason, she may disavow the marriage. Unless he pays her a *sarhaed,* of course. Her honor-price." The need to cry was now so strong, her throat was tight with it. "I cannot allow you to beat me for any other reason."

"You cannot *allow?* You seem to have forgotten that you are a subject of England now, and in England a man can do what he wills with his wife."

"He can beat her just to get in the practice," she said, unable to keep the bitterness she felt from tinging her voice. As a Cymraes she'd had rights and respect; married to him she had nothing at all.

He came up to her, and she had to stiffen every muscle to keep from backing away. Though she thought by the slow, lazy way he moved that he wasn't angry and wouldn't hit her. This time.

She had her hair woven into a single fat braid that fell over her shoulder. His fingers started at her neck and followed the length of it where it curled around her breast. "Have you been stricken with a gambling fever?" he asked.

Startled, she realized he was unbraiding her hair. "Nay, but—"

His voice was flat and hard, but the fingers combing through her hair were gentle. "If I catch you with another man, Arianna, I won't beat you, I shall kill you. And as for my manhood . . . it is pointless to cast slurs upon an object which is unassailable." Something flashed in his eyes. Arianna thought it could have almost been laughter. "So do you understand now where you stand with me?"

Arianna tried to think, though her head suddenly felt slow and thick, like resin on a cold day. All she could concentrate on was the way his fingers felt in her hair. "I am to be your obedient and submissive chattel."

His hand fell to his side. "Then at last we are in agreement about something."

He turned away from her abruptly. He threw himself into a chair with a grunt and began to work loose the heel of one boot with the toe of the other.

Arianna watched him, dazed for a moment. Then she knelt in the rushes before him, her bottom settling down onto her heels. She pulled off his boots, and then his slippers. His chausses hugged the muscles of his calves and thighs, and she remembered how he had looked in the joust, with those legs wrapped around the thick body of his war-horse, how he had controlled the charging, thundering beast with those muscles alone.

He leaned forward, threading his fingers in her hair. He tugged her head up until her eyes met his. "I will be very slow and easy with you tonight, and if you don't fight me it won't hurt so much."

"It will hurt."

"A little, perhaps. At first. You are very small and tight."

"And your male appendage is so very big and thick."

His lips danced on the verge of a smile, and she caught her breath. "Was that a slur you just cast upon my appendage, or a compliment?"

Absurdly pleased that he was teasing her, Arianna lowered her lids. Then she smiled as a memory suddenly came to her. It had been the summer she was twelve. She could almost feel again the hot sun beating down on her head and the warm sand oozing up between her toes, smell the salt and wet seaweed, and hear the sucking, popping sound of the waves.

She spoke her memory aloud, without thinking. "You men are all so vain about your appendages. I snuck up on four of my brothers once, one summer day on the beach near Father's *llys* on the Isle of Môn. They were standing in a half-circle right at the water's edge, and at first I couldn't imagine what they were doing because their braies were sagging down around their knees. They were seeing who could pee the farthest into the ocean, and comparing the sizes of their privy members."

Raine laughed and she laughed with him and the sounds they made—hers airy and sweet, his deep and rich —blended together and filled the room.

He stopped first, and when she heard him stop she caught the last of her laughter in her throat. She looked down. Her hands were clenched in her lap and she flattened them, smoothing them over the pale blue silk.

After their laughter, the room seemed too quiet. His hand had been idly toying with her hair, but now his fingers stroked her neck, stroked, stroked, and a warm, heavy feeling spread over her.

She pulled away from him, stumbling to her feet. She went to the laver and filled an enameled basin with water. She brought it to him, along with a towel she tucked under her arm.

"What are you doing?" he asked as she set the basin down beside him.

She bent over him and her loosened hair fell forward, slapping against his bare shoulder. He turned his face into it, his eyes squeezing shut. But she didn't notice, for she was busy plucking at the edge of the bandage on his arm, trying to see if the cut had mortified. "This filthy rag is stuck to your wound. It'll have to be soaked a bit before it can come off."

"Just rip it off."

"But that would hurt—"

"It couldn't possibly hurt any worse than it already is with you poking at it."

She ripped off the bandage. He didn't utter a sound. But his whole body went rigid and the creases at the corners of his mouth turned hard and white.

Fresh blood welled out of the cut. She wet the towel, folding it into a thick pad, and daubed at the wound. "My lord, I hope you will accept my apology for knifing you. I had my reasons, as you know, but I am sorry for it now."

He shrugged. "It's only a scratch."

"You should have put sicklewort on it to stop the bleeding last night. Now you'll likely as not be left with a scar." Some of the water had splashed onto his chest and it ran in slow rivulets, down over the ridges of muscle, matting the dark hair into swirls around his nipples, sliding into the crease of his stomach.

She jerked her eyes off him and looked at the gilded floral wall above his head. Inside, she felt all tight and hot as if her flesh were swelling and pressing against her skin. "I am waiting now for your apology, my lord husband."

"My what?" He was watching her strangely, with glazed, unfocused eyes, as if he'd just been punched in the head. He had certainly done a number of things to her in the short time they'd known each other that warranted his contrition. Perhaps he was running the long list through in his mind. "Your apology for blackening my eye."

He blinked, grunted. "The hell I will. You deserved it, and besides, it was an accident."

"I apologized to you. First for calling you a bastard, though you are one—through an accident of birth, I mean," she added quickly. "And now I've apologized for stabbing you while you were performing a perversion upon me—"

"I was *trying* to make love to you."

"So the least you can do is apologize for hitting me, accident or no. It's only fair."

"What in God's wounds is fair about me having to apologize for something you brought on yourself?"

Arianna straightened with a snap. "You, sir, are woefully ill-mannered. Even for a Norman."

She snatched up the basin and soiled rag, but he hooked her wrist as she sailed by. "Are you going to yap at me about this all night?"

"I am not yapping. Puppies yap."

His jaw tightened until a muscle in his cheek began to tick. "Very well. I apologize for accidentally hitting you in the eye while I was trying to prevent you from slashing me to death with a ten-inch quillon dagger."

"I don't accept your apology."

"You don't accept—"

"Nay. An apology given so begrudgingly is worthless."

"Blood of Christ!" Raine came up off the stool like a bee-stung bull, knocking the basin she held in her hand and splashing water all down the front of Arianna's bliaut.

The water was cold and wet and she sucked in a sharp breath, looking down. The thin silk had molded to her body and her nipples had drawn up hard and tight so that they looked like two round nuts, and she remembered what he had done last night, how he'd sucked one into his mouth, sucked on it like a babe.

She raised her eyes to his face. Her heart was hammering so hard that it reverberated like a tabor throughout every bone in her body, and somehow she'd lost the ability to breathe. Her eyes focused on his mouth. She wanted him to . . . wanted him to . . .

His lips parted open, she wet hers. Her head fell back, his dipped down.

Oh God, she wanted him to . . .

His breath stroked her lips and she sighed.

Wanted him to . . .

His lips brushed hers, and then he was kissing her.

His mouth slanted back and forth across hers, pressing hard, forcing her lips open. His tongue probed once, twice, then filled her. She stiffened a moment, unsure, and then she began to respond with timid tongue-flickings of her own.

He ended the kiss slowly, touching his lips to hers again and again, as if he couldn't quite bring himself to stop. He groaned into her mouth. "Sweet Jesus, your lips are soft."

His mouth trailed down her jaw, followed the curve of her throat. Her head fell back and her fingers dug into his arms. She felt heavy, aching, her insides all soft and runny like melted butter.

His hands spanned her head and he brought her face down until she was forced to look into his eyes.

"Arianna?"

She hesitated, suddenly afraid again. But she had a lifetime of nights to spend with this man, to spend in his bed, and she could not be afraid of him forever.

She drew away from him. Slowly, her eyes on his face, her fingers trembling, she raised her hand and pulled open the laces of her bliaut.

He smiled, and suddenly she knew there was nothing to fear.

12

She lay naked on the bed, the camlet sheets cool and smooth beneath her back, and watched him undress. Candlelight bronzed his skin, it gleamed in the hair on his chest and between his legs. It cast shadows over his face, so she could not see his eyes.

It was so quiet, quiet enough to hear the hiss and snuffle of coals collapsing in the brazier and the lowing of the wind through the eaves. Quiet enough to hear his breathing, and her own.

He stretched out beside her. He smoothed her hair where it was crimped from the braid. His mouth twisted into a wry grimace and in a sudden movement, as if he couldn't help himself, he buried his face in it. He rubbed first one cheek then the other in it, reminding her oddly of a child cuddling up to a puppy. He made a sound that was halfway between a moan and a sigh. "You smell delicious."

"Are you thinking of eating me?"

His head snapped up, his eyes wide. Then a laugh burst out of him, surprising her into a blush. She should have known better than to try to play at courtly love speech; she'd never been any good at it.

"Lord God, what an innocent you are," he said, his voice a little hoarse. He rubbed his curled fingers back and forth over her mouth, pulling at her lower lip. "I had forgotten there were girls like you. Untouched, unspoiled . . . innocent."

He pressed his other hand into her scalp and pulled her head up to meet his kiss. Her mouth parted open and he sent his tongue deep. He kissed her a long time, spanning the gamut of passion from the barest, tender brush of lip to lip to thorough, tongue-thrusting kisses that sucked her empty. When he finally released her mouth, her lips were swollen and throbbing and no longer innocent.

He leaned above her on his forearms and traced the features of her face—eyebrows, cheekbones, nose, and her wet mouth. His eyes were heavy-lidded and there was the hint of a smile playing around his lips. She held her breath, waiting for that smile. But suddenly his hand shot out, snatching away a pillow.

Startled, she cried out, "What are you doing?"

"Looking for daggers."

His hand stretched out for another pillow and she grabbed his wrist. "I am trusting you this night, my lord. Trusting you not to hurt me. Can you not trust me as well?"

The sinew of his wrist tightened beneath her fingers. His eyes had grown cold and his mouth had pressed into a straight line. He was going to pull away from her, to look beneath the other pillows. He trusted in nothing, she thought. And no one.

His mouth relaxed first, though he didn't come close to smiling. He pulled free of her grip, but he didn't lift the pillow. Instead he lowered his head, his lips finding the hollow of her throat. She drew in a deep breath of air. Her very pores seemed to fill with the scent of his heated skin.

"Do you want this, Arianna?" His breath washed over her. "Tell me you want this."

She wondered what he would do if she said no. Would he take her anyway as he had last night? She didn't want to find out. And to deny him now would be a lie.

"I want this . . . you," she said.

His hands drifted over her, tracing the span of bone at her hips, cupping her belly. Her body felt weighted, heavy, her skin too hot and tight. She gasped at a feeling so piercing it was almost painful when his fingers lightly, lightly brushed her mound.

She pushed his hand away. "I don't think I like for you to touch me there."

"Liar. You like it too much."

But he didn't touch her there again. Instead he massaged her breasts and they seemed to swell and throb in his hands. Heat began to spread from her belly into her limbs as if she were melting from the inside out.

"You are so damned soft," he murmured into her hair. "So soft . . ."

She liked the way his hands looked touching her, dark against pale flesh, his long fingers tracing ribs, fluttering across her heart, enveloping her breasts. He lifted them, whisking her nipples with the rough pads of his thumbs.

She had to touch him as well. She smoothed her palms over the curves of his chest, threading her fingers through the mat of hair. She marveled at how his skin could be silken and warm, while beneath it the flesh was so hard, so unyielding. She could feel the leashed power within him as he moved.

But then he shifted his weight, pulling her tighter against him. His member, burning and heavy, pressed between her thighs. She went rigid, pushing against his heavy chest.

His breath stirred her hair. "It's nothing to be afraid of, Arianna. Touch me."

She wouldn't touch him; 'twould be unseemly. But to her utter shock, he took her hand and pressed it against his stiff sex. He hissed through his teeth when her fingers closed around him.

She marveled at how hard he was. And the heat of him —it was like holding her palm right above a candle's flame.

"Tighter. Harder. I won't break," he said, though he sounded as if he were already in pain.

She tightened her grip, stroking him more roughly. His eyes clenched shut. The bones of his face seemed to sharpen, the skin to draw tauter. His whole body began to shudder. She felt a heady sense of power suddenly, that she could do this to him.

"Jesus, I can't . . ." He grabbed her hand. "Enough." He buried his face into the curve of her neck, then he laughed, his breath blowing hot and moist. "Something tells me you're going to get very good at that very soon."

His hair lapped her neck, brushing across her chest as he lowered his head. His lips poised above a nipple and she watched, eyes wide, as he drew the whole of it into his mouth as if sucking a cherry off a stem. The pleasure was so exquisite she almost screamed. And almost screamed again when he cupped her mound, thrusting a finger deep inside. Her back arched off the bed, and she squeezed her legs tightly together.

He went still, and in the quiet her panting breaths sounded harsh and loud. She opened her eyes to find his lips only inches from hers. His breath filled her mouth, followed by his words, "Spread your legs for me."

Her thighs fell open.

His finger withdrew, entered, withdrew again. With the pad of his thumb, he gently stroked the lips of her sex, sliding upward. It was like touching a candle to a pitch torch—she burst into flames. She was burning, burning up inside, burning and swelling and splintering apart all at the same time. She heard herself whimpering and knew she was undulating her hips shamelessly, and she didn't care, didn't care, didn't care. . . .

Her nails dug into his shoulders and her head thrashed back and forth. She thought if he didn't stop she would explode. She would shatter into a thousand pieces and never find herself. The fire blazed, building higher and hotter, sucking the air from her chest so that she couldn't breathe and her heart stopped and she was sure that she would die, that dying would be a relief.

Yet still she held back, held back, held back. . . .

"Give yourself to me, Arianna," he whispered harshly into her neck. "Give to me. . . ."

"Nay, I cannot!" she cried on a sobbing breath, not sure what it was he asked of her, only that she could not. She couldn't give him this last surrender, it was too much like giving him a part of her soul.

Her chest heaved with the effort to breathe and the blood rushed in her ears. She opened her eyes onto his face. He was not going to have her. He shouldn't have her, because he didn't really want her. Not the part of her that mattered.

He covered her with his body, his sex, hot and smooth, sliding across her belly. He rose up to rub the broad tip of it along her woman's flesh. He spread her with his fingers first, then eased into her. She winced, but the discomfort faded to be replaced by a sense of fullness and of being stretched wide and wider still as, slowly, he buried all of himself inside her.

"Jesus God . . . you are tight."

Her hands moved restlessly over his back and she shifted her hips. He slid in deeper and he groaned. "You feel good, so good . . ." His hands cupped her hips, pulling her tighter to him at the same time that he thrust upward and she gasped.

"It's hurting now. Stop."

"God, wench, I can't stop . . ."

He pulled out of her, then pushed in again, slowly at first, then faster. His hands spanned her hips, moving them in a rhythm with his thrusts, and the pain went away

a little, though not completely. She clung to him without
even knowing that she was doing it. The reality of being
penetrated, of being possessed by him, was frightening.
But it was also in a strange and savage way exciting. A
tense, tight feeling curled low in her belly, spreading out-
ward, filling her chest until she couldn't breathe again.

The skin of his back went slick with sweat and his panting breaths rasped harshly against her ear. He arced upward as he drove into her hard and fast. Then he reared,
throwing back his head as he surged deep inside her. She
felt his shudders and opened her eyes in time to see his
face contort as if in agony.

"Arianna, God, God, Arianna!"

The cry was raw, sounding torn from his throat as if he
had tried to stop it, but couldn't. I didn't surrender, she
thought. I gave him my body but I didn't give him *me*.

So why then did she feel so sad?

It took a long time for him to get his breath back. He
lay partly covering her, one leg pinning her hips to the
bed. His rib cage pushed up and down against her breasts,
pumping like iron-banded bellows.

Her body felt heavy and sore as if she'd been pummeled by a whole army of washerwomen. He was inside
of her still, and it ached there. But when he started to pull
out of her, she tensed her thighs. She didn't understand
why, but she didn't want him to leave her. She felt empty
inside. And sad.

They lay together in silence a while. Then he rolled
onto his side, slipping out of her. He propped himself up
on one elbow. "It will get easier by and by," he said.
"When you fear it less, you can begin to take more pleasure in it."

"I knew my duty was to submit, my lord. Is it now my
duty to feel pleasure as well?"

"Aye, dammit. And don't call me 'my lord' when we're
in bed together." His eyes glittered in the candlelight,

hard and flat like beaten silver, but he traced the outline of her mouth with a finger that was incredibly tender. " 'Tis said a woman is more likely to conceive if she is pleasured."

"That is all you care about—having an heir!"

His head lowered, his breath was warm, as tangible as a caress in her hair. "Not all," he said, soft, low.

His lips brushed over her cheek. Her belly tightened with anticipation. He was going to kiss her and she was beginning to like being kissed very much. She sighed as her mouth parted open.

His head jerked up, and he froze. Then his hand lashed out above her head. A pillow went flying. Within a heartbeat he had the blade of the dagger she had hidden there pressed to her throat.

He held the honed edge a hairbreadth from her skin. Fury narrowed his eyes, his mouth had hardened into a ruthless line. He looked as he had the first time she had seen him. In her vision.

She felt his grip tighten on the hilt. His lips pulled back over his teeth. " 'Trust me,' you said."

He didn't move and neither did she, not even to breathe. His eyes stared into hers, pale and hard, colder than the northern ice floes.

She swallowed and felt a sharp sting as the blade nicked her skin. "It's hard to talk with a knife at one's throat."

He snarled a curse and flung the dagger over her head. It twanged as it bit deep into the headboard; the hilt quivered, then stilled.

He grabbed her between her legs and she swallowed a startled cry. "What did you think I would do, Arianna— stick my tongue into your honey pot again?" He thrust his fingers up inside of her, hard. "Do you still think this too rich for a bastard's tastes?"

"I didn't know *what* you'd do! I am surrounded by Normans and have only myself to defend me. I thought you would want to punish me for all that happened yes-

terday and I couldn't let you—for honor's sake I could
not let you shame or abuse me . . ." She could feel tears
welling in her eyes, but she held them back.

"For honor's sake," he repeated, as if her words as-
tounded him.

He stared down at her, his thoughts inscrutable, his
mouth so hard. His hand was still between her legs, his
fingers inside of her. She felt hot down there, and wet. He
pushed his fingers farther into her and she moaned,
squeezing, sucking them even deeper.

She watched the change come over his face, the tauten-
ing of the skin across his cheekbones, the darkening of his
eyes until they were sooty, hungry. His chest pressed
against hers and she felt the hitch in his breathing.

The words came out of her, without thought. "Kiss
me . . ."

"Ah, hell," he said, and kissed her.

Arianna came abruptly awake. She sat up, pulling the
fur coverlet around her against the chill. With only the
night candle burning, the room was full of shadows. She
held her breath, listening for the noise that had roused
her, but heard only the wind and the scratching of mice in
the walls.

It felt late, deep in the night. She turned her head to see
the time. Much of the candle had burned down; it lacked
only three marks until dawn.

They slept with the bed hangings tied back, for Raine
insisted on fresh air over privacy. Her husband was oddly
contrary in that way, wanting the bed curtains open, the
shutters left unbolted. Just as he did not sleep with a
nightcap. When she had reminded him that evil spirits
could come flying through the open window and snatch
his soul out the top of his head he had only laughed. He'd
said evil spirits were no match for the Black Dragon. In
that he was probably right.

It was because she was thinking of evil spirits that when the candle went out she almost screamed.

But of course it was only a draft, and she laughed beneath her breath at her own foolishness.

Until the music filled the room.

As a child of Cymry she had been weaned on the sounds of the harp, but this music could never have been made by the hands of any earthly bard. Ringing, bell-like chords surged and crested, shattering into a waterfall of crystalline chimes. The music was clear, vibrating, like thin sheets of ice. So piercing in intensity that she could almost see it.

And then she *could* see it. Striated ribbons of color, blues and purples and violets, that swirled through the air. Shimmering, rippling rainbow threads that wove together into a tapestry of sound. They wrapped around her, caressing her skin like a lover's hands. She felt exposed by the music, both beloved and violated.

She reached out, trying to touch the colors of sound, but though they danced around her still, her hands passed through them as if they were wisps of mist. Tears filled her eyes, for the music was so beautiful it hurt.

The bard plucked the strings in a slow, melancholy arpeggio. The chimes faded into a whispering stillness. The banners of sapphirine mist hung in the air for a moment longer, then dissipated slowly, ghostly remnants of the dying chords.

"Taliesin?" she whispered into the night, though she expected no answer. The music had not come from beyond the door, or inside the room. It had come from the same place her visions did, from the circle of time. It could have been played centuries ago or not yet played for another hundred years.

Then as soon as she was sure the music had vanished back into time, a sweet, liquid voice took flight.

A lady in a lake didst dwell,
Fair of bosom, green were her eyes . . .

This time the song wove around her like a river of silver. She could feel it, hot and molten, and where it touched her skin, she burned. He sang and with the music he created a lake where there dwelled a girl, and of a knight who came to claim her body without giving her his love.

The tale was both sweet and melancholy and Arianna smiled through her tears. Suddenly she was *in* the song, and it was as vivid, as real as any vision. She smelled the fecund odor of the algae-scummed mud that bordered the shore. She heard the caw of a crow and felt a summer wind, wet and hot. She was a girl, arising from the flat silver bowl of the lake, a girl who was naked, with long, dark hair, her milky skin slick with water, and breasts with brown, protruding nipples. She waded toward the shore and a knight came to stand before her, his shoulders filling the coppery sky. Silver sunlight bounced off his burnished black mail, surrounding him with a white halo of light. She raised her arms, beckoning, and there were tears in her eyes. Tears and a sad, desperate yearning.

"Oh, please . . ." Arianna cried, feeling already the pain that was to come. But at the sound of her cry the lake and the knight vanished and she was left with only the words, words that told of the knight's rejection and the lady's vow.

"'Possess you I will, fair one.
And rule you all our days.
But my love I do keep for those things of my heart . . .
God and my lord and my trusty steed.'"

"'Possess me thou wilt never, cruel lord. Nor rule me
true.

But I to thou on my soul doth vow . . .
The sun will look upon a dawn, when thou wilt come to
* me*
Naked and on thy knees, and with thy heart in thy
* hands,*
To give to me, sweet lord, thy own true love.' "

Then as suddenly as it had begun, the music stopped.
Arianna waited, her breath suspended, for it to begin
again. But the silver river had thinned to a trickle, then
vanished. The silence now was ordinary, the silence of a
hall at sleep.

Suddenly, the candle beside the bed flared back into
life.

Arianna jerked upright, swallowing the cry that leapt to
her throat. She sagged back against the piled pillows and
waited for her heart to stop its wild beating. As she
waited, her eyes opened wide, her ears straining, she understood that it all had been a dream.

She drew in a deep breath, and slowly she calmed. But
the emotions of the dream stayed with her—the hollow,
empty ache of a girl who loved but was not loved in return. It left a sadness that caught in Arianna's throat.

She looked at the man sprawled beside her, this man
who had made love to her without loving her only hours
before. She could still feel the wet stickiness of his seed
between her thighs. And a tenderness, a hurt.

The hero of her dream song had dark hair and a hard
mouth, and his eyes had been like the lake, flat and silver.
She wondered if the dream had gone on, if the knight
would have ever come to the lady of the lake naked and
on his knees and with his love in his hands.

Because the knight in the dream song had been Raine.

But then she could not imagine Raine, with his pride
and his impregnable mail-armored heart, ever doing such
a thing.

God's death, Arianna. You are being a witless nit. It was only a dream.

She did not want her Norman husband's love. She wouldn't want his love even if he brought it to her naked and on his knees. It was only a dream; a dream that meant nothing.

And if it was not a dream, then that God-cursed squire who called himself a bard had somehow been responsible for it all. The wretched knave—to wake her from a sound sleep with his caterwauling.

She rolled over and punched the pillow. She squeezed her eyes shut, trying to will herself back to sleep. But sleep was elusive, not coming until a long time later, when she had drawn the pillow to her breast like a shield. . . .

As if she were trying to protect her heart.

The next morning, Arianna sat at a table within the bedchamber, chewing on the end of a bent goose quill and trying to make some sense of the Rhuddlan ledgers. Ceidro's seneschal had turned up missing after the battle, and from the way he'd kept the accounts, Arianna was beginning to suspect his disappearance wasn't a coincidence. The man had been skimming the cream off the top of her brother's coffers for months.

She scraped and smoothed a fresh sheet of parchment with the pumice stone and had just picked up a bear's tooth to polish it with, when she felt the change in the room. It was as if the sun had suddenly burst free from behind a cloud. Her blood began to hum and a heat flushed over her skin.

"Good morrow, my lord husband," she said, not looking up. Her hand shook a little, though, as she rubbed the flat edge of the big tooth over the crackling yellow sheet. She had sensed his presence as soon as he was near, without seeing him. Such a thing had never happened to her before.

"I must be getting out of practice," he said. "I used to be able to creep up on an enemy much better than that."

She did look up then. He filled the doorway, leaning against the jamb, with his thumbs hooked into his belt, his legs crossed at the ankles. His face was flushed from the sun, his hair ruffled by the wind.

"And do you think of your wife as your enemy, my lord?"

"Let us say I am careful to remember that she is a Welshwoman."

The bear's tooth squirted out from between her fingers, clattering across the table and onto the floor, to disappear into the rushes.

He pushed himself off the jamb and came toward her. He hunkered down at her feet and sifted through the straw. His chausses pulled across his thighs and the muscles of his back bunched beneath his thin summer-weight tunic. The sunlight streaming through the open window glinted off the blue lights in his hair, and she had to quell a ridiculous impulse to run her fingers through it. It seemed odd to see him like that, kneeling at her feet, just like the knight in the dream song.

His head came up suddenly, and then his hand, as he tossed the tooth at her. Caught by surprise, she snatched the tooth awkwardly out of the air and her elbow sent first the pen and then the scraper rolling onto the floor. He retrieved both implements and handed them up to her, flashing one of his rare smiles. "Is there anything else you'd like to drop whilst I'm down here?"

"Oh, no, no, I'm finished . . . I mean, I thank you for . . ." She realized she was babbling and bobbing her head like a chicken pecking in the dirt, and she made herself stop.

He stood up, towering over her. He had been hunting that morning and she could smell the forest on him, and the kill.

He looked down at the ledgers of bound parchment

and the amusement fled his face. "What are you doing?" he demanded, his voice sharp.

So lost was she in looking at him, that it took a moment for his words to penetrate her fogged senses. "What? Oh, these are the castle accounts, my lord. They're in a sorry shape. You haven't appointed a steward as yet and I thought that—as I've just inventoried Rhuddlan's stores —that whilst I'm about it I might as well . . . that is . . ." She thrust her chin into the air. "If you insist, I will turn the accounts over to your priest. Though if his Latin is any indication, I fear he is a poorly lettered man."

"You, a mere woman, claim to be more learned than my priest?"

Arianna clenched her teeth. "I was taught my letters and how to cipher along with my brothers and all the boys who fostered with us. My father believed knowledge enhanced a knight's stature. And a lady's as well."

Some emotion flared in his eyes and was gone. "Clerking is for priests. A woman has no use for such knowledge. And a knight's value lies in his prowess with a sword."

She decided to ignore his opinion of women, for she knew most all of Christendom shared it. But she could not let the other pass. "It is a very poor knight, indeed my lord, who cannot read and write. A real knight is always a man of learning and honor and chivalry."

His lips twisted into a bitter smile. "Only in the songs of the bards, Arianna. In *real* life, knights kill any way they have to and with no thought for honor or chivalry. They'd cheat their own mothers for the coin to bed a whore, and lie to God Himself to buy one more hour of this miserable life. Their limbs rot off from their wounds and they puke their guts out with diseases. They wind up selling their souls and bartering their honor because after a while anything seems better than dying and—ah, hell!"

He cut himself off abruptly, turning away from her. Arianna pushed to her feet, knocking into the table. The inkhorn teetered and would have spilled if Raine hadn't spun back around, his hand shooting out to steady it.

He laughed suddenly and caught her to him. "You are dangerous, woman." He backed up, sitting down on the coffer beneath the window and drawing her between his thighs. "Dangerous to yourself and to others, with your foolish ideals and your flapping elbows." His voice had turned oddly soft and caressing. "Perhaps I ought to tie you up and gag you, the way that Taliesin did when he dumped you in my tent that day."

His thighs tightened around her hips, drawing her closer to him. She resisted a moment, then yielded. She wanted to yield. Her hands came up between them and her palms wound up resting on his chest. His tunic was warm from the sun and partly unlaced, revealing brown skin and a V of curling dark chest hair. She wanted to kiss him there, but she didn't. She could see a rough spot on his jaw that the tonsor had missed while shaving him that morning. She wanted to kiss him there as well.

His hands settled around her waist and Arianna almost shuddered at his touch. She tried to grab hold of her scattering wits. "I'm glad you brought up the subject of Taliesin, my lord," she said around a strange tightness in her throat.

She felt his chest expand beneath her palms. "What has that wretched whelp done now?"

"In the fortnight that you have been here at Rhuddlan he has managed to bed every single one of the kitchen wenches save for Bertha, and he has now started in on the dairy maids."

"Why did he pass up Bertha? Isn't she the one with the splendid tits?"

"Hunh! They droop and swing about like a cow's udders." She felt a twinge of jealousy that her husband had noticed Bertha's magnificent breasts. Arianna had rubbed gillyflower juice every night for years on her own breasts to get them to grow. "Nay, Bertha was saved from your squire's base lechery because she has a rash."

"Ah."

"Not *that* sort of rash, you dolt." Laughing, she thumped his chest with her fist. He caught her hand, bringing it up to his mouth. He nipped her knuckle, then licked it, sending a shiver up her arm. He was going to make love to her soon; he had sought her out for the purpose of making love to her, and in the middle of the day. She thought of what he had done to her body last night, how he had made her feel, and she knew that she wanted it to happen again.

"God's truth, you must do something about Taliesin, my lord," she said, and was shocked to hear a quaver in her voice. "Else Rhuddlan will be overrun with babes nine months hence."

"What would you have me do—geld the boy? Order your wenches to keep their legs together."

One of his hands had moved up to her breast. His fingers found her nipple and she had to bite her lip to keep from moaning. "I might have known I would get no help from you on this matter, as you are a man and have not a care for how many maids you debauch or bastards you sow."

"You malign me, wife. I've given up debauching maids and sowing bastards, now that I am married."

A part of her was pleased by his words, the other part barely heard him. She could think of nothing but the feel of his hand on her breast, of what his fingers were doing to her nipple.

"I see that I shall have to take matters into my own hands," she said, having trouble getting the words out her tight throat. "I'll give all the wenches brakeroot to take in wine. At least then they won't be gotten with child."

His fingers suddenly fastened around her wrists and he jerked her hard up against his chest. "How do you know of such things?"

For a moment she simply stared at him with bemused eyes. Her breast still tingled from his touch. "Every woman knows . . ."

"Nay, only whores know how to keep a man's seed from taking root."

"You insult me, my lord."

His fingers tightened their grip, digging into her flesh, and his jaw clenched so hard the muscle jumped. He brought his face so close to hers she felt the angry heat of his breath. "And do you know, too, of a way to rid yourself of a babe once the seed has been planted?"

"Aye, but—"

"If you ever, *ever* take anything to abort my child, I will kill you for it, Arianna. Believe this, for I mean it."

She jerked free of his grip and shouted so loudly he blinked. "I would never do such a thing, you worm-witted, bog-headed, moldy-tongued Norman! I want a child."

Raine's head snapped back, his eyes widening. *"Moldy-*tongued?" he said, and for a moment she thought he was actually going to laugh. She couldn't keep up with his abrupt change of temper; she wanted to hit him. Irrationally, she still wanted to kiss him. Or for him to kiss her. God's death. She didn't understand him, and she didn't understand herself.

He gripped her jutting chin between his thumb and forefinger and brought his lips close to hers. "You would have a Norman bastard's child?"

"Whom else's would I have? You are my husband."

For a moment he did nothing, simply stared at her. Then he brushed her lips with his. "Take off your clothes and get into bed."

She pulled away from him and backed up a step. Her lips burned and she had to resist an impulse to lick them. "I will not."

He said nothing, nor did he move. But his face had

assumed that hard look, the look of a conqueror who would not be denied.

She backed up three more steps until her thighs bumped into the table. She crossed her arms over her breasts. "I am no longer in the mood to mate with you, my lord."

He stood up. "It matters not whether you are in the mood. I could strip you naked and tie you to the bed and have my way with you and there is none to gainsay me."

"Aye, that you could, for you are stronger than I. But afterward mayhap you ought to purge the entire castle of daggers. Aye, and the whole of England, too, while you're about it. Else you had better leave me tied to your bed forever."

"The suggestion has merit." He took a step toward her and she scooted around the table, putting it between them. "I'm beginning to think that naked and tied to my bed is the only place for you."

She had never seen anyone move so fast. He didn't come around the table, he came *over* it. Arianna grabbed the back of the chair, but he snatched it away and sent it flying. Whirling to run, she tripped over the clawed foot of the empty brazier. She was back on her feet in a second, but Raine snagged her arm. He hauled her around and slammed against her, pinning her back against the table.

A scream erupted past her lips before she could stop it. He stopped it with his mouth.

And she was lost. She returned his kiss with all the passion she had felt the night before but held back. He let go of her arm and pressed his palm against the back of her head to kiss her deeper. His tongue thrust, slowed, then stayed, filling her mouth, and he turned his head back and forth, slanting his lips across hers.

Arianna's heart thundered in her ears and her legs trembled so violently that only the edge of the table and his hand on the back of her head kept her upright. She rubbed her breasts against his chest and plunged her hand into his hair, twisting her fingers in it, pulling his head back to plant little sucking kisses along the line of his jaw. Her other hand rubbed over his chest. She felt the erratic beat of his heart and his low moan was a vibration against her palm. His hands went around her waist, and he ground his hips against her. He was hard for her.

She flung her head back, her eyes opened wide onto the painted beams that spun and whirled like cartwheels above her. He pressed his lips to the throbbing hollow in her throat and his voice thrummed like a harp string in her blood. "You are mine, Arianna. Mine."

"No . . ." she said. But it wasn't Raine she was trying to deny. It was her own raging need.

He let go of her, so abruptly that she had to grab the table to keep from falling. There was a wildness in his eyes as he stared at her. A sort of bewildered anger. Then he spun around on his heel and left her.

She actually took a step after him before she stopped herself. She looked around the room with glazed eyes, then stumbled back to the chair. She straightened it, then lowered herself into it with careful movements, as if she'd just been stricken with an ague. Her lips felt swollen and bruised and she wet them with her tongue, tasting him.

Her hands fisted on her thighs. There was a yawning, aching hunger low in her belly and he had caused it. He had made her want him and then he had left her.

It matters for naught, she told herself. Aye, it matters not at all. I will show him that I care as little for him as he cares for me, and it will be true, for I care for him not in the least.

Her fingers trembled as she picked up the pen, but she pretended not to notice. She saw that the quill's end had split and she searched through the clutter on the table for the penknife. She slit through a piece of the horny stem, fashioning a new point.

"My lady . . ."

The knife jerked, slicing through the pad of her thumb. She watched, mesmerized, as bright red blood welled from the cut and dripped onto the ledger, and it was odd, for she didn't feel a thing. She looked up into the beautiful face of her husband's squire. "God's death, Taliesin, you fool, look what you've done."

"Milady, 'tis you who have done it. One who is as clumsy as yourself ought not to be allowed around knives."

"Shut your insolent mouth, boy, and fetch me water and a cloth." She wasn't clumsy. She'd never been clumsy in her life until she'd been forced to marry that cursed Norman. If the man wasn't upsetting her inner humors, his wretched squire was popping up out of nowhere and scaring the sin right out of her.

Her thumb began to throb now with pain. Suddenly a white film formed before her eyes and her whole body trembled. Surely she wasn't going to faint over a little cut. She gripped the table with her good hand and looked up to see Taliesin walking toward her. He carried the golden mazer in his hands.

Oh, please, no . . . she said, except the words had not come out her mouth. And Taliesin was holding out the mazer, only it wasn't Taliesin, it was an old man, withered and with yellow skin and sunken eyes, but the eyes . . . the eyes belonged to Taliesin, jet black and shimmering. *Why are you doing this to me?* she cried without sound. *I don't want to see any more.*

But the mazer was in her hands and it was pulsing and hot, and she was looking down into a golden mist that swirled and eddied, enveloping her mind. The mist cleared, became the yellow glare of a morning sun, but the air was cool, the crisp air of autumn. She heard the squeal of a stuck pig and smelled blood, and she laughed.

13

He laughed as the pigsticker thrust a knife into the hog's neck. The animal thrashed and squealed and blood spurted into the air. It splattered in the dirt and on his bare feet and legs, and then his mother shoved a steaming kettle of boiled oats beneath the hog's neck, to catch the blood.

His mouth watered. There would be blood pudding for supper this afternoon and maybe, if there was enough left over, there would be some for him.

"Raine!"

At the sound of his name, he looked up. His brother, Hugh, rode across the bailey on a pony. A magnificent white pony with a long blond mane and tail. The pony was too big for Hugh; his legs could barely grip its fat back. But I am taller than Hugh, he thought. And he wanted that pony. He could taste the wanting of it even more than he could taste the blood pudding.

Hugh laughed. "See what my father the earl has given me for my birthday!"

The earl is my father, too, he wanted to shout, but he didn't dare. Because he was a bastard, a whore's son. He knew what the words meant, exactly what they meant. But he still could not understand why his father didn't like him, was always so angry with him. Why his father should give Hugh a pony and nothing to him.

Hugh shouted and pointed toward the great hall. A knight came down the steps, a man in sparkling silvered mail with hair the color of the ravens that scavenged in the midden, a man so tall and broad he blocked the pale autumn sun. Someday I will be that big, he thought, as big as my father, a knight like my father, and his guts twisted with the bewildered mixture of fear and longing he always felt when he saw the tall, hard-faced man. But then the knight strode toward him and he was smiling, and suddenly he was sure the smile was for him.

"Father!" he cried and he ran, and he wrapped his arms around the man's steel-armored legs. "When is my birthday? Can I have a pony too?"

He didn't see the fist until it was too late. It snatched him by the scruff of his tunic and hauled him high into the air until he looked into a pair of pale-gray eyes.

"You are never to call me that again. I am 'my lord earl' to you, you whore's whelp, and you are never to forget it."

"But will you give me a pony too? When it's my birthday?"

The back of a hand smashed into his mouth and he hit the ground with a smack that drove the air from his chest. He skidded along the hard-packed dirt and into the butchered hog, knocking over the kettle. Blood-soaked oats slopped over him and his mother screamed at him and Hugh laughed. But it was his father's voice, harsh with anger, that squeezed his chest with pain.

"Shut your mouth, boy, or I'll have the flesh flogged from your bones. Aye, I'll have you flogged anyway. Impudent whelp . . ."

His chest heaved as he fought for breath and tears burned his eyes, but he didn't cry because knights never cried.

His mother bent over him. Her hair fell across her face and into her mouth that was red and open with laughter.

She cackled and prodded him with her toe. " 'When is me birthday?' he asks. Well, it's been an' gone and we all forgot it. Tried to forget it, mayhap, 'cause we never wanted ye born in the first place. Paid me an old witch thrupence to purge ye. Puked and bled me guts out for three days, I did. Near killed me, it did. But ye hung on, ye stubborn, tough lil' bastid. 'When's me birthday?' he asks. Well, we forgot it, we did."

But he didn't care about his birthday anymore, because he had seen the marshal coming with his knotted rope, and he turned and pressed his face against the ground that was wet and sticky with the hog's blood and the spilled mush.

The rope slashed across his back, but he didn't cry because knights never cried. . . .

"I won't cry," Arianna said.

"Well, I should hope not, my lady. It's only a little cut, after all."

Arianna blinked against the haze of a bloody sun that dimmed and became the green-spangled walls of her chamber. For a moment she felt a burning pain across her back and she was confused, for Taliesin was pressing a cloth against her thumb. She had opened her mouth to tell him it wasn't her thumb that hurt, when nausea suddenly cramped her stomach and the painted walls tilted and blurred. She clenched her jaws, squeezing her eyes shut. She thought she smelled boiled oats and hog's blood, but that couldn't be, for it was late July, not slaughtering time, and she had ordered no pigs butchered this morning. And then no sooner did she think that then she remembered.

The old bard had put the golden mazer in her hands—no, Taliesin had startled her and she had cut her thumb with the penknife, and that fool boy brought over the mazer and she had made the mistake of looking into it and she'd had a vision. That was all, simply a vision. She had watched a hog being butchered in a strange bailey that must have been Chester, for the old earl was there;

she had recognized him, for he looked so much the way
his son did now. And Hugh was there, he had been given
a pony for his birthday and when she saw it she wanted
one too. . . .

No, *Raine* had wanted the pony. He had been the one
in the bailey and she had just seen that brief moment out
of his past. Except that she had done more than see it, she
had *been* him, been Raine as a small boy and everyone
had forgotten her birthday—no, *his* birthday. It had been
Raine's birthday that was forgotten. There had always
been a fuss made over her on her birthdays.

Arianna clenched her teeth against a shudder that
racked her body. These visions were becoming too real.
To be in someone else's mind and heart like that, it was
too frightening to contemplate, for what if she lost herself
and never came back?

"You're not going to faint over a little bit of blood, are
you, my lady?"

She opened her eyes. Taliesin had ripped off a piece of
the cloth and was tying it around her thumb. A curtain of
flame-colored hair obscured his face. "Why are you doing
these things to me?" she demanded. She still felt queasy
inside, all hollow and sad.

His head came up, and he brushed the hair back with a
pale, thin hand. His eyes glimmered at her, like a cat's
eyes at night. "Because the cut must be cleaned," he said.
"Else it will putrefy and your arm will rot off."

He had hold of her hand still, and it trembled in his.
"Don't play the fool with me, boy. Why are you making
me see these things . . . feel them . . . ?"

"What things? If you mean startling you so that you cut
your thumb, you must acquit me, my lady, for I knocked
ere I entered. I feared something was amiss, for my lord
had come thundering into the hall, all wild-eyed like a
charger with a burr beneath its saddle, nearly knocking
me down, and bellowing at *me* for being in his way. I pray
you haven't bungled things again, my lady." He heaved a

long-suffering sigh. "For, the goddess be my witness, I am being worn to the bone trying to keep the peace between you."

He dropped her hand to snatch up a basin of pink-colored water and Arianna started, for it was the bronze basin from the laver that he held, not the golden mazer. "What did you do with it?" she cried.

"My lady?" He jerked so violently that water slopped into the rushes, but he stared back at her with blank, wide-open eyes, like a puppy caught with a half-eaten shoe between its paws.

"Myrddin's magic bowl—what have you done with it?"

"I know naught of a magic bowl."

"You lie. You stole it from me that day Rhuddlan fell and then put it here in this very chamber to bedevil me on my wedding day. A moment ago you handed it to me and now it has gone missing again and you . . ." Her voice trailed off. He would admit to nothing. It mattered for naught anyway, for the bowl would turn up again, and she didn't want any more of its cursed visions anyway.

The squire had returned the basin to the laver and was edging toward the door. "Taliesin," she commanded, and he froze, then turned, and his face pleated into a comical expression of reluctance.

"My lady, I swear to you I know naught of magic bowls, and I have important matters to attend to. Aye, my lord's armor needs polishing and though that brother of yours is grooming my lord's destrier, I fear the wretch is hopelessly incompetent and I shall be the one to suffer my lord's ire if the task is not done properly. I shall be hung up by my thumbs—"

Arianna's laughter cut through the boy's tirade. "Quit flapping your tongue ere it falls out your mouth from overuse and tell me—do you know the date of Lord Raine's birth?"

He blinked, then a smile flashed across his face. "Strange that you should wonder, for it came to my mind

only an hour ago that my lord was born under the influence of Mars, which explains why he is oft so irascible and
foul-tempered." He heaved a put-upon sigh. "The blessed
event took place twenty-six years ago tomorrow, and thus
was I doomed to this miserable fate."

Arianna failed to see what the one thing had to do with
other. "Fool boy, you were not even a lustful urge between your father's legs at the time of my lord husband's
birth. But you say that his birthday falls on the morrow?"

"Aye. And pity it's a fast day, for he is not overly fond
of fish, is my lord. But doubtless the cook will conjure up
a frumenty for the feast to tempt his appetite."

"We are having a feast?"

"Why, I think that a splendid idea, my lady!" the boy
exclaimed, clapping his hands. "Would that I had thought
of it. Though you should have told me sooner, for I shall
want to compose an ode in honor of the occasion."

She scowled at him, for she suspected that a feast was
precisely what he had been after all along. Perhaps he
wanted a reason to perform on his harp. She wondered
again if the music she had heard last night had been made
by him, not by a dream. But, no, even with an extraordi-
nary talent the boy was too young to be so skilled. And
yet . . . yet, suppose he were *llyfrawr,* a wizard. It was
said that wizards could fashion music out of the very air,
they could assume any shape and travel through the circle
of time, they could make themselves invisible or be in two
places at once, so perhaps they could even conjure visions
and bend the unsuspecting to their will.

*God's death, Arianna, you witless nit! Who ever heard
of a wizard wandering about in these modern times? And
certainly no self-respecting wizard would take on the shape
of that irritating squire.*

Besides, what did it matter from whence the vision
came? It had all happened to Raine, the boy, just as she
had seen and felt it, and she knew with a certainty she
could not explain that it had never been forgotten by the

man. She ached for the man, even more than she ached for the boy. No wonder he had grown up so hard, so unfeeling.

His birthday was tomorrow and this once, she vowed, it would not be forgotten. There was scarce time left to arrange for a proper banquet, but it could be done if she put the whole castle to work. She would give him a gift too. Aye, a gift would be nice. . . .

She wished she could give him a pony. But she was twenty years too late.

"Seventeen, eighteen, nineteen . . ."

Arianna folded her arms across her chest and frowned at the stacks of trestle tables lined along one wall of the great hall. With only twenty tables and all of Rhuddlan at the feast, people would be pressed in rows one upon the other like piglets suckling at a sow's tits. But twenty would have to be enough, she supposed. There certainly wasn't time before the morrow for the carpenter to make any more.

Her frown deepened as she studied the condition of the great hall. It was clean enough, for she had already seen to that. But the rafters were black as the bottom of a well with soot and the walls sorely needed a fresh coat of whitewash. She thought how much plainer was this hall compared to that of her father's *llys*. Except for a few moth-eaten stag heads and rusted weapons hanging on the walls and pillars, there was naught to catch and please the eye. What was particularly needed, she decided, was something bright and colorful in back of the high table. A biblical painting, perhaps, or an array of silken pennons in peacock colors.

Suddenly she knew just what would be her birthday gift to Raine. She would fashion him an enormous banner to hang in back of his high seat. She would make it of the richest silk, the deep red color of fall apples, and on it she would put his black dragon device. Thus all strangers who came to sup and sleep in their hall would see the banner and mark that it was the Black Dragon who was lord here.

Filled with excitement over her plans, Arianna set the kitchens into an uproar preparing for the feast. Then she saddled a palfrey to ride into town to purchase the silk she would need from Christina, the draper's daughter. The day had turned suddenly stormy, and she thought with a sigh that she would probably get wet. Gray clouds had piled up overhead, like mounds of dirty fleece, and the marsh grass rippled in a stiff wind that smelled of rain.

The toll keeper waved Arianna through the town gate —she didn't pay, for the toll went directly into her husband's purse. A pack of dogs chased and nipped at her palfrey's heels, their yapping competing with the cries of fishermen who trolled the river with their nets. She passed by the open, cavernous doors of the mint, where sparks flashed and the air thrummed with the sound of hammers pounding the dies. They were fashioning new coins with Lord Raine of Rhuddlan's likeness on the face of them, just like the Roman Caesars of old.

He had come far, she thought, from the ragged boy who had yearned for a pony and was given a beating instead. As the palfrey picked its way slowly through narrow streets that stank of pigs, she pictured the look of surprise and pleasure on his face when she presented him with the banner on the morrow.

The draper's daughter lived in a large, timbered house that fronted the market square and backed up against the quay. The market square wasn't square at all, but shaped rather like a large, lopsided triangle of packed dirt that turned into a bog in winter. At the pointed end of the triangle squatted the church, with its chunky, square stone bell tower. In the front yard of the church a man sat in the stocks, hunched in misery, with a stinking, rotting mackerel tied under his chin.

In the middle of the triangle stood the large market

cross, carved of granite, and beside the cross a well where a group of women had gathered to gossip, water buckets balanced on their heads. Their magpie chatter ceased immediately as soon as they caught sight of Arianna.

She dismounted before the draper's house just as the first drops of rain left penny-sized patterns in the dust. Skirting around a braying donkey that had been overladen with sacks of wool, she entered the dark cool interior of the undercroft.

A servant rushed forward, bowing low. "Milady!"

"Fetch your mistress, if you please."

The servant left and Arianna looked around her. Stacks of bundled fleece tied up with reed cords took up a good part of the floor, along with barrels of papyrus and indigo and sheafs of woad leaves, all used for the dyes. Shelves on the wall were piled with bolts of cloth in rainbow hues.

A small door opened into another room, from which Arianna could hear the smack and clatter of looms. Another door led out back where bare-legged workers in clogs beat the raw wool in tubs of water and dyers dipped and stirred lengths of cloth in vats with long wooden poles. She stepped into the yard, holding her breath against the stale reek of urine, which was used to set the dyes.

Thunder rumbled overhead and it began raining harder. She was just about to step back inside when a movement to the left caught her eye. Steps led down the side of the house from the upper story. A man stood on the narrow landing, facing an open doorway. As she watched, he leaned into the shadows as if he were imparting a farewell kiss, and indeed, a woman's hands went around the man's neck. Then the man turned and ran lightly down the stairs. He carried a leather bag in one hand, which he thrust through his sword belt, and Arianna thought she heard the jangle of coins.

At the bottom of the steps the man paused to take a look around him, his eyes narrowed against the pouring rain. Arianna got a glimpse of familiar honey-brown hair and a dashing, flowing moustache.

Without knowing why she did it, she stepped back beneath the shelter cast by the eaves, where he couldn't see her. He looked around one last time, then slipped out a side gate. She wondered what her cousin Kilydd was doing here, what mischief he was up to. Doubtless whatever it was, it would mean trouble for the Lord of Rhuddlan.

It was several moments later before Christina joined her in the shop. The girl's flushed cheeks stood out in stark contrast to the dazzling whiteness of the coif she wore on her head. Her mouth looked wet and swollen.

"God's grace to you, milady," she said, curtseying with folded hands. She sounded out of breath, as if she'd just been running. "What brings you here in foul weather such as this?"

Arianna smiled. "If one doesn't venture outdoors in Wales when it rains, one would never go anywhere at all."

"How true, milady." Christina's eyes darted toward the open door that led to the yard, which was now awash with running water. She forced an answering smile. "Not even the Normans have been able to tame our weather."

It was an old jest, but Arianna laughed anyway. A trestle table sat beneath the window, a bolt of moss-green wool lay, partly unwound, on its shear-scarred surface. Arianna fingered the material. She wanted to ask the draper's daughter what her cousin Kilydd had been doing sneaking down the back stairs. She said instead, "I would like to see what you have in the nature of carmine sarcenet."

"If it pleases you, milady." Christina motioned to the servant, who hooked a bolt of purplish-red material from a top shelf and spread it out on the table.

The sarcenet was beautiful and would be perfect for the banner. Next she selected a figured silk of the blackest ebony with which to fashion the dragon. As the servant wrapped up the ells of cloth and carried them out to load upon her palfrey, Arianna realized suddenly that she'd brought no coin with her. She had no money to bring anyway, for what she'd had upon her marriage now belonged to Raine. All she had of value that could be considered entirely her own were her wedding band and the seer's torque she wore around her neck.

Though it pained her to part with it, she reached up and unclasped the bronze circlet of writhing snakes. She held it out the draper's daughter. "Would you accept this as payment?"

Christina backed away from the torque as if she feared to touch it. "My lady, that is not necessary. I shall simply add the price of the cloth to the amount left owed for your bridal gown."

Arianna thought of the exquisite sapphire silk bliaut, wrought so heavily with gold thread, and the poppy-red pelisse trimmed with fur—their cost must have been exorbitant. Though Raine might soon become rich as the Lord of Rhuddlan, he had been poor on the day of their wedding. Yet still he had given her the beautiful gown and a white mule with all the trappings.

She practically pushed the torque into Christina's hands. "But I wish to use the cloth to make a gift for my husband. So I can hardly have him paying for it."

Christina hesitated a moment before her fingers closed around the ancient bronze circlet. She looked up at Arianna through a veil of pale lashes. "You are happy then in your marriage to the Norman? Have you fallen in love so soon?"

"Nay, I love him not at all," Arianna said, too quickly, and felt the blood leap to her face. For she lusted after him, oh aye, she lusted after him. She could not bear to admit even to herself that this man, who cared for her not at all, could make her throat get all tight and her knees go all loose with but one of his rare smiles.

"And what of you, Christina?" she demanded, wanting childishly to share her shame. "Perhaps you speak to me about love because you have the subject much on your mind lately? Does my cousin Kilydd share your maiden's bed?"

Christina's doe-brown eyes opened wide, and she started to shake her head. Then her back stiffened and her chin jerked up. "Aye, we are lovers, Kilydd and I, and I care not if the whole world knows it. For though we are not yet married by law, we have plighted our troth before God."

Christina waved her hand as Arianna opened her mouth to speak. "You need not point out, my lady, that he is Welsh and of noble blood, whereas I am English and naught but a draper's daughter. We love each other, and we share a common enemy, he and I, and a common dream. Someday, when the Normans have been driven back across the sea, we can . . ." Her voice trailed off as tears welled in her eyes. "Oh, milady, I do love him so. . . ."

Lightning flared suddenly, casting Christina's face in a greenish glow. Her last words seemed to echo in the darkening room, *love him so . . . so . . .* Thunder rumbled, and a gust of wind dashed rain against the side of the house.

Arianna wondered how it felt to be so sure of your love, so sure you were loved in return. She shut her eyes trying to recall how she'd felt in her vision when the golden knight had taken her into his arms. But all she saw was Raine charging her with his lance, and the touch she remembered was Raine's touch, fierce and insistent and full of passion, but not love. Never love.

"Kilydd has asked his so-called lord, your *Norman* husband, for permission to marry me," Christina was saying, and Arianna saw how hatred twisted the young woman's face, making it seem for a moment almost ugly. "His petition was denied. Lord Raine wishes for his Welsh vassals to wed Norman girls, so that their lands will then be well and truly conquered. He cares not at all that Kilydd and I love each other."

No one ever marries for love, Arianna started to say, but thunder pounded again overhead and once it had died she held her tongue. It would bring the English girl little solace to hear the truth so starkly spoken.

Christina touched her arm. "But I had thought that you, milady, would understand. You, who were wed against your will and to a man you hate."

Arianna sighed. "It isn't that." She seized the other girl's hands. "Christina, if it is rebellion that Kilydd plans, then you must stop him—"

"Stop him? Kilydd has oft told me that you of all women hold most dearly the dream of freedom for your land and your people. Have only two nights in the Norman's bed changed you so quickly?"

Arianna stiffened, drawing away from the other girl. "I have not forgotten that I am Cymry. I will never forget."

She turned to leave, but Christina seized her arm, and Arianna felt the girl's fear and desperation in the strength of her grip. "You will not betray Kilydd to the Norman?"

"I know naught of what he intends, so there is little for me to betray. But tell me no more, Christina, I beg of you. For a wife's first loyalty must be to her husband, and I would not want to have to choose between my honor and my kin." But she had already chosen, this she knew. For whatever Kilydd planned, it had to mean ill for her husband, yet she would say nothing.

Arianna stepped through the door, drawing her hood over her head against the slashing rain. The joy she had taken in purchasing the cloth for the banner was long gone. Her gift to Raine would be betrayal, for silence was after all a form of deceit. Perhaps the worst deceit of all.

The two squires heaved a simultaneous sigh as they peered through the pouring rain at the lone knight who prepared to charge at them from across a boggy tilting field.

"Please God, not again," one said. "I've bruises on my bruises and every time I open my mouth to breathe, I nearly drown. Doesn't he know it's raining?"

The other whined through his teeth. "You seriously don't expect the Black Dragon to call a halt to a little jousting just because God is pissing on Wales again. The man isn't human, and he's got no sympathy for those of us who are."

He whined again and squinted through the rain, hoping the knight had gone away, but he had not. Again and again they had taken him on, two against one, but so far they hadn't been able to touch him, let alone unhorse him. In truth, they'd barely scratched the paint on his shield. He was going to knock them on their asses in the mud again, God curse his black and merciless heart. They had both spent a good part of the afternoon becoming intimate with Rhuddlan's mud. The knight rarely smiled, but the two squires would have wagered their immortal souls that he was smiling now.

They would have lost, for the man at the other end of the field was not smiling. Cold water poured down his back and seeped into his bones and he had to resist the urge to shake himself like a dog. *I'm getting too old for this,* he thought. He was wet and miserable and his decrepit and battered twenty-five-year-old body had wanted to quit an hour ago. He wanted to sit before a warm fire and drink mulled wine. He thought of Arianna, of taking her to bed.

He wiped the sluicing rain out of his eyes before he lowered his helm. He tightened his right hand around the smooth butt of his lance and brought the long weapon up level with his hip. He winced as its weight pulled against the tired muscles of his arm. The wretched thing seemed to have gained a stone since he had first hefted it a dozen tilts ago.

He had just touched his spurs to his charger when he saw her, riding alone from the direction of the town. He whirled the great beast around on its hunches and bore down upon her, leaving the two squires to stare after him, first with astonishment, then with two fat grins splitting their mud-splattered faces.

The hooves of his steed pounded through the sucking muck, sending up sprays of black water. Lightning brightened the sky and thunder boomed so loudly it sounded as if the very heavens were splitting open. He didn't realize how he must appear, charging out of the storm with lowered lance, until he pulled up before her and saw the stark terror on her face.

She was paler than death, her lips bloodless and trembling, her eyes wide open and dark as caves. Her fist was pressed to her breast as if she feared her heart would burst, and he could see the blood pumping wildly in her throat.

He tossed the lance aside and bent down to take hold of the shank of her horse's bit and keep her from bolting. He looked into her face, wet and pale and vulnerable, and he thought, *God's love, she is so beautiful.*

For that timeless moment, as they stared into each other's eyes, he was certain they had done this before. Not once, but many times. Yet each time had been different. The woman whose beauty hurt his heart was her, always her, but with a different face. It was not always raining; once, the sun had beat down hot on their uncovered heads and again it had been night and the smell of snow had been in the air. But each time he had felt the hunger, the almost desperate longing to carry her off somewhere and love her until she was his, and only his.

He wanted to do that now. He wanted her beneath him, he wanted her nails digging into his back, her legs wrapped around his hips, her tongue in his mouth. He wanted to hear her cry out in ecstasy as he pleasured her with his fingers and his lips and his tongue. He wanted to thrust into her and explode inside her and die a little with her.

"Where in hellfire have you been?" he demanded, his voice harsh. No woman had ever affected him in this way, and he didn't like it. It mattered not that she was his wife, he could never let her have that sort of power over him.

She blinked and awareness came slowly over her face, as if she'd just been awakened from a deep sleep. "I went to Rhuddlan town to . . . to visit with Christina, the draper's daughter. She is a particular friend."

"Where is your escort?"

She blinked again, then looked behind her, as if she expected an army to appear out of the air. "I—"

"You are never to ride off alone again. Anywhere."

Her head snapped around. "I am not a hound to be kept on a leash!" Then she bit her lip, squeezing her eyes shut. He almost smiled, for he could guess that she was now calling on God and all the saints to give her patience. She sucked in a deep breath, but then, to his surprise, she reached out and laid her hand on his arm. "Please, my lord, don't treat me like a child."

"Then don't act like one." His arm was protected by links of tempered steel, yet he could feel her hand, burning, as if she touched bare flesh. He urged his horse back a step, putting distance between them. "There are any number of men within a day's ride from here who would like nothing better than to take you captive so that they could bleed me for a ransom. Your cousin Kilydd, for one."

It had been a lucky cast, a name pulled out of the air. Yet her hands convulsed on the reins, so that the palfrey danced, pulling at the bit. Her lips parted open and two bright bands of color flared across her cheekbones. Raine knew immediately that it was her cattle-raiding cousin, and not the draper's daughter, whom she had met in town, and he wondered why. But he didn't ask her. Because he didn't want to hear any lies coming from those sweet lips. God help him, all he wanted to do was kiss them.

"Kilydd would never harm me," she said.

"But he would dearly love to harm me."

"He gave you his oath of fealty."

"Aye, an oath that holds about as much value as a sieve does water."

He saw her lips tighten with anger, but he didn't trust either one of her cousins and he wouldn't pretend that he did. For that matter, he didn't trust her. They rode toward the gatehouse, side by side, yet in silence. The rain had stopped. Sunlight poured through a break in the clouds, and a rainbow appeared suddenly, directly over the tower of the keep.

"Look," he said, pointing to the shimmering band of colors. "Hurry up and make a wish ere I beat you to it." And then immediately felt foolish. Wishing on rainbows was for children.

But to his surprise she squeezed her eyes shut and her lips mouthed a silent plea. For a moment he wondered what she wished for, if her heart's desire had anything to do with him, and he looked away, disgusted with himself. For if anything she had wished him gone from her life.

"Raine?"

His head jerked around. It was the first time she had ever used his name, and spoken that way, in her low and slightly husky voice, it had made him think instantly of bed and sex.

"Would you really pay a ransom to get me back?" she said.

"You are my wife."

He wasn't sure what response she had expected, but that wasn't it. Yet it was the only one he had to give her, so he could only watch as her face hardened and she gathered up the reins, spurring her horse into a canter.

As he watched her ride away from him he let himself wonder, though only for a moment, what would have happened if they had met years ago, before life had finally ruined him. Back when he had still believed in love and happily-ever-after and that wishes on rainbows could sometimes come true.

14

Arianna tried to catch one of Taliesin's eyes—both of which were preoccupied with a pair of round and creamy breasts. The squire sat at the edge of the dais with Bertha instead of his harp in his lap. The girl laughed as she thrust her splendid cleavage beneath the boy's nose and a cup of hippocras into his hand.

Arianna scowled at the squire; the wretch as usual was slacking in his duties. Some soothing music would be nice, she thought. Her head pounded like the shuttle on a loom from the din that filled the hall. Everyone seemed to be talking at once, shouting over the snarls and yelps of the dogs, who lay among the rushes and waited for bones to be tossed their way. Several of Raine's knights had also brought their falcons with them to the table. The hawks sat on perches at their masters' backs and added their shrill cries to the noise.

The tables sagged beneath platters loaded with eel coffin pies and roasted pike seasoned with cumin. Fire-blackened cauldrons sent spicy steam into the air: the rich smell of sturgeon stew, flavored with saffron and leeks. There were delicacies, too, peeled walnuts and rice with almonds and white loaves of wastel. As a crowning glory, the cook had made a subtlety—a spun-sugar creation sculptured in the shape of a dragon.

All in all it promised to be a fine feast, even for a fast day. The only thing missing was the Lord of Rhuddlan himself.

Just then Sir Odo stepped from behind the screen's passage. He flapped his big arms wildly about, like the sails on a windmill, and a big grin split his face. Arianna threw a piece of bread at Taliesin's head and at last got his attention. The boy hefted Bertha off his lap and picked up his bow-shaped harp. He strummed the heavy brass strings with silver struts, and music, clear and sweet as the chimes of a bell on a clear night, filled and then silenced the hall.

Raine came through the passage and Arianna felt a smile break across her face. Her eyes burned, her back was stiff, and her fingers blistered from pushing a needle again and again through stiff cloth long into the wee hours of the night. But she knew that it would all be worth it when she watched the look of surprise and pleasure come over her husband's face as she presented him with his birthday gift. She hoped that it would mean as much to the man as a pony would have meant to the boy.

Even the dogs had quieted as Raine entered the hall. His step faltered a moment when he noticed the crowd and the sudden hush that greeted him.

Arianna descended the dais. Perhaps she was only imagining it, but she thought his eyes darkened and his mouth softened a bit as he watched her come toward him. He had been training a young destrier and so he wore his leather *broigne,* tall boots and worn chausses, yet she thought he looked stunningly handsome. She hesitated a moment, then she took his hand and led him toward the high seat. His hand was large, swallowing hers, but his touch was gentle.

He dipped his head until his breath brushed her cheek.

"You should have warned me that we had guests, wife. I fear I reek of the stables."

Arianna leaned into him, breathing deeply of his smell —of horse and leather and man. The *broigne* was opened to his waist, revealing a sun-browned chest damp with sweat. She felt a curling ache in her belly as she looked up at him. She wanted to press her face against his chest . . . there, where the hard, scarred muscle protected his heart.

"Nay, husband, there are no special guests this day," she said, and her smile was filled with sweet anticipation. "Or rather you are the guest, for this feast is in your honor. All of Rhuddlan is here to mark the occasion of your birthday, my lord."

His head snapped back and all the gentleness vanished from his face. "My *what?*"

His voice cut through the noise in the hall like the snap of a whip. Taliesin's hands stilled the thrumming harp strings. His brow creased with confusion, then his eyes narrowed on his master and they flared for a moment, like twin fireflies.

"Your birthday?" Arianna said, her smile wavering and then dying as she watched her husband's eyes turn cold and hard.

By now they had reached the dais and as arranged, a pair of heralds trumpeted a signal and Rhodri and Sir Odo's page came forward bearing the banner. They unfurled it between them with a dramatic flourish and a loud cheer and another blare from the trumpets bounced off the vaulted ceiling.

Raine's gaze stabbed at her; he hadn't even looked at the beautiful banner. The closed expression on his face didn't alter except for a slight flaring of his nostrils. "Is this your idea of a jest?"

Arianna tried to swallow around a thickness in her throat. " 'Tis a banner to hang on the wall in back of the high seat. It is my gift to you, my lord husband." The lump was now in danger of choking her. It felt as if she had tried to swallow an egg and it had gotten stuck in there. "For your birthday," she added, as if enough explanation would somehow erase that look on his face.

He stared at her for a long, long while, his eyes cold and hard with anger. Slowly he turned his head and looked at her gift. For a moment she thought she saw a startled pain flare in his eyes before they hardened again. "My birthday gift," he said with a snort of derision. He laughed once, hard and harsh. "Take it out to the midden and burn it."

The boys hesitated, frozen with shock. "Go!" Raine shouted, and Rhodri dropped his end of the banner as if it had suddenly caught fire and whirled, stumbling off the dais. Sir Odo's page gathered up the stiff material into a bundle in his arms and followed more slowly.

The hall was now silent, an echoing silence like an empty church. Raine's gaze flickered down the length of the tables, then back to her. "You are never again to deplete my pantries and my buttery in this fashion without my permission."

Arianna tried to draw a breath and couldn't. She felt as if she'd been punched in the chest. He might as well have used his fists on her, so badly had he hurt her. "Why?" she asked softly. *Do you really hate me so much?*

But he said nothing, simply stared at her with empty, flint-gray eyes. Then he spun around and strode away from her, down the length of the hall.

"My lord, wait!" she cried after him. "What have I done? Why are you so . . . angry," her voice trailed off as she realized he had no intention of answering her.

She stared at his retreating back, fighting tears. She picked up her skirts and ran after him.

"Come back here, Norman!"

Raine lengthened his stride. He heard the soft patter of her leather-soled slippers on the stairs behind him, and then a hand fell on his arm, jerking him around.

Her chin sailed into the air, though it trembled a bit. "If you are angry, then by God's eyes you will tell me why. But don't you dare walk away as if I were of no more account than your lowliest villein."

He pried her fingers loose from his sleeve, but then his hands closed around her arms and with a vicious jerk he brought her crashing against his chest. He looked down into her eyes and saw that they were wide and bright with unshed tears. He stared into those eyes, not moving, saying nothing. His gaze fell on her mouth. To his astonishment, he was filled with such a fierce need to kiss her he almost groaned aloud from it.

His fingers tightened their grip. "How could you pretend to know the date of my birth, when I don't know it myself?"

Her eyes widened even further. "That God-cursed, wretched squire of yours—he said it was today."

"Then he lied. Except, the boy has no reason to lie." He closed his fingers around her scalp and brought his face close to hers, close enough that he could see his own breath stir the wisps of her hair. "But you do. What did you hope to accomplish by this mummery—except to flaunt your contempt for me? Did you think to shame me before all of Rhuddlan by reminding one and all that my birth was so base, no one ever cared to mark the occasion?"

"No!" she protested, but his hand tightened in her hair and he shook her head, hard.

"Pity for you, little wife, but it was a wasted effort. I've been called bastard too often and by too many people. That particular knife has long ago lost its edge."

"No, no, you are wrong!" She laid her palm on his cheek, touching him in a way that was tender and soft, and he couldn't bear it.

He jerked his head aside and let go of her so abruptly she almost stumbled.

"Raine . . ." she said, and her voice broke. She drew

her lower lip between her teeth, then pushed it back out again, and he had to tense every muscle to keep from hauling her back into his arms and sucking that lip into his mouth. Never had he wanted to kiss a woman more in his life, and he almost hated her for it. No one had ever made him want something so badly, and so beyond his control.

Again her hand started up to his face, but this time she let it fall without touching him. "It was not done to hurt you. None of it was meant to hurt you."

His mouth twisted into a mocking smile. "You flatter yourself, wife, if you think that you can hurt me. Not when the only use I have for you is in my bed, where you can breed me sons."

For the longest moment she simply stared at him, while the blood drained from her face as if he'd torn open her heart, and her chest jerked once on a sob. Then she whirled and ran away from him.

He thrust his fingers through his hair. "Ah, Christ . . .

"Arianna!" he shouted, as she darted into the path of a cartload of dung that was being taken to the fields for fertilizer. The cart swerved, clipping a pile of empty ale barrels, which went clattering and rolling like ninepins across the yard. At the gatehouse she disappeared into a crowd of beggars and pilgrims who, having heard of the feast, had gathered for the largesse.

Cursing, he started after her then veered toward the stables. It would be easier to catch her on horseback.

Two hours later he still hadn't caught her.

There were places in the marshlands around Rhuddlan where it was said people had been swallowed up by the shifting sands. The forest to the east harbored wild boar and wolves, and bands of landless marauders who would cut off a woman's head to sell the hair for a few shillings —after, of course, they had taken turns using her, passing her from man to man like a costrel of wine.

The more Raine thought of the dangers that could have befallen her, the more his guts clenched with fear and the angrier he became until he thought he just might kill her himself, if something or someone else didn't do it first.

At last he picked up her footprints and he followed them along the river to the sea. He stood up in the stirrups, searching for her among the dunes that rose in heaps, like frozen waves.

"Arianna, little wife," he muttered through his clenched teeth. "You'll be sleeping on your stomach for a week once I catch up with you."

But then he remembered that there was only a limited list of crimes for which she would allow him to beat her, and he smiled. She stood up to him, his little wife. Even when she was in the wrong, she stood up to him.

Her footprints led him to an old dilapidated fishing pier that listed like a three-legged chair, its pilings sinking into the soft sand. He thought she might have sat here for a while, staring out to sea. Clam holes pockmarked a gravelly beach littered with driftwood and spume spit up by the receding tide. Gray weeds trembled in the wind and screams from the sea birds rent the salt-laden air. The land felt empty here, and forgotten.

A movement to his left caught his eye . . . there, where a group of tall granite boulders poked up like giant gray thumbs on top a nearby rise.

He remembered this place and the circle of stones from the day when his ships had brought him to Wales almost a month ago, for they had landed but a few hundred yards to the north of this spot. The day that he had taken Rhuddlan and started in motion the sequence of events that eventually brought him a coveted title and land.

And her . . . Arianna, his wife.

Thirteen pillarlike stones stood in a perfect circle atop the rise, with two of the pillars connected by a capstone to form an archway. In the center of this cromlech were more boulders in the shape of an altar that had been carved with strange markings and blackened by old fires. Marsh grass swayed among the stones, as if dancing to music only the fairies could hear.

"They are called *meinhirion* . . . the standing stones," Taliesin had told him that first day in an awe-filled voice, accompanied by a dramatic shiver. "The ancient ones worshipped their gods at such places. 'Tis a center of powerful magic."

"It looks like a great pile of useless rocks me," Raine had said.

But now the stones seemed to float in a murky mist dyed golden by the setting sun. She stood within the cromlech, before the altar. His boots made no sound on the marshy ground, and he was almost on top of her before she heard him. She whirled, but there was no surprise on her face. She simply stared at him, her green eyes mirroring the flames of the dying sun.

The sunset bathed the stones so that they glowed with a defused light, like a candle within a lantern. The light spread from the stones, enveloping her with a gentle radiance, and drawing him with its warmth. Slowly, the light shimmered, brightening, from soft gold to blinding white. He felt a sudden and terrible need to lower his head and bury it in her breasts, to beg for the comfort of her woman's arms.

"What do you want from me?" he asked, his throat thick. He was not even aware he'd formed the thought aloud.

He saw her lips move, but it took a moment for her voice to be heard over the sudden rushing of the blood in his ears. "Do you know that these are magic stones, my lord? They say that if a woman can get a man to drink of water that has touched the *meinhirion*, then he will love her forever."

The last of the sun sunk below the horizon. The blaze of light vanished, leaving shadows and a cold wind. Raine looked at the altar. There was a worn spot in the stone where a small pool of water had collected. It was not a lot, about as much as a man could cup in his two hands.

"And does it work the other way about? If a man will get a woman to drink from this water—"

"Then she will love him. Forever." She dipped two fingers into the pool, reverently, as if it were a stroup of holy water. Then she brought her fingers, wet and shining silver up to his lips. But she didn't touch them. If he wanted the water, he was going to have to lick it off, of his own free will.

"All it takes is one drop," she said.

He told himself it was all a game, a silly Welsh superstition. Yet he thought, too, how this was the way Adam must have felt before he took the apple from Eve's hands —knowing he was damning himself and unable to stop . . . not wanting to stop. . . .

He dunked his fingers in the water.

A torrent of sizzling fire coursed through him, as if he had touched a lightning bolt. The air crackled and a blue light, hot and bright, engulfed him. Engulfed him and vanished so quickly, he was sure an instant later that he had imagined it all.

He brought his dripping fingers up to her lips. "You go first."

"No, you."

Her eyes were dark and wide with some emotion he couldn't name, though it seemed to mirror his own. His mouth felt parched, empty. The need to lick the water off her fingers was irresistible. He lowered his head.

The bellowing of his name snapped him around. A man on horseback galloped toward them from the direction of Rhuddlan. As he neared, Raine saw that it was Sir Odo, in full armor. From out the corner of his eye, he saw Arianna wipe her wet fingers on her skirt, and he felt a wrenching sense of loss.

"We've trouble, lad!" The big knight reined his charger in sharply, digging up divots of marsh grass. His gaze fell

first on Arianna and his eyes grew soft with sympathy,
then he turned to Raine and his craggy face fretted into
deep lines of disapproval. Arianna was still a broken sparrow to Sir Odo, and he was still trying to protect her.

"It's those cursed Welsh vassals you acquired upon
your marriage," Sir Odo said. "Milady's cousins. They've
declared Rhos and Rhufoniog free of your suzerainty and
they're both holed up in their castles like badgers in a
burrow, daring you to come and dig them out."

Raine cursed and started toward Sir Odo, but Arianna
held him back, her fingers digging into the sleeve of his
broigne. "What will you do to them?"

"Hang them."

She sucked in a sharp breath. "But you can't! Such a
death is dishonorable—"

He pulled his arm loose from her grip. He would be
damned if he'd justify himself to her. It was always the
case when a new lord took over—those of his vassals who
were not of his own making, who owed only loose allegiance to the new lord, inevitably tested his mettle with
rebellion. If he had any hope to maintain control over his
fief, he couldn't let traitors escape without justice and
Arianna knew that.

She stepped in front of him. "You do this because they
are Welsh—"

"I do it because they are traitors."

"You could exile them instead."

"No."

Tears filled her eyes, though they did not spill over. "If
I were to ask you, for my sake—"

"No."

For once Taliesin seemed to anticipate his master's
needs, for he came trotting up on his cob, leading Raine's
black war-horse.

Raine unhooked his shield off the saddle pommel and
ran his left arm through the two leather grips on its back.
"Sir Odo, you will escort my wife back to Rhuddlan—"

"I can get there by myself."

He loosened his sword in its scabbard, then turned to her. "Aye, I've no doubt you can. But you could just as easily get yourself to Rhos and join your precious cousin." He bared his teeth at her in a grim smile. "I don't trust you, sweet wife."

He started to step into the stirrup, but his charger danced away, gnawing at the bit. Taliesin, who still had hold of the reins, tried to bring the restless steed under control.

Arianna stepped between them, heedless of the sharp, slashing hooves. "Ivor ap Gruffydd killed one brother and blinded another so that he might rule the whole of Rhufoniog after his father died. You'll not defeat him so easily, Norman."

He couldn't help it. He touched his fingers to her mouth and it trembled beneath his touch. "Would you mourn my death, Arianna?" He brushed his thumb along the length of her lower lip again, then again. "I told you once. I never lose."

But it was not Ivor ap Gruffydd he was thinking of defeating. It was her.

His hand fell to her shoulder, then to her arm, and he pulled her up against him. But when he lowered his head, she turned her face aside. He let go of her arm and caught her jaw between his long fingers, jerking her head back around again. And brought his mouth down hard on her lips in a kiss that was swift and fierce, and angry.

Thrusting her away from him, he vaulted into the saddle. He gathered up the reins, looking down at her. She stared back up at him as slowly, deliberately, she wiped the taste of him off her mouth.

He threw back his head and laughed.

Rain poured down on the open bailey. It splashed over the eaves in miniature waterfalls and gurgled in small rivers along wagon ruts and gutters. The night was as black

as the devil's heart. Gusts rattled the shutters in the bedchamber where Arianna paced, as she had paced for two
days and most of three nights, awaiting her husband's return.

She almost missed the bleat of the watchman's horn, so
loud was the storm. She threw open the shutter and the
wind snatched it from her hands, sending it crashing
against the wall like the snap of a catapult.

Leaning out the window, she peered through the dense
night and driving rain. She heard shouts and the stomping
of hooves muffled by mud, the jingle of bits and the clink
of armor, the clatter of weapons. She strained for the
sound of his voice, but heard it not.

And later, a long time later, she heard the clunk of
boots on the stairs. But it was Taliesin who burst through
the door, shouting, "Come quickly, my lady! He is sorely
wounded."

Arianna's knees crumbled, and she had to grasp the
bedpost for support. "W-where is he?"

"In the stables. I fear he is dying."

She ran into the antechamber where the chatelaine's
bag of herbs and balms was kept, along with the spice
chest and penny barrels. Why had they left him in the
stables? He must be so badly wounded they were afraid
to move him. God . . . her fingers scraped with desperate haste at the lock. *Dying.* Raine was *dying.* Damn him,
he couldn't leave her now when she had just barely gotten
to know him. When there was so much left unfinished
between them.

Clutching the medicine bag tightly to her chest, she
hurried back to the squire. "What has happened to him?"

"It's his hindquarters, my lady. They were hurling fire-
pots down on us from a mangonel, and balls of burning
pitch. One struck his hindquarters, setting his tail afire.
He's sorely burned, my lady."

"His tail afire?" Arianna flung the bag onto the bed
and seized the boy by his slender shoulders, shaking him

so hard his teeth rattled. "It's not Raine who's wounded, it's his cursed horse!"

He stared at her with wide, innocent eyes. "Did I not say so?"

"Nay, you did not say so," she said through gritted teeth, giving him another rough shake. "You deliberately misled me!"

A smug grin swept across his face. "And did not your heart stop when you thought 'twas Lord Raine who lay dying? Did you not think that if he died, then so too must you die, for life would be but a barren desert without him? Do not you realize that it is love you feel for this man, your husband—"

"It wasn't love I felt, you pox-faced idiot!" She flung the boy away from her, so violently he tripped over his own feet and landed on his rump. "It was only a wife's natural concern for her husband." She pointed a shaking finger at him where he lay sprawled in the rushes, his laughing gaze daring her to deny the truth of his words. "And if you ever breathe a word of this to your master, you blackhearted, conniving traitor, I swear by your goddess I will set the dogs on you and feed what's left to the crows!"

Snatching up the medicine bag, she ran from the room with the sound of Taliesin's cackles following after.

Arianna stopped off at the kitchens for a piggin of lard, some figs, and a costrel of soured wine. She had to carry it all in the folds of her mantle, so that by the time she reached the stables she was soaked. Once through the door she paused to catch her breath and shake off the water. The air inside was damp and smelled of wet horse and fresh dung. Straw rustled, pawed by restless hooves, and she was greeted by snorts and an occasional nicker. From a stall in the rear, where spilled a pool of lantern light, she heard a man's murmur and the wheezing, belabored breath of an animal in pain.

The soles of her shoes made no sound on the swept,

packed earth. She stopped, her hand on the stall door, and looked inside.

His *broigne* was stained dark with rainwater, his hair plastered to his skull in wet swirls. A two-day's growth of beard shadowed the lower half of his face. She thought the lines that framed his mouth seemed more deeply etched, the skin more tautly drawn across his cheekbones. He sat cross-legged on the hay-strewn floor, the destrier's head cradled in his lap. He spoke softly to the big horse and she was shocked by the tenderness she heard couched within the rough words.

"Don't you go dying on me, you old flea-bitten, mangy bag of bones." His hand stroked the thick black neck, as gentle as his voice. "I promise you'll be fed on nothing but winnowed barley for the rest of your idle, misbegotten days—"

His head snapped around at the creak of the stall door opening. The all-too-revealing pain vanished from his eyes as if they'd been shuttered. "I didn't think you'd come."

"I see no reason why a noble steed should suffer for a Norman's sins."

She knelt beside the great beast, who quieted immediately, as if he sensed her presence would bring relief. She searched her bag, assembling the herbs and other ingredients she would need. The hair had been seared from the horse's left hindquarters, leaving bare hide covered with oozing, bleeding blisters. He followed all her movements with an unblinking eye glazed with pain.

"What star was he born under?"

Raine's hand paused in its rhythmic stroking, then resumed. "I don't know. I got him as a yearling. Does it matter?"

"Of course it matters. All remedies are associated with the stars and planets and certain ones work best on those born under certain signs. Since we don't know the date and hour of his birth . . . ?" She glanced up at him to receive a negative shake of his head. "Then I shall have to use a general remedy for burns."

She mashed up the figs and mixed it with the soured wine, added dandelion and bryony root and stirred it all into the lard. Then she sprinkled in a packet of dried cow dung. She scooped up a handful of the mixture, repressing a shudder at its stink and gooey feel.

"I don't think he'll die," she said. He didn't answer, but the taut lines that bracketed his mouth relaxed a bit.

Except for an occasional shudder of his powerful muscles, the horse didn't move as Arianna smoothed the doctored lard over his burns. She could feel Raine's eyes on her, but when she cast a glance his way she saw that as usual his face was inscrutable. Yet she remembered the achingly tender sound of his voice when he had tried to soothe the stallion. He would speak that way to a woman he loved, she thought.

The horse nickered and she crooned to him, without thought:

> *"But my love I do keep for those things of my*
> *   heart . . .*
> *God and my lord and my trusty steed.' "*

"For mercy's sake, sing anything but that," Raine said.

She looked up at him in surprise. "You know the song, my lord?"

"Every bloody word of it. The first six months he squired for me, Taliesin regaled my ears with that cursed lovers' tale near every night. He only shut up after I threatened to bore a hole through his tongue with an awl."

Arianna tensed her jaw to keep from smiling. But at the same time she felt a chill. So it had not been a dream, after all. Or it had not been *her* dream. She wanted to ask Raine how the song ended, if the lady of the lake ever won her knight's love.

Instead, she daubed on the last of the lard in silence. Sitting back on her heels, she wiped her hands with straw. Raine eased the stallion's head off his lap and stretched to his feet. His fingers closed around her arm to help her up, letting go of it immediately as soon as she was. She felt the loss of his touch as a hollowness in her chest, an ache.

She swallowed, cleared her throat. "There's naught else I can do. The salve should numb his pain."

He said nothing.

After a moment he lifted his hand and smoothed back the wisps of hair that had begun to curl around her forehead as it dried. His thumb brushed her cheekbone. "There's a gentleness in you, a sweetness. . . ."

Arianna's throat felt tight, and her heart began to beat in unsteady lurches. She wanted him to hold her, she wanted it with a longing so intense it made her chest ache. But she could not forget that two days ago he had left her and ridden off to do battle with Kilydd and Ivor and if he was back already and alive, then it must mean that her cousins were dead and that he had killed them.

"What did you do to my cousins?"

He fixed her with ice-pale eyes. "Kilydd escaped. Ivor died in the fighting. I cut off his head and hanged his body by the feet from the ramparts, where it will dangle until the ravens pick clean his bones and serve notice to the rest of you Welsh that the Lord of Rhuddlan will suffer no rebellion—"

She whirled and ran for the door, but Raine overtook her in two strides. He snagged her arm, hauling her around, pinning her to the door of an empty stall.

"You are my *wife*, Arianna. That means you will be loyal to *me*, over all others. You are to give me your respect and your obedience and your worthless Welsh loyalty without question, no matter what the cost. And you are going to give me this"—he thrust his hand between her legs, cupping her sex—"when I ask for it and how I ask for it, and you're going to quit pretending not to want to give it to me because we both know damn well you do."

He went still. Her body shuddered, and her hips arched, pressing upward. His fingers curled ever so slightly, pushing soft silk into the tender folds of her mound.

She could feel her own pulse pounding in her neck. It seemed to match the steady drumming of the rain on the thatch. Away from the light, his face was shrouded in shadows, but his eyes burned. He hadn't removed his hand.

She sucked in a deep breath and the movement caused her breasts to brush against his leather *broigne*. They tightened, swelled, and there was a thick heaviness between her legs, a burning ache, where he touched her still, still. . . . The breath came out again, slow and shaky. He still hadn't removed his hand.

"You're wet for me," he said, his voice rough. "I can feel it soaking through your clothes. Wet and hot."

God's death. She wanted him. She wanted him with a wildness that frightened her. She lost herself in his eyes, eyes that turned dark and moved down to her mouth. With deliberate provocation, she wet her parted lips.

And with slow, erotic purpose he lowered his head, to take her lips in a deep and violent kiss.

He tasted hot, and smelled of wet leather and anger and lust. He grabbed her hair, pulling her head back so that he could deepen the kiss, so that he could impale her mouth with his tongue. She clung to him, digging her nails into the back of his neck. They sank together to the dirt-packed floor.

He pulled at the laces of her bliaut. Her nipples puckered in the sudden wash of cold air against her thin chainse. He lapped a nipple with his tongue, wetting the fine linen. He sucked and nibbled on it with his lips. Tearing open his braies, he took her hand and closed it around his aroused sex. She thrilled to the muffled sound of pleasure that came from deep in his throat.

"You do this to me, Arianna. Does it please you to know that you can do this to me?"

It was only fair, she thought. Only fair that she had the power to make him want her, when he had such power over her. "Do it to me," she whispered. His mouth closed over hers, flooding her with the taste of him. Heat and man and lust.

He yanked up her bliaut, running his palm up the inside of her thigh. His fingers traced the outer edge of the triangular nest of hair, down between the cheeks of her bottom, then up again, sliding deep within the soft folds of her sex, and she convulsed, her hips coming off the floor.

He tried to ruck her skirts up to her waist, but they were caught beneath her. He tore his mouth from hers, swearing. "Get undressed."

"But what if somebody—"

He didn't let her finish. He ripped her bliaut down the middle and then her chainse. She gasped, but not with shock.

"I want you naked too," she demanded.

He pulled off his clothes, flinging them to all corners of the stable. He kept his eyes riveted onto her face as he knelt between her thighs, and lifting her legs, brought them up over his shoulders. He lowered his head and kissed her low on her belly.

She thought she must tell him to stop, that it was wicked, a perversion of the French sort, but instead her fingers became entangled in his hair and she was pressing his head down low and further.

Her muscles jumped and tensed beneath his mouth and then, oh God, he slid his tongue inside her. His tongue plunged and licked. He nibbled with his teeth and sucked the nub of her between his lips, and a fire began to build inside of her, so intense, so hot, she couldn't decide if it was pain or pleasure. She only knew she didn't think she could bear it.

He played her with his tongue, making her blood sing, and there wasn't enough room inside of her for all that she felt. Heart and lungs pressed against her bones and flesh, pressed and pressed until she was sure she would explode.

"Raine!" she screamed, emptying her lungs in a guttural cry as the tremors she could no longer hold back burst over her, going on and on until she thought she was dying.

His name echoed in the stable rafters as he waited for the space of a heartbeat, his mouth pressed still between her legs. He reared up and drove into her. She cried out again because, though she was wet and hungry for him, he was huge and he had driven deep.

He leaned back so they could see where they connected, man to woman, man in woman. "You are mine, Arianna," he said, as he pressed more deeply still within her, until she thought he must surely be touching her heart. "Mine . . ."

But you're inside of me, Raine. And when you're inside of me like this, you're a part of me, you are mine.

His hand splayed her stomach, middle finger inching down and she arched upward on a gasp. He began to move within her, pulling out until only the tip of him remained, then plunging his length in again and again, harder and faster, thrusting, thrusting, thrusting while his finger stroked and stroked and stroked and the tension within her built until she couldn't bear it anymore and she broke apart inside, broke all apart into thousands of little pieces, until she saw herself in little pieces, floating like stars in a black heaven, and she felt his seed spewing deep inside her.

He collapsed on top of her, his chest heaving, his skin slick with sweat. The rain pattered on the thatch above their heads and cool air blew through the cracks in the walls. A horse nickered softly. After a while, a long, long while, she could feel her wildly thumping heart begin to slow, to quiet.

He eased his weight off her chest, bracing himself on his forearms. His sex was still inside her.

"You shouted my name," he said.

"I did not."

"You bellowed, little wife. Like a fishmonger touting her wares. And you came, hot and wet against my mouth. And then you came again when I was inside you. I felt you, gripping me."

She could feel the heat flooding her face. "It was an accident."

He grinned. "I know."

"It won't happen again."

"It will," he said.

He was growing hard inside of her again, already, moving inside of her again, already. And she wanted him again. Already. She squeezed her eyes shut, turning her head aside. But he cradled her cheeks between his hands and forced her around to face him.

"Look at me," he said.

She couldn't look at him. He would be able to see what she was feeling, all that she was feeling reflected in her eyes.

"Look at me, damn you."

She opened her eyes. His own eyes were hot and glittering. "It's not enough, Arianna," he said. "You've given me your body, but it's still not enough. I want more from you. I want more." He buried his face in her neck, arching his back, pushing, plunging, filling her. "I want all of you. . . ."

They didn't hear the stable door creak open, or see a slight figure enter. He smiled when he heard the sounds of sex, the sighs and moans and sucking kisses. And paused to watch the shadows that undulated and danced on the wall—a man's arched back, shapely legs wrapped around pumping hips.

When he left, he was whistling softly to himself. Outside the rain had stopped. The moon broke through the scudding clouds. For a moment silvery light bathed the deserted bailey, glinting off long, coppery curls. Black eyes glowed, moonstruck, and old. So very, very old.

15

It was the sort of day the poets spoke about, a day meant for love.

The rising sun flooded the sky with a blaze of gold. Thrushes, nesting in the sycamores by the river, burst into song. A pair of milk cows, grazing on the grassy banks, added their bells to the chorus, tinkling in merry harmony.

Beggars and pilgrims had gathered for alms outside the gatehouse as they did every morning. But on this day, the lady of the castle was herself administering to the poor. The almoner, with his iron scuttle full of pennies, stood to one side of her. On the other was a servant bearing a flat basket tray piled high with loaves of bread. It wasn't day-old bread, as was given out at most castles, but baked fresh just that morning. Its warm, yeasty aroma mingled with the scent of heliotropes and violets floating over the wall from the castle gardens.

The pilgrims, blessed by God, came first. They had all taken a vow not to bathe or cut their hair while on their travels. In their robes of shaggy wool and scraggly felt hats they reeked of leek soup and human sweat. Arianna dispensed the alms holding her breath.

A man with a withered arm shoved the pilgrims aside, followed by an old crone with a goiter, round and purple like a plum, protruding from her neck. A skinny girl in a tattered tunic and bare legs approached next, leading an old blind woman. Arianna folded the woman's knobbed and crooked fingers around a breadloaf and pressed coins into the thin outstretched hand of the child.

The girl looked up at Arianna with peat-brown eyes sunk into the fleshless bones of her face. "May sweet Mary's grace be upon you, my lady."

"Go with God, child," Arianna said, but her attention was focused across the river, on the hills of Rhos, where a haze hovered like a pall over the balded slopes. The hills of Rhos, where for three days Raine had been hunting her cousin.

She thought of that night in the stable, of the violence of their passion and the feelings he had unleashed inside of her. But she could not change what she was, whom she loved. Kilydd had fostered with her family when they were children; he was as much of a brother to her as Rhodri. She could not deny her family and her land, any more than she could deny herself. Her flesh, her blood were Cymry, and so was her heart.

Within the bailey the chapel bell rang, calling the faithful to midmorning mass. As the peels floated away on the heavy summer air, Arianna heard the warning rattle of a leper's bone clappers. At its dreaded sound the few pilgrims and beggars who were left quickly shuffled off.

The leper, abandoned by God, walked up the road from town. She wore the long gray robe and scarlet hood to mark her as one afflicted by the dread disease. A thin veil swathed her from head to knees so that none might have to look upon her ravaged face. The almoner and the servant were already backing toward the gate, for the leper was almost upon them now, her bone-rattle clacking. Arianna approached the poor woman alone.

"May your soul repose with God," she said, pressing a

handful of pennies into the leper's bandaged hands just as a group of horsemen burst out of the forest, galloping across the tilting fields. The leper, hampered by her trailing robe and veil, took off in a stumbling gait. Arianna stood frozen a moment. Then she picked up her skirts and ran to intercept the band of men.

Raine vaulted from the saddle before the charger had come to a complete stop. "What in God's wounds are you doing?"

"Giving alms to the . . . poor." Her voice trailed away as her gaze riveted on the man hog-tied to a cob, his arms chained behind his back. Raine was shouting at her, saying, "Christ Jesus save us. That woman was a leper!" But she barely heard him, for her thoughts were filled with the horror that her cousin Kilydd had been captured and that now he would die. Her husband would kill him.

Kilydd cocked his head up, shaking sweat-damp hair out of his face. Dirt caked the seams of his brow and cheeks, but his mouth bore a surly smile. One eye was swollen shut, but the other met her gaze, golden like summer honey, and she saw within it a questioning look, and a plea that she would save him.

She had taken an unconscious step toward the prisoner, when her path was blocked by a chest covered in black chain mail. Slowly, she lifted her head.

She had known his eyes to turn dark like that, dark like smoke and smoldering with hunger and passion. But what burned in his eyes this time was rage—hard and hot, and unforgiving.

She flinched at a sudden movement of his hand. But he was only pulling something out from beneath his *broigne*. He dangled it before her face and it caught the sunlight, blazing like a torch. His voice whipped her like a lash. "Is this familiar to you, sweet wife?"

She could not prevent her hand from shaking as she reached up to take the circlet of twisting snakes. Her fingers brushed his . . . *and the sky above them exploded*

*into flames. Fires crackled, spewing oily smoke. War cries
and screams of death. And then he was there, her beloved,
standing tall and strong before her, and he touched the
torque around her neck and he kissed her mouth and
spoke to her of forever. But she knew, because she had
seen, that this kiss would be their last. Tears blurred her
eyes, washing the world in a sea of blood, and above her
the sky burned and burned.*

In the next instant it was all gone, and forgotten by her
next breath. The metal collar was warm in her hand, but
she thought it was from having been carried against her
husband's body.

"He was going to use it to buy an army to take Rhuddlan with," Raine said, his eyes boring into her, his voice
cold, so very, very cold. "An army recruited from the
stews of Ireland. Did you know that, Arianna? But of
course you knew it, that is why you gave it to him."

Her gaze flashed to Kilydd, but he had his head bowed,
studying the ground. She had a vivid memory of him running down the stairs into the yard of the drapery, tucking
a leather bag of jangling coins into his belt. She knew she
could never explain how he came by the torque, not without implicating Christina in her lover's treachery.

But nor could she bear to have Raine think she'd so
deceived him. She laid a hand on his mailed arm. "I did
not give it to him, my lord. As God is my witness, I did
not."

Every muscle in his body grew taut, hardening against
her. He removed her hand as if her touch disgusted him.
"Don't lie to me, Arianna," he said, and for a moment
she thought pain flared in his eyes, before they turned
hard again. "At least don't lie to me."

She could only shake her head, as a sadness closed her
throat, a regret for something gone that had never been.
He did not believe her, would never believe her, nor
could she blame him that this was so.

When he turned away, as if he could no longer bear the sight of her, she cried his name.

A shudder rippled across his back. But he didn't look at her again.

"What will you do to him?"

He didn't answer her. He sat in a faldstool before the brazier and followed her every movement with narrowed, hooded eyes.

An immense sorrow swelled in Arianna's throat. She went around the bedchamber lighting more candles, trying to banish the sorrow with a blaze of light. The pungent smoke from the burning tallow made her sneeze, but her husband did not call on God to bless her.

His face was all sharp bones, impenetrable as a stone cliff. Even the flickering shadows cast by the candles gave no illusion of softness. His long fingers toyed with the filigreed stem of a wine chalice as he watched her, but he had yet to drink.

She tried to will him to raise the cup to his lips, but at the same time she knew that if he did drink she was doomed. She had laced his wine with henbane, just as she had drugged the ale that would be given to the men who guarded the keep. Later, deep in the night, when all were asleep, she would descend into the cellars and free her cousin. Raine would never forgive her for it.

But she could not watch Kilydd die. He was the son of her mother's brother, her blood, and she could not watch him die.

She drained her own cup, hoping it would inspire Raine to thirst. But all she succeeded in doing was making herself dizzy.

Suddenly she could bear the silence no longer. She knelt at his feet, her hands on his thighs. She felt a shudder pass through him before his muscles tensed. She looked up into his hard, implacable face.

"Can we not at least talk about it, my lord?"

The vertical lines that framed his mouth deepened. "What would you have me say, Arianna?"

"That you believe I had no part in this. That you don't hate me."

His lips curled slightly and he looked away from her.

She leaned forward, her breasts pressing into his knees. "Spare him, my lord, I beg of you. Imprison him if you must, or exile him. But spare his life. If not for my sake, then for us, for our marriage. For how can we ever grow to love one another if—"

She cut herself off, appalled at the words that had slipped from her mouth. He would laugh at her now, or sneer. She would deserve it for being such a fool.

But he did not laugh or sneer. His eyes, pale and blank as a pool on a still and moonlit night, impaled her so that she could not move. He stood abruptly, tangling his fingers in her hair and hauling her up with him.

He jerked her hard against his chest. Their faces were now so close she could see herself reflected in his eyes.

He stroked her cheekbone with his thumb, catching a tear that had somehow escaped without her knowing it. "Don't expect love from me, Arianna."

Her chest burned with humiliation, and she felt as if she were choking. She tried to pull away from him, but he tightened his grip.

She pushed against him, desperate now for she was about to cry, and she wouldn't be able to bear the shame of that. "Let me go."

"No," he said. "I will never let you go." He slammed his mouth down over hers in a brutal and punishing kiss.

She resisted him for a moment, pressing against his chest with her clenched fists. But she wanted this, oh how she wanted this. Her lips opened and her tongue met his. There was a desperation to their kiss. As if they both knew that to hunger like this, without pride, was wrong, would only bring them pain.

The door opened behind them and he stiffened, thrust-

ing her away so violently that she stumbled and had to
grasp the arm of the faldstool. Their eyes clashed and
held, and his burned her with his fury. The taste of him
was still hot and wet on her mouth.

Sir Odo filled the doorway. "My lord, I would speak
with you," he said, careful to keep his face blank and his
shaggy-browed eyes focused on the distant wall. "It's
most urgent."

But Raine stood unmoving, staring at her. His lips
parted slightly on an expulsion of breath. She thought of
how he had tried to punish her with that mouth, and of
how she had taken it. At last he turned to Sir Odo, jerking
his head in the direction of the door.

Sir Odo followed Raine out into the stairwell. But with
the big knight's bull-throated voice, Arianna was able to
hear it all. The Welsh crofters belonging to one of Raine's
vassals, a Norman who ruled over the lands of the valley
to the south, had been inspired by the recent rebellions,
taking up cudgels and sickles and attacking their master
while he was hunting. The knight was sorely wounded and
likely to die, and the Welsh were now terrorizing the
countryside.

Then Raine said something she couldn't hear. She wondered if he was ordering Kilydd's death.

The two men reentered the chamber. She saw no trace
on her husband's face of the sexual fire that had raged
between them only moments before. "You will remain
here and guard my lady wife," he said to the big knight,
though he looked at her. "Don't let her set one dainty
slipper outside this chamber."

Sir Odo coughed and studied the floor. "Aye, m'lord."

"And as for you, sweet wife . . . Have you ever seen
what armed knights can do to a group of peasants?"

A low, half-worded cry escaped her. "Raine, I
didn't—"

He flung his arm in the direction of a Virgin statuette
that was tucked within a corner niche. "I suggest you

spend the time praying to Our Lady, Arianna. Pray to her for the souls of those whose deaths you and your precious cousin will have caused on this night." With that he strode from the room, calling for his squire.

Arianna went to the window. She watched him mount a gray destrier that was not quite as spirited and strong as his black, and ride through the gate with a dozen of his knights. Taliesin followed behind, carrying Raine's shield and lance. Moonlight reflected off the squire's golden helmet, turning his head into a blazing torch. She watched the bobbing torch as it crossed the drawbridge and tilting fields, watched it become smaller and dimmer until it was extinguished altogether by the blackness of the forest.

She stayed at the window long after there was nothing left to see but the yellow horn of the moon and a star-filled sky. When she at last turned around she was surprised for a moment to discover Sir Odo hovering in the middle of the chamber, shifting his weight from foot to foot like a dancing bear.

"Forgive me for intruding on your privacy, my lady," he said, flushing so that his pitted face looked like a pulped berry. "But I, uh . . . milord said I was to—"

" 'Tis not your fault." Arianna patted his shoulder, giving him a smile dazzling enough to make him blink. "I should not trust me either, if I were Lord Raine. Come, Sir Odo. I challenge you to a game of tables." She took the big knight's arm and ushered him over to the faldstool, then dragged up an inlaid ivory-and-mahogany chess board. "It will be a long night and I doubt either one of us shall sleep."

Sir Odo hesitated only a moment before sinking with a sigh into the chair. His gaze fell on the carafe of wine and he wet his thick lips.

"Mayhap you are thirsty, sir," Arianna said, and smiling again, she picked up the chalice from off the floor where Raine had left it and pressed it into the knight's hand. "It is good wine, this. It comes from your King Henry's Aquitaine, or so I'm told."

"You took the devil's own time, Arianna. Half the night is gone."

Arianna bit down on a curse as she scraped her knuckles on the rusted shackles, trying to force the stiff key to turn in its hole. "A little more gratitude would not be amiss, cousin."

"Just quit nattering and get the damn thing off me."

The lock tumbled open with a groan and the chains clattered onto the cellar floor. Kilydd kicked them aside and stood, stretching the kinks out of his muscles. Arianna was already at the door, waiting. "Hurry," she whispered.

The slumbering guards slouched against the wall, their open-mouthed snores echoing in the stairwell. Kilydd paused to poke one between the ribs with his toe. "Look at him, cursed Norman whoreson—"

"God's death, Kilydd, will you hurry?"

She dashed up the narrow mural stairs. Kilydd bumped into her when she stopped abruptly to peer around the corner at the entrance to the hall. Night sounds came through the screen's passage—drunken snores and the shuffle of restless sleepers, the click and rustle of mice foraging in the rushes and the *whump-whump* of a dog's hind leg pounding the floor as he scratched his fleas.

Sucking in a deep breath, she scurried across the opening, motioning behind for Kilydd to follow. They were almost through the shell keep when one of the guards, who had stepped outside the gatehouse to relieve himself against the wall, spotted them.

Kilydd grabbed her, thrusting her into the shadows and clamping his mouth down over hers. One of his hands groped for her breast while the other rucked up her tunic, baring her thigh to the guard's leer.

She heard the man's lewd laugh through the blood that

rushed in her ears, for she hadn't had time to snatch a breath. Her head whirled and lights flashed before her eyes. She pushed against Kilydd's chest, but he only kissed her harder, mashing her lips with his teeth.

It was the oddest thing, for when she was thirteen, the same year she had rubbed gillyflower juice on her breasts to make them grow, she had promised the Virgin a wax statue in her image if Kilydd would only be seized with a wild desire to kiss her. The desire had never seized him, and her infatuation with her cousin had eventually been transferred to the beekeeper's son. Now, here, six years later, he was finally kissing her and all she felt was a desperate need to breathe.

The guard reentered the gatehouse and at last Kilydd released her. Arianna drew in a wheezing breath.

She tried to rub some feeling back into her lips. "Did you have to maul my mouth as if you were mashing grapes?"

"Hellfire, Arianna, you've been wanting me to do that to you for years. Don't tell me now you didn't like it."

"You kiss like a boy, all soft and mushy."

Kilydd snarled and shoved her in front of him. He followed in fuming silence down the long wooden stairs of the keep, across the drawbridge and into the bailey.

They paused within the black shadow cast by the hulking tower at their backs. The night was so clear that the stars looked close enough to gather in baskets, and the moon, though only a quarter full, bathed the yard with such light it seemed that hour before dawn when the sun was but a promise away.

"I couldn't drug the entire castle, and the gatehouse is crawling with guards. But you can slip out through the postern door," Arianna said, and had started forward when Kilydd seized her arm, drawing her up short.

"Give me your knife."

"I haven't got one."

His hand snaked out, reaching under her tunic and

whipping her dagger from its sheath before she could draw breath to protest. His teeth flashed white in a grin. "You forget, we had the same teachers, cousin. Now, where's that soulless bastard you call husband? I've a score to settle with him."

"He's not here."

He stroked Arianna's cheek with the flat of the blade. "You wouldn't be lying to me, would you, Arianna *geneth?* You wouldn't, perchance, be trying to save your husband's handsome neck? Do you like *his* kisses, eh? Mayhap you've grown fond of his perverted French ways."

Arianna's fingers wrapped around his wrist, pulling the knife away from her face. "He isn't here, I tell you." She gave him a little shove. "The postern door is over yon, between the farrier and the mews. Get you gone before someone else wakes up needing to piss and stumbles upon us standing here, flapping our jaws as if we've nothing better to do."

He pinched her chin between his fingers, giving it a rough shake. "Have you pease porridge for wits, woman? I can't walk all the way back to Gwynedd. I'll need a horse. I'll keep an eye out whilst you fetch one from the stables."

"God's death," she hissed at him, jerking her chin from his grasp. "I'm beginning to wish I had left you to hang."

Arianna did as he bade, anxious now only to be rid of him. She found the palfrey she'd been using during the past month—a chestnut gelding with a soft mouth and just enough fire in his disposition to make him a challenging ride. The horse felt enough like her own that it didn't seem so much of a thievery to be giving it to Kilydd. She had the horse saddled and bridled in no time. She nuzzled its neck with her cheek as she gathered up the reins.

"I just knew you'd be up to something like this."

Arianna whirled, her hand to her throat, where her thudding heart now resided. When she saw who it was, her heart pounded even harder. "What in God's mercy are you doing frightening me like that?"

Taliesin stood in her path. His long, lanky legs were spread in a stubborn stance, his full mouth turned down sulkily at the corners—looking no different than one of her brothers in a pout. But there was something strange about him. The stable was shadowed in the bit of muted moonlight that managed to filter through the cracks, but his body seemed outlined in a faint luminescence, as if a lamp burned brightly at his back. He wore a simple squire's tunic over leather leggings, but the golden helmet on his head shone as brightly as the noon sun. For a moment Arianna thought the helmet pulsed and shimmered. But she blinked and the illusion disappeared.

A low growl, like thunder, rumbled in the distance. Arianna heard the sound but her mind instantly rejected it, for the sky had been filled with stars a moment ago; there hadn't even been the thinnest wisp of a mist, let alone a cloud.

"You mustn't run away, my lady," Taliesin said.

Arianna opened her mouth to tell the boy she had no intention of running away, then slammed it shut. How else would she explain the need for a horse in the middle of the night? Her hands clenched around the leather reins. She hoped Kilydd would have the sense to stay out of sight until she had dealt with the squire. And damn Taliesin, anyway. Surely she had seen him ride out the castle gate at Raine's side, yet here he was. It was just like the wretched boy to pop up like a weasel when he was least wanted. If only she could get by him and out the stables with the horse, perhaps Kilydd could manage his own escape after that.

So she now thought to try the same trick on the squire that she'd plied so often and to such good effect on her brothers whenever they'd tried to deny her something she wanted.

She made her lips go all trembly and her eyes all soft

and imploring. "Oh, Taliesin, I do truly fear for my life. Earlier this night Lord Raine beat me." When the squire appeared unmoved, she embellished on her lie. "Beat me most cruelly so that I'm covered all over in bloody welts and near faint with pain. He thinks me a traitor along with my cousin and there was naught I could say to convince him otherwise."

All the while she spoke, Arianna nudged the horse forward. Thunder rumbled again, closer this time, and the wind had kicked up. It rattled the barn door that the squire had failed to latch behind him, and whistled around the eaves.

Taliesin's teeth had sunk into his lip and his eyes narrowed with uncertainty. Arianna had started to think her ruse was succeeding when his chin jutted stubbornly. "Lord Raine wouldn't have beaten you if you hadn't provoked him. He is not by nature a violent man."

"Not a violent man!" Arianna nearly shouted, only stopping herself in time, so the words came out in a strangled growl. They were drowned out anyway by the howl the wind was making outside. Lightning flared so brightly it penetrated through the cracks in the warped wooden walls. A loud crack of thunder followed, ripping through the air, and the palfrey shied.

Taliesin stepped in front of her. "You'll not be leaving the castle."

A gust slammed against the stables and the unlatched door flew open, banging against the wall. The palfrey reared and Arianna clung to the reins as she gaped open-mouthed at the fury of the elements outside. Lightning flashed again and she saw a milking stool go tumbling across the yard. The sky was as black as the pit of hell. The clouds suddenly opened and water poured down on the ground of the bailey turning it into an instant sea of mud.

"You can't run away in the middle of a storm," the boy

said, and his thin hand looked blue in the flashes of lightning as it closed around her arm.

At his touch a torrent of fire sizzled through Arianna, as if the power of the storm had been transferred into the boy. *Or was coming from him* . . .

Her mind shuddered at the thought even as it came to her. The light around the squire flared and shimmered, and his black eyes glittered silvery as if lit by the moon from within. Lightning flared again, crackling and spitting around them, so bright and hot it seared her skin. She screamed, instinctively flinging her hands over her head. She smelled brimstone and golden spots danced before her eyes. But when the spots faded and she focused onto Taliesin's face, she saw only a boy, who looked even more frightened than she felt.

"Glory," he said on a sharp intake of breath, his eyes wide. "That was close . . ."

She tried to calm the horse, which was now thoroughly panicked by the storm. She led it toward the open door. Taliesin kept after her with his tongue.

"If you will only pause to think, my lady. My lord is going to be very, very angry about this. It does not auger well for your future happiness, if you stab your husband on your wedding night and then run away a scarce week later. He will only have to go after you and it will put him in a foul temper." Suddenly Taliesin threw himself in front of her. "Don't do this, my lady, I beg of you."

"Let me by, boy. Else you'll only get hurt."

The squire clenched his fists and ground his teeth. "Nay, I won't try to stop you, for it isn't allowed, goddess spare me. And curse you both, for she surely hadn't reckoned on the pair of you when she made up the rules."

"What rules? What—" Arianna nearly choked on a scream as Kilydd suddenly reared up out of the swirling, howling darkness.

And thrust the dagger to the hilt between Taliesin's ribs.

The boy's eyes opened wide and light flared out of them, like twin rays from a white sun. In that same instance lightning flashed, followed by a crack of thunder so loud the earth shook. Taliesin's lids fluttered closed and he slumped forward, all jointless and floppy like a rag doll. Arianna caught him as he fell and his weight bore her down to the floor.

There was a wet, black stain on the boy's tunic and his face was pale and still, like a wax statue. Arianna held him in her arms and looked up at her cousin. He was of her blood and she had betrayed Raine because of this man. "You've killed him," she said, unable to believe it, not wanting to believe it. "You've killed Taliesin."

"Good riddance." Kilydd reached down and yanked Arianna to her feet. Taliesin's body rolled over, his arms flinging out flat like a broken crucifix. "Let's get out of here. It's pouring hard enough to drown a duck out there. We could ride right through the front gate and no one would see us."

Arianna jerked out of his grasp. "Then go, damn you." She fell back onto her knees before the body on the floor. *Taliesin . . . Oh, God, he's killed Taliesin.* Lightning flashed again, glinting wetly off the red, red blood on the boy's tunic; the tunic was drenched with blood. If he bled still, perhaps he wasn't dead yet. She should summon the castle leech. And Raine, she would get Raine. Except, Raine wasn't here. . . .

Kilydd hauled her up again, by the hair this time. "Oh, no, little cousin. You're coming with me. You'll bring me a pretty enough ransom to pay for a half-dozen armies."

Arianna swung her fist at his head, but he ducked it easily. He twisted her hair around his forearm, pulling so tightly she had to bite her lip to keep from screaming. "Don't be a fool. Raine hates me. He wouldn't give you a sow's ear to get me back."

Kilydd laughed. "He'll pay. For the sake of his pride he can do naught else."

She struggled harder, though she was helpless against his strength. "Kilydd, please. I have betrayed my husband and destroyed all hope for my marriage to save your life. Don't repay me in this way."

"Arianna, *geneth,* forgive me, but there are some things a man must do . . ." The howling wind snatched away the last of his words as he swung her around.

She saw his balled-up fist in the second before it connected with her jaw.

An icy spray that tasted of salt slashed against Arianna's face, reviving her. Kilydd had her mounted on the saddle in front of him, his arm wrapped like a smithy's vise around her waist. They were by the river. She couldn't see it, for the night was too black, but the sound of the rushing water battered her ears like the flapping wings of a million birds.

She thought Kilydd was making for the bridge that crossed from the Tegeingl into Rhos, but the storm was disorienting. The wind seemed to be coming from every direction at once, driving the rain at them in sheets that slammed against their faces, swirling up spume from the river, so that it felt as if they were being sucked into some giant tidal pool. Water burned Arianna's eyes and clogged her throat. She wondered if it were possible to drown in rain.

Lightning snaked across the sky, making it suddenly as bright as a midsummer's day. Arianna gasped, for the gentle Clwyd was now a raging torrent. The waters had burst over the banks, completely swallowing the piers and had almost reached the walls of the houses that fronted the quay.

The squat lump of the toll house wavered before them through a curtain of water. Arianna thought at first that the bridge had been washed away, for the pilings were completely underwater. But then the timbered span emerged for a moment, before being covered again by the rushing river.

Kilydd kicked his heel into the palfrey's side. The horse reared, then stumbled, and Kilydd cursed. His arm squeezed Arianna's middle, cutting off her breath.

She clawed at his smothering arm, fighting for air. The palfrey balked against crossing the bridge, then suddenly darted forward. They were nearly thrown from the saddle.

Lights pricked at Arianna's eyes as she struggled to breathe. It felt as if her chest had been crushed by a boulder. She twisted, pulling against the arm that pinned her. But Kilydd thought she was trying to get away, and tightened his grip.

The horse's hooves slipped on the wet planking of the bridge. Several inches of water swirled around his fetlocks. Suddenly the bridge heaved beneath them, as if the thing were alive and was trying to buck them off its back. The horse stumbled to his knees.

The abrupt movement broke the grasp Kilydd had around her waist, and Arianna sucked in a life-saving breath of air. Over the screech of the wind and the rushing of the blood in her ears, she heard the wail of splintering timbers. Suddenly, she was flying through the air. The world became a maelstrom of sucking, swirling water and splintering wood. Something brushed against her. She tangled her fingers in it, and thought it might be the horse's tail.

She opened her mouth to scream, and swallowed blackness instead.

16

"Gwynedd! I've come for my wife!"

The Black Dragon sat astride his charger, facing a gate banded with iron and studded with wicked brass points. Behind him ranged a mere handful of men—men who sported bloodied limbs and dented shields and determined faces. The knight's face was as blank as the bleak cliffs that surrounded him, but his challenge bounced off the rocky crags.

"Gwynedd!"

His wife watched from a window in the tower. Her hands pressed hard into the rough wood of the sill and her eyes were riveted on the knight seated tall on his charger. He was silhouetted against a fire- and blood-streaked sky, the setting sun at his back, his pennon snapping in the hot summer wind.

He had come for her. Never would she have believed his reckless pride would compel him to come after her.

Perched high like an eagle's nest on a dramatic rocky outcrop, her father's fortress of Dinas Emrys dominated the narrow defile and broken hills below. It was not the most luxurious of Owain's royal *llys,* but it was one of the more impregnable. It lay hidden within a land of haunted forests and mist-enshrouded mountains, of steep peaks all jumbled together in confusion, as if dashed to earth by the hand of an angry god.

Raine's voice slammed against the castle walls. "Gwynedd! Send down my wife!"

"I hear you, Norman." Owain, Prince of Gwynedd, emerged onto the battlements. He faced his son-in-law with his hands on his hips, his legs splayed wide. "You are far from home, Lord Raine of Rhuddlan."

The prince's scarlet mantle billowed in a sharp gust of wind and Raine's horse reared. The muscles in the knight's legs flexed as he turned the great beast in a tight circle, bringing it under control. He threw back his head, bare of any helmet, and his raven hair glinted blue under the dying rays of the sun. "Where is my wife?"

"She is here," Owain answered, his words echoing down the narrow defile.

The two men stared at each other, unblinking, faces hard with challenge.

"Send her out to me."

"Come and get her."

No knight no matter how brave and reckless could take Dinas Emrys with so few men. But the Black Dragon merely laughed. His charger danced aside, and the wedge of men in back of him parted a moment to reveal Rhodri tied to a cob. The boy was unharmed but frightened, his eyes taking up the whole of his pale face.

And though it seemed he spoke softly, Raine's voice carried clearly to Arianna in her chamber. "Aye, I will come, Owain of Gwynedd. Alone. And I will come out again. With my wife. Your son is simply here to ensure that you behave."

Arianna held her breath. She knew Raine would never harm her brother, but her father would not be as sure, could never take such a chance. Her husband sat motionless on his charger, waiting. After a long look, Owain turned and signaled to his guards. The gate groaned open and the portcullis rope screamed as it was wound around the winch, drawing up the timber and iron-fitted grill.

Raine came on alone. The sun slid behind a mountain, and the world fell into shadows just as his horse's hooves clattered across the drawbridge. Then he was inside the fortress, with her. There was nowhere left to run.

It was an irony when she thought about it, for she had never set out to run away from him in the first place.

The flooding river had thrown her up on a rocky slope, though she hadn't known it at the time. When she opened her eyes it had been to warm sunlight and the smell of wet. It was as if the whole earth had been plunged into a wash trough and left to soak. Trees dripped water and the marsh grass was so soggy it could have been wrung out into buckets. Even the wind was damp. But the sky above was clear and as blue as a field of cornflowers.

The palfrey grazed among the rocks beside her, but there was no sign of her cousin. She searched for him among the tangled brush along the river, whose silty waters still rushed madly as if fleeing from the devil. She called Kilydd's name until she was hoarse, but got only silence in return.

It was an empty silence, as if she and the horse were the only living things left on earth. The terrain was unfamiliar, which meant she had probably been carried several rods downstream from Rhuddlan. She had been dumped on the west side of the river, the wrong side for getting home.

It was strange, she realized suddenly, that she had so easily thought of Rhuddlan as home. Though it wasn't so much those bloodred walls she belonged to now, as their master. But the combination of the freakish storm and high tides had swollen the Clwyd to three times its normal girth. It would be days before the river could be crossed, save by boat.

She sat down on the bank, hugging her knees, and

looked across the river. The ground over there was much
like the ground she sat on, lumped with lichen-mottled
rocks and matted tangles of soggy weeds. So close, yet it
might as well have been on a different world.

*But then we have never been of the same world, Raine
and I,* she thought. The differences between them were
ones of the heart, and could never be bridged.

In truth, she would have to be witless to go back to him.
Because of her, his squire was most likely dead and
Kilydd set free to stir up more rebellion. Raine would
never want to see her face again, unless it was mounted
along with the rest of her head on a spike atop his castle
wall.

Nay, she would do better to go to Gwynedd and wait. If
Raine still wanted her for his wife, she would soon know
it. If he did not, which was far more likely, her father
could petition Rome to dissolve the marriage. Doubtless
they would never have to set eyes on one another again.

So she had ridden the palfrey overland to Gwynedd, to
the fortress of Dinas Emrys, where her father usually
spent the waning summer months.

She arrived in the middle of the night, exhausted and
nearly fainting from hunger. Her mother had stopped her
father's shocked questions with a single, sharp command.
She filled Arianna's cramping stomach with a mild beef
broth and bundled her aching body into a bed of warm,
soft down blankets that smelled of sandlewood. The next
morning, before the fortress awoke, Arianna had walked
down to the nearby lake to be alone, to think, and to
decide how best to explain to her father all that had happened.

A thick mist rose up from the water to wrap around the
rocky shore like scarves of gauze. A grove of the sacred
oak encircled the lake, and the gray-leafed branches,
thick with mistletoe, seemed to weep and shiver in the
wind. It was said that once, long ago, two dragons had
fought to the death in this lake. She tilted back her head

and stared up at jagged black and purple peaks that cut into a metallic sky. The wind screeched through the rocky crags. When dragons died, so it was said, they made such a sound. Sad and lonely.

Arianna shuddered, hugging herself.

"You'll catch your death out here. 'Tis damp enough to rust gold."

The mist curled around her father's booted legs as he walked toward her. He was a big man, bigger than normal in his thickly padded leather gambeson. His gray-streaked hair fell unbound around his shoulders and fluttered like a banner in the wind. The face he showed her was carved in stern, forbidding lines. He looked more the warrior that morning than a prince.

He stopped beside her. At first they didn't speak, but stared together out over the lake that was like a beaten silver platter beneath the cloudy sky. A sad ache squeezed her chest, a wrenching loneliness. Her father would tell her it was the *hiraeth* that haunted her, that wistful longing for things lost or left undone, for places far away but not forgotten. For a love and life that might have been.

A sob started deep in her chest, bursting out her throat before she could stop it. Her father turned and she went into his arms. "There, there, *fy merch,* my daughter, don't cry. I will take care of you. Your papa will take care of you."

Arianna poured out into her father's chest the story of all that happened—Kilydd's rebellion, her betrayal, the storm, Taliesin's death. And Raine, Raine, Raine . . . When she had done, she pulled away, sniffling and wiping at her nose with the sleeve of her bliaut. "He will hate me now," she said, "and who can blame him?"

Owain cupped her cheeks with his rough palms. "You are home, my daughter. You've nothing to fear from the Norman bastard, he can't touch you here."

She wrapped her fingers around his wrists and leaned

back so that she could look into his eyes. "No, Papa. You don't understand. I want to go back."

He shook his head. " 'Tis too late for that." He reached up and stroked her head, his callused fingers snagging in her hair. "Don't despair, sweetling. I can have the marriage annulled. I will find you another man, a better man this time. A Cymro, eh? One of our own."

"But the treaty—"

"The treaty be hanged. The Norman isn't likely to forgive what you have done. I will not send my daughter to her death. Not even for Wales."

She thought of all the tales she had heard of the Black Dragon. Ruthless in battle, merciless in victory. She had seen this side of him, but she had seen another side as well.

"I know Lord Raine will be angry with me, very angry. Yet I don't think he will hurt me. Not in any irreparable way."

Owain searched her face. "You are sure of this?"

Arianna wasn't sure. But for her father's peace of mind, she nodded. "I want to go back to him, Papa. Please try to fix it so that I can go back to him."

Owain turned aside. He tugged at the ends of his thick, drooping mustaches, a habit of his when he was deep in thought. "What is he like, as a man?"

"He is much like you. He is hard, yet fair. He is brave, yet he never boasts of it. He would growl at me for saying so, but at heart he is much the chivalrous knight: steadfast in his honor and loyalty, generous to those less fortunate." Though she didn't know it, a soft smile touched her lips. "And when he lets himself, he can be gentle, tender. . . ."

Owain looked askance at her, pretending to scowl. "You compliment us both, and overmuch, I think."

Smiling, she stretched up on tiptoe and kissed his weathered cheek. *"Fy nhad* . . . I compliment you, my father. I could be wrong about the Norman. But if I'm not, I think . . . I think that I could come to love him."

His heavy hands fell on her shoulders and he turned her to face him. "Ah, *geneth*. I want so much for you to be happy." He hugged her close to him, stroking her hair with his big hand, kissing the crown of her head. She ought to have been comforted, but she was not.

I want so much for you to be happy, he had said. Yet for Wales he had delivered up her and Rhodri as hostages to the English king. For Wales he had allowed his only daughter to be married to the enemy. For Wales he had sacrificed the life of one of his sons. For all his gentle ways, her father was a hard man. Hard as the granite cliffs above their heads, practical and ruthless when he had to be. There was nothing Owain of Gwynedd would not do for Wales, and the dream of freedom.

Now Arianna stood at the window of her father's *llys* and watched the coming night swallow the last of the day. He had come for her, her black knight, a man just as hard, just as practical and ruthless as her father. He was here in the great hall below. She remembered his face the way it had been when last she saw it. Hard with anger. Hot with lust. Two weeks ago she had thought she would never look upon that face again. But he was here now, he was here, he was here, and she couldn't wait a moment longer.

She paused on leaving the chamber and met the jeweled eyes of the saint's statue that guarded the door. He was Dafydd, patron saint of Wales, and the expression on his wooden face was one of stern disapproval. "I don't care," she told the saint. "I want him and I shall do anything, bear any punishment, if only he will take me back."

Raine walked down the length of the hall, his hand on his sword hilt. Members of Owain's *teulu* lounged around a central hearth, which crackled and hissed in the silence. Their swords and spears glinted in the firelight, and they watched, with narrowed eyes, as Raine approached their prince.

A bard took up his crwth and began to play, his mournful lament floating up into the smoky rafters:

> *Our hall is dark tonight,*
> *No fire, no bed.*
> *I'll weep awhile and then be silent. . . .*

His voice, Raine thought, was not near as fine as Taliesin's.

The hall was aisled like a church, with a lofty ceiling supported by double rows of wooden posts. The ancient carvings on the pillars and the paintings on the walls were like images from a nightmare: disembodied heads, writhing snakes, and monsters with forked tongues and curled claws. He walked by a mounted horned head that looked half-stag, half-human, and Raine could have sworn the beast's yellow eyes followed him, its red lips pulling back into a snarl.

Prince Owain sat on a raised dais, on a massive faldstool beneath a purple canopy. In his late fifties, the prince's face was shaped like a rache hound's, long and thin-boned and scored by lines. Gray streaked his flowing brown hair and drooping mustaches—legacies of battles fought, sacrifices made to keep his land free from the Norman conquerors. He watched Raine from beneath heavy lids that concealed his thoughts. There was a Welsh word for the elusive color of his eyes—*glas,* meaning neither green nor silver nor blue, but a little of all three. The color of the sea reflecting a cloud-whipped sky.

Raine's sharp voice snapped the prince's guard to attention, their hands flying to their swords. "Where is my wife?"

Owain said nothing, but he signaled to a servant to bring forth the mead horn. His men relaxed then, for the *hirlas* was a symbol of Welsh hospitality, brought out only for family and friends, not foes.

The servant placed the ancient blue buffalo drinking horn into the prince's hands, and he in turn passed it to Raine. The vessel was intricately carved and ornamented with silver that flashed in the rushlights.

Raine was about to drink when his gaze was caught by a movement in the smoky haze that hung over the clerestory that ran along the upper part of the hall. He saw a flash of blue silk disappear behind a pillar and a slender shadow cast on the wall behind.

"It is my daughter's intention and her wish to honor the vows of her marriage," the prince said. "Else you would not be here, in this hall, drinking from my *hirlas*, Norman." His mustaches lifted in a slightly disdainful smile. "Regardless of your threats."

"She is my wife, and she will remain my wife." Raine's lips curled in an answering sneer, though he pitched his voice for the listening ears above. "Regardless of her intentions or her wishes."

He tilted the *hirlas* and poured a good draught down his throat. The spiced, fermented honey burned as it flowed into his gut. Again his gaze flickered up to the patch of blue in the clerestory.

You are mine, Arianna. Mine.

Arianna carefully closed the door behind her. She pressed her forehead onto the smooth wood, her heart pounding so hard it hurt to breathe.

She is my wife, he had said. *And she will remain my wife.*

When, what seemed like a long time later, she heard the clink of spurs on the stairs, she backed away. And continued backing up until her legs bumped against the carved and ivory-studded bedstead.

The door flung open, bouncing off the wall, and the wooden saint rocked on his wooden feet. "Goddess save me," she gasped, drawing unconsciously on Taliesin's favorite incantation.

He filled the doorway. She searched his face for some sign of the extent of his anger, but Saint Dafydd bore more expression on his wooden countenance than Raine did on his.

He ducked his head, stepping into the room, shutting the door behind him with the heel of his boot. He took a step toward her. To Arianna's utter humiliation her stomach rumbled loudly with fear, sounding worse than a pair of rooting sows.

His gaze moved over her in an insolent manner that caused Arianna's chin to jerk into the air. She spoke to him in a fierce, proud voice. "I will not plead for forgiveness, my lord, for I would do it again. Aye, and again and again, if I must. You are my husband before God, but before God I could not watch you hang my cousin."

A draft caused the rushlights to flare, throwing light on his face and casting black shadows beneath the sharp bones of his cheeks. He looked as cruel as a painting of the devil. He took another step and she clenched her hands behind her back, her nails digging into her palms.

"Because of you," he said, and his voice was colder than midnight in the dead of winter. "Because of you, I had to leave my lands at a time when they are most vulnerable to attack. Because of you, one man is dead, and four are wounded fighting through this godforsaken country to get you back. Does this please you, Arianna? Do you think yourself worth this trouble?"

"Taliesin is dead, then? Oh, Raine, I am so sorry—"

"Sorry? Do you think *sorry* is fair exchange for a brave man's life?"

Arianna pressed her lips together and shook her head.

He spun around and took a step away from her, as if he could bear to look at her no longer. He stopped, his back moving with his jerking breaths as he fought for control.

"Taliesin isn't dead." He pivoted to face her again, and

she almost winced at the blaze of fury from his eyes. "Though you ran away and left him there to bleed his life onto a stable floor."

"I did not run away! I drugged your guard and helped Kilydd to escape, this is true. But I would have stayed to face your punishment. I am no coward, my lord. Whatever else you think of me, you must know that. I would never willingly have left that boy to die."

He stared at her down the length of the room, his expression remote but for the bitter slant of his mouth. She wanted to scream at him to say something, to do something. But when he finally did speak, her heart stopped, and then began to beat again in unsteady lurches.

"Come here," he said.

The rushes crackled beneath her feet as she walked down the length of the room. She stopped when she was right before him and made herself lift her head and look him full in the face.

The room fell so quiet that she heard a pile of embers collapse in the brazier and the scratch of mice behind the walls. There was a fine sheen of sweat on his face, and a feral smell to him—of horses and hot metal and anger. There was no feeling in those hard gray eyes. None at all.

He reached between them and grasped his sword hilt. It made a hissing sound, like shears cutting through silk, as he whipped it out the scabbard. "Kneel."

For a moment she had the wild thought that he was going to execute her with his sword. That he would cut off her head and put it on a spike where it would rot and the crows would pluck out her eyes.

And the words poured out of her before she could stop them, though immediately afterward she felt immensely foolish. "You can't kill me in my father's own house!"

His eyes widened a bit and a strange expression flitted across his face. "Kneel," he repeated in a strained voice.

Arianna didn't know whether she knelt willingly or her legs simply collapsed beneath her.

"Put out your hands."

It wasn't her head he was going to chop off, it was her hands. She would be an outcast then, doomed to go from castle to castle, begging for food with nothing but gory stubs for appendages. She'd heard how the heathen Saracens mutilated their wives for misbehavior. He must have seen it done in his travels and marked it as a most efficient way to discipline a recalcitrant wife.

She had to fight a wild impulse to laugh. "If you would but think a moment, my lord husband. I cannot fulfill my wifely duties without hands," she said. "What will you lop off when next I anger you? Mayhap my nose will be the next to go, or my feet . . ."

He almost smiled that time, she was sure of it. She knew then that whatever troubles they would face in their turbulent marriage, she trusted him. Against all logic, and because of a smile that never quite happened, she trusted the Black Dragon not to hurt her.

"Arianna, put out your hands."

Arianna held out her hands, and she was pleased to see they only shook a little.

Yet though a moment before, she had felt like laughing, now she almost wept from some feeling she couldn't name when his callused palms enveloped hers. Then he was wrapping her fingers around the hard, cold metal of his sword hilt. His deep voice drummed through her. "You will swear homage to me, Arianna."

It took a moment for her to understand. And a moment longer for the full impact of his words to sink in. *Homage to me . . . Swear homage to me . . .*

His hands tightened their grip, pressing her flesh into the hard metal. "Swear your homage to me, Arianna. Swear this and as your liege lord I will protect you, care for you, keep you safe from hunger and cold and harm. I will give you my loyalty and my trust, and you will give me yours. You will serve me and give me counsel and fight with me against the world if you must. You will stand by my side, Arianna. By my side."

If she swore her fealty, then she would be a true wife to him. She would share his bed and give birth to his babies. She would be the chatelaine of his castles, spend her life at his side—and at the end of it she would have still her honor and her pride. But she would have to surrender so much in return. She would have to place in the hands of this man, this Norman, her loyalty and her trust.

But there was no shame in the act of homage. The squire gave it to his knight, the knight to his lord, the lord to his king. It was a system of mutual respect and loyalty that had bound men for centuries. But no women had ever been asked to swear fealty, for no woman was thought to have honor or pride or any value beyond the use of her womb and the lands she could bring as her dower price. No man had ever taken his wife as his vassal, for she would be not a chattel in his eyes then, but his equal in honor. And no man surely would want to look at his woman in such a way.

No man except this one.

"Swear it, Arianna, say the words."

She opened her mouth, but nothing came out.

He started to pull away.

"Wait, my lord!" She recaptured his hands, looking up into his face with blurring eyes. "Wait. I will do it. . . . I want to do it."

Tears, hot and salty, rolled down her cheeks and into her mouth, and she didn't care. She looked down at their hands clasped together around the sword hilt—hers small and white, his larger and brown. Flesh pressing against flesh, yet it was more. It seemed as if her blood flowed into him and his into her. She could feel his heart beat within her own breast.

She spoke the simple oath of homage, changing only one word.

"I, Arianna of Gwynedd, enter into your homage and

become your . . . woman. And I swear by God and all his saints to keep faith and loyalty to you against all others."

He pulled her to her feet, and she lifted her face to receive the ritual kiss of peace. But he tossed the sword aside, and snagging his fist in her hair, he yanked her up on her toes to meet his descending mouth. His lips slanted roughly back and forth across hers, pressing hard, forcing her mouth open. He tasted of warm mead, and of himself, and Arianna thought she could kiss him forever.

He bent, and catching her behind the knees and back, he swung her off her feet. He carried her over and fell with her across the bed.

They rolled over and over, back and forth across the broad width of it, their mouths locked together in a kiss. He ended up on top, straddling her. He raised his head and looked down on her with eyes that were no longer cold and remote, but bright and hot with hunger.

"You are mine," he said. "My vassal."

"Aye, my lord. I am your vassal."

He started to lower his head to kiss her again, then stopped, casting a glance back over his shoulder. He rolled off her and strode across the room.

"Raine?"

"I don't want a pious audience for what I'm about to do," he said, turning Saint Dafydd around to face the wall.

Laughing, she welcomed him back within the circle of her arms. "Does this mean you are about to perform a French perversion on me?"

"Mayhap," he answered with the smile, that wonderful smile, that never failed to pull at her heart. "And mayhap, if you are an obedient and most deserving vassal, I will teach you how to perform a French perversion on me."

* * *

The prince of Gwynedd pressed a *hirlas* brimming with mead into Raine's hands. The knight's long brown fingers wrapped around the ancient drinking horn and he smiled at his father-in-law. There was a challenge in that smile, though no word passed between the two men. The hall quieted as they stared at one another, then Raine tilted back his head and drank of the fiery, fermented brew.

Arianna watched the muscles of his strong throat move as he swallowed. He lowered his head, wiped his mouth with the back of wrist, and met his wife's eyes down the length of the hall. His eyes glinted at her, silver in the smoky torchlight, hot and intimate as a kiss.

Arianna flushed and looked away.

She sat with her mother in front of the central hearth, skeining wool. Arianna held two short sticks between her outstretched hands. Her mother twisted and wound the yarn around the sticks, her small hands quick and deft and looking in the firelight like the fluttering white wings of doves.

Skeining wool was not a task Arianna particularly enjoyed, yet it brought back sweet memories to her, of winter afternoons spent working at household tasks, while her brothers fenced and wrestled and practiced their archery. She was always torn between wanting to join her brothers in their boisterous games and spending that precious, private time with her mother. In such a large and politically important family, one rarely got Cristyn of Gwynedd alone.

Even with a tapestried screen in front of the blaze, the roaring log fire was hot. Smoke drifted up to hang in floating clouds among the painted and gilded rafters. The *bardd teulu* wandered the hall, singing about a red dragon who lived in a cave on the great mountain, Yr Wyddfa Fawr.

"Do you remember," Cristyn said, as the last haunting notes of the bard's crwth wafted upward to mingle with the smoke. "Do you remember how when you were little, you would awake screaming in the middle of the night convinced that there was a little girl–eating dragon skulking beneath your bed?"

Arianna laughed and nodded. Oh, aye, she remembered. She remembered, too, the soft comfort of her mother's arms holding her in the dark, remembered pressing her face into her mother's neck and smelling roses. She remembered the brush of her mother's sun-bright hair, the feel of cool lips on her cheek.

"You would always give me peony seed in hot wine to put me to sleep again."

"But before that I would take your hand and together we would look under the bed. We never found a dragon."

Raine's husky voice floated down the hall. Arianna looked at him, where he sat beside her father on the dais. The wariness between the two men had eased. They were deep in conversation. The flaring tapers cast their shadows onto the wall behind them, creating a monster—a two-headed dragon.

"I think I know what you're trying to tell me," Arianna said.

Cristyn's laugh tinkled brightly, like silver chimes. "I'm pleased that you do, since I'm not sure myself what it was that I was trying to say."

"You're saying there is no such thing as a dragon, except in my mind."

Raine turned his head and again his gaze met hers. Arianna felt a warmth in her belly, a tingle, as if she were the one drinking the mead. Again she looked away.

She felt her mother's eyes upon her and glanced up. There was a faint crease between Cristyn's pale brows; it was a look she wore when she was worried. In that one moment, Arianna felt a kinship with the older woman that went beyond blood. A kinship that went back to the first woman that walked the earth . . . and loved a man.

There had never been any doubt in Arianna's mind of the fierce love her parents bore for one another. Cristyn had never been too busy to spare a word or caress for any of her children and stepchildren, but they had all known that Owain was the sun of her world. When he was home she blossomed like a bright gold sunflower; when he was gone she faded and drooped.

Cristyn removed the sticks and passed one end of the skein of wool yarn through the loop at the other. Arianna looked down at her mother's bent head. "When you first married Papa—did you love him?"

Cristyn glanced up. There was a softness to her face now, as if Arianna saw her through a veil of mist. "Love him?" Cristyn said. "Oh, no. Not at all, for I scarcely knew him and he frightened me. He seemed so distant, so severe. Yet I wanted him to bed me, almost from the first moment he touched me." She stared into the distance, a faint smile on her lips. "It was like an oil fire—hot, raging, melting. Impossible to put out by any ordinary means."

Arianna was disconcerted by this revelation, and a little shocked. She turned aside, unable suddenly to meet her mother's eyes.

Her gaze was drawn up to the dais. Her father sprawled in his high seat, one hand draped over the chair's carved back, the other nursing the mead horn. Raine laughed at something her father said. His hands flashed with surprising grace, dancing through the air as if he waved an imaginary sword. No doubt he was reliving one of his many tournaments.

She could still feel a warm, wet tenderness between her thighs, the legacy of his lovemaking. She tried to picture her parents doing the things that she and Raine had done that afternoon, but her mind shied away from the thought. Before, she had always looked at Owain and Cristyn of Gwynedd from the perspective of being their daughter, and they were like gods to her, all wise and invincible. Now she suddenly saw them as human, beset with human frailties, driven by human passions.

Owain stood up suddenly and bellowed down the

length of the hall. "Cristyn, my love! Rhuddlan and I are going raiding! Merfyn ap Hywel has a herd of sheep that I've had my eye on all this summer. Plump sheep they are, and with fleece white and thick as clotted cream."

The two battle-hardened warriors helped each other step down from the dais as if it were the sheer face of Yr Wyddfa Fawr itself that they were descending. They walked very slowly and carefully toward the hearth, but stools and benches took a malevolent pleasure in leaping up into their path, so that there was a lot of banging and swearing before they finally arrived, safe but breathless, at the hearth.

Owain laughed and the fumes of his meady breath nearly made Arianna swoon. "A rogue like Merfyn doesn't deserve such a nice herd of sheep. 'Tis against the laws of nature, is it not, Rhuddlan?"

He gave Raine such a hearty slap on his back that the younger man swayed on his feet. Raine was smiling lazily at Arianna, undressing her with hot, and slightly unfocused, eyes.

"The Norman and I," Owain proclaimed loudly, "have decided that it is our duty as Christian knights to restore order to the natural . . . uh . . . order of things."

They didn't wait for permission to leave, but began to pick their way through the sleeping servants and warriors who had bedded down in the aisles of the hall.

"Do not forget your sword and buckler, husband," Cristyn called out after him.

Arianna turned on her mother. "How can you encourage him in this foolishness? They are so drunk they will never be able to sit a horse, let alone ride all the way into Llyn and do battle with Merfyn ap Hywel."

"If I forbid him to go, he will turn stubborn. His manly pride will demand that he prove to your Norman husband that the Prince of Gwynedd wears the braies in this hall." She lifted her slim shoulders in a shrug. "Besides, they won't get far."

Arianna scowled after them. "They are behaving like children."

"That is the way of men. Girls grow up, you see. We become wives and then mothers. But men remain forever at heart little boys. A wise wife learns when to humor her man's childish whims. And when not to."

There was a firm set to her mother's small pointed chin that Arianna had never noticed before. Arianna couldn't remember many arguments between her parents, but on the few occasions when her mother had gone nose to nose with her father, it was Owain, the mighty Prince of Gwynedd, who had backed down. Arianna made a resolution that before she left Dinas Emrys with Raine, she would speak with her mother and learn all she could about how to tame a black dragon.

Suddenly a loud splash disturbed the quiet of the hall, followed by a string of bloodcurdling curses.

"God's death . . ." Arianna stifled a giggle with her hand. "They've fallen into the moat!"

Mother and daughter carefully laid aside their skeins of yarn and went to the rescue of their men. They went slowly, as if taking a stroll on their way to Mass. By the time they arrived at the gatehouse, some of Owain's *teulu* had already fetched a rope and were preparing to haul the men out of the slimy water. Putting a finger to her lips, Cristyn relieved them of the rope and waved them inside.

It was a dark night, deep and still, with only a few fading stars and a sliver of a moon to cast any light. Cristyn, looking small and slender as a girl, danced over to the thick chain that raised and lowered the drawbridge. She slung the coil of rope over the chain, but she didn't lower it.

"What in God's wounds is happening up there?" Owain bellowed. "Where did everybody go? We're freezing down here, man. And it stinks!"

Grasping the chain with one hand and raising her skirts with the other, Cristyn lowered herself so that she was sitting on the edge of the bridge, her legs swinging free. Smiling to herself, Arianna did the same. The moat stank of stagnant water and rot. Fortunately for the two warriors now floating down there in the sludge, the castle's sewage did not drain into the moat, but was carried away instead by an underground stream within the bailey.

Cristyn put her weight on her outstretched arms and leaned down to peer into the darkness. "Owain, my love. Why have you decided to go swimming this time of night? I thought 'twas your intention to steal Merfyn's sheep."

"Cristyn, sweetling, is that you? Do not natter at me, woman. Fetch a rope and be quick about it. And for the Virgin's sake, cover up your legs!"

Cristyn pulled her skirts up higher, revealing the tops of her stockings. The pale skin of her knees were like two silver oranges in the dim moonlight. "It seems these big, brave knights need our help, daughter. Shall we give it to them?"

Arianna looked down into the moat, but, although she could hear a lot of splashing going on, she could see nothing. "Nay, why should we? If they are such big, brave knights, they ought to be able to help themselves."

Raine's voice drifted up to her from out of the black hole beneath her feet. "Arianna, my sweet vassal. Remember this afternoon and the oath you gave me."

Arianna remembered the afternoon, all of the afternoon. In truth, she felt hot and weak and slightly dizzy whenever she thought of that afternoon. "'Tis my thought," she said to her mother, though she spoke loud enough to be heard above all the splashing and cursing, "that a night in the moat will go far in teaching them both that to go a-raiding with a belly and a head full of mead is a dangerous undertaking."

"Arianna!" Raine roared, abandoning all pretense of the gentle lover.

Her father spoke in a wheedling tone that she'd never heard before. "Cristyn, wife of my heart, love of my life

. . . surely you do not mean to leave me to drown?"
When this elicited no response, he changed tactics.
"Woman, if you don't help us out this instant, when I do
get out I will make you very, very sorry."

Cristyn began to hum a lilting little song. From below
there came a lot of loud whispering, like the rustle of
crows in a corn field. The men were no doubt plotting
their next strategy. Arianna wondered whether it would
take the form of promises or threats.

"Arianna, are you listening?" Raine demanded.

Arianna swung her legs. "Very well, I'm listening. Since
I've nothing better to do."

"Your father informs me that a wife's willful disobedience of her lord and husband—a disobedience that results
in an endangerment of his life and health—is on the list.
On the *list*, Arianna. If you continue in this defiance, it
will be my veriest duty to punish you, and you must grant
your permission for this punishment. For such is the law
and you cannot deny it."

"What list does he speak of?" asked Cristyn. "What
law?"

Arianna was grateful that the dark hid the sudden color
that flooded her face. "It must be the mead talking," she
said to her mother. She pretended to study her nails,
though it was so dark she could barely see her hand.
"Your threats are like needles pricking the hide of a water
buffalo, husband. I feel not a thing. In truth, I believe I
will return to the hall now and resume my skeining."

Mother and daughter stood up and made a great show
of leaving, rattling the suspension chain and clomping on
the hewn-log decking of the bridge. More bellows and
threats echoed up from below. At the gate they paused
and pretended to reconsider.

"I suppose," Cristyn said, "much though they deserve
it, it would be unnecessarily cruel to leave them floating in
the moat for the entire night."

"Mayhap you're right," Arianna said. "A guard could

mistake Raine for a Norman rogue and put an arrow in his arse."

Raine's voice came at her out of the dark. It sounded as if he were speaking through his teeth. "That is not at all amusing, little wife."

Arianna smothered a laugh with her hand and met her mother's brimming eyes. "Shall I fetch the rope?"

"I suppose . . ." Cristyn heaved a sigh of defeat, like a woman moved by pity in spite of her better judgment. "Else they will likely become waterlogged and drown afore morning."

They tied one end of the rope to the chain and lowered the other into the moat. After a brief argument about who was to go first—during which Raine pointed out that age went before youth and Owain insisted that youth must go before beauty—the rope suddenly pulled taut as it took a man's weight. Arianna felt a quiver of fear in her stomach as it occurred to her that she and her mother might have gone a little too far with their jest.

Owain's head came over the edge of the bridge, followed by the rest of him. He looked like some slimy creature that had crawled out of a bog. Rearing up, he made a grab for his wife. "Come here, woman, and give me a kiss."

Mother and daughter both ran off, shrieking and laughing, for the safety of the hall.

Owain turned his head aside and spat moat water out of his mouth. "Women!"

"Can't live with 'em, can't live without 'em." Raine hauled himself onto the bridge. He shook his head like a wet dog and wiped the reeking slime off his face. "The first man to say that was probably Adam."

Owain snorted a laugh. "Aye, no doubt. No doubt." He bent over to wring out the skirt of his tunic, looking up through slanted eyes at the Norman, his enemy. The knight's pale eyes were focused on the gate through which Arianna had disappeared. Owain straightened and laid a heavy hand on the younger man's shoulder. "You will cherish her, you will cherish my Arianna?"

Raine stiffened, but he did not shrug off his father-in-law's hand. "She will come to no harm as my wife," he said.

It was not precisely the promise that Owain had wanted, but it would do.

For he had seen the way the Norman looked at his daughter. Love did not make a man look at a woman like that. But hunger did. He had felt that sort of hunger for Cristyn the first time he laid eyes on her, felt it still after nearly twenty-five years. How well he knew that out of such a hunger, love could grow.

Sunlight glinted behind Arianna's closed lids, and she opened them slowly onto the gilt-spangled canopy of her marriage bed. She stretched out her hand, but the place beside her was empty. She turned over, pressing her face into the sheet, breathing deeply of his smell.

Their marriage wasn't perfect—far from it. But in the week that had passed since they'd left her father's *llys* and come home to Rhuddlan, they had reached an accommodation. Aye, accommodation was the word for it. They had laughed and made love and spoken truths in the quiet of the night that neither one of them quite yet believed in the light of day. They were like two feuding enemies, she thought, enemies who had somehow grown fond of each other and weary of the fight. So they had buried their swords and sat down together to drink a cup of mead and tell tales and laugh together. And perhaps . . . perhaps become friends.

He brought her with him now when he toured his commotes. The land ruled by the Lord of Rhuddlan encompassed thick forests and bleak moorlands, all rock and coarse grass, and wild salt marshes where wading birds bred among empty tidal sands. But there were also rich open fields of oats and barley and rye, all patched together haphazardly like a ragpicker's scraps, and lumpish, cross-cropped hills dotted with flocks of wool-bearing sheep.

"It must please you to know that all of this is yours," she had said one day as they stood on the crest of a hill admiring the view of the wide, rich green valley that bordered the band of blue water that was the river Clwyd.

"And yours," had been his response, and she realized with a warm jolt of surprise that his were not empty words. He saw the Honor of Rhuddlan as hers to share— both in the bounty and the responsibility that came from ruling.

She stretched now, curling her toes. She really should be getting up, before Raine came to get her, calling her a slug-a-bed. They were to spend the day together supervising the harvest. Already the breeze coming through the open window smelled sweet from the freshly mown grain.

She had just swung her feet over the side of the bed, when a horrible nausea gripped her. She knelt in the rushes beside the bed, and was violently sick into the chamber pot. Breathing deeply, afraid for the moment to move, she sat hunched over and tried to will the nausea to pass.

A pair of lanky legs appeared before her. Her blurred gaze moved up the long length of them until it rested on a white face surrounded by locks of fiery red hair and an impish grin.

"What are you doing on the floor, my lady?"

"What does it look like I'm doing, you fool?" Embarrassed at having that wretched squire catch her in so undignified a position, Arianna stumbled to her feet. "And what are you doing up and about? You'll rupture your wound."

One moment, it seemed, she was talking and taking a step toward the squire, and the next thing she knew she was lying on the bed and Taliesin sat beside her with a bowl, her golden mazer, in his lap. He leaned over to wipe off her face with a dampened cloth and a soothing heat seemed to flow into her, over her, as if she were sliding into a tub of warm, oily water. She looked deep into black eyes, eyes that glowed, moonlit from within.

He is no squire, she thought. No human boy could have survived such a wound she saw Kilydd give him, survive and then be up and about causing mischief in so short a time. And those eyes, something in his eyes . . .

"You fainted, milady. Nothing to worry about." The voice was Taliesin's, clear, melodic, the trained voice of a bard. But the eyes, the eyes belonged to someone else, somewhere else. . . .

She squeezed her own eyes shut. Her stomach felt so queasy. She swallowed around the sour taste in her mouth and tried to ignore her pounding head.

"Do you need the chamber pot again, my lady?" Taliesin said.

Arianna's lids slowly opened. "I fear that some Norman has tried to poison me."

His mobile lips curled into a smile, his black eyes glittered, brightening. "Some Norman has certainly made you ill, milady. You are with child."

"I can't be."

His eyes flashed brighter. "Don't be foolish, girl. Of course you can be." The light in his eyes faded. He looked himself again, all mischievous boy. His face bore a smug look. "My lord will be pleased," he said.

With child. Arianna pressed her hand against her womb. She was going to have a baby. Raine's baby.

Emotions crowded in on her, so many and so fast that she couldn't settle on any one—joy, fear, excitement. *Baby. I'm going to have a baby.*

She became aware of Taliesin's cheerful chatter as he danced around the room. " 'Tis morning sickness you've got. You won't die from it, you only think you will. It's a good sign actually. It means the babe is taking."

He appeared before her again, a blackjack mug in his

hand. He helped her to sit, tilting the leather mug to her lips. "This should help—it's rhubarb, licorice, and wood-bane. The woodbane tastes awful, I fear. The licorice helps to disguise it some, but not a lot."

Arianna swallowed the draught, grimacing at its bitter, oily taste. He started to pull the mug away, but she grabbed his hand. "Taliesin, you will leave me to tell my lord husband of this."

"Of course, my lady. That pleasure should be yours alone."

He flashed a ravishing smile, patting her cheek as if he were soothing a child. She couldn't help smiling back at him. "You look mighty pleased with yourself, boy. You'd think this was all your doing."

A mischievous, secretive look came into his eyes, and they shimmered, like twin stars in the blackest of nights. "Goddess be with you," he whispered.

He sauntered from the room, humming a lilting tune. At the door he turned and, grinning broadly, put words to the music. It wasn't a lullaby, as she had thought, but a love song.

> *"Lady, take me, body and heart,*
> *And keep me for your one true love . . ."*

The door swung shut on Taliesin's sweet, liquid voice. *You are with child.* Raine would be pleased when she told him. Oh, more than pleased. It was what he wanted most, the culmination of all his ambitions.

She rubbed her stomach. How strange it seemed to think that at this very moment a babe was growing within her. How strange and how wondrous. She tipped her head, looking down at her flat abdomen, and she tried to picture it swollen with child. She saw a fat, waddling Ari-anna with a belly shaped like an ale barrel, and she giggled. She pictured herself with a babe in her arms, suckling at her breasts, and her smile softened.

With slow, careful movements, Arianna tried sitting up. She felt weak and heavy, but she was no longer nauseated. The golden mazer sat beside her on the bed where Taliesin had left it. She pulled it into her lap, cradling it in her palms. She looked down, but saw only her own face reflected back to her from the clear flat surface of the water.

She dipped her finger in the water. The reflection shattered and disappeared. She didn't care if the magic bowl had suddenly decided to guard its secrets. She was living her future.

She had bred the Norman a son and all she could feel was joy.

17

Raine leaned on one outstretched arm, trying to hold a piece of curling parchment flat on the table, while at the same time adding a sum by pushing beads up the wires of an abacus. One corner of his mouth turned down in a frown and his hair looked mussed, as if just moments ago he had raked it with impatient fingers.

Arianna stood in the door of the antechamber. The sight of him caused the oddest sensation in the pit of her stomach, a sort of vibration, like a loud hum in a hollow cave, and a compulsion to touch him. She wanted to smooth the hair back out of his eyes and kiss his mouth into softness. But he had a visitor.

She started to turn away, but she must have made some sound, for Raine looked up. "Arianna . . . Come here. Have you met Simon?"

A fat, bandy-legged man waddled forward to greet her. He was richly dressed and sported a fancy beard that had been waxed and tufted and then interwoven with gold threads. The pointed yellow hat he wore, along with the big circle of saffron-colored cloth sewn on his breast, marked him as a Jew.

"Ah, the lovely Lady Arianna," he said, with a flourishing bow. His breath smelled sweet, of fennel seeds. "Your reputation does not do you justice, my lady, for your brow is whiter than the foxglove, your cheeks do glow pinker than apple blossoms. And your lips . . . ah, your lips are redder than . . . than summer poppies!" he exclaimed, looking pleased with his floral metaphors.

"Red as the bristles on an old sow's ear, more like," Raine muttered out the side of his mouth. Laughter gurgled up Arianna's throat, but she caught it between her teeth.

"Skin whiter than a fish's belly."

Another snicker almost escaped out of Arianna's pressed lips. She thumped her husband in the stomach with her elbow, and he hacked and wheezed and sounded as if he were choking to death.

Simon turned worried eyes onto his host. "My Lord Raine, that cough of yours is fierce. Might I suggest a poultice made from the fat of a hanged man to purge your chest. These summer agues have been known to turn deadly."

Arianna couldn't help herself, she laughed, for though the remedy was indeed a common one—when a hanged man was available—her fearless knight had turned quite pale at the suggestion. Thinking she might have affronted their guest, she quickly said, "I was admiring your beard, good sir."

"Were you?" He stroked the object with obvious pride. "It's all the fashion at the French court, they say. Though no man's beard is allowed to be more magnificent than the king's, of course. It wouldn't be good politics." He boomed a laugh that was rich and deep as the beat of a kettledrum. Arianna was shocked to see gold in his teeth as well.

She tried not to stare rudely at the man as he took his leave, but she had never met one of the Jewish race before. Except for the gold in his beard and his teeth, the man appeared quite ordinary, rather nice, in truth, with

his compliments and his remedies. Hardly the sort to kid-
nap Christian babies for sacrifice in heretical rites.

But he did lend money at interest, which made him a
usurer and thereby a sinner in the eyes of Holy Church,
and Arianna wondered what sort of dealings Raine could
have with the man.

Simon the Jew let out another burst of hearty laughter.
Raine strode back to the table to pick up the abacus. He
flipped more beads with fingers that were smudged with
charcoal and frowned some more. But she was beginning
to know him better now, to know that the tautness of the
skin over his cheekbones and the sooty color to his eyes
meant he was excited about something. His brow creased
in concentration, and he bit his lower lip, and she suddenly felt the most incredible desire that he would kiss
her. Pregnancy must be affecting her wits as well as her
stomach.

"Have you borrowed coin from the moneylender, my
lord?"

"Aye, and I had to hock my soul in the process, the
devil take the man."

At Arianna's gasp of shock, Raine laughed, tossing the
counting board back onto the table. "I was only jesting,
Arianna. In truth, Simon's rate of interest was more than
fair."

"Are we so poor then, that we must borrow gold to
live? Perhaps I could ask my father—"

He put his fingers to her mouth. His touch was warm
and soft. It was all she could do not to purse her lips
against them. "We are not poor. I have borrowed coin
from the Jew to finance the building of a castle."

He let his hand fall and her mouth felt naked now. "A
castle? You are going to build a new castle? Here at
Rhuddlan? But why?"

"If you would quit spitting questions at me like peas
out a blowpipe, I will show you." He led her over to the
trestle table where a thin sheet of vellum lay curling on

the scarred surface. Handling the parchment with care, for it was dry and crackling with age, she held it up to the cresset lamp that swung overhead. The vellum smelled of must and mildew, like clothes that had been packed away into a chest and forgotten.

"The keep here at Rhuddlan is outdated," he said, leaning over her shoulder, so that she felt his breath on her neck. "It's better than the old wooden fortress of the Conqueror's time, but there have been great improvements in castle-building in the last ten years. The infidels especially are good at fortifications. I learned a lot from them when I was on Crusade. What you have in your hands is but one example of the kind of castle I could build here at Rhuddlan."

The parchment was covered with a complicated drawing rendered in confusing black lines. Then, slowly, the lines took shape, became a castle. A glorious, impregnable castle with round towers, bristling with crenellations. And from the top of the highest turret a banner flew—a black dragon on a bloodred field.

She blinked and the castle vanished, became fading black lines again. "Did you acquire this map in the Holy Land then?"

Raine took the parchment from her and returned it to the table. "It's called a design. And, aye, I got it from a Saracen architect who once built a castle such as this for the great sultan Nureddin."

She pushed out her lower lip into a deliberate pout. "Aye, I have heard tales of your brave deeds whilst on Crusade, my lord, and I have oft thought how grossly unfair it all is."

His gaze had fastened onto her mouth and his head started to dip . . . then his brows snapped up. "What isn't fair?"

"That simply because you have taken the Cross and kissed the Holy Sepulcher and killed the infidel for Christ, you are now assured of salvation. Which means that after we are dead, you—whose soul is doubtless much blacker than mine—will be reposing on a golden chair in heaven. Whilst I shall have to suffer thousands upon thousands of years in purgatory. It isn't fair."

His lips twitched and Arianna leaned forward, her eyes half-closed. "I believe one has to die while on Crusade to warrant the guarantee of heaven," he said. "But if I do reach the pearly gates before you, perhaps I can intercede with the saints on your behalf. Are you angling for a kiss, wife?"

She straightened with a snap, her cheeks burning. "Don't be a dolt, Raine."

"Have you bitten down on something sour then? Perhaps that's why your lips keep puckering like a hungry fish's."

She turned away, feeling hot, and wishing herself in a deep, deep hole somewhere on the other side of the world. She pretended to be fascinated with the infidel's drawing. There was writing in one corner, beneath the castle's southern fortifications. But it was unlike any writing she had ever seen, not script or even block letters, but more like bird tracks left on a crust of snow.

"This writing is most strange. What does it say?"

When he didn't answer, she glanced up at him. For some reason the sweet, teasing laughter they had been sharing a moment ago was gone, and his face had hardened against her.

"It's in Arabic, my lady," Taliesin said, appearing suddenly at the door. "Though he speaks some of the infidel tongue, my lord does not read it." The squire had his crwth and bow tucked under his arm and he was grinning, as if they shared a secret.

The boy sauntered into the room without invitation. He hooked his hip onto the table and propped the lower bout of the crwth on his thigh. "So, you have borrowed money from Simon the Jew and you are now all set to build your castle. Have you given thought, my lord, of where you will dig the stone to build it with?"

"There is a fine granite quarry on the abbey lands of St. Asap," Arianna said. "Though the monks are very jealous of its use."

Taliesin giggled. "Aye, the Bishop of St. Asap once shot an arrow smack into the arse of the Earl of Shrewsbury himself when the man tried to raid stone from the quarry. 'Twas in the dead of a moonless night, blacker than a witch's soul, so mayhap the bishop was aiming for Shrewsbury's heart and missed. Nay, my lady is right. Not only is the Bishop of St. Asap a handy man with the longbow, he is very hard to deal with when it comes to matters of his quarry." The squire winked at Arianna. "For one thing, he is Welsh. And you know how unreasonable the Welsh can be."

Raine grunted in agreement. Arianna grunted back at him. Raine didn't quite smile, but the corners of his eyes crinkled.

Taliesin's slim fingers plucked at the crwth's strings, creating a mournful wail. "Might I suggest a bribe, my lord."

Raine was still staring at Arianna, and he took a moment to respond. "What and how much?"

"Oh, a couple cartloads of grain should suffice. Though I should not try to deal with him myself, my lord, were I you. He hates most men, does the Bishop of St. Asap, but Normans do top his list of those he considers most vile. He has small regard for women, too, I fear, they being the inferior of the species and put upon earth in the way of tempting men to sin with their seducing ways. But the Lady Arianna, as she is of the noble blood of Gwynedd, he at least does tolerate. I suggest you send your lady wife to negotiate in your stead, my lord. With three cartloads of grain and Sir Odo and a troop of knights as escort."

The face Raine turned on her belonged to the black knight of her vision—hard, flint-gray eyes and a ruthless

set to his mouth. Yet his voice, when he spoke, was oddly
gentle. "Would you do this for me, Arianna?"

Her throat tightened, and to her shock a rush of tears
blurred her eyes. "If you wish it, my lord husband," she
finally managed.

Taliesin lowered his head and a swatch of red hair fell
forward to hide his secret smile. He tucked the crwth beneath his chin and pulled the bow across the strings.
"Now that we have that settled, I should like to play
something, my lord. A love song, mayhap?"

Raine growled a curse. "As long as it is not that damna-
ble tale about that fool wench who dwells in a lake and
that even bigger fool of knight who tries to woo her bare-
arsed naked."

Arianna smothered a laugh with her hand, while
Taliesin sighed and his face, his whole body, seemed to
wilt like a day-old nosegay. But he drew back the bow
again. The crwth erupted into a joyous spurt of sound as
he launched into a wicked ditty about a bishop who was
unholy fond of the baker's wife.

Raine rolled up the drawing of his castle, tying it with a
frayed riband. Arianna studied his averted profile, thinking about the child she carried in her belly. Would he
have his father's thin nose and sharp cheekbones, that
raven black hair and those pale, pale eyes? She had
searched him out to tell him about the child, but she decided now to wait until after she returned from St. Asap,
for if he knew of her pregnancy doubtless he would not
let her go. She wanted this opportunity to show how she
was truly his vassal now, that his trust in her was not
misplaced.

Yet she felt a niggling unease about the trip. She wondered if both she and Raine had been nudged into the
plan by that wretched, interfering squire, the way cows
are led to a feeding trough. Just as he had so easily ma-
neuvered her into planning that birthday disaster. Oh, he
had protested his innocence most soulfully afterward. In

truth, he had wept copious tears and fallen on his knees to beg her forgiveness. But she had never quite believed that it had all been some dreadful misunderstanding, as he had claimed.

But the plan did make logical sense—Raine would need the St. Asap stone for his castle and she, better than anyone else at Rhuddlan, would be able to negotiate with the intractable bishop for the rights to quarry there. After all, she had been the one to bring up the existence of the stone in the first place. With Sir Odo and a half-dozen knights as an escort, what could possibly go wrong?

No sooner had they set out on the road than it began to drizzle. Though Arianna checked the oiled leather tarpaulins that covered the carts a dozen times, still she fretted that leaks and seeping damp would ruin her cargo. Before long, mud coated her palfrey's legs to the hocks and the knights' armor shone slick with the damp. The rain was cold and smelled of winter.

At first they passed by scattered hamlets, the glow of their fires burning in the murk. But the stubbled fields with their grazing cattle soon gave way to wild and empty moorlands and stretches of black forest. The road narrowed until there was barely enough room for the carts to pass. Arianna's palfrey crowded into Sir Odo's destrier and their wooden stirrups knocked.

The big knight grinned, his teeth flashing white in the dim light. "Miserable weather, my lady."

Arianna tilted her head back to catch the moisture on her tongue. It tasted sweet. "I've always liked the rain."

"That's 'cause you've never had to fight in it." He shrugged, rubbing a pawlike hand over his face. "I mean, it's devilishly difficult to grip a sword when your hand is slick as a whore's—er, as a . . . God's wounds!" Sir Odo's jowls had turned the dark purple color of an overripe apple.

Arianna hid a smile. They entered a gorge, silent and

dark as a church, strangled with rocks and thick tangled
oak and mountain ash that crowded out what little light
pierced through the dripping clouds. The trees would be
turning soon, she thought. There was an old waxy look to
the fading leaves.

"It doesn't rain much in the Holy Land, I'm told," she
said.

Sir Odo heaved a sigh of relief and plunged gratefully
into this safer topic, as their horses plunged deeper into
the gorge. "Nay, it is the armpit of hell, the Levant, for all
that it is the birthplace of Christ. Hot enough to blister
wood." He cast her a sheepish smile. "Well, a soldier is
never content with his lot, my lady."

Is anyone? Arianna wondered. She had felt many
things since the black knight had charged through the
whirling mists of her vision and into her life—felt fear and
excitement and the fiercest passion. But never had she
thought herself to be content. Yet it was there, this contentment, wrapped around her heart, soft and warm like a
thick cloak. It must have been there all along, waiting,
like a flower buried deep under snow that slowly takes
root as it waits for spring.

*Do I love him? Nay, it is too soon. But I want him and
need him, oh aye, I do need him, his touch, his kisses, his
thick, hard rod thrusting inside of me, filling me, my
woman's womb . . . my woman's heart.*

Sighing softly, she wrapped her mantle tighter against
the cold and the wet. A bare two months ago she could
not envision how she would ever make a life with him,
now she could not imagine a life without him.

The drizzle had turned into a swirling mist. Vapory tendrils snaked low along the ground, wrapping around the
gnarled and knotty trunks and curling among mold-spot-
ted rocks. One of the men called out, pointing to a hawk
that floated overhead, wings outstretched like dark gray
banners against the lighter gray of the sky.

Just then a hare broke cover from a clump of bracken,

and Arianna's horse shied, pulling at the bit. The circling hawk spotted the hare. Her flight seemed to stall in the air, then she dove with sudden, deadly swiftness, striking her prey with clenched talons. The knights, avid hunters all, had paused to watch and sighed in unison at the beauty of the kill.

Arianna was about to urge her horse forward again when something heavy fell from the tree boughs overhead and landed on the cantle of her saddle. She grasped the palfrey's mane to keep from falling as it skittered beneath the sudden added weight, its hooves sliding on the rain-slick leaves and stones. She opened her mouth to scream, and held it open as the blade of a knife bit into her side.

A man rode out from among the oaks, followed by another on foot and then another. Until the carts and their small band were surrounded by men with longbows nocked and pulled. Only the one man was mounted. He clicked his tongue, urging his horse forward. He had smeared the black mud of Wales on his exposed skin, the better to blend into the forest, and his tawny hair, worn long and free, was wet and matted with twigs and leaves.

"Kilydd!" Arianna cried.

"Leave your swords to lie in their scabbards, and keep your hands where I can see them," he said, and his mustaches lifted in a grim smile.

A man's cackle grated in Arianna's ear and a glob of spit sailed past her cheek. "Aye, ye do as me lord says, ye coddled-livered, white-bellied sons of Norman whores. Or answer to the Black Dragon as to how ye let his wife get her guts spilt." As if to punctuate the point, the knife in Arianna's side pressed harder, breaking the skin.

She could see a dark, hairy hand, caked with dirt and black, broken nails. She could feel the bellowing motion of heavy breathing as the hard leather of a gambeson pumped against her back. He smelled rank—of fish and sour ale and layer upon layer of human sweat.

"Kilydd," she said again, more softly this time.

Her cousin's gambeson had a tear in it and was losing its stuffing. His cheeks were hollowed and creased with haggard lines, and his honey-brown eyes glittered with an unnatural brightness, a hunted, haunted look. "Well met, sweet cousin. As you see, I received your message."

"What message? I sent you no—"

An angry bellow bounced along the gorge, followed by a muffled curse. Arianna twisted around, setting her teeth as the blade dug deeper into her flesh. Kilydd's men were dragging the drivers off her grain carts. Sir Odo tried to stop them and had taken an arrow in the arm for his pains.

Kilydd *tsk*ed and shook his head. "Tell your good knights to behave, Arianna. Explain to them how it's the grain we've come for, not their blood."

Arianna made a soft sound of protest deep in her throat. "Sir Odo—"

The big knight's full lips pulled sideways into a sneer. "Your friends can have the bloody carts for all I care."

"They are not my friends," Arianna said, though she could see by the bruise of disillusionment in his eyes that he did not believe her.

Kilydd sidled his horse up to hers. His eyes widened at the sight of the blood on her bliaut. "God's sake, man, I told you not to hurt her!"

A querulous voice whined in her ear and she nearly gagged from the waft of fishy breath that bathed her face. "Ye said t' make it look real."

The knife disappeared, but Arianna's heart still thudded hard against her chest. She imagined trying to convince Raine that none of this was her fault, that she had not betrayed him.

Kilydd leaned over and patted her cheek. "Why such sad eyes, *geneth?* It has all happened as you promised. For a female you are uncommonly resourceful. We would have starved hiding from the Norman whoreson's patrols and trying to scrounge food from the barren hills of Rhos during a Welsh winter." He flashed a boyish smile. "Aye, our belly buttons would have been rubbing against our spines come spring, were it not for your generosity with your husband's grain."

"Why not go to my father? You know that he will give you sanctuary."

Kilydd's tawny eyes blazed at her. "I don't want sanctuary. Rhos is *mine,* and treaty or no treaty, I'll be no vassal of a Norman cur."

He twisted around in his saddle and waved, and the carts started forward, their iron-rimmed wheels clattering over the stony road. Another hare darted across their path, but the hawk was long gone. The mist had grown thicker, seeming to boil up from the black ground, like steam from a cauldron. Before long it had almost swallowed the carts.

Kilydd turned back to her. "Don't worry, sweetling, you'll be coming with us. Though I fear our accommodations are not fit as yet for a lady's presence."

The man behind her shifted his weight forward, wrapping a thick arm around her waist, and snatched the reins from her hands. He dug his bare heel into the side of Arianna's palfrey and the horse darted forward. "No!" she cried, but the sound was muffled as the man tightened his grip, cutting off her breath.

The man was a poor rider; the hand that held the reins flapped like a chicken's wing. Arianna seized his wrist and bit down hard, so hard her teeth broke through the hairy skin. He screamed and let go of the reins, just as she rammed her elbow into his chest. Swaying backward, he clawed at her mantle. The material ripped and she twisted around, driving her fist into the man's face.

He bellowed again as he slid off the horse's rump. At last Arianna was free of him, but she was nearly free of the horse as well. She had lost a stirrup and only saved herself from falling by snatching at the horse's mane. She clung for a moment as the ground rushed past her eyes at an incredible speed. She pulled herself upright again.

She felt for the loose stirrup with her foot but couldn't find it. Her hair snapped like a flag and branches whipped her face. Somehow she managed to jerk the horse around so that they were heading away from Kilydd and his men. She heard his angry bellow and then nothing but the blowing of the wind past her ears and the pounding of her horse's hooves.

She galloped, clattering through the gorge, and then up ahead of her she saw Sir Odo and the other knights, milling casually about as if they were out for a day's hunting. They looked surprised to see her, but not pleased.

"Why aren't you riding after them?" she cried.

Sir Odo said nothing. He gave a great gusty sigh and shook his head. "There'll be men strung out all along that defile, just waiting to ambush us with their cursed longbows should we be such fools as to go charging in after them."

One of the knights snarled deep in his throat. "Aye, but then charging in after them, and getting ourselves killed for it, is just what she'd like us to do. Cursed Welsh bitch!"

The others grunted and nodded in agreement. They stared at her, their thoughts plain in their eyes, and their hatred rolled over her, thick as the mist.

Arianna slid from the saddle before Rhuddlan's great hall and pressed her face into the palfrey's neck. His hide was wet and warm and smelled of horse sweat. She felt movement around her, heard shouts, and she pushed her face deeper into the animal's flesh, until the pumping of his blood drowned out the world. *He will hate me,* she thought. *Raine will hate me forever.*

She lifted her head and turned, half-expecting to see a black-armored knight on a rearing charger, silhouetted against a slate sky.

He wasn't there. Though the entire bailey was certainly crowded with horses and carts and wagons and retainers, all bustling about. She remembered that the manorial high court was to meet on this day. Normally Raine held it in the open air by the river, but he must have moved it inside to the hall because of the foul weather.

Arianna spotted her younger brother sidling up between the bakehouse and the hen coop. At first she thought he was after the tray of hot cross buns that sat cooling on a stone shelf, but then she realized it was herself and her escort he was interested in. His gaze passed over them and then his mouth curled up into a satisfied smirk, and in that instant she understood it all.

"Rhodri!"

The boy spun around, sprinting across the yard, dodging and jumping puddles. Arianna ran after him.

"Rhodri, damn your cursed hide! Get back here!"

She caught up with him as he rounded the corner of the farrier. They struggled a moment, Rhodri flailing at her to get away and Arianna just as determined that he would not. The smithy, who was putting a new link into a mailed shirt, paused, his hammer halted in midair and curiosity alive on his face.

She seized Rhodri by the arm and thrust him ahead of her, toward the mews and away from the blacksmith and his cocked ears.

Rhodri squirmed. "God's death, let go, Arianna, afore you wrench my arm out its socket."

Arianna gripped him harder. "I ought to wrench your head off your neck." She swung him around and shoved him up against the wall of the mews, so hard that his head knocked against the boards. The hawks protested this disturbance with a cacophony of shrill cries. "Are you playing traitor with your liege lord?"

Rhodri spat into the dirt. "The Black Knight is not my liege lord."

"Don't tilt with me, boy. Did you send a message to Kilydd about the grain for St. Asap?"

"What if I did? Your man is Norman and so 'tis no dishonor to cheat him when I can."

Arianna relaxed her grip and turned to lean beside her brother against the wall. A thick, coppery stink wafted to them from the buckets of raw meat that were to be the hawks' dinner, but she barely noticed it. She was shaking with useless anger and so filled with despair that she was nauseated by it. Always, always she was being forced to choose between her husband and her family.

Rhodri started to edge away, but she flung out a hand, stopping him. "You are not to brag about it. Do you hear me, Rhodri? You are not to admit to a soul what you have done."

"What does it matter?" His eyes grew wide and he let out a soft whistle. "You want Lord Raine to think that it was you. Why? Because he'll go easier on you than me? Well, I—"

"Just do as I say."

"Aye, and mayhap you and Lord Raine will wrestle again and you will acquire another black eye."

"He won't hit me."

Rhodri shrugged. "Aye? Well, 'tis your own wake."

He pulled away from her and ran off toward the stables. Arianna stood staring after him a long while, then with dragging feet she made her way to the great hall.

A sooty haze from a roaring log fire hung over the rafters. The hall was packed with people, some sitting on the cushioned benches that lined the walls, but most milling about in the aisles. Scores of torches burned, adding to the eye-stinging smoke.

Raine sat on the dais, on a gilded faldstool padded with a folded tapestry. He supported his head on his fist, his long legs stretched out before him, and all the power of his unyielding authority focused on a quaking boy who'd been caught pilfering from an honest villein's cabbage patch. Arianna hung back, keeping to the shadows cast by the pillars, yet somehow his gaze found her and the stern expression on his face softened just a little.

A questioning look came into his eyes, for he had not expected her back so soon.

She tried to smile at him, but could not. Her heart lay in her chest like a big, cold stone. She raised her gaze from his face to the wall above him and saw the banner she had made—the one he had ordered burned—spread in all its glorious colors across the whitewashed wood. He saw where she was looking, and this time he smiled.

"Oh, Raine . . ." she whispered.

"You should order the boy's ears chopped off, my lord," she heard the castle chaplain say. An old man with a skull-like visage and palsied limbs, the priest stood on the other side of the high seat. It was his job to administer the oaths, and the silver relic box he now held in his hands shook so hard, the saints' bones rattled. "Aye, off with his ears and he'll steal no more."

The boy, on hearing the priest's counsel, fell to his knees and began to wail.

"You'll give me six months' boon work, boy," Raine said. "And don't give me reason to see your face before me again."

The boy backed down the hall, sobbing still, though with relief. My husband is a fair and merciful master, Arianna thought. Perhaps he will be fair and merciful with me.

Yet stealing cabbages was not the same as betraying one's lord. He would think she had told Kilydd about the grain—he could think naught else, for she could not acquit herself without damning her brother. He had accepted her homage as if she had the honor of a knight, and now he would think she had betrayed him worse than the lowliest churl. He would never forgive her, or trust her again. He would believe her honor worthless.

But she had not lied to Rhodri when she'd said Raine
wouldn't hit her, even though there was many a man who
would kill his wife for less. No, he wouldn't beat her only
because she would tell him about the child—for the sake
of the fragile life she carried, she must. She felt a fresh
wave of anguish at the thought, because to tell a man he
was about to become a father should be a thing of joy, the
creation of a sweet memory that was now lost to them
forever.

Arianna leaned against the pillar, waiting, while Raine
excused a pregnant villein woman her annual tribute of a
shrovetide hen, and fined a pepperer—who had adulter-
ated his product with ground nutshells—a month's profits.

She saw Sir Odo cross the hall and approach the dais.

The big knight leaned over and spoke in Raine's ear
and even from where she stood Arianna could see the
change come over his face. His head snapped around and
his cold gaze lashed at her down the length of the hall.
She started forward, then she began running. But Sir Odo
was there in front of her, blocking her way.

"I must speak to him."

"I am to escort you to your chamber, my lady."

"But—"

"Now, my lady."

Head stiff, shoulders back, Arianna turned and walked
down the long length of the hall.

She stood before the window, looking out over the
green tilting fields and the silty brown water of the Clwyd.
He saw her through a bloodred haze of rage.

At the sound of the door hitting the wall, she swung
around. She wrapped her arms tightly around her waist,
as if she physically had to hold herself together. But she
looked at him out of calm, sea-foam eyes.

"You traitorous bitch!"

He advanced on her, and he expected her to cower or

cringe, but she did not. His clenched fists trembled and his chest jerked. "I trusted you."

"I know. Oh, Raine, I'm so sorry—"

His hand lashed out, his fingers spanning her neck, pushing her chin up. He could feel the pulse beating in her throat, hard, fast. "Sorry," he repeated, his voice raw. "You are profligate with your apologies, Arianna. And you play the innocent so well. You would stab a man in the gut and then pretend not to understand how the knife came to be in your hand."

He felt her throat work beneath his hand as she struggled to speak, but then she merely shook her head, her eyes squeezing shut. "I ought to kill you," he whispered.

"Raine—"

He swung away from her and slammed his fist into the wall. "I *trusted* you. You swore your fealty to me and I believed you. Jesus God, I should have known better." He laughed harshly, flinging his head back. "But then I deserve no less for thinking with my prick."

She lifted her hand, but then she let it fall without touching him. "Oh, Raine, don't . . . Whatever else, there is the joy we share in bed together. Don't destroy that or we will have nothing."

He turned back to her. A coldness descended over him, numbing him. He had things in perspective now. She was his wife, his chattel, to use as he willed. To be punished when she disobeyed him and to be kept in her place with a mailed fist. A man didn't have to trust his wife, he only had to rule her.

"Aye, we do have that," he said, his voice flat and cold. "Me hard for you, and you hot and wet for me and loving every bit of it. You are good for only one thing, Arianna, and that is spreading your legs for me."

He grabbed her by the arm and hauled her over to the bed, flinging her down on top of it. He stood looking down at her—at her hair spread out on the fur, at her mouth partly open, lips trembling, and at her eyes, dusky and deep, and growing wider and wider as she saw his intent on his face.

She reared up, but he threw her back down, falling on top of her, pinning her to the bed with his weight. He tangled a fist in her hair, pulling her head back so hard the tendons stood out taut on her neck. She shuddered once and then stilled.

"Raine, don't—"

He slammed his mouth onto hers, so hard their teeth grated, and out of him poured all his rage and all his pain, and his hate. He hated her for betraying him, and he hated himself for believing in her, believing in anyone again when he should have known, had always known that to trust like that was just asking for a kick in the gut.

She bucked against him, tearing her mouth free. "Not in anger, Raine," she cried. "Not like this or you will hurt our babe."

The words stretched between them, like a drawn bowstring. He froze in place on top of her, one hand still tangled in her hair, his mouth just inches from hers. The room fell so silent, his ragged breathing sounded as loud as ocean breakers and he could feel her breaths harsh and hot against his face. There was a tiny drop of blood on her lip where his teeth had cut her.

He rolled off her. He lay on his back, staring up at the green damask canopy. She lay beside him, unmoving but for the rapid rise and fall of her chest. She wasn't crying. She had cried when she'd given him her worthless oath of fealty, but she wasn't crying now.

"You're pregnant," he finally said.

"If you don't believe me, ask Taliesin."

A baby. A son. The words finally sank in and for a moment his chest swelled, warm and full of joy . . . and then he remembered how she had betrayed him.

He pushed himself off the bed, the interlaced leather springs creaking loudly in the silent room. At the door he paused. The hand that gripped the latch trembled, until he made it quit. "Damn you," he said softly. "And damn me for a fool." He wanted to turn around and look at her, but he didn't think he could stand it. So he just left.

Taliesin was in the stairwell, playing on his crwth, and at the sight of Raine he burst into song:

> *"Lady, take me, body and heart,*
> *And keep me for your one true love. . . ."*

A snarl of rage tore from Raine's throat. He grabbed the crwth from the boy's arms and swung it against the wall. The delicate wood shattered and the strings broke and sprang loose with a grating twang of discordant sound.

Taliesin stared down at the broken instrument at his feet, then up again at Raine's retreating back. He knelt and picked up what was left of the fingerboard, and then a piece of the soundbox. Slowly he stood and continued up the stairs to the lord's chamber.

The door was partly open. Arianna lay across the bed, her fingers clenching and unclenching in the thick marten fur, her shoulders heaving. *"And keep me for your one true love,"* he sang in a soft, sad whisper.

Turning, he leaned against the wall. He looked down at the jagged pieces of wood still clutched in his hands. He let his hands fall and the wood slipped from his fingers to clatter onto the floor, unheard by the girl who lay weeping nearby.

Raine stood at the edge of the tide, looking out to sea, not thinking. Not even allowing himself to feel. The water slopped and sucked at his boots. From time to time he would pick up a piece of driftwood, white and dry as an old bone, and toss it into the breakers, and then he would watch the sea carry it away. Only when the setting sun began to turn the water into a pool of molten copper did he return to Rhuddlan Castle.

Sir Odo stood at the top of the steps to the great hall. His head was sunk deep into his shoulders like a toad's and his eyes watched his lord approach with grim disapproval. Raine felt betrayed all over again, that his best man would still take her side in the face of her obvious treachery.

"Fill your mouth with her name," Raine snarled as he came abreast of the big knight, "and I'll put my fist in there with it."

Sir Odo's lips pulled back from his teeth. "The midwife had to be sent for. To tend to the lady whose name you don't want me to mention."

Raine felt his heart stop, but he nodded, saying nothing. He allowed no expression to show on his face, and he made himself walk at a normal pace across the hall toward the stairs that led to his chamber.

It was dark in the stairwell—the servants had forgotten to fire the rushlights. A shadow loomed up at him out of an embrasure, and with an instinct honed from too many years of fighting just to survive, Raine whipped his knife from its sheathe, nearly taking out the eyes of the figure that wavered ghostlike before him.

"My lord, don't! 'Tis I, Rhodri."

"God's love, boy. Don't ever spring at a man out of the dark like that."

Raine put up his knife and the boy materialized out of the shadows again, more slowly this time. In the half-light his face looked pinched and drawn. Tear tracks stained his cheeks.

He grabbed Raine's arm. "I was the one who sent the message to Kilydd about the grain, my lord. She always tried to take the blame for us when we were little, because Father wouldn't whip her near as hard as he would us. . . ." His voice faltered for a moment, and he wiped his nose with his sleeve. "I just thought you should know the truth in case she . . . well, I just thought you should know."

The words seemed to hang in the air, pulsing to the beat of Raine's heart. Something shifted inside of him. He sucked in a big draught of air, his eyes squeezing shut.

"I will discuss this with you later," he finally said. He tried to make his voice stern, but the words came out sounding tired.

Still, Rhodri's throat worked as if he'd just swallowed a minnow, though he squared his shoulders. "Aye, my lord."

The door to their chamber was closed. Raine thought about knocking, then changed his mind. His fingers grasped the latch and he wondered for a moment if it would be barred against him. But the iron bolt lifted easily.

The boy's voice drifted out of the darkness. "She won't die, will she?"

Raine set his jaw and pushed the door open with his fist.

A woman turned from bending over the bed, having just pulled the covers over Arianna's still form. For a moment Raine thought his wife was dead, and then her hand moved, clenching at the sheet.

The woman who had been tending to her came toward Raine. She was of middle years, slab-jawed, and with a nose hooked like an eel pole. "I am Dame Beatrix," she said.

Raine nodded at the midwife. It was a moment before he could speak. "Has she lost the babe?"

"It's only a little spot of bleeding. This can happen sometimes in the first months. But you must have a care for her, my lord." She had little slits for eyes and they narrowed even further as she studied him. "A man cannot expect to beat his wife and not have his unborn babe suffer for it."

"I didn't beat her. I . . . we had an argument, but I didn't hurt her." *But there is more than one kind of hurt, you bastard, and you hurt her.*

"A babe's hold on the womb can be weak, my lord," the midwife was saying. "I always tell man and wife, they should have a care."

"I will. I'll care for her," Raine said, and he spoke the words as a vow.

He approached the bed on legs stiff as stilts. She looked so small and vulnerable, lying alone on the big expanse of white sheet. Her lips were bloodless. Her skin had the pale translucent shade of an eggshell; he could see the blue tracery of veins on her closed lids. He had seen too much of death not to know how easy it was to die, how quickly and mercilessly death could come. As he looked at her pinched, drawn face, it was not only the child he thought of. He didn't want to lose either one of them.

He leaned over and almost kissed her, then picked up her hand instead. "Arianna?"

She pulled her hand from his grasp and turned her face away, pressing it into the pillow. She had not opened her eyes to look at him.

"Arianna . . . your brother told me the truth."

"Go away, Raine."

He didn't go away. He sat on a chair beside the bed throughout the night, watching her sleep. In the morning, when she at last looked at him, he did something he had sworn he would never do. He asked for forgiveness.

18

Raine stood on a windswept bluff and watched his wife walk along the high road toward town.

He watched as she stopped to speak to a strange youth in a dashing saffron mantle—a traveling minstrel and a good one, by the look of the fancy gittern strapped to his back. She stroked the neck of the boy's piebald pony and the wind carried the sound of her laughter to Raine, where he stood upon the hill.

A hand fell on his shoulder and he turned to look into the face of Reynold, the master mason from Chester. The man held one of Raine's drawings spread wide between two big-knuckled fists.

"This says you intend to dig a canal and divert the Clwyd so that ships can sail right up to the castle." The man was built like a haystack, round and squat. The tools of his trade hung from his belt: foot iron, compass, level, and plumb line. His breath was wheezy from years of inhaling stone dust.

At Raine's nod the man's face screwed into a fierce frown, which he aimed in the general direction of the river. "You're talking about digging a ditch wide and deep

enough for a ship to navigate and it's got to be at least a
league long. Man, it'll cost you a fortune."

"Just tell me if it can be done."

"Oh, aye, it can be done all right. My lord." A gleam
came into the mason's eyes, which were the pale, washed-
out blue of a winter's sky. "It won't be easy, mind you.
But it can be done. Aye, aye . . ." He wandered off, muttering to himself about sluices and dock-gates and the
vagaries of the tides.

Raine turned back, expecting Arianna to have passed
through the town gate by now and saw instead that she
came right toward him, climbing the bluff with long-
legged strides.

The wind pressed her skirt against her legs, and he
watched the play of her muscles beneath the silk, lithe
and slender, yet strong. She panted a bit from her climb,
so that her breasts strained upward against her tightly
laced bliaut. Her mouth was slightly parted, and as she
approached he saw a film of moisture glistening in the
tiny valley above her upper lip.

"Good morrow, wife."

"Good morrow, husband."

Her gaze slid away from his, and she looked around
her. The master had already put a gang of men to work,
excavating trenches for the castle's foundation. One of
the workers passed by, wheeling a barrow filled with dirt.
The man tipped his cap at her and smiled, showing a
mouthful of stubby, brown teeth, and he greeted her in
Welsh, calling her Lady of Gwynedd. Her lips broke into
a wide smile in answer, and Raine would have given just
about anything to have had the warmth of that smile
turned on him.

"So you have begun to build your new castle," she said.

"Aye." He studied her profile. The sun and wind had
put a touch of pink in her cheeks, but the rest of her face
was pale. Too pale. She had done up her hair into a white
linen coif and veil that framed her face and emphasized

the regal elegance of her bones. He thought he preferred it when she wore her hair in the Welsh way, flowing freely down her back and held in place only by a flower or metal chaplet. But this way was nice as well, for a man could then have the pleasure of taking it down. "Would you like to look at the designs?" he said.

Not giving her a chance to say no, he slipped his hand beneath her elbow, and he thought she might have shivered at his touch, but it could have just been the wind. He led her over to the shelter of a giant oak, where his drawings were spread, held down by rocks. He squatted on his heels and after a brief hesitation, she knelt beside him. She had to put her hand on his shoulder for balance while she did so, and her touch raised the fine hairs on his neck. He breathed deeply, filling his nostrils with the smell of musty parchment, freshly dug dirt . . . and her.

"This is just a rough rendition, but you can get an idea." He showed her how the inner ward would be shaped like a squashed square, with two opposing gatehouses and single towers at the other two corners. He explained to her how the keep and all the towers would be round instead of square, which would make them more defensible against sapping. He told her how he planned to give the castle access to the sea and all the while he watched her face, not quite sure what it was he hoped to see there.

She twisted her head to look up at him, and he got lost in a pair of depthless green eyes. "You will use this great castle to make war on the Welsh," she said.

He felt the muscle begin to throb in his cheek. "I'm building this for our sons. They will be half Welsh. And they won't want to make war on their mother's people."

"And if their father's people makes war on their mother's people? What will they do then?"

"Perhaps they will find a way to avoid taking sides." He scooped up a handful of dirt and held it out to her. "Just as this land is ours, Arianna, so it will be our sons'. Their land, their home. If they have to fight to defend it, my castle will help them to do so."

When she said nothing more, he let the dirt trickle through his fingers. He dusted off his palms, then helped her to her feet, his hand beneath her elbow. In spite of himself he left it there to linger a moment, before he let it fall to his side.

A silence came between them. He wanted her. God, he wanted to take her back to their bed and make love to her, and not just once, but again and again. But he didn't even have to shut his eyes to see the image of her lying dead from a miscarriage. He was a man, damn it, not a rutting beast. He had gone for months without a woman before, and he could do so again. He would not allow his lust to kill her or their child.

She made a sudden movement, as if she were going to walk away from him, but then she didn't. A coil of hair slipped free of her coif and she caught at it. She tried to push it back up beneath the fold of linen, but didn't quite get it in and the wind whipped it across her eyes. Raine caught the curl and tucked it up for her. He let his fingers trail down her cheek.

She avoided his eyes. "I was on my way to the market," she said.

"It's too hot for walking. You should have ridden, and brought Taliesin along to carry the things you buy."

"Oh, I don't intend to buy anything, I only want to look. Well, perhaps if I saw a cradle . . ." Her eyes flashed to his, then away again. "There's a man I've heard of who's supposed to be good at working wood."

He drew in a deep breath, then blew it out. "Do you mind if I come along with you? I could use a new pair of boots."

She didn't look at him, but her color heightened. "Oh, no, no. Not at all."

* * *

Arianna's lips softened into an unconscious smile as she watched Raine come toward her, carrying a bucket of ale in one hand and a long, speckly sausage in the other. He stopped in front of her and she eyed the sausage in his hands. She had been to market days with her brothers and she knew where this was leading.

"If you're going to stop for a sample every time our path crosses food, you'll have a bellyache by the end of the day."

"I haven't eaten my way into a bellyache since I was twelve," Raine stated. He pressed the end of the sausage against her lips. "Want a bite?"

The sausage was plump and shiny with juice. It smelled delicious. Arianna opened her mouth wide and sank her teeth into it. Dipping his head, Raine nipped a big chunk off the other end.

The sausage was also spicy. Very spicy. She swallowed it down, gasping, and her eyes bulged. She sucked in a breath of cooling air. "God's death!"

"Don't look now, but I think there's smoke coming out of your ears." Raine handed her the bucket of ale, his eyes watering. "Bit too much pepper."

He tossed the rest of the sausage into the road and it was snatched up by a spotted dog with a bent tail. The dog swallowed the meat in one gulp and Arianna and Raine both burst into laughter at the expression on the dog's face. His lips curled back over his teeth and his eyes opened wide. He whirled around in circles nipping at his crooked tail and then took off for the river to put out the fire.

Their laughter trailed off and they stared at each other. Raine's eyes had turned the color of black smoke and his gaze roamed over her, as intimate as a caress. Arianna thought she could feel it on her skin, like a breath, moist and hot.

She backed away, putting distance between them, though it seemed to do little good. Her heart thudded so

loudly, she was surprised he couldn't hear it. She wiped
her sweating palms on her skirt. Though the wind blew
briskly, she felt suddenly very warm.

The market filled the town square. Though some business was conducted in tents, most of the merchants had
set up stalls that were no more than crude, temporary
wooden structures, although some did have signboards
with pictures advertising their wares. Space between the
stalls was narrow and first their hips would bump and
then their shoulders kept brushing. Finally, Raine slipped
his arm around her waist, and the feel of his hand pressing
into her became like a harp string thrumming in her
blood.

They passed by a meat vendor, where deer and stag and
rabbit carcasses hung by poles in the hot sun, dripping
blood into the dirt. The smell of the curing meat sent a
wave of nausea roiling through Arianna. Unconsciously,
she turned her head, burying her face in Raine's shoulder.
But then a fishmonger came next and the briny odor of
salted herring and the oily reek of whale meat was almost
her undoing. She stumbled into Raine and his arm tightened.

"Arianna, are you all right?"

"I tripped over something," she lied, for she didn't
want to leave him, and he would make her go back to the
castle if he knew she felt ill. It was a strange and constant
ache, this need to be with him, like a bruise on the heart.

Aye, she wanted to be with him, to hear his voice, feel
his touch. Yet, though he knew now that she hadn't betrayed him, still he barely spoke to her, sometimes it
seemed he went out of his way to avoid even being within
sight of her. And though they shared the same bed at
night, he never touched her. A wide expanse of sheet
stretched between them, barren as a desert.

It's because I have conceived, she thought. Before her
only use for him was to provide him with an heir, and now

that this service had been rendered, he no longer wanted or needed her.

Smells of clove and cinnamon floated to them on the wind from a nearby spice stall, and she began to feel better. And better still when they had passed another stall filled with the sweet odor of tallow and beeswax from the candles that hung on cords, swinging by their wicks.

They paused to listen to a wandering friar who preached from beside a stall displaying saints' pictures and relics, most of which were probably false: pig bones in a glass, slivers of wood meant to be the True Cross. And drops of cow's milk that were supposed to have come from the Virgin Mary's breasts.

My breasts will produce milk, too, Arianna thought, and the babe will suckle there. As Raine had once liked to do when they made love.

Raine's attention had been caught by a cutler's booth. His face was turned partly away from her, his eyes narrowed against the dazzle of sunlight that glinted off the blades of hundreds of knives and daggers, sickles and hoes. Even relaxed, as he was now, there was still a hard edge to his features, a wariness. Yet there had been times when he had pressed his face to her breast, like a child, and she had seen a sweet vulnerability there. In the sweep of lashes as his eyes fluttered closed, in the hollows made in his cheeks as he sucked.

"Buy a gift for yer lady t'day, milor'?"

A fat woman with unnatural, peach-colored hair thrust herself between them, a brightly colored bird in a golden cage swinging from her red, pudgy fist. The cage's gilt was chipping and it was bent at the bottom, but the bird was the most beautiful thing Arianna had ever seen. The iridescent crimson feathers on its head were shaped like a blossom and it sported a black band around its neck like a collar, and a blue-and-yellow tail.

"Been taught to talk, she has, milady."

"Oh, Raine, imagine—a talking bird! What can she say?"

The woman's three chins bobbed in unison and she flicked a blunted finger at the cage. The bird squawked: *Pretty lady, pretty lady.*

Laughing with delight, Arianna turned to Raine. "You shall buy me a present today, husband."

He angled his head to one side and cocked a brow. "I don't know if I can afford to. That castle I'm building is going to be ruinously expensive."

Naughty boy, naughty boy, the bird scolded.

Arianna laughed again. "A present would be very nice."

Raine pretended to be deeply engrossed in the wares offered for sale at the toothdrawer's booth next door. The toothdrawer began extolling the curative properties of a crushed tooth taken from the mouth of a deranged man, but Raine discovered something that interested him more.

He picked up a pair of artificial teeth made of ox bone and clacked them in Arianna's face. He assumed a very serious expression. "If your heart is set on receiving a present, I suppose I could part with the coin for these."

She gave him a thoroughly insulted look, which was immediately spoiled by a giggle. "I'll have you know, my lord, that I've yet to lose a single tooth."

His eyes gleamed back at her, full of laughter. "But it never hurts to be prepared for all eventualities."

A hawker, sensing that here was a man about to be persuaded into parting with his money, pushed a two-wheeled cart into their path. The cart overflowed with everything imaginable for sale, from pins to gloves to rabbit skins. Arianna spotted a mirror with a carved ivory back and she picked it up for a closer look.

"I definitely think, my lord, that you will buy me a present today. . . ."

When he didn't answer she turned and saw that he held

an orange in his hand. It was a piece of fruit not found very often, a delicacy and quite expensive.

"You must try one, my lord, if you haven't tasted them before. They're delicious." But then she realized that surely he must have run across oranges on his travels. There was a strange, wistful look on his face as if he were caught up in a pleasant memory that was also a little sad. "But then I suppose you have . . ."

"Once," he said.

He put the orange back into the peddler's cart and smiled at her. But the smile was forced, and she caught the lingering trace of sadness in his eyes. The wind caught his hair, blowing it into his eyes. Without thinking, she reached up and brushed it back from his brow. His hair was soft and warm from the sun.

She still held the mirror. He turned her, and reaching around, cupped his hands beneath hers and lifted the glazed metal up to her face. She saw a girl with bright eyes and flushed cheeks and a wide, smiling mouth.

"You're very beautiful, little wife," he said, his lips just brushing her temple. A warm happiness flooded through her. She waited, breath suspended, for him to say more, sure that what happened next would banish forever that constant ache in her chest.

Something wet and hairy caromed off them. Arianna let out a shriek of surprise, and Raine pulled away from her, laughing. The spotted dog with the bent tail made a big loop around them before lumbering off, a salmon the size of a hearth log dragging from his mouth. He was being chased by a screaming man in a scale-splattered leather apron.

The spotted dog disappeared among the stalls, but Arianna's eye had been caught by a row of boots hanging from a rope across the front of a striped tent. "Look, my lord," she said, pointing. "There's where you can get your boots."

She returned the mirror to the cart, thanked the disappointed peddler, and pushed her way through the crowd, and it wasn't until after she'd arrived that she realized Raine hadn't followed. The tent was filled with tooled leather goods: saddles, belts, harnesses. Arianna breathed deeply through her nose. She loved the smell of leather. It was a manly smell; it reminded her of Raine.

She studied the boots but she realized she really had no idea of his preferences. She was about to go off in search of him, when she felt a presence behind her. He stood there, looking pleased with himself, the caged talking bird in one hand, the ivory-backed mirror in the other, and a mysterious-looking wooden box tucked under his arm. Arianna was seized with a sudden, ridiculous desire to cry.

"Come here," he said. "I've something to show you."

He wouldn't tell her what it was, but as soon as she saw the joiner's signboard, she knew. She ran forward, her gaze falling immediately on a pair of painted cradles that the proprietor had already set out front for her to see.

She knelt before the cradles. They were alike yet different. Carved of wood, both were shaped like miniature boats, and they swung from sinews on a framework of delicate bronze tracery. They were both painted with a riot of vines and flowers, though in one the predominant color was red and in the other blue. On the headboard of each the craftsman had embedded in silver and gold a sickle moon balanced on top of a blazing sun, the design taking the shape of the zodiacal symbol of Taurus, the sign their baby would be born under.

She looked up at her husband through blurry eyes. His arms were full of presents, and he was smiling that rare and ravishing smile. "They're both so beautiful, I can't decide which one I like the best," she said around the lump in her throat.

"We'll get them both."

"Don't be a dolt. We'll have the red one," she told the joiner.

It took her ten minutes to argue Raine out of buying both cradles, but eventually money changed hands and arrangements were made to have the cradle delivered to the castle that afternoon.

They walked back along the riverbank, stopping to watch a cock fight. Raine bet on a red-breasted bird and lost. Arianna became fascinated by a contortionist who had managed to tie himself into a sailor's knot, while a juggler tossed scimitars over his head. The young minstrel she had met earlier on the road to town danced by, reciting a jingling verse that, when Arianna picked up the words, caused her to blush and made Raine laugh.

They had reached the town gate when Taliesin came riding up on his cob. "The master mason's demanding to see you, my lord," he called out, sliding from the saddle. "Something to do with sluices and winter tides."

Raine dumped his purchases into Taliesin's arms and ordered Arianna to ride the cob back to the castle. He hesitated a moment, his gaze on her face, searching her eyes, but revealing nothing in his own.

"I have to go," he said. They stood close together, close enough that if he wanted to he could have pulled her into his arms and kissed her. His head dipped and she waited, her breath short, her head light . . . and then watched him walk away without another word, without even one last smile.

Arianna pressed her face against the gilded cage. "Pretty girl," she prompted, puckering her lips into little kisses. "Pretty girl, pretty girl."

The bird stared back at her with unblinking black eyes. Then it cocked its colorful head and opened its big orange beak in what Arianna could have sworn was silent laughter. The cursed bird hadn't let out so much as a squawk since Raine had bought him at the market that morning.

Arianna gave up on the talking bird that wouldn't talk. She prowled the room, searching for something to do. She picked up a distaff, but she'd always hated spinning, so she tossed it back down again with a scowl.

She went to the window. She could see the bent shapes of men, tiny as gnomes, digging along the top of the bluff that overlooked the town, the bluff where her husband was building his castle, a castle that—though he denied it—would most likely be used to further subjugate her people. She pressed her face against the rough wood of the window frame and squinted, trying to make out which of the men was Raine.

Several times that afternoon she had almost walked back out to the bluff, but she had already approached him once today. Now it was his turn to do the approaching, for she still had her pride. It might be tattered and in shreds, but she had it still, and she wrapped it around herself now like an old worn cloak.

Lifting her head, she turned away from the window. The ivory-backed mirror that Raine had bought for her sat on a dormant table nearby, along with the mysterious wooden box. Since he hadn't exactly said the box was for her, Arianna was being virtuous by not opening it. But she couldn't help rubbing her fingers across the smooth wood. The box was made of walnut, plain with no carving, but it had been sanded and oiled. She hefted it in her hand. Something rattled inside, something heavy.

She let go of the box with firm resolution and picked up the mirror. She stuck out her tongue at her own reflection, then set the mirror down again. Her eyes drifted back to the box and her fingers curled. The cursed thing was like a flea bite she couldn't stop scratching.

She chewed on her lip. Well, she had never claimed to be a saint. . . .

She lifted the lid off the box and . . . frowned. For whatever she had expected to find, it was not this. Inside, stacked in neat rows, were beautifully carved and brightly painted letters of the alphabet.

She picked the letter *A* out of the box. It was green

with a delicate pattern of diamonds and circles painted in gold gilt along the front. She couldn't imagine what had prompted Raine to buy these. It wasn't the sort of thing one would get for a child not yet born. A doll or a toy sword perhaps, but not a box of teaching letters. He could have bought them for her, but again that made little sense. For he knew that she could read.

The crunch of boots in the rushes brought her spinning around, the wooden *A* still clutched in her hand. Raine stood just inside the doorway. His gaze went from her face, to the letter, and back up to her face again. His eyes were opaque, flat as a pond on a windless day.

She looked into those eyes and saw the truth in one intuitive flash. "You don't know how to read," she said.

His mouth curled into a bitter twist. "In between shoveling the dung from my father's stables and killing infidels for Christ, there was hardly an opportunity for me to learn."

He came into the room, all the way up to her. He took the letter from her hand and returned it to the box. He smelled of the hot sun and dust and leather, and her heart ached for him.

She heard the echo of the words she had flung at him not so very long ago. *It is a poor knight who cannot read or write.* She thought of her own childhood, of leaning over her mother's shoulder while they read together from a Psalter. Of sitting in a circle with her brothers, wax tablets in their laps and styluses clutched awkwardly in their hands as they practiced drawing their letters under the strict instruction of the castle priest. The Earl of Chester's heir would have similar memories.

But not the Earl of Chester's bastard.

"I could teach you," she said, then instantly wanted to bite off her tongue.

He kept his head averted from her, but for once he was unable to keep all that he was thinking off his face. She saw the struggle that he was having with his pride, in the tightness of his lips and the tenseness around his eyes.

He turned to look at her and she expected him to dismiss her offer with mockery, or even cruelty. "I would like that," he said.

His face was inscrutable again, but not his voice. There had been a quiver there, of uncertainty, as if he half-expected her to laugh at him, or to sneer. She looked down quickly, obscuring with her lids a sudden rush of tears. He had trusted her with his pride. Of all the gifts he had given her today, she would forever cherish this one the most.

"The priest who taught us used to rap our knuckles with a stick when we made a mistake," she said, babbling to fill the silence. She emptied the box onto the table in front of them. There were four complete sets of the alphabet and they scattered across the board with a loud clatter. "I suppose we should begin by naming the letters."

His fingers brushed her neck, making her jump. He unpinned the brooch that fastened her coif, pushing it off her head. It landed among the letters on the table without a sound. "You'll take this off first," he said, his voice a little rough. "It makes you look much too prim and strict." He threaded his fingers through her hair, pulling it down. It spilled over his arms, catching the light that poured through the window, so it shimmered like ice in the sun. "I'd be afraid that if I were to make a mistake, you'd rap my knuckles." He smiled, and she couldn't help the little moaning sound that escaped from her throat.

He pushed her hair back over her shoulders, then let his hands fall to his sides. Her own hands shook as she arranged the letters in their proper order. He stood close beside her, his shoulder brushing against hers.

When she got to the letter *R* he stopped her, taking it out of her hand to stare at it. It was painted black and had a design of stars in gold gilt. A wistful look came into his eyes, the same look he had worn that morning while holding the orange. "There was a girl . . ." he said. "She taught me once how to make my name."

Arianna felt a sudden spurt of jealousy. She knew she should be glad for him, that there had been someone in his past who cared enough about him at least to teach him how to write his own name. But though he hadn't said who this girl was, Arianna knew—she was Sybil, his lost love. The knowledge hurt. She had wanted this time to be special between them, but he'd already shared a similar moment with someone else. Someone he had once loved.

She took the wooden *R* from his hand and put it in its proper place on the table. She named all the letters for him, illustrating their various sounds and how they were used in words. The words she picked were in his language, French, even though most books and correspondence were written in Latin.

"This is a *B*, remember? Now I'll spell something that begins with a *B*."

She glanced up to find his gaze on her mouth. *"Bouche,"* she said, her voice low and throaty, picking the French word for mouth. She started to moisten her lips, then stopped herself. *"Bouche* begins with a . . . with . . ."

His eyes had darkened and turned stormy, like thunderclouds just before the rain came, and they hadn't left her mouth. "Spell it out for me," he said.

She fumbled with the letters, so they kept clicking against the table. The room suddenly seemed too quiet. She could hear her own breathing. And his. He leaned so close to her, his breath disturbed strands of her hair. His lips moved and she felt them.

"Very good," he said, as if he were the teacher.

"Baiser is another word that begins with *B*," she said. The word for kiss.

He went still beside her, saying nothing; it seemed he wasn't even breathing. "Why don't you pick out another

B and I'll spell it for you," she said, barely able to breathe herself.

His arm brushed her breasts as he reached across the table for the letter, and her nipples hardened instantly. He turned his head slightly. Now their lips were only inches apart. She willed him to kiss her.

He lowered his head, covering her mouth with his.

The kiss was ravishing in its gentleness. His tongue touched her lips, coaxing them to part, then took possession of her mouth. When at last his lips released hers, her body felt so languid and heavy she was clutching at the edge of the table for support.

She sucked in a deep, steadying breath. "Raine . . ."

His mouth tightened, and he backed up a step, putting space between them. "Get on with the lesson," he said, and his voice sounded angry. Except she knew that he wanted her, she had felt it in his kiss, she could see it even now in the way his eyes were dark with the look he always got when he was hungry for her, how his face was taut with it.

She took a step so that they were close again. She leaned over, deliberately rubbing her breast against his arm as she selected more letters from the table. She saw a tiny tremor shake his chest, and she hid a smile. "See if you can tell what this word is, my lord."

It was not a very polite word, but it was the only one she knew for the act in French. It was the first word of that God-cursed tongue her brothers had made sure to learn, and naturally, they had taught it to her.

She watched his mouth sound out the letters and then his eyes widened slightly. "You are horribly vulgar, little wife."

"But now that you've mentioned it, let's do it."

He laughed. "I didn't mention it, you did."

She made her eyes go round and pointed to her chest. "Me? I haven't said a word."

He smiled at that. His beautiful, heartbreaking smile

. . . and the breath left her chest all in a rush, seeming to take her heart right along with it. She was so aware, oh so very aware of the man standing beside her, of how much she wanted him.

She leaned into him, entwined her hands around his neck, and pulled his mouth down to hers. For a moment he responded, sliding his tongue over her lips. Then his hands tightened on her shoulders and he thrust her away from him.

"Damn you, wench," he said, his chest heaving. "If you don't stop, I'm going to throw you down right here and now and take you among the rushes and wind up killing both you and the babe."

The babe! That was it—he was worried about harming the babe. And her too. He was worried about her as well.

A smile blazed across her face. "We could do it on the bed."

"Jesus." He spun around, shoving his hand through his hair. "You aren't *listening*. Dame Beatrix said—"

"She said to be careful. She didn't say we must abstain altogether."

His jaw jutted forward. "I am abstaining and this discussion is finished."

The man, Arianna decided with a sudden spurt of anger, was behaving like a stubborn sheep that wouldn't go over a stile. Well, there was more than one way to get over a fence.

She thrust her chin into the air. "You may abstain if you so desire, my lord, but I shall not. I will take a lover."

She had expected him to turn instantly jealous and possessive. Instead, one black brow quirked up in an amused fashion. "You don't have my permission to take a lover, Arianna."

"I don't need your permission. In Wales, if a husband denies his wife the marriage duty, she has the right to take a lover. It works both ways, of course. If a woman denies her husband, then he may take a leman. In such circumstances, no permission is required by either party."

"In this castle, permission is required."

She decided to try a different tact. "You know how men get when they have not had a woman in a while."

This time both brows went up. "Do *you?*"

"Aye. I had nine brothers, after all, and so I know these things. Well, it is the same for women. Once they have known a man's pleasuring they cannot go long without it before they become—"

"Horn-mad? Crazed with lust?" He twisted his face into a particularly lecherous leer. "When it gets real bad do you start foaming at the mouth?"

Arianna had to press her lips tightly together to keep from laughing. "This is hardly a matter for jesting, my lord. This is a serious problem affecting the delicate inner humors of the body for which there is, happily, an easy solution. I shall take a lover."

"Taliesin!" Raine bellowed and Arianna jumped. A head ringed with long, coppery curls poked around the door jamb, and Raine went on in his flat, controlled voice. "You might as well come in and do your listening in the open."

Taliesin sauntered in the room. He winked at Arianna, then assumed an affronted look. "My lord, you malign me. I just happened to be passing by on my way to somewhere important."

Raine hooked his hip onto the edge of the table, bracing his weight on his hands and crossing his long legs at the ankles. "As you have no doubt just heard on your way to somewhere important, my sweet wife has decided to take a lover. You will provide one for her before the end of the week."

Taliesin's red brows disappeared into his hair. His eyes flashed over to Arianna. "Any particular type, my lady? Yellow hair, brown? Long of limb or short and stocky? Slender, brawny? Sharp of wit or pleasant of face?"

Raine waved an idle hand. "Bring her a selection and she'll choose one. But be sure he is well versed in perversions of the French sort," he added. "The Lady Arianna likes them."

Taliesin bowed before Arianna's suddenly flaming face. "As you command, my lady."

She watched the squire leave the room. She could feel Raine's eyes on her, and she strove for a look of nonchalance. Damn the man, he had seen right through her ruse, and now she had plowed herself into a corner she had no way of getting out of without appearing the fool.

"I'm gratified that you see the wisdom of this course of action, my lord husband," she said. She dared a glance at him. She might have known his face would bear no more expression than a grave marker. "I thank you for your understanding and generosity, my lord."

"You are quite welcome, lady wife."

Arianna felt a terrible urge to burst into tears. She fumbled for the coif and jammed it back on her head. It went on crooked, but she didn't care. "If you will excuse me, my lord, we'll have to finish our lesson later. I've remembered something I must see to in the . . . kitchens."

She sailed around him and headed for the door, half-hoping he would stop her, but of course, he didn't. At the threshold she paused and looked back at him. He was still in that lazy, relaxed position, but his mouth now wore a superior little smirk.

"After I have had him, my lord, would you like me to let you know how he compares with yourself? Mayhap he'll know a few perversions you have not mastered yet."

And that, she thought with satisfaction as she glided out the door, had at least taken care of the smirk.

19

Heavy mist muffled the sounds of the hunt—the lowing notes of the olifant and the baying of the hounds, the thunder of hooves on mulchy ground. The mist obscured the colors of the forest, muting the hues of gray, green, and purple. The air smelled of the earth, fecund and old.

Raine studied the averted face of the woman who rode beside him. Somehow the rest of the hunting party had ridden ahead of them, and it was the first time they had been alone together in two days. Since the afternoon in their chamber, when she had taught him the alphabet, and he had been within a heartbeat of making love to her.

The deer were fattest this time of year, but Raine also hoped to find a boar that was ruining the peasants' crops. Those who claimed to have caught a glimpse of the beast said its hide was white. A white boar had special powers, magic powers, and only the bravest of knights could corner and kill one.

In direct defiance of his orders, Arianna had come with him, claiming she had always yearned for a sight of the legendary white boar. But Raine knew differently—she had ridden along to torment him. His little wife, with a determination that was driving him mad, had set out to seduce him.

She reined in, and Raine pulled his horse up beside her chestnut palfrey. The delicate ermine trim of her scarlet *chaperon* emphasized the paleness of her face. The wet had spiked her lashes and curled dark tendrils of hair around her forehead. She looked ethereal, like one of those fairy creatures of the lakes who appeared but once, gave themselves to a mortal man, and then vanished forever.

"Are you all right?" he asked.

She looked at him in silence for the longest time. Then she sank her teeth into her full lower lip. "My mount seems to be favoring his left foreleg," she said. "I think there could be a stone caught in his hoof."

Raine threw his leg across his horse's withers and slid to the ground with a jingling of spurs. He lifted her out of the saddle, his hands disappearing into the thick folds of her scarlet mantle. He let her down slowly so that the front of her body slid along the length of his. This close to her, he could feel the slow rise and fall of her breasts, see the pulse that beat in her throat, faster than normal. Her nostrils flared as she sucked in a deep breath, and she pulled out of his embrace.

It was misting so heavily now that droplets could be seen swirling around them. Arianna reached up and closed her fist around air, as if trying to catch the mist in her hand. "They say when the weather's like this, the fairies are crying."

"Why do you think they're weeping today?"

"I don't know . . ." Her gaze roamed over his face, searching. "Perhaps they weep for us."

Raine jammed his hands under his belt to keep from hauling her up against him. Beside them, the chestnut pawed the ground and blew a fog of warm breath out his nostrils. A pair of ravens took flight from a nearby clump of bracken, with a staccato burst of raspy caws and a flap of black wings. Arianna shuddered and pulled her mantle tight to her chest.

Raine turned to the horse, his movements stiff. It was a known medical fact that bleeding purged the body of noxious humors and diminished lust. Monks, living their celibate lives within their abbeys, had themselves bled five to six times a year for that very reason. Raine thought he would soon to have to get the castle tonsor to open a vein.

He bent over, and bracing the chestnut's cannon bone against his thigh, began to scrape and dig the caked mud and dung out of the hoof with the point of his dagger. He glanced up at Arianna from time to time. She had gone to stand beneath the shelter of a big oak, but she watched him.

Raine let the hoof drop to the ground. He ran his hand along the horse's leg, feeling for heat or swelling. The animal seemed to be standing square, his weight evenly distributed.

He wiped his dagger on his boot and sheathed it. As he walked up to her, he saw two bright spots of color flush across her cheeks and the pink flash of her tongue as she dampened her lips. "There wasn't any stone," he said.

The color on her cheeks deepened, from rose to ruby. "Oh . . . I guess I was mistaken, then."

Her gaze swerved away from his. She shivered, drawing her mantle up more tightly beneath her chin. The forest was thick here—oak, birch, thickets of aspen and hedges of hawthorn. Though he couldn't see it, Raine could hear a spring gurgling nearby. The hand that held the fold of her mantle trembled. "This is a place of strong magic," she said.

"Is there no place in Wales that isn't magical?" Raine said, though he, too, couldn't help but be affected. The oak, under whose bower they sheltered, looked like a ruined gray tower, hollow and broken. Its gnarled, deformed branches dripped with mistletoe.

He felt her gaze on him, and he turned his head, meeting her eyes, eyes like the forests of her land—dark, haunted, impenetrable. She made a soft sound in her throat and Raine's next breath came out in a hiss from between his teeth.

"Looking at you now, so tall and strong and dark . . ." she said, and her voice held a strange kind of awe. "I can almost believe you are the wild huntsman, Gwyn ap Lludd. God of war, hunter of men's souls . . . hunter of women's souls. Riding your demon horse across a blood-shot sky, a pack of spectral hounds flying on your heels."

He shook his head and traced the strong line of her jaw with the tips of two fingers. "I'm only a man, Arianna. A man who—"

The bracken exploded behind him and he whirled, just as a boar hurtled into the clearing and skidded to a stop. Raine reached for Arianna, to shove her behind him. But to his horror she dashed away from him, *toward* the deadly beast, and then she froze. Girl and boar stared at one another, unmoving, like two bees caught in a pool of resin. Nor did Raine move, afraid he would trigger the boar into charging her. He had a spear, hanging from a sheath on his saddle, but too far away. Just as Arianna was too far away from him now. If the boar went after her and not him, he would never get to her in time.

Froth bubbled from the boar's snout. Tusks, thick as a man's wrist, curved out from his jaws, and the smaller grinders, the killing teeth, looked dagger-sharp. Bristles spiked along his pointed back and his eyes glowed red. His hide was white. Not the white of the mist, but of old snow, layered with soot.

The boar's heavy head dipped and he pawed the ground. Dirt and pine needles flew up, then settled. All was silent, but for the sound of breathing—theirs, and the low snoring groans of the boar.

Slowly, Arianna's hands moved up her throat, to the heavy gold brooch that fastened her mantle. Her face was stiff with fear. Raine eased his dagger from its sheath. He pushed the air from his lungs and tensed the muscles in his thighs. If he launched himself forward, the beast would probably turn those deadly tusks onto him and Arianna could run for the horses and safety.

"Arianna . . ." he began in a whisper, to warn her of his intent.

The great beast's haunches bunched, gathering, and he charged—just as Arianna tore off her mantle and sent it sailing through the air. The scarlet cloth billowed and flapped like a flag. The boar saw it, or heard it, and he swerved at the last second, goring the mantle.

The boar's tiny feet became tangled in the cloth, and he stumbled to his knees. It gave Raine the time he needed to spring to his horse and pull out the spear, and to throw himself in front of Arianna. He knelt, bracing the spearhead against the ground, holding it tight in his sweating hands, just as the boar staggered upright and charged again, and Arianna screamed.

The barbed iron point broke through the tough hide of the boar's breast, piercing the heart. Incredibly, the boar kept coming. The crossbar snapped off the spear, and the shaft, driven by the force of the animal's charge, burst out the other side, through his shoulder blade. And still the boar came. . . .

Fetid breath blasted Raine's face. Yellow tusks, gleaming wetly, flashed before his eyes. The boar slammed into his chest, knocking him onto his back and driving the air from his lungs. He saw the gray of the sky above him and then he saw nothing at all.

Soft hands fluttered over his face, like the wings of a hundred moths. "You big, stupid Norman. If you're dead I'm going to kill you."

Raine opened his eyes onto Arianna's face. There was a crushing weight on his chest; he couldn't breathe. Dizziness engulfed him and black spots danced before his eyes. "Raine, you dolt," he heard her say, and her voice echoed at him as if coming from the bottom of a well. She covered his mouth with hers in a hard, desperate kiss. He still couldn't breathe.

At last she let go of his mouth, and he sucked in air. His nostrils filled with the sweet, musky scent of her skin, followed by the coppery reek of blood. He pushed at the dead weight against his chest. "Help me . . . get it off. . . ."

They rolled the monstrous white boar off him. He sat up, relieved to discover that nothing important had been pierced or broken. Warm, stinking blood covered the front of his jerkin, but none of it was his.

Arianna's eyes had widened at the sight of the blood. Her mouth pursed as if she were about to scold him again, but it trembled instead. "Where are you hurt?"

He was still having trouble drawing a deep enough breath. "Not my blood," he gasped, pulling off the soaked and reeking jerkin and flinging it behind him. He brushed the tears off her cheekbones with his thumbs. She was crying for him. His brave little wife was crying for him. "I'm all right."

The eyes she had fastened onto his face were wet and dark. "I owe you my life, my lord."

Raine started to smile—and then he remembered everything that had happened, and his hands closed around her upper arms. "And I owe you a damned good thrashing with my belt!" He gave her a rough shake, then hauled her up against his chest. "You ran right at that damned boar! What in God's wounds possessed you to do such a thing?"

"I was afraid he was going to charge you."

"You . . ." He pushed her away from him, then crushed her against him again. "You did a very stupid thing," he said, but his voice had grown softer.

She threaded her fingers through the hair over his ears and snuggled into him. "I admit that it was very foolish what I did. I could have been killed." She leaned back against the band of his arms and stared at his face, as if memorizing his features. "But I will not apologize, mark you, for I would do it again, husband. And thus, since I am not at all sorry, you have my permission to beat me."

Groaning a laugh, he stood up, bringing her with him. The smell, the feel, of her made him slightly dizzy. His sex, which had been momentarily distracted by the danger to his life, surged full of blood again. He had to kiss her. He twisted her hair around his fist, pulling her head back, smothering her mouth with his.

The force of his kiss caused her mouth to open, and he thrust his tongue inside, slowly retreated, and thrust again. She tasted hot, of fear and hard hunger.

He let his breath trail across her lips, while he roughly massaged her breasts with the heels of his hands. His voice grew raw with need. "Damn it all, damn you . . . I want you, Arianna. So bad I'm dying." She clung to him and he tilted his hips forward, rubbing his hard sex across her belly in a slow thrust and grind. "Sweet Jesus, I'm about to burst. . . ."

Her panting breaths steamed against the tender skin of his neck. "Do it to me, Raine. Do it, do it."

He couldn't have *not* done it. He was beyond stopping himself. His lips fastened again over her hot and eager mouth. She sucked at his tongue and he gave it to her.

He began backing up, bringing her with him, his mouth still locked on hers. When he bumped against the scaly bark of the oak tree, he turned so that she was braced against the trunk. He bunched her bliaut and chainse up around her waist. His hand groped between her legs, while the other supported her weight, gripping her bottom. He rubbed his thumb along the wet, swollen lips of her sex, parted them and plunged his fingers inside. Her head fell forward onto his shoulders, and she breathed his name on a ragged groan. Her slick inner muscles closed around his fingers, and he clenched his jaw so tightly the bone throbbed. His need for her, to bury himself deep inside of her, was like a scream on his mind.

He fumbled beneath his chainse, pulling his stiff rod out through the slit in his braies. Bridging her hips with his hands, he lifted her. Her legs wrapped around his hips, gripping him—and he sheathed himself in the hot wet mouth of her sex.

She cried out, arching into him, her eyes squeezing shut, sucking him in deep, and he grunted, almost coming again, pulling back just in time. He surged upward until she accepted the full length of him, grinding against her, fitting so tightly into her, so deeply inside of her, and he was so lost, so lost, so lost, he wasn't going to be able to stop, didn't want to stop, ever stop, he heard his own keening breath, felt the tremors rack his muscles, thought this time, this time, this time, I will have her, all of her, she'll be mine, mine, mine . . .

Every muscle in his body tightened violently and he exploded inside of her. Long and hard and deep.

She sagged against him, her body heavy. He relaxed his arms, and she slid to her feet, though she clung to his shoulders. She exhaled in a long, shuddering sigh and looked up at him.

Her eyes held a glazed, stunned look and her lips were red and wet and swollen. They quivered as she sighed again.

God, Raine, you stupid bastard, you were too rough. He smoothed back damp wisps of her hair, cupped her jaw and rubbed his thumb across her mouth. "Did I hurt you?"

She pushed out her lower lip against his thumb. "I think my bottom's scratched."

"Let me see."

Before she could protest, his hand spanned her scalp and he bent her over, pulling up her bliaut. There was a faint red mark on one finely muscled cheek. He fell to his knees and pressed his lips to it.

She gasped, squirming away from him. "You, sir, are a perverted man."

Raine knelt among the wet mulchy leaves and black earth of Wales and flashed his wife an unrepentant grin.

Laughter bubbled out of her. She tried to catch it with her hands but it spilled out, full and joyous, to be swallowed by the mist.

He stretched to his feet, reaching for her, to pull her into his arms, but she came willingly. She traced his features as if she were sightless and needed touch to know him. This time his lips met hers with a fragile tenderness.

But the kiss, that began with slow and easy sensuality, soon turned raw and hot with lust and he couldn't bear it. He pulled away from her and walked off. He dragged in an aching breath, shocked at the effort it took to control himself. She was his wife, his pregnant wife, dammit, and she deserved better than to be taken up against a tree.

The wild white boar lay on its side in the sodden black earth. Steam rose from the hot blood where it pooled among the soggy, decaying leaves. The spear that stuck out the thick, hoary hide of its shoulder seemed much too slender and fragile to have killed it. A single eye stared sightlessly up at the canopy of leaves that dripped, wet from the mist.

"The white boar . . ." Arianna had come up beside him. "The tales were true, Raine. Only the bravest of knights could have killed such a beast."

The gaze she turned on him was full of a strange, shining light. Since he'd never seen it before, it took him a moment to realize what it was. Arianna was proud of him. Never in all of Raine's life had there ever been anyone to care enough about what he did to take pride in his accomplishments. If a dragon had come bursting out of the bracken just then he probably would have slain it, too, just to keep that shining look in Arianna's eyes.

"He had me done for, Arianna, if it hadn't been for you. It was a lady's bravery that slew this particular beast."

A self-conscious flush suffused her cheekbones, but she shook her head. "Nay, I was so scared my knees were clacking together worse than a pair of timbrels. And after the boar charged you, I just stood there screaming like a witless nit. You were the true hero."

He reached out and pinched her chin between his thumb and forefinger, giving it a little shake. "You argue too much, wife."

"Only when it is necessary to set you straight, husband."

Arianna suggested they cut off the boar's head and have it paraded through his fief. Raine told her not to be a witless nit. As a concession he agreed to send someone back to butcher the meat.

Arianna's horse had taken flight during the boar's attack, so Raine mounted her in front of him on his charger. Her mantle had been trampled and torn by the animal's sharp little hooves and Raine's leather jerkin was now stiff with its drying blood, so they rode through the chill mist without protection, and with his arms wrapped around her.

The saddle's pommel was built high in front, forcing Arianna's back up against Raine's chest and her bottom in his lap. He scooted her forward, but as soon as he kicked the horse into a canter, she slid back onto him again. He kept pushing her forward and she kept sliding back. Her flesh seemed to mold itself into the cradle made by his spread thighs, and her breasts bounced and swayed against the forearm that he had braced across her chest.

"God's love, woman," he growled into her ear. "You are riding my rod instead of the horse."

But she only laughed and squirmed harder.

As they emerged from the forest, nearing the castle, the sun began to melt the mist. Defused light bathed Rhud-

dlan's sandstone walls, turning them the ruby-pink color
of newly ripened strawberries.

The castle gate gaped open. Strange sounds came from
inside, cackling, rustling sounds, like a field full of crows.
Raine sent his charger cantering across the drawbridge
and pulled up short. He slid from the saddle and Arianna
followed, not waiting for his help.

"God's death," she exclaimed softly, turning in a slow
circle.

The bailey was full of men. Hundreds of men. Red and
brown and yellow heads, bald heads, coifed heads, even
one tonsured head. Men in dung-colored rags and men in
gem-bright silks. Men with bulging muscles and necks
thick as tree trunks and thin, flitty men with rice powder
caked into seamed and pitted cheeks and rouged lips.
Men with faces of all humors—some round and red as
August berries, others weathered, hard, tough as cured
hide. Boys barely old enough to know what to do with the
rod between their legs and one withered, toothless man
who looked too old to remember.

Raine searched among all these men for the obvious
culprit. A flash of copper caught the corner of his eye.

"Taliesin!" he roared. "What in bleeding hell is going
on here?"

The boy danced up, his face bright with excitement.
"These are the Lady Arianna's lovers, my lord."

"God's death!" Arianna said again.

"God and all his angels . . ." Raine echoed, looking
around the bailey again, not sure he wanted to believe the
evidence of his own eyes. The cursed squire had gathered
every male in northern Wales from fourteen to sixty.

Raine heard a choked giggle, and he turned to his wife.
She, too, was looking around the bailey and then her gaze
settled on the squire. She put her hands on her hips and
tried to glower at the boy, but her mouth kept twisting
and puckering as she struggled not to laugh. "What in

God's holy love did you think I was going to do with all these men?"

The boy's chest puffed out like a rooster's and he grinned, looking inordinately pleased with himself. "I thought to give you a wide variety to choose from, my lady."

"Get rid of them," Raine said.

Taliesin's black eyes grew round as cartwheels. "*All* of them, my lord?"

"Not so hasty, husband." Arianna pretended to give serious consideration to a handsome youth with long, curling black locks and soulful brown eyes. The boy gave her a shy smile in return. He was wearing, Raine saw, a short tunic and very tight chausses that showed off a pair of shapely, muscular legs.

"Get rid of them," Raine said again. "Every bloody one of them." He pointed at the smiling youth. "Him first."

Laughing, Arianna slipped her arm through Raine's, leaning into him. "Perhaps I really should keep one or two prospective candidates on hand, husband. Should you again become negligent in the marriage duty."

Taliesin's head bobbed eagerly. "Aye, 'tis a known fact that a well-loved wife makes a malleable wife, and with some women it takes more than one man—"

"Shut your mouth boy, else I'll have the tailor sew it shut for you." Raine grinned at his wife. "The Lady Arianna is merely trying to make me jealous with her foolish suggestion. A ploy that only a witless nit would fall for."

Taliesin's gaze flashed from Lord Raine to his lady and back again. Thick-lashed lids lowered quickly to cover a sudden flash of moonlight glimmering in jet eyes. He heaved a put-upon sigh. "You might have told me so before I went to all this trouble."

The watchman's horn shattered the din within the bailey, signaling the approach of riders. "Taliesin," Raine growled. "That sure as hell had better not be any more prospective lovers."

Dazzling sunlight broke through the dissipating swirls of mist, flashing off the silver mail of a knight on a white destrier. A squire bearing shield and lance and a falcon followed.

"Why, it's Earl Hugh," Arianna said in a tone of voice that brought Raine's head sharply around. She smiled, looking pleased to see his brother, and Raine felt a stab of sick jealousy that he told himself to ignore and knew he wouldn't.

Earl Hugh rode up to them with a jingle of bells and a flash of silver. He dismounted, turning as he did so, his blond brows rising higher and higher as he took in the turmoil within the bailey.

By the time he had made a complete circle, amusement shone like sunlight on his handsome face. "Dare I ask what this is all about?"

Arianna stepped forward, hands folded at her waist, and curtsied prettily. She flashed Hugh an impish smile, which Hugh returned with a slow, lazy smile of his own and a look that started at Arianna's muddy shoes, took in her torn and stained bliaut, the leaves and bits of bark in her hair, and the well-bedded, thoroughly-bedded, look about her that Raine knew his brother would not fail to miss.

The look he *hoped* his brother wouldn't fail to miss, just as he hadn't failed to miss the look of hunger that had flared in Hugh's cornflower-blue eyes at his first sight of Arianna.

Hugh's mocking gaze moved over to Raine, and he didn't try to hide the desire he felt for his brother's wife. The message Raine sent back through eyes flint-gray and hard was just as unmistakable: *She is mine, and if you so much as think of touching her, I will kill you.*

"Are you giving something away here today?" Hugh

drawled. "Or is it always this crowded at Rhuddlan on Tuesdays?"

"I had it in my mind to take a lover," Arianna said, unaware of the currents of rivalry and antagonism that flowed between the two brothers. "And now I've changed it. Poor Taliesin is not pleased."

Hugh's brows shot up even higher. "If you should change it back again, do let me know."

Raine slipped his arm around his wife and drew her against him. "It was only a little jest that got out of hand."

Hugh sighed, feigning disappointment. "I see. . . . Well, I bring you tidings"—he cast another amused look about the bailey—"which might be welcome tidings, given the overcrowded conditions of your poor little castle. King Henry has laid claim to the title of Toulouse. He's assembling an army at Poitiers and he's calling all his vassals to arms." Hugh's smile was dazzling. "You, big brother. He particularly asked for you. His best and bravest knight."

Raine said the one thing he knew would wipe that smile off his brother's face. "Henry picked a damn poor time to start another war. Arianna's pregnant."

Six years of marriage had yet to give his brother an heir, and Sybil was twenty-seven and getting older every day. Raine knew how Hugh would envy him his pretty wife with her young womb that was already bearing fruit.

Hugh only did keep his smile in place with a visible effort. He bowed slightly in Arianna's direction. "My felicitations on your fertility, milady."

Raine had felt Arianna stiffen as soon as he'd told Hugh of her pregnancy. Now she pulled out of his embrace. "Thank you, my lord earl. My husband is most pleased. It seems he is at last to get what he most wants in life. And I have done my duty, so he is pleased about that as well."

Hugh turned his gaze onto Raine. "Will you be obeying the ban then? Or will you elect to pay the scutage?"

Scutage was money paid by a knight in lieu of military service. But all of Raine's funds, even funds he didn't have yet, were tied up in the building of his new castle. There was no way he could afford to buy free of his duty to answer Henry's ban, the call to arms owed to his king.

"I'll go and fight," he said.

He glanced at Arianna, but she was looking at Hugh.

"Pity you are to lose your husband so soon after your wedding, Lady Arianna," Hugh said. "Alas, I will not be here to console you." He shrugged, flashing an insouciant smile. "Duty calls and Chester has been boring of late."

"My lord Raine, too, must do his duty by his king," Arianna said. She sent him a look he could not read. "At least this time it won't be Welsh mothers who will be burying sons killed at the Black Dragon's hands."

The tangerine light of a summer's dawn broke upon the bailey. A group of armored warriors milled within the shadow of the gatehouse, having breakfast. A varlet walked among them, carrying a pot of ale and a broad flat basket piled with bread loaves. He poured ale into leather blackjacks and passed around the loaves, and the men dunked the bread into the ale to soften it before stuffing it into their mouths. The smell of the bread and ale mingled with the aroma of horse and metal and leather . . . and excitement.

Arianna stood at the foot of the steps to the great hall, watching Taliesin, his golden helmet flashing in the sun, as he fastened a breastplate to the saddle of Raine's charger. The big black horse pawed the ground and tried to take a bite out of the squire's leather tunic. There was a gray-and-pink splotched bald spot on the animal's rump where the hair had never grown back properly after his burns had healed.

Beside her, shifting his bulk from one big mailed foot to the other, stood Sir Odo, who would be staying behind with a troop of men to guard the castle. Together they waited as Raine, armored in his black hauberk, strode toward them.

He had made love to her throughout the night with a desperation that frightened her, as if he feared he might never return. That desperation had been there, in a lesser degree, during all the times that they had made love during the past week. They made love, but they never spoke.

He stopped before them, and she saw that he carried in his hand his seal, the symbol of his lordship. She expected him to give the seal to Sir Odo, so she was surprised when he took her wrist and laid the heavy, embossed piece of latten into her palm.

"Whatsoever is done by my wife, the Lady Arianna of Rhuddlan, shall be done in my name," he said, loud enough for all to hear.

"I will serve you well, my lord," she answered, her throat thick.

In front of Sir Odo and all his men gathered within the bailey, he brushed her lips with a sweet, fleeting kiss.

It took forever and seemed only seconds before the provision and armor carts rolled out the gate, followed by the arbalesters and the men-at-arms. The knights, mounted and therefore able to move at a faster pace, got a more leisurely start, but soon they too were gone. Only Raine and his squire and a chosen handful of his men remained.

The others, mounted already, waited for Raine just inside the castle gate. For the second time that morning, Arianna watched him walk toward her and she thought, *This time he will say it, he will say the words.*

He said nothing, not even good-bye. He only stroked her cheek once, then turned on his heel, mounted his horse, and left her.

She waited until he was halfway across the tilting fields before she ran after him, crying his name. For a moment she was afraid he wouldn't turn back. But then he did, sending his men to ride ahead of him and dismounting to wait for her.

She ran across the field, the dew-wet grass dampening her skirt, hampering her legs, so that for a moment it seemed as if she ran forever and got nowhere. Then she was throwing herself into his arms and the doubled rings of his hauberk bit into her chest, and he was kissing her hard in that rough, fierce way of his.

He held her at arm's length, rubbed his knuckles across her cheek. "God's love, what a babe you are. Don't cry, little wife. I'm coming back."

"I'm not crying," she said, though tears blurred her eyes. "And I don't care if you come back or not, Norman."

His smile was very male and pleased with himself, for he knew she lied. "You chased me all the way out here to tell me that?"

She fumbled at the girdle around her waist, where she had stuffed a wadded ball of silk. "I forgot to give you this."

He smoothed out the crumbled, wrinkled ball. It was a pennon for his lance; she had made it for him. On the rectangle of bloodred silk she had woven his black dragon device, using strands of her own hair.

He said nothing, but he smiled at her, that beautiful, heart-stopping smile. He pulled her into his arms to kiss her again, a kiss that was deep and rough and full of hunger.

When the kiss ended, she clung to him still. "Oh, Raine, I—" She stopped, shocked at what she'd been about to say. "I'll miss you so," she said instead.

"I'll miss you, too, little wife." His hands moved up and down her arms. "I must go," he said. But he didn't.

Instead, he pulled her back to take her mouth one last time, then set her purposefully away from him and strode back to his horse without looking around. He mounted, and still without looking he cantered down the road, catching up with his men. And still without looking he rode with them south toward the channel and France and King Henry's war.

Arianna stood in the green grass of the tilting field and watched his figure get smaller and smaller, hoping he would turn around one last time, knowing he wouldn't. Just as he was about to disappear over the last rise, he whirled his rearing charger about, and she saw his arm lift in farewell.

She ran back to the castle. She raced across the bailey, clattered up the wooden steps of the motte and into the keep. She took the stairs up to the top of the tower two at a time.

She crawled out onto the little catwalk that wound along the edge of the oak-shingled roof and from there, if she stood up, stretching tall, she could see him still, a tiny black dot shrinking on the horizon. She watched that dot get smaller and smaller until it had vanished completely.

She turned away from the empty road, and pressing her back against the rough shingles, she sank slowly to the ground. She lowered her head and rubbed her eyes against the hard bones of her knees.

I should have told him, she thought. I should have told him that I love him. Now he was gone.

20

"Milady, you should see the commotion in the hall!"

Edith burst into the chamber, bringing shouts and laughter with her. Her round, pockmarked face glowed bright as a torch from too much Christmas ale.

Arianna had sat on a stool before the brazier to comb her hair, though at the moment she was amusing herself by running her thumb over the ivory teeth, creating an irritating whine. She planted a listless little smile on her mouth and glanced up at the huffing servant. "What is happening?"

"The Lord of Misrule has just commanded Bertha to name all her lovers before the entire hall. Oooh, saints deliver us! I tell you, my lady, there is many a married man squirming like a worm at this moment."

Edith fell into a fit of giggles. Arianna burst into tears.

"My lady! What is amiss? Why do you cry?"

"I'm not crying," Arianna said. "I never cry. God's death!" She flung down the comb and buried her face in her hands.

Edith patted her shoulder. "It's your condition, milady. It makes you weepy for no reason."

"Aye . . . I suppose so."

Nay, it is because Raine is not here, Arianna thought. *Oh, God, I miss him so.* It was a constant ache, this yearning to see him, to touch him. An ache deep within her chest, like a wound that was bleeding from within.

Edith closed the door, shutting out the discordant blare of a sackbut and the smell of ale and smoke that billowed from the great hall below. All of Rhuddlan had come, napkin and mug in hand, to partake of the lord's Christmas feast.

At first Arianna had been excited about the Christmas preparations. It gave her something to do, a few moments at a time when her thoughts were occupied with something other than Raine. She had the hall decked with so much holly and ivy and bay boughs it looked like a summer's day had been captured and brought indoors. The Yule log had been burning in the hearth for twelve days—a log so huge it had taken twenty men to carry it in. She had cajoled the cook to turn out all the traditional Christmas foods—gingerbread dolls and frumenty, tripe pie and sweet pear wine. As a crowning glory to the festivities, a sack of pennies and a tun of wine had coaxed a traveling band of mummers into stopping by to pantomime the baby Jesus's birth in a stable.

Ralph, the cowherd, had been the one to find the bean hidden in the Christmas bread loaf and so had been crowned Lord of the Misrule. His first command had been for the Lady Arianna to sing a solo whilst dancing a jig atop the table. Thanks to her brothers, Arianna knew a considerable repertoire of bawdy songs. She chose one that was risqué enough to delight the crowd, but not so shocking as to stop the heart of the castle's palsied priest. But it wasn't long afterward that she had pleaded fatigue and left the hall.

She hoped Raine's people would think her health was the reason she did not stay for the ringing of the midnight bells and the singing of the Christmas carols. But it had really been the laughter and the sight of couples kissing and dancing that had driven her away.

Edith took up the comb and began to work out the tangles in Arianna's hair. "I heard many comments tonight on your beauty, my lady. You are blooming with the babe."

Arianna huffed an unladylike snort. She picked up the pretty ivory-backed mirror that Raine had bought her that day they went to market together. Her wavering image glared back at her from the glazed metal surface. If he rode into the bailey this very moment, she thought, he would find a wife with a protruding belly, bloated ankles, and a disgusting pimple on her forehead.

The baby kicked and Arianna winced. It was said the harder and more often a baby kicked, the more likely he was to be a boy. If that were true then surely she was breeding a knight who would grow up to be a champion jouster like his father, for he pummeled her day and night.

Arianna sighed. In truth, she did feel tired. Though she doubted she would sleep. Her gaze went to the marriage bed. It filled the room, on its carved platform, with its heavy curtains of green sendal. It was empty without him.

She burrowed deeper into her robe of soft vair and drew closer to the brazier. She sought warmth, though she wasn't cold. It was this time of the evening, in the hours before sleep, when she thought most often of their last night together.

They had made love again and again, until they fell exhausted into sleep, he still inside of her and they so tightly entwined together it seemed there wasn't a place their bodies didn't touch. But not once in all those hours of loving had they touched one another's soul. She had waited all through that night for him to say the words, the tender words. But the words had not come and so she had held close to her heart the thoughts she longed to speak aloud. What was it he felt when he held her and kissed her? she wondered now. When he entered her body and filled her with his own?

"Milady?"

She looked up, and was startled to see Edith standing there, with Myrddin's golden mazer in her cupped hands. "What are you doing with that?" Arianna demanded, more sharply than she'd meant to.

"There was a pilgrim wandering by today, milady. He sold me a flask of holy water from St. Winifred's spring. I thought it might be fun to see whether the babe shall be boy or girl." She looked around the room, confusion mottling her face. "I saw this drinking cup sitting on the chest over yon and thought to pour the holy water into it. 'Tis all right, isn't it?"

Arianna smiled suddenly and reached for the bowl, setting it into the cradle of her spread knees. It was said a pregnant woman could discover her baby's sex by pricking her finger and letting a drop of her blood fall into holy spring water. Perhaps using Myrddin's bowl would enhance the magic.

Edith handed Arianna an eating knife. Grimacing in anticipation, she pricked the ball of her thumb with the small sharp point. But then she hesitated.

"If it sinks, it will be a boy," Edith said. "If it floats, a girl."

"Aye, aye . . . I'm scared of a sudden. Mayhap I don't want to know."

Edith bent over to pick up the bowl. "No, wait," Arianna said. She held her thumb over the mazer and squeezed out a drop of blood. The drop started to sink, then floated back up to the surface again. "What the devil does that mean? Is it to be a boy or girl?"

"I don't know, milady. Mayhap you ought to try again."

But the water had already turned a deep red, too red for such a little bit of blood. She stared at it, at the bleeding water, and felt its pull, sucking her in, down, through.

Her hands wrapped around the bowl and a torrent of fire
flared up her arms. She felt the power, drank it in. *No,* her
mind cried, *I don't want to see.* But the thought was a lie.
She wanted to see, wanted the power of seeing.

The water swirled, faster and faster, like a whirlpool,
throwing up a bloody mist. A light shot up out of the
whirling vortex, a clear, cold light that bathed her with its
radiance until all around her was the crisp, sharp white of
ice.

A war-horse thundered at her from out of the light,
ears back, nostrils flaring. Then the light faded, became a
forest, cool and damp, the air heavy with the mulchy
smell of crushed leaves, and the odor of fear, like sour
sweat. The ground quivered with the sound of clashing
metal and screaming men. Among the fiery autumn
leaves there was a sudden bright, piercing flash, the sun
shining on chain mail. She flung her hand up in front of
her eyes.

> *A glint of metal flickering among the orange and red
> leaves of the trees . . . he flung up his shield. Crossbow
> bolts landed on the varnished hide with a clatter that
> rattled his bones. He spurred his horse forward, crashing
> through the forest, yelling, "À moi, À moi . . ."
> Branches whipped his face, the dying leaves catching in
> his hair and eyes as he struggled one-handed to fasten
> his helm.*
>
> *Men and horses, colliding, wheeling, charging, and
> falling. Flashing blades, battle cries. Screams and lurid
> oaths. Damning God and calling on the devil to save
> them. Everywhere, everywhere, the sweet, hot smell of
> blood.*
>
> *Charging, charging . . . He peered over the end of
> his lance point, saw it dip as his hand, slick with sweat,
> slid along the painted wood. He tightened his grip until
> the tendons in his wrist burned. The point came up, held
> true, caught a man beneath the armpit. He felt the point*

*sink through flesh, strike bone with a grating sound. He
let go of the spear and charged on.*

Screamed. God, the man had screamed.

*He had his sword in his hand and he swung it up to
stop a descending blade. Steel clashed with a ringing
sound that battered his ears and made his teeth ache. He
thrust upward, aiming for the man's neck, felt the soft,
sucking pop of flesh giving way. A mace flew by his
head, so close that it caressed his cheek like a sigh. He
whirled his charger, swinging his sword in a wide arc,
sunlight flashing like lightning off the steel. His sword
met a scream that ended with a gurgle as blood spurted
over him, wet and warm and stinking. He swallowed
down the hot taste in his mouth that was rage and blood
lust and fear. He killed and killed and killed.*

A horn sounded retreat.

*Quiet, for a moment. Then moans, the scream of a
horse in pain, ravens shrieking. Something wet, warm
. . . blood in his lap. Not his, thank God.*

*His hand began to shake and he sheathed his sword,
hiding the shaking from himself. Arianna . . . she filled
his mind, warm and soft, touching him. He thought he
saw her, lying on their bed in sleep, candlelight glinting
in her long, dark hair. She twisted and turned, crying out
in her dream, crying his name, warning . . .*

*He spun around. A man in silvered mail emerged
from the fiery trees. He wore no helmet and his hair
glowed golden, brighter than the yellow leaves, brighter
than the sun. He carried a Welsh longbow in his hands.*

*The bow came up. An arrow, bright and sharp and
fletched with peacock feathers, pointed at his heart. The
man in silver smiled. "Did you die this day, big
brother?"*

"Not yet, little brother."

*He laughed, because they had played this game be-
fore. He stopped laughing in the second it took him to
realize that this time he'd left it until too late to duck.*

*The arrow struck his chest like the blow of a fist. He
expected pain but felt nothing. He heard someone
screaming his name and then he was falling, falling, falling into a soft white light. . . .*

Arianna . . .

"Raine!"

Arianna jerked upright. There was the taste of a scream
in her mouth, and the echoes of it in her ears.

She was lying on the bed, on top of the coverlet, still
wearing her vair robe. But the cresset lamps had been
doused, only the night candle burned. "Edith?" she whispered, though she knew the room was empty. There was a
smell in the air, a hot, sweet smell. A familiar smell,
though she couldn't place it.

She got out of bed, fighting down dizziness and nausea.
Something gleamed on the chest beside the window. The
golden mazer.

It all came back to her then, with such a rush it was like
a punch in the chest, and she doubled over as if from pain.
Raine, fighting in a forest in France, the killing and the
blood and the screams, then quiet . . . She had turned,
no *he* had turned, and Hugh had been there, lifting the
bow, and she had left it until too late. Falling, falling,
falling into a soft white light . . .

"No!" Arianna cried.

She stood in the middle of the room, battling down a
paralyzing fear. His name was like a drumbeat in her
mind, *Raine, Raine, Raine* . . . She had to warn him. She
prayed she had been given a glimpse of the future and not
the past.

She dressed for hard traveling, arming herself with a
quillon dagger. She bumped her protruding stomach
against the jamb on the way out the door and a slightly
hysterical laugh burst out her throat. She kept forgetting
there was more of her than there used to be.

A thought pushed into her mind of what hard traveling

might do to her and her unborn babe, but she pushed it out again. Peasant women harrowed a cornfield in the morning, stopped to birth their babies in the afternoon, and were carding wool before the fire that evening. If they were that strong, then she was stronger. The blood of Cymry warriors pumped through her veins. Tough as old bacon were the princes of Gwynedd, how often had she heard her father say that. Tough to bring down, tough to kill . . .

With all the carousing still going on in the hall, it was easy to slip out unnoticed. But once in the bailey she pulled her fur-trimmed *chaperon* over her face and kept to the shadows. The ground felt encrusted in a mail coat, cold and hard. But there was no snowfall as yet this winter, and the sky above was clear as ice, sparkling with stars.

Rushlights burned outside the stable doors, though at the moment there was no one about. She ducked inside and began quickly to saddle her palfrey.

"Goddess spare me! I knew this would happen sooner or later. One must watch you every second, else you rashly set off on some foolish escapade."

Arianna whirled, her hand at her throat where her breath had caught.

"Taliesin!" Her first thought was that Raine had returned, and her heart swelled with the joy of it. Then slowly collapsed again when she realized that the guard would have announced the lord's arrival with a blast of trumpets to rouse the entire castle. "What are you doing here? Where is my husband?"

"My lord is in France. My lady, may I ask why you are again saddling a horse in the middle of the night?"

The squire's golden helmet pulsed and glowed. A blue light surrounded him, shimmering, like a flame disturbed by a draft. And his eyes . . . his eyes were two shining stars floating in a black sea. *I am not imagining this,* she told herself. *I cannot be.* "I—I am going to France."

Outside, a strong wind had come up. The stable walls groaned beneath the force of it; a door banged somewhere. It had grown suddenly cold. Her breath left her mouth in vapory white clouds.

He stepped toward her and she backed away. The wind whistled through the cracks in the walls, stirring up little whirlpools of dust and straw. She pulled her mantle tighter against her throat to close out the creeping cold.

"My lady, you cannot be such a fool," he said. "You are heavy with child and 'tis not as simple a matter as riding to town. The south coast is leagues away and then you must take a boat to cross the channel waters. And if through the grace of the goddess you did manage to make it safely to France, do you know where you are going once you get there?"

Arianna shook her head, mesmerized by the glimmering light in his eyes.

"I thought not," he went on. His mouth took on a smug curl that was all boy. But he was no boy, she knew that now. The wind screamed and something that sounded like gravel pelted the walls. "And, besides," he said, "it's kicking up a blizzard out there."

"You lie, boy. The sky was as clear as spring water a moment ago." But it had grown so cold, and the wind . . .

She ran to the front of the stable and flung open the door.

And looked into a blinding, undulating maelstrom of whirling white. Ice crystals whipped past her face, and the wind slashed and cut like a knife, so cold it flayed her cheeks and made her eyes water.

He's doing this. He's making it snow, just like once before he made it storm with lightning and thunder and so much rain the river flooded and the bridge washed away.

Suddenly he was standing in front of her again, though she had not seen him move. His helmet blazed, bright as a summer sun. The blue lambent sheen that surrounded

him, throbbed, grew brighter. "You are *magi*," she said.
"Llyfrawr."

The squire erupted into a fit of boyish giggles. "Would
that I were a wizard, milady. I'd change Sir Stephen into a
toad. He beat me this afternoon for not cleaning Lord
Raine's hauberk properly when it wasn't his place to do
so. My lord never beats me, though he does growl a lot
and—"

"If you were being beaten in France this afternoon,
how come you to be here in this stable tonight?"

God's death, even I am no longer making sense. I must
be dreaming this, she thought. Yet it felt so real. She
could hear the horses shuffling in their stalls, smell the
pungent odor of straw and dung. She could feel the tickle
of her fur *chaperon* against her cheek. She had seen . . .
she had held the magic mazer in her hands, felt its heat,
its power.

She grabbed his arm, and a jolt of fire coursed through
her, as if she'd just touched the golden mazer. "Taliesin, I
don't know how you come to be here, but you must go
back to Lord Raine, you must warn him that his brother
will try to kill him—"

"He is safe, my lady. It is not his destiny to die in
France. You must believe me," And the word echoed
back at her, *believe, believe, believe.* . . .

His eyes glimmered, star-filled, possessed of the wisdom of the ages. Time is a circle, she thought, and those
eyes see it all. All that was, all that is, all that is yet to be.
A white light blazed from his eyes, filling her mind. She
embraced the light to ask of it the only question that really mattered to her.

Is it Raine's destiny to love me?

She saw his lips move and knew that he answered her.
But she couldn't hear. The white light was a scream in her
mind, drowning out his voice and the wail and whistle of
the wind, drowning out her fears. For one single joyous
moment she thought she understood it all. But then the

white light shattered, exploding into thousands of glittering crystals that floated and melted away, like snow-
flakes.

"Milady, are you awake?"

Arianna opened her eyes onto Edith's round, berry-
colored face. The maidservant had a steaming cup that
smelled of mint in her hand and she held it up to Arianna's lips. "You were sleeping so late, we had begun to
worry."

Arianna pushed the cup aside without drinking. She got
up, and pulling on her robe, went to the window. A pale,
watery winter sun hung low in a washed-out sky. There
wasn't even a dusting of snow on the ground.

She turned away from the window. Edith bustled about
the bed, straightening the covers. "Did you hear the blizzard last night?" Arianna asked the maidservant. "There
was snow and wind and it was cold, so cold."

Edith covered her mouth with her palm to catch a giggle. "Oh, no, milady. Mayhap you dreamed it."

Arianna crossed the room to stand in front of the brazier. She held her shaking hands out over the burning
coals. "Have you seen the boy Taliesin this morning?"
she asked, oh so very casually.

Edith's forehead crinkled. "Taliesin? Why, he is in
France, squiring your lord husband." She came up to Arianna, concern on her normally placid face. "Milady, you
do look pale. Mayhap you ought to spend the day abed
after all."

Arianna allowed the girl to lead her back to the bed.
"Edith? Last night, did we look to see the sex of the babe,
using holy water from St. Winifred's well?"

"Aye, milady."

"What . . . happened?"

"Why, at first we couldn't tell. The drop of blood
seemed to sink, but then it floated up to the top again. So
we did it again and . . . and . . ." The girl stopped. Her

eyes went blank a moment and her mouth fell open. Then she blinked and went on. "It sank that time, my lady. Aye, that was what happened. 'Twill be a boy."

Arianna got back into the bed. She didn't protest as Edith pulled the covers up, tucking her in like a child. She was sure the maidservant had not remembered one way or the other what had happened last night. Edith had imbibed so much Christmas ale doubtless it was all a hazy, drunken blur.

I could have dreamed it, Arianna thought. Dreamed the vision, dreamed Taliesin in the stables, dreamed the blizzard. What did it matter anyway, dream or real, she could change nothing. In the light of the day, she knew she could not go to France, not six months pregnant, with no idea where Raine even was at this moment.

It had been autumn in her dream-vision, the trees dressed in orange and yellow and crimson. The wind would have stripped the branches naked by now, the ground would be hard and crusted with ice and snow. Whatever she had seen had happened already. If he were dead . . .

If he were dead, she would know it. There would be an empty hole in her heart that nothing could fill.

The coral-tinted sea smacked against the bow as the ship jibed, turning up the wide mouth of the river Clwyd. A flock of gulls led the way, and a westerly breeze filled the square leather sails, carrying him home.

Home.

Raine stood at the pointed prow of the ship, heedless of the salty spray that wet his face. He narrowed his eyes against the setting sun. A soft haze hung over the shore where, silhouetted on a hill, a man gripped the handles of a plow, while a woman walked ahead, wielding a goad to drive the oxen. The colter cut deep into the black earth, leaving a fresh furrow across the land. His land.

It had been September when he had left and the crops

had just been harvested. It was the end of April now, the plowing and sowing season. Yet it was not the land he had missed, or the safe walls and comfort of his castle, or even the dreams and ambitions he had left behind. It was her.

Arianna . . . his wife.

He would see her soon. He would drown in those sea-foam eyes and taste the sweetness of her lips. He would hold her softness in his arms.

"The tide's in, my lord," Taliesin said, coming up behind him. "We'll be able to tack right up to the quay this time."

Raine acknowledged his squire with a nod. The blood-red walls of Rhuddlan Castle appeared suddenly around the bend. On the spring wind he heard the clamor of bells. The sonorous toll of the village church bell clashed with the tinny peals from the castle chapel until they filled the sky with a glorious noise.

"They've spotted our sails," Taliesin said. "They're welcoming you home."

They moored the warship among the fishing scows, near the tidal wheel of the stone mill house. A man who was fat as a muffin emerged from the open door of the mill house, wiping his hands on a flour-smeared apron.

"Why do the bells ring, miller?" Raine called out to the man who looked up at him from the wharf, squinting against the glare of the setting sun.

"They be ringing to induce the saints to ease the Lady Arianna's pain. She be in labor with . . ." Recognition dawned on the man's face, as he finally made out the features of the man he spoke to. He bowed low, scraping the weathered boards with his cap. "With your son, please God, milor'."

Fear slammed into Raine's chest like a fist. "Taliesin, fetch me a horse."

The boy jumped onto the dock, rocking the boards. "Oh, there's no need to rush, sire. First babes are always a long time in coming. It could be hours yet—"

"Taliesin, if you don't shut your mouth and find me a bloody horse before my next breath, I will hang you up by your thumbs until you rot!"

In the end he didn't wait for a horse, he ran up the road to the castle on foot. It was a sight they were to speak about for years to come—the Lord of Rhuddlan arriving home from the wars in France, pelting up the road as if all the devils of hell were after him, to be home in time for the birthing of his first child.

By the time Raine crossed the drawbridge into the bailey, his heart seemed to be squeezed up into an area just below his throat, so he couldn't breathe. The yard seemed unusually empty of life for just past sunset. Even the mews and the kennels were silent.

The door to his chamber opened halfway before it was blocked by the formidable bulk of Dame Beatrix, the midwife. "My lord! You are not supposed to be in here. It isn't allowed."

"I make up the laws in my own castle," Raine snarled, then drew in a deep breath. He knew that men were strictly barred from the birthing chamber and in principle he applauded the sentiment.

In reality, he was damn well going to see his wife. "I only want to see her, then I'll leave," he said, and he used one of those rare smiles that had captivated women's hearts from Jerusalem to Paris.

Dame Beatrix's hooked nose quivered as she glowered at Raine. But in the end she was no more immune to that smile than any other female. "Oh, very well," she said in a voice tart as vinegar. "But only for a moment, mark you."

She stepped aside to let Raine enter. So many torches blazed within that it was like stepping into the belly of a forge. The chamber had been prepared for the lying-in, with fresh rushes spread on the floor and sweet herbs burning in brass bowls on every available surface.

Arianna emerged from behind an osier-reed screen,

supported by Edith. The thin chainse she wore was so drenched with sweat, it clung to her body. Her hair hung in damp, matted tangles down her back. The torchlight glazed a face that was the waxy white of an old candle, and shadows lay like old bruises under her eyes. But his gaze was filled mostly with the sight of her belly, heavy and swollen, monstrous with his child.

Raine's throat closed up and, to his shock, tears stung his eyes. "Could you not have waited a day or two until after I returned, little wife?"

She saw him then, and her eyes opened wide. Then joy suffused her face; he could not have missed the joy, and it warmed him. She took a stumbling step, and he covered the room in three quick strides to take her in his arms.

She felt as fragile as blown glass, for all the bulk of her pregnancy. He smoothed back the wet strands of her hair and kissed her mouth. Her lips were dry and cracked, but they were smiling.

She stroked his cheek, then pressed her own cheek against his. "I thought you would never come. That you would never come home to see your son."

He tried to pull her tighter into his arms, but just then her body jerked and spasmed and a low moan escaped past her clenched teeth. The contraction was fierce and violent, and he felt it against his own stomach.

Sweat started out on his face, and he eased her carefully away from him. "Arianna . . . I must go."

She clung to his arms and her eyes blazed up at him. "No, you will stay, Norman. This is all your fault in the first place and you will see it through with me to the end."

He stroked her back. "I mustn't, Arianna. It isn't done."

"Huh! Since when has the Black Dragon ever let what isn't done stop him from doing what he wants?" But he saw the fear lurking in her eyes, and her voice quivered with it. "Stay, Raine. Please . . ."

The midwife shoved her face between them. "My lord—"

Raine's head snapped around. "I'm staying."

"But—"

"I'm staying."

The midwife pressed her lips so tightly together they all but disappeared. She shrugged as if to say, *so be it on your head,* and turned away.

Edith came up to them, and she gave Raine a shy smile. Then pressed an opaque green stone into Arianna's hand. "It's jasper, milady. For luck. The babe will come soon now," she said to Raine. "Milady's waters have broken and not an hour ago she was given a draught of vinegar and sugar with powdered ivory and eagle's dung."

"Eagle's *what?* Jesus . . ." His gaze met Arianna's, and he saw laughter in her eyes, before they darkened with pain as another contraction wracked her. A strange emotion swelled in his chest, constricting his heart. He didn't know what it was, for he'd never felt it before. To him it merely seemed a fierce sort of pride—he had never known another woman like her, and she was *his.*

He slid his arm around her waist, taking her weight. "Shouldn't you be lying down?" he said, his voice rough.

"Nay, I want to walk awhile yet. It seems to make it easier."

But before long the contractions sharpened, came closer together, and the midwife announced that it was time. Edith pulled the chainse off over Arianna's head and led her over to the birthing stool.

Dame Beatrix slapped a clay crock into Raine's hand. "If you're going to be here underfoot, you might as well make yourself useful. Rub this on her belly, it will help to ease her."

Raine knelt between his wife's legs. He poured some of the oil into his palm. It was cool and smelled of roses. He glanced up and his hand paused in midair. There was something terribly erotic about the sight of her, though it stirred not his manhood, but his mind. It was the pure femaleness of her, he supposed. Her belly heavy with child, her legs spread wide, and the hair, dark and wet and mysterious, between her thighs. She was all things to him then, wife and mother and goddess.

He smoothed the oil over her belly. Her flesh quivered and lurched beneath his hands, as it worked to expel the child. A child is being born, he thought. *My* child. The thought frightened and humbled him, for he realized his part in this was small, and he could do nothing now to help her.

The midwife touched his shoulder, and he started. "Stand you behind her there, my lord, and hold her."

A wooden plank protruded from the stool, and Raine straddled it, bracing Arianna against his back. She stiffened and writhed against him as her belly clenched and spasmed.

"I will not shame you by screaming, my lord," she panted through clenched teeth.

"No," he said, and planted a kiss in her sweat-damp hair. Her back arched, and her head flung back until the corded muscles of her throat stood out like white ropes, her lips pulled back in a rictus of pain. Unable to bear it any longer he looked away, and his gaze was caught by the bowl of holy water sitting on a stool nearby, on hand for the last rites, and his belly caved in at the sight of it. He tried to pray, but he couldn't think of any words.

Her body wrenched, twisting violently, and a small sound escaped from her taut lips. It sounded to Raine like the last chirp of a strangled bird.

"Oh, Christ. Is she dying?"

Dame Beatrix's thin lips lifted in a superior smile. "It hurts, my lord. A kind of hurt you men know little of."

He wanted to know it, he wanted to bear it for her, to take her pain into himself. He remembered how small and tight she had been the night he had so roughly consummated their marriage. He had brought her pain then, and he was the cause of her pain now. If women had to risk suffering agony like this every time they lay with a man, it was a wonder they didn't wish all men to perdition.

The midwife greased her hands in a waxy mixture that smelled of chickpeas and put them between Arianna's thighs. Edith began to pray aloud, calling on St. Margaret to deliver her mistress safely of the child.

Suddenly he saw something round and dark emerge from between his wife's legs and he realized it was the babe's head. Arianna's stomach convulsed again, and the whole child slid, bloody and slimy, into the midwife's hands. Its reedy wail was nearly drowned out by Arianna's harsh, panting breaths.

"She is a girl, my lord. And she is whole."

But Raine's gaze was riveted on his wife's face. Her eyes were closed and she seemed so still now after the violence of a moment ago that he was convinced, in spite of her heaving chest, that the last contraction had surely killed her. The midwife had to speak his name again and then again, before he turned his numb gaze onto his daughter.

She was very red and wrinkled, and so incredibly tiny. The midwife cut and tied the navel cord and then put the baby in his hands. He held her as if she were a fragile butterfly and he a gross giant who could crush her with his big, clumsy strength. Love swelled in his chest, swift and fierce and overwhelming.

He turned and lay the babe against his wife's breast and kissed her dry and trembling lips. "We have a daughter, little wife."

"Oh, Raine, I'm so sorry. I have failed in my duty." Tears filled her eyes and spilled over, running down her pale cheeks. She, who refused to cry during the pain of labor, now wept because she thought she had disappointed him, and he almost wept with her, though not for that reason.

"Nay, she is beautiful," he said, and he could not hide
the wonder in his voice. He didn't even try. "She is the
most beautiful thing I have ever seen."

A hand touched his shoulder. "Come, my lord. The
child must be bathed. Edith will see to your wife and the
afterbirth."

Raine hovered over her while the midwife washed and
massaged his baby with salt. She plunged her tiny feet
into cold water to toughen them to the cold, and touched
her fat cheek with a gold coin to make her rich, and
rubbed her tongue and gums with honey to give her an
appetite. Then she swaddled her in bands of soft wool and
placed her once again in her father's waiting arms.

Arianna had been put to bed. She stared up at him with
tired, glazed eyes as he sat beside her. He peeled back the
swaddling cloth, and they looked together at their daughter's face, and he saw pouring out of Arianna's eyes the
same all-consuming love that he knew was in his own.

He leaned over and kissed the smiling mouth of the
woman who had given him this wondrous gift.

"Little wife . . . thank you."

21

"If thou carest not for meeeeee, I will care no more for theeeeeee . . ."

Taliesin swept into the room with a jingle and a jangle and a laugh. He was draped in ribbons and flowers like a maypole. A pair of cowbells hung around his neck, and he waved a shepherd's pipe in the air like a marshal's baton.

He danced around the bed where Arianna sat, braced against a hill of pillows. Leaning over, he dropped a garland of roses onto her head. He laughed in her face, and her nose was assaulted by the spicy, grapey fumes of hippocras. "You are drunk!" she exclaimed, brushing falling rose petals out of her eyes.

"Nay, nay, my lady. I only had a tot or two, I do swear on the honor of my mother," he proclaimed, hand over his heart. Then spoiled it by hiccupping.

"Your mother's honor! I doubt you even know the wench."

The squire laughed again. He sucked in a deep breath, stuck the reed pipe into his mouth and blew, dancing a jig so wild that the bells around his neck jangled discordantly.

"Taliesin!" Raine bellowed. He crossed the threshold

bearing a small, white, squalling bundle in his arms. "If you don't cease pelting our ears with that noise, I swear by Christ I'll have you stretched on the rack."

The pipe cut off in midnote, and the bells tinkled into silence. The baby in Raine's arms ended her wailing with a gurgle.

Taliesin looked worried for a moment, then his face brightened. "You haven't got a rack at Rhuddlan."

Raine bared his teeth in an evil smile. "I'll have the carpenter make me one."

Arianna smiled as she watched her husband walk toward her. He looked so handsome in a new tunic and mantle of emerald satin set off by a fine leather belt with a silver gilt buckle and a silver crescent brooch. She had never seen him so happy, and she wanted to kiss his laughing mouth until he begged for mercy.

She held up her arms, and he filled them with baby. She felt a tightening in her chest as she looked down at the tiny head covered with a lacy crison cap. She planted a kiss on the soft pink brow, taking care not to touch the greasy mark left by the holy oil.

She made a face at her daughter and laughed, for it seemed the baby made a face back at her. "We never talked about a name," she said.

He sat down next to her on the bed. "You were sleeping. I wanted to wait, but the bishop grew impatient."

Babies were always baptized as soon as possible upon their birth, for too many died within hours to risk hope of paradise by waiting. Earl Hugh and his lady wife had already stood as godparents in the ceremony that morning, and Raine, knowing Arianna thought her a particular friend, had asked Christina the draper's daughter to be the second godmother.

Arianna wouldn't have been allowed to attend the christening anyway because she had not yet been churched. In a week's time she would don the clothes she had been married in and enter the chapel, carrying a lighted candle, and thus receive the absolution and blessing of God. But until she was purified, she couldn't attend any religious ceremonies, prepare food, or touch holy water.

"I thought to call her Nesta," Raine said. "I've always liked that name."

She looked up at him in surprise. "It is a Welsh name."

"Aye, I know."

"Nesta . . ." She had rosy skin, a heart-shaped face and her father's hair, black as sin. "It suits her, I think." Arianna held little Nesta up for her father's inspection. "There, see, she likes it. She's smiling."

Taliesin capered around the bed, cackling like a demented chicken. "Babies don't smile. 'Tis only gas."

"What do you know of babies, you dolt of a squire? Aside from the making of them, you—"

Laughter, warm and rich as mulled wine, filled the room. The Earl of Chester, wearing a smile as bright as a sunbeam, stood in the door, flanked by his wife and Christina, the draper's daughter. "We have come to pay court to Arianna, fairest of all mothers," he proclaimed. "May we enter?"

An image flashed in Arianna's mind of a man in silvered mail emerging from a grove of fiery trees, a bow and arrow in his hand. She sat staring at her husband's brother, unable to say a word, until the silence became noticeable.

Christina came up to lean over and kiss Arianna's cheek. "Oh, milady, she is the most beautiful baby. I am honored that you wanted me to stand godmother to her and you can be sure I'll do all in my power to look after the welfare of her soul." She rubbed her little finger across Nesta's pursed lips. "Kilydd sends his love," she whispered. Arianna squeezed the girl's hand in answer.

Suddenly Nesta opened her mouth and let out a wail, her eyes clenching into tight, angry slits. Arianna groaned. "Surely she cannot be hungry again already."

"Aye, she is a little glutton," Raine said, beaming down at the squawking babe with fatherly pride. "And she has a pair of lungs fit to be a smithy's bellows."

Feeling a bit self-conscious, Arianna opened her chainse, thumbing up her nipple and poking it into the baby's mouth. Though most women of her station had a wet-nurse, she had chosen to nurse her babe herself. It was pride, Arianna knew, and thus probably sinful, but little Nesta had the blood of Cymry warriors in her veins and she did not want it contaminated with a commoner's milk.

The room fell silent and she knew they all watched her. Her cheeks grew warm and she lifted her head to look into eyes the pale-purple color of lavender. They were the most beautiful eyes Arianna had ever seen, and they belonged to the woman her husband had once loved.

The Lady Sybil drifted closer to the bed, and Arianna caught the expensive scent of ambergris. The countess looked as slender as a hazel wand and beautiful in a pale-pink bliaut embroidered with jewels and bead work. Gold threads had been woven through her thick silver-blond braids. Her face was so pale, Arianna decided she must sleep with a mashed-bean poultice on it near every night.

Whereas my face is fat and blotchy and I smell of milk, Arianna thought. Just like an old house cow.

But there was such a look of pained yearning in Sybil's eyes as she watched Nesta suckle at her breast that Arianna knew she should feel no envy of the woman's beauty. She remembered how the gossips said Sybil had been married for six years but had yet to conceive. It was her punishment, they said, for continuing to love a man not her husband.

Raine began to stroke the dark fuzz on Nesta's head with a crooked finger. Sybil's gaze rested on his bent head and the feelings in her heart shone plainly out of her face, like a sunbeam though the sheerest veil.

Unable to bear it, Arianna looked away . . . and

caught Hugh staring at his wife. Some dark emotion flashed across the earl's face, before he masked it with his sardonic smile.

Does he know that his wife loves his brother? she wondered. Of course he does—all of England knows it. Such a thing would hurt a man's pride, if not his heart. It was the sort of thing that would drive a man to shoot an arrow into his brother's chest.

But it could not have happened as I saw it, Arianna thought. For Raine would not welcome a man who had once tried to kill him into his castle, he would not ask that man to stand up as godfather to his firstborn.

Not that it wasn't possible for brother to hate brother enough to do murder. In Wales, where land was not passed on whole to the eldest, but divided among all the sons, it was common for brothers to blind, castrate, and kill one another to increase their share of the inheritance. It was, Arianna knew, a recurrent fear of her father's— that when he died, his sons would commence slaughtering one another.

Nesta decided she'd had enough of eating. She let the nipple fall out of her mouth and heaved a loud belch.

Hugh laughed. "She has her mother's beauty and her father's manners. It's a pity she's a girl-child, though. She can't inherit and she'll cost you a fat dowry when it comes time to buy her a husband. Especially as she is a bastard's daughter."

"But you forget, my lord earl," Arianna said in a sugar-sweet voice. "That she is also the granddaughter of a prince, and I am young yet and have proven most fertile. Doubtless I will breed my husband many sons."

Taliesin giggled, Hugh looked taken aback, and Sybil paled. Raine frowned at her, but she ignored him.

She refused to sit silently while Hugh used words like knives on the man she loved. Though she knew that Raine truly did not care that their first child was a girl. Already he loved Nesta with such a fierce gentleness. Arianna couldn't watch her man holding their baby without her throat closing up and tears blurring her eyes.

A soft breeze wafted through the open window, carrying with it a mingled scent of the sea and of freshly plowed earth. It was a sweet day, a day meant for laughter and giving. She looked at her husband's averted face and she was filled with such a love for him that she ached with it.

Lord God, she did so want to take him in her arms and tell him how her life and heart were now linked with his, as tight and intricately as the rings of steel on his coat of mail. Yet something stopped her. Perhaps it was because she'd never heard the words from him. Oh, she knew he loved her, she had felt it in his touch, heard it in his voice the night of Nesta's birth, when he had kissed her and called her his little wife. Perhaps the words themselves weren't necessary.

But she wanted them just the same.

"Did you see what Hugh and Sybil gave her?" Raine said, holding up a jewel-encrusted silver christening cup.

"It is beautiful," Arianna said, though in truth she thought it a bit gaudy.

It was evening now, and they were alone together. It seemed odd, after all those days and nights without him, to have him suddenly here. She felt awkward around him, unsure of what to say, sensitive to his every word and expression. They had been too long apart, and now they were strangers again.

He wandered over to the cradle and bent to study his daughter, who was fussing. He pushed the rocker with his toe and sang in a smoky voice:

> *"Dinogad's speckled petticoat*
> *Was made of skin of speckled stoat.*
> *Whip, whip, whip along . . ."*

He looked up and caught Arianna watching him. The song died on his lips and Arianna would have sworn that he blushed. "Dame Beatrix says that rocking a babe will make the fumes from the humors in her body mount to her brain and thus help her to sleep," he said gruffly.

Arianna hid a smile. Raine was taking fatherhood so seriously. One would think he was the first of his species to procreate.

"Will you leave off gloating over your daughter for a moment, and come kiss her mother?"

He sat down on the bed beside her and gathered her into his arms.

His mouth was hot and moist, and it moved easily beneath hers, letting her lead the way. But not for long, for soon she felt his tongue slide into her mouth. She let him end the kiss when he was ready, though she almost passed out from lack of breath.

"You should rest now," he said.

He started to pull away, but she held him to her. She had her face buried in the crook of his neck, her fingers threading through his hair. "Lie next to me, husband. I want to know you lie beside me whilst I sleep."

He said nothing, but she felt him tremble as he held her, and she thought she heard him sigh.

She wormed her hand beneath his tunic and chainse. She pressed her palm against his bare flesh, felt his stomach muscles spasm. She inched her fingers lower, beneath the belt that held up his braies, her nails scraping along the edge of his pubic hair. His sex stretched and thickened, pushing against the back of her hand.

His breath hitched, and the hand that had been stroking her hair clenched, pulling at her scalp. He started to shift his hips away from her, then didn't.

"Arianna, we can't . . . Ah, Jesus. If you don't stop I'm going to spill my seed all over your hand. I've been too long a time without you."

"My brother Cynan says a hand is better than a whore because it can't give you the pox."

He started to laugh, and then his breath caught again. For she had moved lower to lightly, lightly caress the inner skin of his thighs. He leaned back on his hands and she saw the muscles in his arms quiver. "Are you offering to perform a perversion on me, wife?"

She merely smiled.

She wanted to pleasure him slowly, so she moved back up his stomach, to his chest. The smell of him, tangy and male, seemed to enter through her skin. His rib cage expanded as he took a ragged breath. She could feel the pumping of his heart beneath her palm. She rubbed her hand across his finely molded flesh and felt the ridge of a fresh scar. It was a long diagonal cut, left by the slash of a knife or the glancing blow of a spear or . . .

An arrow.

She pushed away from him so hard that he rocked back on the heels of his hands. "He did shoot at you! Your brother tried to kill you and yet you ask him to stand godfather to our Nesta. How could you?"

He stared at her with glazed eyes, his chest heaving. "Hugh wasn't trying to kill me. He's never been any good with a bow and I left it until too late to duck this time. It's a game we play—" He broke off and his eyes narrowed.

In one swift movement he was over her. He pressed her down into the pillows, bridging her shoulders with his hands. His eyes turned the bleached gray of a winter sky as he studied her face. "How did you know it was Hugh who gave me this wound?"

"Taliesin told—"

He moved his head back and forth once, slowly. "Taliesin doesn't know. He thinks I got it during the battle." His fist snaked out, grabbing her hair, yanking her head back so hard that tears started at the corners of her eyes. "Did Hugh tell you? I wondered why he went running home as soon as his forty days were up. Mayhap, it was to visit my bed? Was it?" His hand tightened and jerked, pulling at her hair. He brought his face so close to hers she could see the black specks in his eyes and feel the heat of his angry breath. "If you've put horns on me, sweet wife, I will strangle your pretty neck. But first I will bring my brother's balls to you on the tip of my sword."

She dug her nails into his wrist, trying to loosen his grip. "God's death. I have waddled about your hall fat as a stuffed goose for months. How can you seriously think I would take a lover?"

He searched her face, trying to decide whether to believe her, until she wanted to punch him right between those opaque gray eyes. "You are a fool," she shouted. "And you make me so cursed angry sometimes that I could spit!"

He leaned back, letting go of her hair. He took a deep breath, then another, closing his eyes. "Then how do you come to know of an incident that took place unwitnessed between my brother and myself in a forest in France? Explain this to me, Arianna."

She would have to tell him the truth, and he would hate her. He would feel invaded, his very soul exposed and flayed. No man with any pride at all would be able to accept what she was about to tell him.

She sucked in a deep breath as if she could draw courage from the air. "You know that I am *filid,* a seer. I have visions, and in them I can see the future and sometimes the past. Usually they come to me in pools of water. Lately they've come most often in my golden mazer. I saw you in the battle. It was fall and they charged at you out of the trees and you killed a man with your lance and four more with your sword. And then Hugh came; with his bow . . ."

His gaze had jerked over to the mazer where it sat on the chest beside the window. She wondered if he could see the way it pulsed and glowed, if he could feel the beckoning force of its power.

"What else?"

"There is nothing else."

"What other times have you spied on me with that damned thing?"

"It isn't like that! I can't control what I see."

"What else have you *seen* then?"

She couldn't look at him, afraid of what she would find in his eyes. She kept her gaze on her hands, which clutched and twisted the sheets in her lap as she told him about the first time she had seen him, charging her with his lance. "I knew you would bring me pain," she said. She wanted to add: *I couldn't know how I would fall in love with you,* but he would be able to accept, she knew, only one confession at a time.

Instead, she spoke of the other visions, of being with him in the bailey here at Rhuddlan on the day they had come to put out his eyes, and that fall morning in Chester when he had asked for a pony and gotten a beating instead.

Only when she was finished did she raise her eyes . . . to find him looking at her as if he were looking into the face of the devil.

"Raine . . . It doesn't have to be what you're thinking. To be that close to another—it can be a beautiful thing. More beautiful than—"

He pushed himself up from the bed and walked away from her, his back stiff. He went over to the cradle and looked down at his sleeping daughter. Then he turned abruptly and started for the door.

"Raine!"

He stopped with his hand on the latch. He did not turn around.

"I know what every inch of your body tastes like. I have taken you inside of me, inside my womb and my mouth. Is it so awful to think that for a moment I dwelled in your mind, that I felt a bit of your pain?"

His fist slammed into the door, shoving it open. "Stay out of my past and out of my head, Arianna. Just stay the hell away from me."

22

Arianna couldn't help smiling as she watched her husband's fingers weave the bell heather into a tiny garland. The baby, swaddled tightly in folds of soft linen, swung between them, hanging from a low branch of a big horse chestnut tree. They had stopped beneath it, she and Raine, for an outdoor nooning on their way to the summer's fair at Chester.

Raine finished twisting the flowers into a circle. He stretched up onto one knee to put it on Nesta's head as if he were crowning a queen. A little too big, it drooped over one eye. Laughing, he dipped his head, rubbing her tiny nose with his. "Now don't you look like a saucy May Day wench?"

Arianna laughed, too, and leaned against him, pressing her breasts into his back. "And where, husband, did you learn to plait a lady's chaplet so prettily?"

He moved away from her so that they were no longer touching. He sat down, his back against the trunk, one leg bent, his wrist resting on his knee. She thought he wouldn't even bother to answer her, but then his head swung around and his eyes were as hard as the sunbaked hill they sat upon. "I used to make them for Sybil when we were children. But then I'm surprised you didn't see that, Arianna. When you were peeping into my past."

"I've never had a vision of you and Sybil."

His lips pulled back from his teeth in a travesty of a smile. "How fortunate for you. For I doubt you would have liked what you'd seen."

A rush of tears stung Arianna's eyes, and she looked quickly away so that he wouldn't see them. When they got to Chester they would stay in the castle there as guests of his brother. And Sybil.

A conker fell into her lap from the branch above her head, startling her. She picked up the big glossy brown seed. There was another on the ground beside Raine's hand. She stared at it, and at the hand, at those long brown fingers that could wield a sword and plait a garland of flowers. And caress a woman's breast.

She reached for the conker, letting her fingers brush his.

To be touching him, even in so small a way, made her ache with a fierce longing. After a moment he moved his hand away, but it didn't matter, for she had seen the hairs rise on his arm and the swift hard jerk of his chest.

The white sun blazed down so hot that even the tree, with its wide, palm-shaped leaves, managed to cast little cool in the shade. Sweat trickled down between her breasts. She pulled at the front of her bliaut, flapping the silk like a fan, trying to stir up some cooling air.

She felt Raine's eyes on her, but when she glanced up, he looked away.

Her mouth felt dry. She picked up a costrel of wine from among the scattered remains of their dinner. The liquid sloshed in the cask as she tilted back her head and drank. Some escaped out the corner of her mouth, running down into the hollow of her throat. She caught the wine with her fingers and stuck them in her mouth, sucking them clean.

Again she felt Raine's eyes on her, but this time she did

not glance his way. Let him look, she thought. Let him want. . . .

She stood up, shaking the burrs and hooked seeds off her tunic. She started off down the road, in the direction of England.

Several rods or so from where they had stopped to eat, a great ditch slashed diagonally across the land. On the east side of the deep trench an earthen barrier rose up twenty feet high. It spread as far as she could see in either direction. Taliesin had told her it was called Offa's Dyke, after a Saxon king who had dug the great ditch to shut out the Welsh from England. Now it divided her husband's land from that of his brother.

As she stood on top the escarpment, looking down into the deep trough, Arianna felt a hankering to go exploring as she would have done were she still a young girl with nine brothers to impress. But it was choked with knee-high brambles and saw grass, and the only male she wanted to impress now didn't seem to care anymore what she did with herself.

A lone cloud passed across the sun, casting a shadow upon the withered yellow grass. Shading her eyes, Arianna turned and looked back at the chestnut where it stood lonely upon the rise. Some distance away was the retinue of servants, men-at-arms, and sumpter beasts they had brought with him. But Raine still sat alone beneath the tree, but for Nesta, swinging on her bough.

Was it a marriage, Arianna wondered, if you slept in the same bed but did not share it? She was healed now, but she didn't know how to tell him. She was afraid to turn to him at night, for fear that he would turn away.

Her ears picked up the sound of gurgling water. Among the sunbaked browns and grays was an oasis of bright color—of purple speedwell and white charlock and more bell heather. She walked toward the splash of flowers, her skirts swishing through the tall grass. The water sounded cool and wet.

She disturbed a bird that flew off with a flash of white-barred wings. The grass was green here, the bright green of new growth. The spring must have surfaced recently, she thought, as she knelt among the grass and flowers. She cupped the water and brought it up to her face. How odd, she thought, for it smelled of oranges.

He bit down and juice exploded against the roof of his mouth. Sweet and tangy, cool and wet. He had never tasted anything so fine. He looked at the girl and grinned. Except maybe for your lips, sweet Sybil . . .

"Do you like it?"

"Aye. Give me another."

She put another section of the strange, exotic fruit against his lips. He sucked it in, then sucked in her finger as well. He cupped her neck and pulled her face to his and kissed her mouth. She tasted of the orange, tangy and sweet, cool and wet.

"Another."

"You are greedy, sir."

"You never complained before." He kissed her again, and then again.

"Do you love me, Raine?"

"Yessss . . ." The word came out in a hiss, for her hand had just closed around his sex. She stroked him down to the root. The ache was sweet and tangy, like the taste of orange, the taste of her mouth. Fine, so fine . . .

"Then don't leave me," she said.

He bore her down to the yellow summer grass. He worked at the laces of her bliaut. Her breasts filled his hands.

But he would leave. If he stayed he was afraid, so afraid that he would never get out of the stables.

She spoke into the side of his neck, her breath warm, fruity. "Will you marry me?"

He lifted his head. He stared deep into her eyes. Lavender-blue, the color of a summer sky at dusk. "You are Hugh's. You cannot stand against your father and mine."

*"I can and I will." She beat her balled-up fists against his
back. "I am yours, Raine. Yours!" She cupped his cheeks,
giving his head a little shake. "I asked the priest. He said a
girl cannot be married against her consent. I lied. I told
him I wished to be a bride of Christ." Her laughter lilted,
curling up at the ends like rose petals. "Oh, Raine, can you
imagine me as a nun?" Her mouth softened, became pouting. He didn't kiss it, though he wanted to. "When you
leave, I shall go with you."*

*"Aw, Sybil, sweetling . . . You can't come with me. I go
to join Matilda's army."*

*"And do you think when you walk up to this great
queen in your rags and your bare feet that she will make
you a knight?" She tried to sound scornful but her voice
trembled. "They will put a spear in your hand and make
you a foot soldier and you will die in your first battle."*

*His sex throbbed against her belly and his chest felt
heavy. He rubbed his face in her hair, breathed in her
scent, sweet and tangy. Oranges. He would never be able to
think of this day without smelling oranges.*

*He rolled off of her onto his back and looked up at the
sky. It was clear, empty, as big as the world. "I won't die.
And I will come back again, but when I do it will be as a
knight."*

*She touched his cheek, turning his face until their gazes
met. "And I shall be here, Raine. Waiting . . .*

"Waiting," Arianna said.

"We're in no hurry. Don't sit up until the dizziness
passes."

Her head was in Raine's lap. His thighs were hard,
warm, and somehow comforting. But he was angry with
her. It seemed that lately he was always angry with her.
"What happened?" she asked, and in the next instant remembered it all.

"You fainted." He hauled her half-upright, his grip so
hard she missed the fear in his voice. "Jesus God, Ari-

anna, you toppled over like an axed tree, face first into the spring. You would have drowned if—"

She jerked, trying to pull away from him and sit up. "Quit shouting at me."

The abrupt movement brought nausea rising in her throat. She rolled aside onto her knees and threw up into the grass.

His fingers were in her hair, smoothing it back from her face. He put something white and dripping wet into her hands. It was a piece of swaddling cloth. She felt an irreverent urge to laugh. God's death. The Black Dragon, most fearsome knight and champion jouster in all of Christendom, was going about the countryside with swaddling cloths tucked about his person.

"You just had another of those cursed visions, didn't you?" he said.

She buried her face in the wet cloth, so she wouldn't have to look at him.

"Whose soul did you possess this time?" he said.

She pushed her face harder into the cloth, shutting out the bitterness in his voice.

He had been crouched down on one knee beside her. Now he stood up abruptly. Only when she heard the sound of his boots crunching through the grass did she raise her head.

She watched his broad back walk away from her. A hot wind bathed her wet face. It held within it the smell of oranges.

Once they crossed Offa's Dyke into England, the road to Chester spread wide enough for sixteen knights to canter abreast. But she and Raine rode side by side, so close their stirrups bumped from time to time. It was his choice to ride practically on top of her like that, yet not once since she'd had the vision by the spring had he looked at her.

This part of Cheshire was mostly yellow-green salt

marshes and meres dotted with grazing cattle. The summer sun beat down so hard on the road that the air in front of them seemed to ripple, like fumes from a fire. The thick, dusty smell of cow dung and nettles tickled her nose as she breathed.

It occurred to Arianna that for the first time in her life she was in the land of her enemy. As a young girl she had pictured England as a flaming cauldron full of cavorting devils, much the way their priest had described the pits of hell. It was, she thought with a wry smile, certainly hot enough today to match the England of her childhood imagination.

They rounded a bend in the road and there, meandering across the plain, was the fat and slumberous river Dee. Reflected in its placid waters were the rusty-red towers and walls of Chester. A soft haze hung over the riverbank, melting as it crept up the town's castellated walls. Raine pulled up sharply and stared at what had been his home for so much a part of his life.

Arianna studied his face. His mouth was set, his eyes shuttered. But she knew him better now, knew he worked so hard at hiding his emotions only because he felt them deeper than most. He was returning to Chester in triumph just as he had vowed, but the triumph must surely taste empty. For the girl he loved had not waited for him after all, and the man he wanted most to impress was dead and so would remain forever contemptuous.

She almost reached out and touched his arm, to let him know she understood. But in the end she kept her hand to herself.

They had to take a flat-bottomed ferryboat to cross the river. They passed through a gateway in the town wall and onto a street crowded with houses of magpie-black timber and white plaster, packed as close together as a pile of barrel staves. Most of the houses had shops that opened directly onto the street with stalls in the manner of Oriental bazaars.

There were few towns in Wales, certainly none the size of Chester. Arianna thought her eyes probably looked to be popping out of her head as she took in the congestion of people, all scurrying about like rats in a grain bin, and the streets, so narrow that rooftops touched, blocking out the sun. The very air seemed to vibrate with the clatter of cartwheels, the peals of church bells, and the raucous shouts of the shop vendors touting their wares. The town teemed with life. Perhaps too much life, Arianna thought, for she wanted to hold her breath against the stink of night soil and dung and refuse that clogged the gutters.

They passed a side street and Arianna saw the rounded pink sandstone nave of an enormous church. She supposed this was the cathedral and she had heard a tale about its windows—that they were fashioned of colored jewellike glass. She gave herself a crick in her neck trying to catch another glimpse of this wonder.

They crossed a drawbridge suspended by iron chains as thick as a man's waist, then they passed through another great gatehouse and into the paved courtyard of the castle itself. Arianna put more strain on her sore neck, tilting her head back to look up the length of a huge square keep that was pierced by small round-headed windows and topped by a banner bearing the White Horse of Chester. The flag hung limp in the hot, still air.

Raine clasped her waist to help her dismount. She thought his hands might have lingered a moment before he released her, but she could not be sure. It was an unconscious gesture, to help a woman down from a horse, nothing more. Yet she had been so aware of the feel of his palms resting on her hips, the brush of his leg against her skirt, the nearness of his face. Though the sun beat down bright and hot on the stone courtyard, she shivered.

But then he turned away from her and helped Edith, who carried Nesta in her arms, to dismount as well.

The Earl of Chester came toward them, his hair glinting in the sun, bright as a newly minted florin. He greeted them both with the kiss of peace. "Well met, brother. Sister-in-law, you look as pretty as a pear tree in bloom."

Arianna heard a small cry of delight and she looked around. Sybil glided down the long, sweeping steps of the great hall, but her eyes were on Raine and her smile was for him alone. She wore a bliaut with so much embroidery she looked like a meadow of fresh flowers, and the tippets of her sleeves were so long they dragged on the ground. She looked beautiful and Raine answered her smile with one of his own.

Arianna looked away.

"Welcome," Sybil said, with a sweeping gesture of her arm, "to our hall."

She watched, hiding a smile, as the little Welsh princess's eyes grew wide and then wider still as she turned in a complete circle, looking around her.

Tall and vaulted like a cathedral, the hall had a central hearth big enough to roast two whole oxen in tandem on a spit. Sideboards displayed bowls and dishes of gold and silver and exotic cups made of ostrich egg and agate. Palls of silk and tapestries draped the walls and the entire space in back of the dais was filled with a painting of Delilah cutting off Samson's hair in glowing colors with a sparkle of gold gilt. Their footsteps echoed on a floor made not of wood, but enameled black and brown bricks, and covered with skins and furs instead of rushes.

Sybil had been nine the year she was affianced to the Earl of Chester's sole heir and sent here, as was the custom to be brought up in the household of her future husband's family. Her own father had been a rich and powerful man, but even she had not been prepared for the ostentatious wealth displayed at Chester.

She touched Arianna's arm and the girl started. "Come, I will show you where you and Raine are to sleep."

She led them up to the gallery above, to one of the

many small private sleeping chambers built into the thickness of the wall. Guests at Chester did not clutter the hall with their sleeping pallets at night.

Sybil pushed open a door and ushered the Welsh girl inside. "I've put the child and her nurse in an attic room. This chamber is somewhat shabby and cramped, I fear." It was false disparagement, for in truth, the room was furnished with such luxuries as candles made of twisted beeswax and its own bed, whose coverlet was of green silk lined with beaver.

Raine's wife whipped around when she saw that her child and its nurse had continued on up the stairs, led by a servant. For a moment, Sybil feared she would run after them. "Your babe will be well cared for, you mustn't fret."

Arianna turned back and a sudden smile brightened her face. Hers was a spare, striking beauty, Sybil thought with a pang. A beauty that men would find irresistible.

"I didn't mean to be so rude," Arianna said. "Of course she'll be well cared for. And Edith can bring her to me when she grows hungry."

"How I envy you the babe," Sybil said, striving to spin a thread of friendship between herself and this self-contained girl who was Raine's wife. She sensed a core of iron in Arianna of Gwynedd, hard and endurable like the ore mined from the black hills of her land, a strength that she herself had always lacked. *Perhaps if I had been stronger,* she thought, *I would have waited for Raine as I had promised.*

"I've tried everything to conceive," Sybil went on, to fill the silence. "From hanging mistletoe over the bed to drinking anise in wine. I've sent so many prayers up to St. Margaret, the poor woman's ears must ache—if saints do have any ears."

She stopped her babbling, feeling swamped suddenly with the old, familiar ache. God, God, she so wanted a child. For what sin was the emptiness of her womb a pun-

ishment? For not loving Raine enough, or for loving him
too much? If she had waited . . . What would have been
their fate if she had waited?

To Sybil's surprise Arianna took her hand and there
was true sympathy in her dusky green eyes, but then she
said, "You are young yet." Sybil felt a flash of anger, for
twenty was young, not twenty-seven.

As if to underscore her own youth, Arianna suddenly
blew her breath out in a loud, gusty sigh, the way a child
would do, and flapped her hand in front of her face.
"God's death . . . Is it always so hot in England?"

In spite of the closed shutters and thickness of the castle's stone walls, it was warm in the chamber. Sybil was
about to comment on the weather when Raine, who had
lingered in the yard with his brother, appeared suddenly
at the door. His gaze went directly to his wife, who had
yet to notice him.

She stood in the middle of the chamber and pulled off
her coif, shaking out her hair, and it fell like a cataract of
autumn leaves down her back—red and gold and brown.
She ran her hands over her breasts in an unconsciously
erotic gesture, smoothing her bliaut. Raine watched his
wife's movements and Sybil saw his face grow taut and his
eyes darken. But then Arianna glanced up at him, and he
looked away.

For a moment Arianna simply stared at her husband's
averted face, and the tension between them could be felt
in the air, as thick and stifling as the heat. "I'll go see how
Nesta has settled in," she finally said, going to the door.
She brushed past him as she left, but she no longer looked
at him.

"She doesn't like me, I fear," Sybil said.

"She has little use for any Norman. Can you blame
her?"

Sybil was taken aback by the hard edge to his voice.
She had not expected him to leap so swiftly to his wife's
defense.

Raine unbarred the shutters, pulling them open with a squeak of leather hinges. He looked out toward the west, toward his land. The blue-gray hills of Tegeingl could be seen from this window. It was why she had put him in this particular chamber.

She came up and stood beside him so that she could see his face. "Do you find Chester changed since last you were here?"

"No. Not especially."

There was the tiniest, almost imperceptible tick in one cheek. The last time he was here had been the day she married Hugh. He had come striding into the hall in the middle of the wedding feast. He had marched down the length of it, had stopped before her, had looked at her where she sat frozen in her chair, joy and fear and despair all churning within her breast at the sight of him, and she would never forget his eyes. Because there had been nothing in them, not pain or anger, not even regret. There had been nothing in his eyes at all.

He turned abruptly away from the window to prowl the chamber. He stopped for a moment to toy with the perch put beside the bed for a hawk that he didn't have. But then hawking was a nobleman's sport; it had not been a part of his childhood.

Servants appeared at the door just then bearing a tub filled with scented, steaming water. It was expected of the lady of the manor to assist the guests in bathing upon their arrival and Sybil felt a flutter of panic. She wondered how she would be able to touch him without going into his arms, without his knowing just how very badly she wanted to be in his arms.

But he did not exhibit the least embarrassment at the sight of the tub or at the thought that she would be the one to bathe him. She had undressed him before, though not for such innocent matters, and it was the memory of all those other times that caused her hands to tremble as she pulled off his boots and helped him off with his tunic.

She could feel the heat building on her face, and she could no longer look at him. When he was completely naked, he walked with unselfconscious grace to the tub and stepped in.

She took up a cloth and began to wash his back. From behind him, where he could not see her, she could look her fill of him. She noted the changes in his body. He had the hardness and strength of a man now, and the scars of a man as well. She looked down at the bowed nape of his neck, vulnerable for all his warrior's strength, and in her imagination she kissed him there. She discarded the cloth, and with her bare, soaped hands she kneaded his shoulders, down over the battle-sculpted muscles of his chest, to the flat planes of his stomach. And though she felt wicked to be doing so, she looked to see if he had become aroused. He had not.

A sound brought Raine's head up sharply. His wife stood just within the open doorway, caught fast within a beam of sunlight blazing through the window. It flashed off the bronze torque she wore around her neck, encircling her throat with a ring of fire. And as they looked at one another, she and Raine, something leapt between them, hot and bright, like the fiery circle around her neck.

Sybil knelt beside the tub, forgotten.

The alewife took Taliesin's penny, cut it in half and gave him back the change. The squire passed to Arianna one of the clay flagons brimming with ale, keeping the other for himself. He touched his cup to hers with a clink of pottery and flashed a wicked grin. "To love."

"I'd rather drink to something else."

The squire's grin deepened, putting two dimples the size of half-pennies in his cheeks. "To swiving then," he said, and Arianna couldn't help but laugh.

The ale was hot from the sun and tasted leathery, but it quenched her thirst. Trying not to be obvious about it, she looked around to see if she could spot Raine. They had all set off to walk to the fair together, but somehow she and the squire had gotten separated from the others.

Taliesin took her arm, steering her down the crowded path. Tents and stalls filled with a dizzying array of goods, and flaunting bright pennons lined the way. Soon Arianna began to notice how every female turned her head as they walked by. But then Taliesin, in his cloak of peacock feathers, outdazzled even the booths displaying silks and tapestries. He carried a gittern strapped to his back and several of the prettier girls called out to him, begging him for a song.

Up ahead a crowd had gathered, spewing cheers and shouts. Taliesin elbowed their way in to see what was happening.

It was a band of performing mountebanks with trick dogs, a tired old dancing bear, and a mangy lion in a cage. But what had drawn the crowd was a man who had woolly hair like a sheep's and skin as black as soot, and with a flaming firebrand in his hand. Arianna watched with fascinated horror as the man tipped his head back and stuck the torch down his throat, seeming to swallow the fire.

Beside her Taliesin sniffed with disdain. "It is a base trick, milady. Easily accomplished."

Arianna opened her mouth to ask the boy if he could do better, then thought better of it. If he really were *magi,* he could doubtless spit fire out his mouth like a dragon as well as swallow it, and she didn't want a demonstration.

They had started to turn away from the fire-eater when a cloth merchant and his assistant stretched out a length of scarlet silk across their path, separating them. By the time she had walked around the shimmering river of silk, Taliesin was nowhere to be found.

Arianna felt a silly moment of panic to find herself abandoned and alone in the middle of the crowded fair. She spun around and nearly backed into a carved wooden soldier that was modeling a hauberk and helm for sale.

She walked fast, nearly running, past stalls selling copper pots, leather saddles, wooden tubs, and Saracen carpets.

Earl Hugh appeared suddenly before her, laughing as he rescued a tray of strawberry-jam tarts that she'd almost tipped into the dirt. "Arianna!" he exclaimed. "You look lost. I thought Taliesin was taking care of you."

"That wretched squire," she said, with a laugh that sounded slightly strained. "Doubtless some pretty wench caught his eye."

Hugh led her down a path that was less crowded. He tinkled as he walked, for he bore a falcon with silver bells and varvels on his wrist. The hawk was dressed nearly as splendidly as his master in a hood embroidered with gold thread, pearls, and bright feathers.

They paused before a spice booth, and the smells of cinnamon and clove reminded Arianna of the day she and Raine had gone to the Rhuddlan market together. Somehow their problems had not seemed so insurmountable then. But that had been before he'd learned of her visions and turned away from her in fear and disgust.

Above the shouts of the moneychangers and the shopkeepers, she heard his laugh.

He had a distinctive laugh, deep, smoky. She turned and saw him, with Sybil at his side. They were watching the antics of a display of pet monkeys. Sybil tilted back her golden head and her laughter joined with his. Hers was light and tinkling, like a falcon's bells.

She is too beautiful, Arianna thought. She was so fair, so fragile. Her mouth was small and soft and always appeared on the verge of trembling open. Arianna felt ill as she looked at Sybil's beauty. Beside this white-and-gold perfection, she was awkward and plain. This woman, who had known Raine's kisses, had felt Raine's body thrust into hers. This woman, who once knew Raine's love.

Suddenly his head snapped around. Their gazes clashed and held, but, of course, she could tell nothing of his thoughts from the expression on his face.

She heard the trailing sound of Hugh's voice, and she laughed although she had no idea what the man had said. But she turned to him and flashed her brightest smile. "You, my lord earl, are most skilled at gay and flattering talk."

She let Hugh take her arm and lead her away. She knew Raine watched them. Let him be jealous, she thought. But she was the one who was jealous, she was sick inside with jealousy.

"I possess other skills as well," Hugh was saying. His voice had turned low, urgent. "Certain skills in particular, which you might come to appreciate should you bestow on me the gift of your mercy, sweet Arianna."

The gift of mercy. It was chivalry's euphemism for sex.

She pulled her arm from his grasp. "I am married, my lord earl. To your brother."

Hugh shrugged. "As if vows could bind a lady's heart. Love does not belong in wedlock, my sweet. Besides, it would be a folly of the worse sort to give your heart to Raine."

Too late. I already love him with all my heart. She knew by the way Hugh was regarding her that her thoughts must show on her face, but she no longer cared.

Hugh seemed neither dismayed nor insulted by her rejection. "You and my wife both," he said with a sigh, and then a ragged laugh. "Christ, I love him myself. When I'm not hating him."

It was a strange sort of love Hugh must feel for his brother, Arianna thought, if he could so nonchalantly play with his brother's life, and then try to bed his brother's wife.

> " 'But my love I do keep for those things of my
>   heart . . .
> *God and my lord and my trusty steed.' "*

The song carried to her pure and sweet, over the tent-tops and heads of the crowd. "Listen!" she cried.

"What?" Hugh said, but she was already dragging him in the direction of the music.

It was Taliesin singing, she was sure of it, even before she saw him. He sat on an upturned ale keg, the gittern in his lap. When she pushed her way to the fore of the audience, mostly female, that surrounded him, he looked up at her. He brushed the fall of red hair back off his face and winked at her before singing:

> *"Bereft of a way to buy his lady's love*
> *The knight did set out to earn it fair,*
> *By the strength of his sword and many brave deeds.*
> *Sore with love-longing, he embarked on a quest*
>   *To win a maiden's heart."*

At last, she thought, I will hear the rest of the story. She would know if the lady of the lake got her man. It seemed important to Arianna suddenly, as if the lady's life and her own moved on parallel lines. If the lady won the love of her brave knight, then so, too, might Arianna win the love of hers.

She felt a presence beside her, and she knew without looking that it was Raine. She barely stopped herself in time from leaning against him, seeking the shelter of his arms.

In the song the knight had come back to his lady of the lake, defeated in his quest, and she taunted him, as well he deserved it.

> " *'What wilt thou givest me now, poor knight?*
> *Stripped as thou art of thy wealth and thy pride.'*
> *And the knight once so strong*
> *Onto his knees he did fall,*
> *On the green mossy banks of the lake,*

And besought of his lady with gentle pleading:
'I have naught to give thou, fair one, but my heart.' "

Taliesin paused, and the warm summer breeze carried away the last of the vibrating chords from the gittern. In the silence Arianna heard a choking sob, and she realized to her horror that it had come from herself.

The gittern erupted again into an explosion of sound. Taliesin's voice dipped low, taut and aching, before soaring upward to a fevered gaiety.

"So she took her dear knight into her bower
And bound him she did, fast with her love.
The knight through his lady of the lake he was given
Knowledge and joy, and the gift of life eternal."

Her own knight touched Arianna on the shoulder and turned her to face him. "What a babe you are," he said. He tried to wipe the wetness off her cheeks with the pads of his thumbs. "You shouldn't cry. It's only a foolish story."

She twisted her head away, and missed the tightening of his mouth. "You could never begin to understand," she said, the breath shuddering in her throat. "All her life a girl dreams of that happening to her, of finding a man to love her that much."

He laughed harshly. "How much—enough to slay dragons?"

Suddenly she could bear it no longer. She pulled away from him and ran.

She heard his voice calling after her, but she kept running. The fair had been set up beneath the shelter of the castle, along the grassy, sloping banks of the Dee. Somehow she found her way to a postern door that had been cut into the wall and stumbled into the courtyard.

"Arianna!"

She whipped around, surprised that he had come after

her. She hadn't fled to have him chase her, and she didn't think she could bear to face him, to be with him any longer. Let him go to Sybil.

She whirled and ran up the long sweeping stairs and into the great hall. She felt like a hunted animal, running for her lair. If she could only make it to their chamber she would be safe from him. She raced across the hall, slipping on the enameled bricks. The staircase was set into a tower wall and she fled up the twisting mural stairs. Her legs tangled in her tunic and she fell to her knees with a hard jar that skinned her palms and rattled her teeth.

"Arianna!"

She glanced back over her shoulder as she pushed herself back to her feet, her breath sawing in her throat, her raw hands burning. He was almost upon her, his spurs striking sparks on the stone. His figure flashed in and out the splashes of light that poured through the arrow slits in the wall, getting closer. And then he was upon her.

He hauled her around and slammed against her, pinning her to the wall.

"Damn you." He was panting, and his eyes were throwing off sparks, brighter than his spurs had done on the stairs. He eased his weight off her, but he kept her trapped by placing his hands of either side of her shoulders. "Don't run away from me when I call you."

"Why don't you just whistle for me as you do with your hounds and save yourself the expenditure of breath?"

He brought his face close to hers, so close that if she so much as breathed her lips would brush his. She could see the rough stubble of his beard, the lines at the corners of his mouth. And his eyes, smoky gray and growing darker, like lowering storm clouds.

"If you want to have a fight, I shall be pleased to oblige you." He growled the words, low in his throat.

A part of Arianna knew that she would never get her husband back into her bed by behaving more shrewish than an alewife, but her anger with him was now a hot cloud in her brain. She shoved him, hard, in the chest. "Let me go."

His head went back, but his arms remained braced around her. He looked down the length of her body. She wore a double girdle of plaited gold thongs that wrapped once around her waist, and then again around her hips, and knotted in the front to form a *V*. Until now she'd never noticed how the fashion blatantly called attention to the round parting of her thighs.

Now she could feel his eyes on that part of her body, and she burned there.

His gaze came back to her face and the bright heat of sexual hunger glowed in his eyes. "I won't woo you naked and on my knees, Arianna."

"I haven't asked you to."

He lowered his head, and he kissed her. His mouth was rough and hungry, and it had been so long, so long. She thought she would never get enough of the taste of him.

His hand cupped her breast. She became aware suddenly of how heavy her breasts felt, aching, filled with milk. He worked the laces of her bliaut free and slipped his fingers beneath the neckline of her chainse. Her nipples were so sensitive she nearly screamed into his mouth when he oh-so-lightly brushed one with his thumb.

From above their heads came the sound of a baby's piercing wail.

"My daughter is hungry," he said against the corner of her mouth.

But he didn't let her go. Instead he looked down at her exposed breast. She watched as his fingers, so dark against the paleness of her skin, gently squeezed her distended nipple until a drop of milk appeared.

A soft, strangled sound tore out her throat.

He caught the drop of milk on his thumb, and slowly, his eyes on hers, he brought it up to his open mouth. His tongue came out, and he licked it clean and Arianna moaned his name.

"Milady?"

Edith stood at the top of the stairs, a squalling bundle in her arms. The maidservant's cheeks were pink, but her mouth was drawn into a tight line of disapproval. "Forgive me, milady. But Nesta . . . she is hungry."

Raine watched his wife's dark brown hair sway back and forth, caressing her bottom as she disappeared up the stairs, and his hands trembled to touch her.

He knew that if he rubbed his face in that hair it would smell of lemons. He could follow her into the chamber and watch her nurse Nesta, and he could imagine the feel of her nipple budding up hard and round in his mouth, and the taste of her, ah God, the taste of her. Afterward, while their babe slept, he could lay his wife on the bed and undress her slowly, and then kiss and touch every inch of her skin. He could spread her legs wide and bury his face between them and lick and suck her there until she shuddered and quivered against his mouth. Then he could bury his heat inside of her and die a little. Just the thought of doing those things made his sex so hard he had to lean against the wall and squeeze his eyes shut, his chest jerking as he fought for breath.

He wanted her. Christ, how he wanted her.

But he couldn't bear the thought of how she had seen him in those visions, seen him vulnerable and scared, alone and aching. It was too intimate, more intimate than sex. Or perhaps as intimate as sex with her could be if he let it. He knew he couldn't stay away from her forever, no man had that much will. But he would take her again only when he was ready, when he was sure he could come out of it at the end without her possessing him utterly and forever, body and soul.

So instead of doing what he wanted to do, which was to follow her up those stairs and spend the rest of the day and night loving her, he went back down into the hall.

He spotted Taliesin immediately, lounging against one of the pillars, the gittern slung across his chest by a strap.

For some reason the sight of the squire brought anger squeezing up into Raine's chest. It was the wretched boy's constant romantic babble about wooing maidens and quests and love everlasting—Christ, it had even gotten him started thinking along those lines.

He advanced on the boy, wagging a stiff finger. "Not another peep out of you, wretch. Or I'll wrap that God-cursed noise-box around your head."

Laughing, Taliesin held up a hand in surrender. "My lord, if you care not what you do to my head, at least spare a thought for the gittern."

Raine growled a curse and flung himself through the passage screen. He found himself back out in the court-yard with no clear thought of how he'd gotten there. He needed to buy some things, a good breeding horse for one, but he didn't go back to the fair. His legs of their own accord seemed to carry him instead to the tilt yard.

His boots stirred up puffs of dirt as he walked the length of the field. The quintain stood at the end of the run—a mannikin covered with an old coat of mail and a shield, set on a post. From this distance, with the setting sun in his eyes, the quintain almost looked like a real man, an old battered knight who had fought for too long, seen too much.

Raine had not been weaned on destrier and lance as Hugh had been, as was any boy who hoped to be a knight. Instead, he had snuck out at night on a horse borrowed from his father's stables to tilt at the quintain by the light of the moon. Often he was caught and flogged for it, but that hadn't stopped him.

It had hurt him at the time to think that his father thought more of his blooded horses than his own son. But he understood a little better now the earl's anger. A good war-horse cost more money than a common man could expect to earn in a lifetime. An unschooled boy could endanger the training and health of such a valuable beast.

Yet somehow on those borrowed horses and with no

one to show him, he had taught himself how to hold a
lance steady while charging, to turn and move a galloping
charger without using the reins. In all those hours he had
been sustained by a dream—that one day he would kneel
before his father and receive the buffet of honor, a blow
for once delivered in pride, not anger, and hear the words
from his father's lips: "Be thou a good knight."

It had not happened that way. Instead he had been
knighted in a far-off land by his father's enemy. When he
came home it had been on the day of his brother's marriage to the girl he loved, and he had stood before his
father, all of nineteen, proud and maybe a little scared, in
his armor and his spurs and with his knight's sword girded
round his waist.

His father had looked right through him and said,
"What churl is this?"

"Your bastard stableboy, my lord earl," he'd answered,
so full of himself he could have conquered dragons.
"Don't you recognize me?"

But the earl had dismissed him, as easily as flicking a fly
off his sleeve. "I thought Matilda's men had made a blind
eunuch of you," he'd said with a laugh. Others joined
with him. Hugh, and even Sybil.

Look at me, Raine had wanted to shout into that impassive face. *I am your son, damn you. Your son!* Aloud he
said, "Nay, instead they have made me a knight."

His father had looked right at him then with cold gray
eyes, eyes so like his own, and had seen not a knight, or
even a man, but a whore's bastard still. He'd known then
that between them things would never change.

He picked up a stone now and threw it at the quintain,
missing. He wondered if Arianna had seen it in one of her
cursed visions—that day in Chester's great hall during the
banquet of Hugh's wedding, when he had stood before his
father and been rejected for the last time.

"Raine . . . I have been looking for you."

He spun around. A small, slender figure walked toward

him across the field. She had her hair down, like a girl's. It swung, brushing her hips, glowing silver in the sun. Not all the memories, he decided suddenly, were bad.

"Sybil," he said, and he smiled.

They walked in silence from the tilting yard to the castle gardens. It was quiet here, sheltered from the wind by the walls and enclosed by whitethorn hedges. And cool, as it was shaded from the sun by old yews and oaks. Beds of flowers and herbs lay in geometric patterns, like the designs on a Saracen carpet. The air was almost cloyingly sweet with the smells of roses and lilies, of mint and sage and coriander.

They walked around the fish pond, and Raine caught the flicker of a silver carp among algea-scummed lily pads. The leaves above rustled and the trill of a wren floated down upon their heads.

Sybil's fingers toyed with the brooch that fastened her mantle. It was a cheap trifle, made not of silver, but tin, with no ornamenting jewels. It was fashioned in the form of a love knot.

Sybil noticed his gaze on the brooch, and she said, "Do you remember this, Raine? You gave it to me that summer you left."

"Aye," he said, though in truth he had no memory of it at all. He certainly hadn't bought it for her, as he'd never had any money when he'd worked in Chester's stables. He must have stolen it from a peddler's cart one market day. And he had not *left* that summer, he had been taken, tied to the end of a rope and driven like a slave to Rhuddlan—a hostage his father intended all along to abandon.

She stopped and turned to face him, her hands clasping his forearms. "Why won't you ask me why I married Hugh?"

"I know why."

Her mouth curled into a funny smile that trembled on the edges. "You were gone a long time, Raine."

A lock of hair drifted across her cheek, and he brushed

it back. "I never really expected you to wait," he said. He spoke the truth. He had hoped, but he had never really believed. He couldn't remember a time in his life when he had ever really believed in anyone or anything. "You were Hugh's affianced and a lady, born to be a countess. I was nearly as low as a serf, worse really. A bastard stable-boy. I never thought you would wait."

"Then you were wrong, because I waited, oh I waited and I prayed. I thanked God every day that the old earl was in no hurry for Hugh to marry, because he didn't want his heir to start thinking too soon about inheriting. But then we began hearing the stories about you, how you were so brave and took such chances. First, to win your spurs, and then in the tournaments afterward. Hugh said once that . . . that you would be dead before the age of twenty. He said it with such certainty, and I thought . . . I thought if I married him that you wouldn't have to risk your life anymore."

His surprise must have shown on his face, for she covered his lips with her fingers before he could speak.

"I know," she said, softly, sadly. "Too late I realized that you weren't doing it for me at all, but for yourself. For power, money, glory. You would have gone on risking your life no matter what I did. You always will."

Not any longer, Raine thought. He had learned that in France, when he had never been more scared of dying. Because now he had something to live for.

"Raine . . ." Her hand moved up his arm to cup his cheek. "I never stopped loving you."

The words should have warmed him, but they did not. He realized with a sudden, sharp pain that was like a spearpoint in his gut that they were being spoken by the wrong woman. *I love you. . . .*

Arianna. It was from Arianna's lips that he wanted to hear those words.

He looked down into Sybil's face, with the tiny pleats at the corners of her mouth and the freckles across her nose, and he saw a young girl who had cared for him when no one else had. He owed her so very much, and he didn't want to hurt her.

He brushed her cheek, once, lightly, with his curled knuckles. "Sybil . . . It was so long ago. We were children."

She shook her head so hard, tears splashed out the corners of her eyes. "It doesn't matter. I've never stopped loving you."

He looked past her and up, to a twilight sky, of soft and shadowed lavender. The color of her eyes. He had loved her once, but it had been a boy's love, not a man's. Yet he couldn't help wondering. . . .

He spanned her pointed chin with his fingers and tilted her face up, and he kissed her.

Her mouth was still sweet and soft. But the passion was no longer there. Perhaps it had never been there, except in his memory.

He heard a small sound. It might have been a bird, or even the wind, brushing across the hedges. But somehow he knew that it was not. He let go of Sybil and slowly turned.

Arianna stood at the edge of the pond, so close she might almost have risen from its dark, green depths, like the lady in the song. Though he wasn't close enough to see the hurt on her face, he felt it.

She brought her fist up to her mouth as if to stop a scream, or a sob. Then she turned and ran.

23

"Arianna, open the bloody door!"

"Go to hell, Norman."

Raine rubbed his fist, which throbbed from beating uselessly on the iron-banded, oiled, and slightly worm-rotted slabs of wood. He considered trying to kick the door in, then thought better of it. He spun around and tromped back down the stairs to the hall.

He found what he was looking for immediately, hanging, along with a broadsword and pair of crossed spears, on one of the mighty pillars that supported the rafters—it was a battle-ax with a three-foot shaft. Its thick, trumpet-shaped blade was a bit dull, but would suffice.

He hefted the heavy weapon in his hand and smiled grimly. The wench needed to learn that he would never tolerate her locking him out of a bedchamber, any bedchamber. It was important that she learn this now, for he suspected there were going to be many more little rough spots like this in their marriage in the years to come.

He took the stairs two at a time and strode down the length of the gallery, tossing the ax from hand to hand. "Arianna!" he called out. "Will you quit behaving like a child and let me in?"

This time she didn't even bother to curse him. He allowed five beats to tick by, and then he swung the ax with both hands and all his strength at the door.

He thought he heard a scream, abruptly smothered, but he could not be sure, for the wood cracked with a loud splintering wail. He pulled back the ax and swung again. A dozen more whacks and the door sagged in the middle like a deflating bladder, hanging by one hinge. He punched it in with his foot and burst across the threshold.

And nearly skewered himself on the tip of his own sword.

She held the weapon out in front of her with both hands, for it was heavy. But she held the blade true, and he had never seen her angrier.

They stood facing one another, both breathing heavily, he with the ax in his hand, she with the sword pointed at his middle, and he realized he had no idea what he was going to do next.

He tried a smile. "Will you kill me with my own sword, little wife?"

She did not smile back. "I ought to geld you with it."

He tossed the ax aside. He took a single step toward her. The sword did not waver. The muscles of her wrists and arms tightened.

"What you saw . . . it was not what you think."

She gave him one of those sneers she could do so well. "What do I think?"

"I have been faithful to you, Arianna. Even through those long months when we were parted, I lay with no other woman, not even a whore."

"I'm sorry you suffered on my account. But then Sybil was not in France to tempt you."

"Sybil is a childhood friend and that is all."

"You are lying in your teeth!" She flung the sword down into the rushes and spun away from him.

"I am not lying about this, Arianna, and you know it."

She walked the length of the room, then turned back.

She folded her arms across her breasts. "I'm going home to Rhuddlan."

He drew in a deep breath of relief that she had said home to Rhuddlan, not Gwynedd. He didn't want to have to keep her by chaining her to his bed. But he liked even less the idea of another confrontation with the Prince of Gwynedd, should he have to fight his way through Wales again to drag her back.

"We'll leave soon," he said, trying to make his voice sound calm and rational. "I've a brood mare to buy first and some other things."

Her head snapped back and forth. "I'm going now. You may stay if you like. Stay forever. I care not what you do."

This time he caught the telltale quiver in her voice. Her eyes were wet and dark, filled with pain. He ached to hold her—hell, he ached to do more than hold her. But part of his success in war was due to an ability to know when to press on and when to retreat.

"Go home, then, if you want, and I'll follow you in two days," he said. "But I won't let you leave until the morning. It's already growing dark and it's too dangerous to travel at night."

"What do you care what happens to me?"

"I have said you may leave tomorrow, Arianna. Do not push my temper further."

Her chin jerked up and he expected her defiance, but instead she said, "Very well. But I will not share a bed with you this night."

His jaw tightened. "Aren't you afraid I will spend the night with Sybil?"

"I've told you. I no longer care what you do."

He kept his face blank as he turned away from her and started out the room. Splinters of wood and split bands of iron were strewn like giant jackstraws over the floor. He pictured the look on Hugh's face when he saw the ruined door, and he almost laughed. He paused with his hand on the jamb and looked back. She stood at the window, her back stiff, her eyes focused on the distant blue hills of the Tegeingl.

"On my honor, Arianna, she is not my lover. Nor will she be."

Her shoulders jerked, but she did not turn around. But then her voice, proud and strong, came to him as he stepped over the broken door and into the gallery.

"I'll be waiting for you at Rhuddlan, husband."

Arianna reined in her horse and looked back across the Cheshire plain. A gust of wind whipped at her mantle, bringing with it the smell of rain. Thunderheads billowed thick on the horizon, the flat gray of steel. The color of his eyes.

Just then, clouds of orange-and-black striped butterflies, sensing the coming storm, rose up from the flattened grass, obscuring her last sight of Chester's pink towers.

Taliesin's saddle creaked as he leaned over to study her face. "This is not like you, my lady. To run like a corncrake over a little competition."

"I am not running away, for Sybil is not my competition."

His red brows arched up. "Oh? Why, then, are we leaving the battlefield?"

"The battlefield is not here, it's at Rhuddlan. And it is not another woman I must fight, but a man's fool pride."

"You do mean to fight for him then?"

She pulled her horse's head back around, kicking him into a trot to rejoin her escort and Edith, who carried Nesta. "God's death, you fool wizard. I love the man. Of course I'm going to fight for him."

Taliesin cantered to catch up with her, then eased down to her gait. He rode well, but then he did everything well, as was to be expected of someone who had doubtless lived for centuries.

He heaved a huge sigh, his eyes on a stray butterfly that

danced between his cob's ears. "I am not a wizard, my lady. Where you acquired this ridiculous notion, I do not know, but if my lord comes to hear of it the blame will be mine. He will string me up by my thumbs—"

"Stop flapping your jaws, churl. I need quiet to think."

Taliesin let her think for the space of two heartbeats. "What are we going to do to get him back into your bed?"

"*We* will do nothing."

"I was thinking a love philter might suffice."

"You would. And I would have a husband on my hands crazed with lust and trying to tup every female within a day's ride. Nay, you will have one small part in this plan, boy, and see that you do not bungle it."

Taliesin did not look pleased to be relegated to a small part of any plan. "What is it I'm supposed to do?"

"Bring him to me at the standing stones at midnight on Lugnasa night. Get him there if you have to use magic to do it."

"I know no magic, my lady."

Arianna snorted so loudly her palfrey craned its head around to see what was making the racket.

They rode in silence awhile, then Taliesin began to hum the chorus of a bawdy song. He tried again, "I still think a love philter might help—"

"Do you wish to be flung from a catapult into a cauldron of boiling oil, you worthless wizard?"

"Nay, my lady, please! And, my lady, I am not a wiz—"

"Or spitted on a pike and roasted over a slow fire like a fat goose? No love philter, do you understand me?"

He sighed. "Aye, my lady."

They crossed Offa's Dyke and there, beside the road, was the chestnut tree where she and Raine had eaten their dinner two days before. She thought of the vision she'd had on that day—of a young Raine bearing Sybil down to the grass, his man's sex hard for her. There had been a violence in his masculine need, she remembered, a fierce and raging urge to possess. But there had been softer feelings there, too, a yearning to give pleasure, to protect and cherish. Once he had not been too proud to reveal his love.

"Taliesin? Would your goddess send Raine to me if she never meant for him to love me?"

"I fear I do not understand what you mean, my lady. The Black Dragon loves you. Even the most witless of females could see that."

Sighing, she turned and looked at him. "I do know he loves me, but I want to hear the words. For only when I hear him say the words, will I know that he has at last admitted the truth of them to himself."

He thought how very good it felt to be home.

The setting sun washed the castle with a soft orange color. The wail of a horn echoed over the flat marshlands and the smell of burning oak and green yew came to him on the wind. Normally the hayward's horn marked the end of work, but today had been one of rest, a holiday to celebrate the festival of Lammas and the beginning of the rye and wheat harvest. This evening the peasants would dance caroles around bonfires and drink the lord's ale.

And perhaps, Raine thought, perhaps the lord and his lady will do a little private feasting of their own.

He smiled as he patted the purse that hung from his belt, heavy with the trifle he had bought at the Chester fair. It was a very expensive trifle—a brooch in the shape of a dragon, set with pearls, rubies, and emeralds. It was a trifle he really couldn't afford, but then it was a known fact that a man lured no hawks with an empty hand.

She was not in the hall where he expected to find her. The hall, in truth, was empty but for Sir Odo's page and Rhodri, who were heating pokers in the fire to mull cider. He called out a cheerful greeting to the boys and actually smiled. At this uncharacteristic good humor, their mouths fell open in shock, then they looked at one another, shrugged, and went back to their cider.

He was about to ask them the whereabouts of their mistress when Sir Odo came lumbering in, tally sticks and abacus in hand and a scowl on his brow, to discuss the expected income from the harvest. Raine spent the next hour with his bailiff—it wouldn't do, anyway, he thought, to appear overanxious. But when he finally mounted the stairs and entered their chamber, she wasn't there.

Taliesin was, sprawled on the padded chest beneath the window, a harp in his lap. "Where is the Lady Arianna?" Raine asked of his squire.

"Out and about."

Raine flexed his jaw. "Out and about where?"

The harp erupted into a sudden tinkling glissando. Taliesin glanced up through a veil of fox-red lashes. "Do you want your wife back in your bed, my lord?"

"She never left my bed." Raine strode the length of the room. He took off his sword and sent it sailing with a clatter onto a table, then pulled off his *broigne* and flung it at a stool, missing. He spun around. "What is it to you, anyway, where Arianna sleeps?"

"You are horn-mad and irritable with it, and I grow weary of putting up with your foul temper."

Raine advanced on the boy, thinking to give him a good taste of his foul temper, but Taliesin tossed something at him, grinning. "Don't hit me, sire. Save your strength. You'll need all of it for later."

Raine snatched the thing that Taliesin had thrown out of the air. It was a small leather bag, closed together with a bit of string. "What's this and why will I need my strength for later?"

"It's a love philter, my lord. A bit of that in a cup of wine will make the one who drinks it near mad with desire."

Raine pulled the string loose, opening the bag. He

sniffed its contents, which was a soft brown powder, like fine dust. It smelled musky. "What's in it?"

"Mandrake root, of course. Also the pulverized liver of a toad and boiled hedgehog fat. Among other things."

"God's blood."

"No. Not that," Taliesin said, and laughed.

Raine growled another curse, but he stuffed the packet beneath his belt.

Taliesin plucked at the harp strings, creating a lilting, dancing tune. "Aye, that'll put a good stiff bone in your braies, milord."

"*I* don't need it, you fool. I've been walking around hard as a battering ram for months. Are you sure this will make her mad for me?"

"Tonight is Lammas night as you know, though in Wales they do call it Lugnasa. In the time of the ancient ones, the women gathered around the *meinhirion* and offered up prayers and sacrifices to the god Lleu for a bountiful harvest. Arianna is a seer and so a part of her is drawn to the old ways. She will go to the standing stones tonight and there she will perform the ritual dance . . ." Taliesin lowered his voice, and his black eyes took on a strange and shimmering light. "Naked."

In spite of himself, Raine felt a tingling in his groin. He scowled at the squire. "Why do I get the feeling I'm playing with loaded dice? You're arranging something, and whatever it is, I doubt I'm going to like it."

The squire tossed a fiery lock over his shoulder and looked up with wide eyes, innocent as a maid who'd spent her life in a convent. "Oh, no, my lord. Goddess forfend. Arranging things—that isn't allowed."

"Damn right it's not allowed."

The girl danced among the stones. A night wind, thick with the smell of the sea, bathed her face. The air was soft, warm, caressing her flesh like a lover's hands.

A curlew cawed a warning, and she whirled, to see a knight on a black charger riding toward her.

He bore down on her and his hair, black as a raven's wing, floated behind him like a banner on the wind. The charger's hooves struck stone, and sparks flashed as he pulled the great beast to a halt, for he had seen her. The girl shivered, but it was not with fear.

She began to dance again.

Moonlight splattered the dunes with silver. The sea slashed across the beach, cutting between the rocks like scythes. He dismounted before he entered the circle of stones. He paused to watch her dance, watched as a white mist rose out of the ground like steam, enveloping her and the stones, until it seemed they danced with her. The wind whispered, telling tales long forgotten and best not remembered.

She danced, legs flashing silver, like the sea, among the grass.

She stopped suddenly before him, so close that the tips of her breasts almost brushed his chest. She had a wreath of mistletoe in her hair, which flowed over her shoulders, dark and thick, like a living mantel. But the rest of her was wondrously, gloriously naked.

He was afraid to touch her for fear she would disappear from the earth forever. She is a fairy, he thought, a creature of dreams, of yearnings that come deep in the night. Elusive, ephemeral, woman—he had never felt stronger, more powerfully male.

She took his hand.

And led him to the altar. Candles burned in melted pools of wax, surrounding the dip in the stone. The flames shimmered in the water . . . liquid fire.

They say that if a woman can get a man to drink of water that has touched the meinhirion, *then he will love her forever.*

Love her forever . . .

He waited for her, his breath suspended somewhere

between the earth and heaven and hell, waited for her to move, but she did not. So he did it for her.

He took her finger and dipped it in the water.

A crackling stream of fire leapt up her arm, flooding her in an incandescent light. Slowly, he raised her finger, wet and shining golden, up to his lips. A single drop glistened on the end of it, throwing off rainbows of light, and he caught the drop of water-light with his tongue.

Heat blasted through him like a Sahara wind, searing him bare. He felt a shiver of fear, but it was too late to go back. He didn't want to go back. He lowered his head and rubbed his tongue, wet from the water, across her lips.

Her mouth closed over his with a sudden, shattering hunger.

His fingers dug into her buttocks, and he crushed her to him hard. The wind flayed his skin. He was burning, melting, like silk held too close to a candle's flame. He could feel their pulses beating, hear them, pounding, pounding, pounding in tempo with the surf at their backs, until it seemed the pumping of their blood was at one with the tide, one with the pulsating, driving force of life. Together, beating together.

Her mouth parted from his, and he groaned at the loss. His lips felt naked, his mouth empty, his tongue lonely.

But then she was undressing him, her mouth following her hands as she pulled off his tunic. She rubbed her palms over his chest, her fingers tugging gently at his hair. "You are a warrior," she said. "My black knight." He pushed out against her hands in a deep, unconscious breath.

She knelt before him, her mouth to his belly, and she kissed the arrow of hair where it disappeared into his braies. He shuddered beneath her lips. A groan escaped his clenched teeth, and he pressed his fingers against her head.

She opened the belt that held up his braies and let it fall unheeded to the ground. His braies sagged around his

hips and she pulled them down further, freeing his sex.
She cradled it in her hands.

"You are so strong, so hard," she said, and the words
made him stronger still, harder still.

She lowered her head and took him in her mouth, and
his breath left him on a soft keen.

But it was too much, the pleasure was too much and he
couldn't bear it. He pulled her down with him into grass
wet by a silver dew.

She straddled his hips, poised above him on her knees.

He slid two fingers into her and opened her slowly. She
arched, her head falling back so that her hair brushed his
hips, and her breasts thrust up high and full. Her thighs
began to tremble first and then it spread like ripples over
her body until she was shuddering and convulsing and
then shouting his name, and his eyes stung with a sweet,
hot joy—that he could bring her to this, that it was his
name she cried.

She lowered her head and looked at him with eyes wide
open and dark with desire, her mouth swollen and slack.
He dug his fingers into her hips, and lifting her high, he
sheathed himself slowly, slowly inside of her. He wanted
it to last. He wanted it to last forever.

His hand reached up to cup her breast, but then the
wind blew and the candles flared, catching the torque
around her neck, setting it afire. So he touched that instead.

Burned. Oh God, it burned. He could feel her pulse
throbbing through the hot metal, as if he touched her
heart. It thundered through his own blood like a violent
sea beating against rocks. A curling silver mist blurred the
edges of his vision. He looked beyond her face to the
heavens and all the stars, and constellations began to
whirl like a vast millwheel and the sky, the black, black
sky bled into a white hot light.

*He stood within the circle of stones with his beloved in
his arms while around them chariot-mounted warriors*

wheeled, brandishing swords, long hair spiked, naked bod-
ies painted blue, and priests in white robes whirled in a
frenzied dance, pouring forth imprecations. A trumpet of
sound battered his ears, men shouted war cries, screams of
rage, howls of pain. Smoke stung his eyes, and the sky
burned, and he was afraid to die, for he could not bear the
thought of leaving her, even knowing that beyond death
she would be there still, waiting, his, always his. His be-
loved . . .

The sky burned red and the stars whirled and fell, raining fire, raining light. The light flooded through him, until
he became the light and the light was her, and it burned,
burned, and then was gone, and he was looking into Arianna's face, Arianna's eyes.

She was riding him, pushing up on her knees until he
touched but the edge of her, then sliding back down his
length, clenching around him, and he felt the first shudders of a release he knew he wasn't going to be able to
stop, even if it killed him, sure that it would kill him.

He shouted, spilling hot and deep inside of her.

She slumped forward onto his chest, her face nestled
within the crook of his shoulder, her heart beating hard
and loud against his chest. There were pieces of him up
there floating among the stars, but most of him was inside
her still, where he belonged. For she had stolen his soul,
this woman, his wife. He would never fully belong to himself again.

"*Cariad,*" he whispered in Welsh, a word he didn't
know he knew, a word he couldn't remember hearing.
But he knew what it meant . . . *beloved.*

And so it was as the weeks passed and summer faded to
autumn, that the Black Dragon came to understand the
meaning of joy.

He watched his people harvest the land. Villeins and
cottagers mowed the golden fields with scythes, while others followed, threshing the grain from its husks with

wooden flails. Still others fanned and tossed the grain into the air to winnow it from the straw and shaft. The breeze smelled pungently sweet from the freshly mown wheat.

But it was not Rhuddlan or the land or his place as the lord of it that was the cause of his unbounded joy. It was Arianna and their child. He needed them. More than his next breath, he needed them.

One day, after all the fields had been reaped and gleaned, Raine thought to celebrate by putting on an exhibition for the pages and squires, an exhibition of knightly horsemanship and lance play.

He let his knights do the showing off, but it wasn't long before his men were clamoring at him to put on a little exhibition of his own. They set up a dozen small rings set on stakes at intervals down the length of the tilting field. The object was to spear, while riding bareback on a galloping horse, as many as one could with the tip of one's lance. A perfect score required a feat of horsemanship, balance, and strength few men could master.

But Raine had bought himself a suit of Damascus mail with the money he had won performing that particular trick on the jousting fields in France.

He set his black charger full tilt at the row of stakes. He leaned out and away from the horse's side, legs gripping hard, lance pointed at a downward angle. Too low and the point would stick into the ground, vaulting him off the horse's back and wrenching his arm from its socket. Too high and he would humiliate himself by missing the rings entirely.

He did it perfectly—he should, after all those stolen hours of practice as a boy, paid for with beatings. The metal point scooped up the rings with neat clicks. At the end of the list, he wheeled his horse to the sound of cheering, his lance wearing all twelve rings like bracelets. He saw Arianna standing at the end of the field.

He spurred his horse, charging at a hard, free-shouldered gallop. The wind bit at his face and flattened his hair. Hooves struck the ground with a steady thunder, like a barrage from a catapult. His thighs gripped moving flesh, powerful muscles flexing and releasing, flexing and releasing, blood pumping hot and fast in his veins. She stood with her head held high and watched him come.

At the last moment he swerved and pulled up hard beside her. His destrier reared, pawing the air. She looked up at him, sea-foam eyes wide, mouth parted. But with excitement, not fear.

She is mad for me, he thought, and almost smiled. She was his, and he hadn't even had to use Taliesin's philter to get her. But she had never once said she loved him. Lust —too many women had come to him out of lust. He wanted more from Arianna.

He dismounted, turning his horse over to a page. Closer to her he could see that she looked tired, with shadows like bruises beneath her eyes and a wan tint to her skin. Nesta had kept her awake throughout the night with a cough.

Nesta . . . Every time he thought of his daughter he felt a soft warmth, a feeling of coming home. "How is our girl?" he asked. His hand slid beneath the fall of her hair to caress her neck. Arianna reached up and clung to his forearm, twisting her head up and around to smile at him.

Her smile was sweet. The warmth within him swelled, cocooning his heart, so that he had to blink a wetness from his eyes.

"Sleeping peacefully," Arianna said. "I gave her a bit of ale and mustard seed and put a poultice of burdock on her chest." She pointed toward the head of the lists. "Look, Rhodri is about to tilt now. How is he doing? Will he make a good knight?"

"He's strong. A bit reckless, but he'll grow out of that. He's got the Gwynedd guts." He saw that his words pleased her, and he smiled.

Rhodri caught Arianna's eyes and waved, grinning. He

buckled his helm, hefted his lance, and spurred his horse into a gallop toward the quintain.

The quintain was dressed up like an infidel, but with a hole in his chest. The object was to put the lance through the hole. If a rider hit the quintain anywhere else it would spin around, thwacking him off his horse.

Rhodri struck a good solid blow, but he hit the mannikin smack on its right shoulder. He tried to duck but the quintain spun, catching him on the back, and sent him flying into the mud.

Taliesin, who had been sitting on the fence, hooted and cackled and slapped his knee. "You're dead, Gwynedd!" he jeered. "Killed by old Quinty the Infidel, a better man than thee."

Rhodri pushed himself onto his outstretched arms, shaking mud out his eyes. He was so covered with slime he looked like a tarred scarecrow.

"Not only are you a dead man, Gwynedd. You're a dead man that stinks of horse piss!" Taliesin hooted and cackled some more.

Rhodri let out a bellow of rage and launched himself at the squire.

The boys tumbled together, end over end, like a bucket rolling down a hill. Taliesin kicked himself free, and both boys stood up, but Rhodri's fist shot out, quick as a bolt from a crossbow, smacking into the squire's nose and knocking him back onto his rump. Mud splattered into the air.

Arianna cried out, starting toward them, but Raine held her back. "Let them fight. It's time they got it settled between them."

Rhodri tried to settle it by kicking Taliesin in the groin. But the squire nimbly spun aside, rolling back onto his feet. He grabbed Rhodri by the hair and threw him to the ground, and Rhodri plowed a furrow in the mud with his nose.

Arianna winced and covered her eyes with her hands. But then Raine caught her peeping through her fingers.

The knights and other boys had gathered around to watch the fight, and wagers flew through the air. Amidst all the shouting at first no one heard Edith's screams. She ran across the fields, her skirts hiked up around the knees, her coif hanging askew on her head, her face twisted with fear.

"Milady! Oh, milady, come quickly. 'Tis Nesta. She is . . . oh, milady, she is so very sick."

Raine stood alone in the deepening twilight of the deserted tilting ground. His eyes, black in the hollowed-out flesh of his face, stared at the window of their bedchamber. No glow from cresset lamps bled through the shutters. Beyond them, hidden away from the air and the light, in a red cradle gaily painted with vines and flowers, lay Nesta. Six months she had lived and now she was dying.

Oh God, God, God . . . But there was no God, and there was no mercy. And he was no brave and honorable knight, no knight in silvered mail. He couldn't make himself go in there and face this particular dragon, not this one. His own death—hell, that was easy. But not his Nesta, not his baby.

Still, he had taken a step toward the castle when a tortured scream floated out the opened doors of the hall. Raine jerked to a stop, his eyes squeezing shut as anguish closed around his heart like a fist. Eventually, because he had to, he began walking again, toward the hall that now, after that single unearthly scream, was silent.

The air inside the darkened chamber was close and still. Arianna stood beside the cradle, rocking it and singing to Nesta as if she still lived.

Edith laid a hand on his arm. Her cheeks were thick with tears, her eyes nearly swollen shut. "The Lady Ari-

anna has gone mad with grief, my lord. She cannot accept—"

"Get out," he grated, and the maidservant, sobbing,
scurried out the door. He did not go all the way up to the
cradle. Nothing was going to make him look at Nesta
dead. Nothing.

He stood in the middle of the room, unable to breathe
for the pain that squeezed his chest. A fierce and terrible
anger gripped him, anger with Arianna. He had trusted
her with his heart and now he was hurting again, and this
time the pain was unbearable, and it was all her fault.
Somehow she had wormed her way in under all his careful armor, she had made him start caring about things
again, even though he knew better. Start caring, even the
least little bit, and he knew he was just asking for a kick in
the guts.

Even in the midst of his agony he knew his thinking
wasn't rational, that Arianna could not be blamed for
Nesta's death. Still, he could not stop it from coming out
his mouth. "How could you let this happen?"

She turned her head and looked at him out of lifeless
eyes. "Don't worry, Raine. It's only a little cough."

He could feel his face hardening. *Stop it,* he told himself. *Stop it now.* But he could not. "You're so good at
seeing things, Arianna. Why didn't you see this?" He
flung his arm out in the direction of the cradle. "Why did
you give her to me in the first place, if you were only
going to let her die?"

She made a fluttering motion with her hand. She turned
back around and looked at the crib, blinking as if dazed.
Her hands wrapped around the edge of it, and she
hunched over. A sob tore out of her, and then another
and another and another, until the sound of her tearing,
broken weeping smothered the room.

"I'll go speak to the wainwright about a coffin," he said
to no one in particular.

He turned and walked toward the door, not really see-

ing where he was going, lost in a hell he knew there was
no coming back from.

"Raine!"

He kept walking. She twisted around, falling onto her
knees, one hand reaching out for him. But he didn't
know, for he had not looked back.

A crucifix lay across her tiny chest. She rested upon a
bier, draped in a black pall. Around her tall candles
burned. Flames flickered in the empty darkness, glowing
off the wooden rood and glinting in the gilt of the saints'
effigies and the gems in the reliquary.

Beside her, Arianna stood and grieved, alone.

She tried to pray, but the words were a jumble in her
mind. Every time she breathed, the sweet smell of incense
made her want to choke. She felt as if red hot awls had
been thrust into her eyes. They were empty sockets now,
incapable of any more tears.

I cannot bear this, she thought. *God must end this right
now, for I cannot bear it.*

The chapel door creaked open. Slowly, she turned,
wanting it, needing desperately for it to be Raine.

Candlelight glinted off red hair. Taliesin walked down
the chapel's squat nave on silent feet. He stopped before
her, his young face grave, his eyes glittering and old. "Oh,
my lady . . ." he said, that was all. But there were worlds
upon worlds of sorrow in those three words.

Arianna turned back to the bier. Tears . . . there were
fresh tears on her cheeks. God, where were all these tears
coming from? Grief was endless, she knew that now. It
didn't stop, it just went on and on and on.

"We must bury her soon . . . Oh, God, Taliesin.
Where is he?"

"He loved her, my lady."

She whipped around. "But I loved her too! Can't he
see how . . ." She stuffed a fist into her mouth.

"He is hurting, my lady."

"Does that give him the right to hurt me?" She pounded her chest with her fist. "I love him and he is *killing* me."

"Love always hurts, my lady. Even at its most wondrous there is that sweet agony underneath—the knowledge that to risk loving, is to risk losing and hurting. To risk sometimes destroying the one you love . . . or being yourself destroyed."

Raine felt things too deeply, she understood that now. It was his one weakness—when he loved, he loved too hard. "He will never risk that sort of pain again," she said. *More loss,* she thought. *More tears. Without him, without his love, I cannot bear it. But with me, with my love, he is the one being forced to give more than he can stand.*

Taliesin touched her shoulder. A soft heat flowed into her, a golden light. She felt it deep within her, in her soul.

"He will love again, for you will show him how. Go to him, child. He needs you and this time it is you who must be the strong one."

She wasn't sure how she knew where Raine was. Perhaps Taliesin had put the place in her mind. *Go to him, child,* he had said. Yet the words hadn't sounded strange coming from someone younger than she. But then he was not really a beardless squire, he was *llyfrawr,* a shape-changer, and he was older than time.

Dark gray stones against a pale gray sky, the *meinhirion* stood as they had always stood, anchored to the earth, reaching for the stars. The wind moaned through the dry grass, buffeting the stones. Yet still they stood.

One night they had come together here in shattering passion and possession, and it had seemed their love was older than the stones. A love so strong that even the passing of centuries could not kill it. Like a boulder on the beach, she thought. The sea came and swallowed it, but when the tide left again, the boulder remained—endurable, enduring. Forever standing, like the *meinhirion*.

He was on the beach, at the very edge of the sea. The waves reached for him, nearly touched, then receded. He stood with his hands fisted at his sides, his head thrown back. As if he were screaming, though she heard no sound.

She did not call his name. Yet he turned.

Something had broken inside of him. His face had shattered, his eyes bled pain. He could hide nothing from her anymore. He stood naked before her, down to his soul.

She took the first step, but he was the one who came stumbling to her across the sand. He fell to his knees and pressed his face into her thighs, turned his cheek over and over against her thighs, like someone blinded.

Her hand hovered over his hair, and then she touched him.

"Oh God, God, Arianna . . . hold me." A silent sob shuddered through him, and then another. And then they were no longer silent—but the harsh, tearing sobs of a man who had never learned how to weep. "Please hold me . . ."

24

"Raine!"

She ran up the hill, skirts held high, bare legs whipping through the grass.

Ox-carts carrying timber and stone groaned to a halt; big wooden hammers paused in midair over chisels and stone; diggers leaned on their shovels and laughed—all work on the lord's new castle stopped, while the men watched the Lady Arianna run.

"Raine!"

He waited for her, legs spread, hands on his hips, his mouth fighting a smile. "There are forty men working here, and every one of them just got an eyeful of your legs," he said when she had danced to a halt in front of him.

Her head tilted back, her eyes laughed. "And a piddling lot of men they are if they've never gotten a look at a woman's legs before. Quit scowling at me, Raine. I've wonderful news. I tossed up my breakfast into the chamber pot this morning."

"Shall I send out the heralds?"

"Not for eight months or so."

But the significance of what she'd said had just struck

home to Raine. Joy blazed across his face. "Morning sickness!"

She opened her mouth to give him all the details, but he seized her around the waist and pulled her up to crush his lips to hers. He whirled her around and around, mouths locked together, her toes skimming the ground, her hair billowing away from her head like a sail.

He stopped spinning, and they clung together a moment while the world went on whirling dizzily around them. He laughed against her neck and she twisted her fists in his tunic, and his heart was hammering so hard he thought his chest would crack.

She touched his cheek. "Let's go for a walk by the river."

Their feet crunched on the frozen mud along the shore, crushing the ice into star-burst patterns. The river ran flat and gray, reflecting the pale winter sun like polished mail.

A biting wind carried the smell of burning lime, which was used for the mortar. And sounds as well, the hawing and chiseling of stone, the screech and groan of pulleys, the shouts and curses and the hoarse laughter of men at labor. From here, looking up at the bluff, he could barely see the beginnings of the bailey wall and mural towers. The main keep, already two man-lengths high, was embraced by a scaffolding of ropes and sapling poles. Twelve feet of stone a year it took to build a tower.

It surprised him sometimes to think that he had dared to start a project that would take so long to see to fruition. He had always been a man who had measured his future in hours, not years.

They walked along the riverbank hand in hand. She rubbed her thumb along the calluses on his palm, then stopped and turned into him and brought his hand up to her lips and kissed his curled knuckles.

"Raine, I'm afraid."

He threaded his hands through her hair, tilting her face. He knew what she feared; he feared it as well. That the child would die. His own fear was compounded—she, too, could die.

He let his hands fall to her shoulders, then worked them up over the neck of her bliaut until he touched the bare skin of her throat and felt her pulse. "It will be all right," he said, and drew her to him, held her tightly against him, stroking her back. Her arms went around his waist.

They were empty words, yet she took comfort from them, or from the arms that held her. God knew, he took comfort from hers.

They stood that way for a long time, wrapped in each others arms, chest pressed against chest. She drew apart. She looked up at him, and he saw the truth in her eyes before she spoke it.

"I love you, Raine."

The warmth, the sweet, soft warmth, enveloped him, and he knew that at last, at last, he had come home. No, that was wrong. He'd never had a home before, and now he had found one.

He tried to tell her he loved her, too, but the thought got stuck somewhere between his heart and his throat. So instead, his lips came down to caress hers in a tender, endless kiss.

He walked her back to the castle, the old one. But he did not go with her up to their chamber. He went to the chapel.

Once, in a field in France that was already stained red with the blood of men who'd died the day before, a priest had told him it wasn't necessary to have faith, only to pray and that God would heed the words. He hadn't believed it at the time. The God he knew never listened.

He hesitated at the chapel door, knowing himself for a hypocrite. The smell of incense and burning candle wax wafted out the opening, black like the mouth of a cave, bringing with it a jumble of memories, of childhood hours spent going through the motions of a worship he had never believed in. The sculptured saints that flanked the portal seemed to smirk at him as he entered.

Though it was the lord's duty to set a good example, he rarely attended the Mass, and so he had not often been in here. The paintings on the walls glowed like brocades, but he could not feel God in them, or in the sacred vessels of silver and gold. He laid on the floor before the altar in the attitude of prayer, arms stretched out from his sides. The stone was cold against his face and smelled dank, like a grave.

He thought he would have a hard time with the words, but they poured out of him, silent, beseeching, from the heart.

Dear Lord . . . Don't take her. Do anything else, take everything else, but leave me Arianna. Don't take Arianna from me.

Two months later, Arianna found herself leaning against a cruck that supported the thatched roof of a hovel, dripping rainwater into the dirt.

Christina, the draper's daughter, dipped a ladle into a black iron cauldron that hung by a chain over the fire. She spooned soup into wooden bowls and cast a nervous smile at Arianna over her shoulder. Then her gaze slid to the tawny-haired man who lay, sweating and flushed with fever, on a straw pallet against the wall.

Rain cascaded like a cataract over the lintel of the door, left open to let in the day's meager light. Gusts of wind sent water splashing across the threshold that had been whitewashed, as they were in all Welsh homes, even the most humble, to keep the devil from entering. This home was indeed humble. It was a *hafod*—a summer hut used by Welsh herdsmen. It was not a pleasant place to spend a winter's day.

Circular in shape and made of tightly woven osier reeds, the hut had no hearth. But a makeshift one had been scooped out of the floor and vented through a hole

in the roof, that let in more rain than it let out smoke. The
fire of wet vine branches crackled and spat. In spite of the
open door, the air inside was close, smelling of wood
smoke and soup, and underneath, of wet sheep.

From his pallet in the corner, Kilydd, his brow lowered
into a frown, watched his woman carry the bowls of soup
and wooden spoons over to the table. His eyes flashed to
Arianna and his scowl deepened.

Christina set the bowls onto the scarred, ringed-marked
boards, then she cut off hunks of brown bread from a
stale loaf. There were two other men in the hut. One
already sat at the table, a battered harp in his lap. His
fingers moved nimbly over the strings, picking out a plain-
tive melody. His voice, dark and rich and so very Welsh,
like the smell of the soup, filled the tiny hovel:

*"No one shall dare to trod on my mantle,
No one without bloodshed shall plough my land . . ."*

The other man tapped into a barrel of ale and brought
two brimming leather jacks to the table. He started to
straddle the bench.

Kilydd's voice, weak but irritable, came from the pallet.
"Get out of here."

The man stopped, half crouched over the bench. "It's
bloody pissing out there!"

"Out!" Kilydd bellowed, and the men, grumbling,
picked up their food and left. "You, too, Christina,"
Kilydd said. Then he added, his voice softer, "Please."

The girl gave him a look that was halfway between hurt
and anger. Taking a mantle from a peg off the wall, she
stepped out into the rain.

"They'll get wet," Arianna said.

"There's another *hafod* just down the hill." Kilydd's
gaze took in the slight swell of her stomach and his honey-
colored eyes narrowed. "You're breeding again. You
shouldn't have come out in this weather."

"It wasn't pouring good Welsh sunshine when I left."

He started to laugh, but then the laugh turned into a tearing hack that jerked at his chest, leaving his face purple. "Did you bring something for this bloody cough?" he said when he had gotten back his breath.

Arianna pushed her fur-trimmed *chaperon* off her head and reached within the folds of her mantle for her medicine bag. She poured a jack of ale and mixed into it a measure of horehound.

She sat beside him on the pallet, putting the jack into his hands. The wind coming in through the open doorway lifted the sweat-dampened hair on his brow. This close to him she could see that he was sicker than she had thought. His flesh burned with the fever, and his skin had a papery look, like a dried-out husk. But she no longer felt love for him, not even pity. She would never forget or forgive how he had thrust a knife between Taliesin's ribs.

She made both her face and her voice hard. "I wouldn't have come to you, cousin, even knowing that you were ill. But I am here because Christina said you wanted to talk about surrendering to my husband. Did she lie?"

Kilydd's head fell back weakly onto the pillow. "Nay, she didn't lie. But I'm not committing suicide, Arianna. I'll want a guarantee of mercy first. Can you get it for me?"

"Would you swear to give up all claim to Rhos and go away, leaving us to live in peace?"

"To him I would swear."

"No, to me. You must swear it to me. Your blood kin."

He flushed, his eyes shifting away from hers. He would break his oath to Raine, this she knew. But not an oath given to blood kin. No Welshman would dare, for on Judgment Day, it was said, the Welsh would have to answer to God in Welsh.

"Aye, curse you," he said. "I'll swear."

"Now. I'll hear your oath now, Kilydd ap Dafydd. On peril of your soul."

He glared at her. "On peril of my soul I swear before
God that I will give up all claim to Rhos and make no
more war on that Norman bastard you call husband, God
rot *his* wretched soul."

"That was a very poor oath, and I don't think I believe
it. Why do this at all if you are so unwilling?"

His fist thudded on the cot. "It's Christina, damn the
wench. She's latched herself to my side like a leech." His
wide mouth spasmed, and he swung his hand in an arc.
"Look at this place. Another month up here and her
beautiful white skin will start to look like a ham cured in a
smokehouse. She's rail-slat thin as 'tis and wasting away
even as I look at her. I told her she should leave me the
hell alone and go back to her shop in Rhuddlan." He
looked down, punishing the blanket with his fists. "We
had a fight."

"Small wonder, that is. I would have clouted you with a
broom for such sweet words."

Kilydd's head came up, and he flashed a smile. "She
poured a jack of ale over my head."

Arianna contemplated her cousin. In truth, he was
handsome, with his flowing blond mustaches and soft,
golden eyes. But there was a spitefulness in him, and a
cravenness that Arianna didn't like. There was no ac-
counting, she thought suddenly, for some women's tastes.

But she did still like Christina, and so she tried to explain to Kilydd what he was being too obtuse to see.
"When a woman loves a man all she wants is to be with
him, to spend her life with him and bear his children."

"Pity then that your papa the prince married you to a
Norman bastard," he said, a sour curl to his mouth.

Suddenly, through the splashing rain, they heard the
rumbling thunder of approaching hooves followed by a
thin scream like a trapped hare. Arianna ran to the door,
while from the pallet, Kilydd blistered the air with his
oaths.

Rhuddlan knights surrounded the hut. Kilydd's men al-

ready lay flat on the ground, their arms trussed behind
their backs. Two horsemen had bracketed Christina
against a tree. She had her hands to her face, weeping, but
she was not being hurt.

Arianna turned from the doorway and looked at
Kilydd. His face, even with the fever, was blanched with
fear. "And a pity it is that my Norman bastard has captured you, cousin . . . *before* you had a chance to surrender."

She stepped out into the rain.

The black knight looked down at her from the height of
his horse, menacing in his dark armor. She wondered if he
had expected to find her here, for he did not appear surprised to see her. Perhaps he had followed her.

Without a word, he dismounted before her.

With his face like this, wiped free of all expression, he
looked as he had on the day they first met—ruthless and
cruel. But she knew him now, as surely he must know her.
He must know that if she were here with Kilydd, then
there was a reason for it, and that she would tell him.

One of the men brought over her horse. Raine made a
step of his clasped hands and boosted her into the saddle.
"Sir Odo, take the Lady Arianna back to Rhuddlan," he
said, his voice flat. He still had not spoken a word to her.

"Aye, sir." Sir Odo's face was as blank as his liege
lord's. But not his eyes. The last time something like this
had happened, the big knight had looked at her with disgust and disillusionment. This time she saw only worry in
his kind eyes.

He, at least, thought Arianna, *no longer believes me capable of betrayal.*

The clouds had emptied themselves for the moment. A
cold wind flattened the grass and whipped at the edges of
Arianna's mantle. The scudding storm cast shadows on
the land. The cries of the crows were brittle in the air.

She gathered up the reins and urged the horse into a
canter, leaving Sir Odo to follow.

* * *

It was evening before Arianna sought out her husband.
She appeared at the door to their bedchamber, as he was
just stepping into a copper-banded, wooden bathing tub.
He had his back to her. Steam wafted up from the tub to
wreathe him in a perfumed mist. The only light in the
room came from the brazier and a single wall cresset, so
that a soft, golden glow bronzed his skin.

Edith stood beside the tub, there to assist with his bath.
With a silent jerk of her head, Arianna sent the maidservant from the room.

She knelt behind him, and taking up a cloth, began to
lather his back.

He flexed his shoulders, sighing. She lowered her head
and planted her lips on the nape of his neck.

"A little lower, Edith, love . . . ah, that's it."

She nipped his ear, hard.

He grabbed her wrist and pulled her around. Her chest
landed with a splat in the water and her face wound up
bare inches from his. Hot water lapped around her
breasts.

"You knew it was me."

"I smelled you, little wife."

"Are you saying I stink?"

He showed his teeth in a strange smile. "Not at all."

He let her go, and she straightened. Cooler air bathed
the warm, wet silk of her bliaut and she felt her nipples
tighten. She wondered if he saw them, and glanced up to
see that he did. But no warmth softened his eyes. They
remained as hard and flat as the flint that was their color.
Her eyes locked with his, she lathered her hands with the
soap and rubbed them over his chest.

His flesh was hot. The steam, smelling of violets, rose
between them, so that the features of his face blurred and
softened. The water lapped against the sides of the tub.
Rain rattled against the shutters. A single bead of sweat

trickled down her neck into the valley between her breasts.

Her rubbing, stroking palms moved steadily lower, across the planes of his chest, over the ridges of his stomach, and lower still. He grabbed her hands, pushing, and they slid off his flesh with a soft, sucking sound.

"You have not asked me what I will do with him," he said.

"You will do what you must. . . . You have not asked me how you came to find me there with him."

"He wanted you to arrange for his surrender."

"He told you that."

"Aye." He let go of her hands and cupped her cheeks between his wet palms. "I trust you, Arianna. You are my staunchest vassal. But I have come to think that I was wrong to force you to chose between me and your blood kin, your people. It is an unnatural thing—"

She stopped the flow of his words with her fingers. "I have chosen." She moved her fingers back and forth, once, across his hard mouth. "I love you above all others, Raine. I always will." She replaced her fingers with her lips, giving him an unhurried, deep kiss.

She ended the kiss first, saving more for later. She began to wash him again, her hands moving over his legs. But only going so far up between his thighs. Still, she heard the catch in his breathing.

"I put him and the girl on a ship for Ireland," he said.

He had spared Kilydd for her, and she loved him all the more for it because she knew he had done it against his better judgment. He believed he risked future trouble, yet to please her, he had been willing to take that risk.

"You might come to regret it," she said. "He probably won't stay there."

"Aye, in that you are right. He probably won't."

She rubbed her thumb across the sharp angle of his hipbone, following it to the meeting of his pelvis. But her eyes were fastened onto his. "If he does not stay there, if he comes back to make war on you again and you must hang him," she said, "then I will stand by your side and watch you do it, and I will not weep for him."

He said nothing. He had already said it—she was his staunchest vassal.

Her hands moved down between his legs. "There is, I think, a soft side to you, husband."

"Like hell. I have no soft sides."

Her hand enveloped him, and she smiled.

25

The alewife took a sip of the ale, swished it around her mouth, threw back her head and swallowed loudly. She screwed her face up in concentration and a silence descended on the crowd as it held its collective breath.

" 'Tis fit to drink," she finally said, with a solemnness worthy of a bishop. The crowd let go of its breath in a single sigh.

A sloshing leather jack of the brown liquid was pushed into Arianna's hands. She took a sip, pronounced it delicious, and the villagers cheered. Raine, too, was given a jack. He up-ended his and drank it down at once to the accompaniment of more cheering. The ale left a residue of foam on his upper lip, and he licked it off with his tongue. Arianna, watching, thought how she would have liked to lick it off for him.

But they were in too public and holy a place for such a display. They were the special guests of honor at the town of Rhuddlan's annual church-ale. Kegs of the special brew had been rolled into the cemetery. It would be sold by the jackful, along with loaves of fresh bread, with all profits going to the church.

At the moment the church was being used to store the

surplus hay from the harvest and the smell of the freshly
mown grass was so thick in the air, it tickled Arianna's
nose. A late June sun, yellow as gorse flowers, beamed
down from a flawless sky, and Arianna would have
laughed for the joy she felt—if she also didn't feel more
pregnant than a sow carrying a double litter.

Jack after jack of ale were purchased, consumed, and
purchased again. Taliesin, gittern swinging from his shoulders, gathered up a little makeshift group of musicians
and a tabor, a sackbut, and a pair of timbrels launched
into a rousing tune that made up for in volume what it
lacked in style. The villagers joined hands and whirled
furiously in the carole, singing at the top of their lungs,
and the church bell set up such a clamor that Arianna
winced, fighting an urge to clap her hands over her ears.
The dancers whirled faster and faster until they blended
together like the spokes of a spinning cartwheel.

Arianna's foot began to tap. "I would like to dance,
husband."

"Absolutely not."

She poked at her enormous stomach. "Look at this. I
am fat as one of those ale barrels. I want this baby to
come."

Raine patted the spot where she had poked. "Our
daughter will come when she is ready. You are not to
jiggle her out of you."

"I keep telling you, Raine, though you do not listen.
This time it is a son that I am breeding for you."

They stayed to drink another cup of ale and then
walked back to the castle, his arm supporting her. "I
shouldn't have let you talk me into this," Raine said,
when she had made him stop for the third time so that she
could catch her breath. The babe rode so high it pushed
against her lungs.

"Dame Beatrix said a good long walk might make it
come," she answered him. "You've never been pregnant,
Raine. You don't know what it's like."

"God be praised for that. When we get home you will do something quiet. How about a game of tables?"

She made a face. "Tables are boring."

"You only say that because I always win."

Arianna's fingers hovered over a whalebone bishop and a smile played around her mouth. With a decisive movement she pushed the game piece down the board. "I believe I have just checked you, husband."

Raine grunted. "The game is not over yet. In truth, I have you right where I want you, little wife."

Arianna's smug smile suddenly turned into a grimace. Raine jumped to his feet, sending knights, bishops, and pawns into the rushes. "Did you feel a pain?"

She sucked in a deep breath. "Nay, 'twas only gas."

"You're going to lie down this instant. If you put up any more arguments, I'll turn you over my knee."

"I'd like to see you get me over your knee with me in this condition. It'd be like turning a turtle onto its back."

Nevertheless, he was relieved to see that she allowed him to lead her over to the bed. She wasn't the only one anxious for the babe to put forth its appearance. His guts had been tangled into knots like snarled gittern strings for weeks now.

Arianna had just fallen asleep, and Raine was about to leave the room, when the trumpeter at the gatehouse announced a visitor. He went to the window, surprised to see a lone woman ride into the bailey. He was even more surprised when he saw that the woman was Sybil.

He met her at the bottom of the steps of the great hall. She pushed the hood of her mantle off her head and looked up with big lavender-blue eyes. Eyes that stared at him above a cheek that bore a livid bruise in the shape of a man's hand.

He guided her inside with a light arm around her shoulders, taking her up onto the dais and into the small antechamber that led off the end of the hall.

He turned her around to face him. He tilted her chin up, and he brushed his thumb along her cheekbone, just above the bruise. "Did Hugh do this to you?" They were the first words he had spoken to her. Her eyes fluttered closed and she nodded. "Why?"

"We argued. He . . ." She stopped, lifting her shoulders in a helpless little shrug. "It's for a different reason every time, and the same reason." She pulled away. Her fingers twisted around the love-knot brooch he couldn't remember giving to her, and when she looked up again, he saw that her eyes were wet and shining with unshed tears. Her lower lip trembled open and she caught it with her teeth. "I wish that I could just leave, Raine. Sometimes I want to go away somewhere and never come back."

She looked so hurt and bewildered, like a little girl who has just been punished and doesn't know why. But there was nothing he could do for her. She was Hugh's, and he could not come between his brother and his brother's wife.

Suddenly her shoulders hunched and she buried her face in her hands, muffling her words. "I shouldn't have come here. I know it's wrong, but I . . ."

He made the mistake of touching her, and she fell into him, wrapping her arms around his waist, rubbing his chest with her breasts, burying her head in his neck. "Don't say it's too late. Say you still love me. Tell me you still love me."

He grabbed her shoulders, stilling her. He felt the wetness of her tears on his neck, the beating of her heart against his chest, the softness of her. And the wrongness of her.

"Sybil . . ."

She lifted her head and looked at him.

He stared into eyes that were soft purple, the color of an evening sky one summer day when they had made love in a field of grass. In a sad and futile way, she was right, he hadn't stopped loving her. But it was the girl of that summer he loved, not the woman of today. Because of that girl, in memory of that girl, he didn't want to hurt her.

But he was going to have to.

"It's over with us, Sybil. It ended on the day you married my brother."

The words came out harsher than he'd meant them to. Her chest jerked and her hands clenched into fists against his chest. "But I still love you."

He gave her a little shake. "You're in love with a memory. But memories are only pieces of the past. Whatever might have happened or could have happened, didn't. We are married to other people now, for better or worse. Go home, Sybil. Go home and keep the memories, but let go of the past."

Her head fell forward and she laid her brow on his chest. Slowly she straightened and when she looked up at him this time, a smile trembled on her lips. "But you did love me once. For a while you were mine."

He answered her smile with one of his own. "It was a sweet summer, Sybil. I will never forget it."

His hands had closed around her shoulders, to push her off of him, when he heard a sharp, angry intake of breath. He jerked his head around and there stood Arianna, looking at him with Sybil in his arms.

He relived a thousand years of hell in that one moment, while she stood there and looked at him, saying nothing, just looking at him with blank sea-foam eyes. She turned and walked away, her stomach leading the way before her.

"Hell," Raine said. And then he said it again. "Ah, hell."

Sybil had let go of him and taken a step back, but he didn't notice because he was still staring at the now empty doorway. She had to say his name twice before he turned and looked at her.

She smiled, a smile from the old days that dimpled the

corners of her mouth. "Oh, Raine, I do believe you've gone and fallen in love with your little Welsh princess."

Raine took a deep breath and let it out slowly. "Aye, I love her." It was an odd thing, but the words, once said, tasted good in his mouth. In truth, they tasted so fine, he said them again. "I love her."

"But you haven't told her, have you?"

"Well, I . . . Well, not exactly. But, dammit, she knows I love her."

Her smiled faded. She touched his cheek, once, lightly. "Tell her anyway, Raine. Tell her before it's too late. It's a rare thing, is love. And too easily lost."

They looked at one another—she thinking of the past, he of the future. She stood up on her toes and pressed her lips to his in a light, fleeting kiss that spoke of good-bye.

He escorted her out of the hall and put her on her horse, but he didn't even wait long enough to watch her ride out the gate. Instead he bounded back inside and up the stairs. He stared at a thick expanse of iron-banded oak and sighed. He really didn't want to take a battle-ax to his own bedchamber door.

"Arianna, let me in so that we can talk."

Silence.

"Arianna, you are judging me falsely again, and I grow weary of it."

Silence.

"Arianna, I can't tell you I love you through a bloody door!"

Somebody snickered.

Raine whipped around. Taliesin slouched against the wall, his arms folded over his chest, and a smirk on his pretty mouth. "Have you tried opening it, my lord?"

"Huh?"

"The door. Mayhap it isn't even bolted."

Raine grabbed the latch and the door swung open easily beneath his hand. He shot Taliesin a quelling look before the boy could start flapping his jaws again, then he took a deep breath, girded his loins . . . and stepped into an empty chamber.

"She went to the *meinhirion*," Taliesin said, appearing suddenly at his side. The boy heaved a huge sigh. "Once again you have bungled things. This is getting to be a bad habit with you. Why the goddess ever thought—"

Raine's hands clamped down hard on the boy's shoulders. "She didn't try to ride there, did she?"

"Nay, she couldn't. She walked."

Raine lifted his eyes heavenward, thanking God for small favors. "I'll wring her neck for this!" he bellowed, giving his squire a rough shake because the boy was in his hands and handy.

He felt anger boiling up within him and he let it rise, reveling in it. It was the anger of righteous indignation, of a man who has found himself in love with a woman who bewilders him and drives him mad, but whom he couldn't possibly live without.

The squire watched his master's broad back disappear down the stairs and his eyes shimmered, shooting out sparks like falling stars.

The light faded. He rubbed his aching shoulders—he would be sporting bruises for a week at least. The kitchen wenches and dairy maids would all feel sorry for him, they would want to kiss him and make him better.

He threw back his fiery head and laughed at that. His laughter, rich and deep, echoed down and up and through the years.

She had known him to keep his anger tightly under control, and she had felt the full blast of his icy rages. But never had she seen him hot-blooded and bellowing. If it wasn't for the memory of once again catching him with that wretched Sybil in his arms, she would have laughed.

He leaped from his horse and came charging up to her, huffing and puffing and breathing fire, just like the dragon he was named after. "What in hellfire is it that you think you're doing?"

She jerked her chin into the air and looked down her nose at him, because she knew he hated it. "What are you doing here, Raine? Shouldn't you be with Sybil? Already she probably grows lonely for you . . . for the feel of your arms around her."

He flushed slightly, then his jaw tightened and jutted forward. "What am *I* doing here? What are you doing here?" He flapped his arm. "You're about to have a baby and you're out wandering the bloody moors."

A part of Arianna was suddenly aware that her skin felt clammy and the roots of her hair were damp with sweat, but most of her was more preoccupied with making her husband suffer just a bit before she forgave him. "Why should you care what I do, or where I am? When it's Sybil you love."

Raine let loose with a string of curses that shocked even Arianna's experienced ears. "I love *you,* you thick-headed wench! I love you!"

"You say that now."

"Aye, I say it now," he said, somewhat calmer, only battering her eardrums a little. "I say it now . . . I love you, little wife."

"Now doesn't count."

"What do you mean, now doesn't count?" He was bellowing again. Nice dragonlike roars. "Why doesn't it count?"

"Because I've put the words into your mouth. They didn't spring from your heart."

"Jesus wept." He pushed his hand through his hair in that typical masculine gesture of exasperation with a female. He pointed his finger at her, shaking it like a scolding alewife. "I know what you want. Well, fine—that's just what you're going to get."

He pulled his tunic over his head with a vicious jerk and sent it sailing through the air. His chainse followed.

He leaned against one of the standing stones and yanked off one boot, switched feet, and then yanked off the other. He started to peel off his chausses.

It suddenly occurred to Arianna that he was taking off his clothes. All of his clothes.

Surely, he couldn't be thinking he was going to—no, of course he couldn't. "Raine, stop." Off came his braies. He was definitely naked now. "Raine, what are you *doing?*"

He fell down onto his knees before her, seizing her hands. "You wanted me naked and on my knees, just like in that cursed song. Well, here I am." His voice had softened. She had never seen his face look the way it did now. All that he was feeling was there, in the tautness of the skin across his cheekbones, in the curve of his lips, in his eyes—turning smoky and warm. "I love you, Arianna, my wife, my lifemate. *Cariad* . . . Beloved, beloved. I love you."

He knelt naked at her feet and offered her his love, and she was so moved by the silly, romantic gesture that tears filled her eyes. Oh, Lord, how she loved this man.

She opened her mouth to tell him so, and screamed.

Raine grabbed her as she fell forward, settling her down into the grass. "Arianna!"

She clutched at her middle as another savage pain racked her. "The baby, Raine. It's coming."

"Oooh, God . . ." He started to get up, sat back down again, started to get up, then sat down again. "All right. Don't panic. There's no reason to panic," he said, sounding like a man on the edge of hysteria. He patted her cheek, then stood up for good and all, and dashed around the stones, snatching up boots and tunic and braies. He looked so funny that Arianna wanted to laugh in spite of the fierce pains that tore through her middle.

Raine hunkered down beside her again, breathless, his arms full of clothes. She heard in his voice the effort he was making to sound calm so that he wouldn't frighten her, when he was scared witless himself. She loved him so much in that one moment that it made her throat hurt. "Arianna, little wife, I'm going to have to leave you for just a few minutes. I'm going to ride back to the castle and fetch a cart."

He was behaving so sweetly, she almost hated to have to do this to him, but . . .

Another pain ripped through her. She seized his arm, almost pulling him down on top of her. "Now, Raine. The baby is coming now."

He stared at her, his eyes wide, and then he looked down at her convulsing stomach. "Oh, sweet heavenly Jesus. Damn you, Arianna, you are doing this on purpose." He started to lift her bliaut, hesitated a moment, then shoved it up around her waist. "Christ Jesus save us . . . I can already see her head!"

"It's a son I'm giving you, husband. Not a daughter," Arianna said in between panting grunts.

"She's as bald as an old man."

"He, not she. He has dark hair, black as a raven's wing. And beautiful gray eyes, soft like smoke."

"The rest of her is coming . . . I think. Push." She lifted her head to see him reaching between her legs. "Arianna, for the love of Christ, will you push!"

"I'm *pushing,* curse you!"

"Well, push harder. I can't do this all by myself."

She pushed harder. She pushed so hard it felt like she was pushing herself inside out. He would be sorry, yelling at her when she was in the middle of having a baby. " 'Push harder,' he says. I'd like to see you do any better, Norman," she muttered between clenched teeth.

She felt the baby come out of her all in a rush. She heard a rusty squawk and a man's deep laughter of relief. She lay, looking up at the blue, blue sky, and she smiled. Unlike the last time when she'd felt so exhausted after the birth, this time she felt euphoric.

She turned her head and saw Raine, with the baby in his hands. The poor little thing looked like a red and wrinkled old pod. Yet she experienced again that heart-soaring love that a mother feels when she sees her child for the first time.

Her husband was, she noticed, behaving most efficiently—cutting the navel cord with his dagger and wiping the blood and mucus off the baby with his chainse. Arianna began to giggle, then her giggles turned into loud whooping laughter.

Raine loomed over her. "What's so cursed funny?"

"You. You'll do Dame Beatrix out of a living, you're so good at midwifing. And you're naked, Raine. As naked as the day you were born."

He laid the babe, now wrapped in his tunic, gently onto her breast, and his face broke into that smile she loved so well. "As naked as my son."

She started to smile back at him, but it twisted crooked up on the ends, turning into a grimace. "Raine . . . something very strange is happening."

"Don't worry," he said, sounding like quite the authority. "It's only the afterbirth."

"Nay, husband, you forget I have done this before, I . . ." She stopped, gasping as a fierce pain racked her. "It's happening again. I'm having another baby."

His face disappeared from her sight, then reappeared. "You're right," he said, looking disgustingly cheerful. "It's another baby. Start pushing."

"Go to hell, Norman," she gritted out between her clenched teeth. But she pushed.

Five minutes later Arianna gave to her husband another little girl.

26

The babes thrived.

One hot August afternoon the lord and lady of the castle disappeared into their chamber, and all who saw smiled and shook their heads, for they were in love, were those two, and mad with it.

Arianna went to the window, while Raine poured them each a cup of wine. Below, the beekeeper was walking across the bailey, covered from head to toe like a leper and carrying his drums in a yoke across his back. There will be honey on our manchet loaves tomorrow morning, she thought with a smile, for it was one of Raine's favorite things.

She had turned around to tell him this, when she caught him tipping a small leather packet over one of the wine cups. He must have felt her eyes on him, for he whipped around suddenly, his fist closing over the packet and his hand going behind his back.

She advanced on him. "What is that you are hiding?"

"Nothing." He turned in a half-circle, presenting her with his chest and keeping his hand out of reach.

She feinted to the left, then dashed to the right. Her hand snaked behind him, seizing his wrist. "I can see that it is something. A something that you just put into my wine." She tried to pull his clenched fingers apart. "Are you trying to poison me, Norman?"

He opened his fist, surrendering its contents. "It's a love philter." There was a faint blush on his sharp cheek-bones.

"Oooh, a love philter," she cooed, examining the small leather bag. "Have I demanded so much of your poor male member lately, that you must use magic to assist you in fulfilling your husbandly duty?"

To her delight his blush deepened. "I was just sort of curious, is all. Taliesin gave the cursed thing to me on that Lugnasa night when you danced naked under the moon, back when you were being a stubborn wench about sharing my bed."

"You have a faulty memory, my lord, about who was being stubborn about what. That squire is a scheming, interfering trickster!"

He grinned suddenly. "You must admit, though, that it might be fun to try it. Look, we'll both drink it." He picked up the wine goblet, stirring it with his finger, then held it up to her lips. His voice turned husky. "You go first."

Arianna grasped his wrist with both hands, pulling the cup away from her face. She looked down, half expecting to see a white light and swirling mist, but all she saw was wine with a faint brown scum floating on the surface. But she had more sense than to trust that wretched squire, and Raine, too, should know better.

"It could be powerful magic," she said.

"It's some kind of root and hedgehog fat and toad liver. It'll probably just give us a bit of a tingle." He wriggled his brows in a comical leer. "Mayhap I will be moved to perform even more perverted French perversions upon you." He lifted the cup to his own lips.

"Don't!" She grabbed his wrist again. "Raine, you

must have realized by now that Taliesin is not really a squire. He is *magi, llyfrawr* . . . a wizard."

"Aye, a wizard at getting out of work and into trouble."

"He can conjure storms out of clear air and be in two places at once."

"It's been my experience that he's never where he should be."

"But that helmet of his came from the ancient ones. There is magic in it—"

He leaned over and kissed her to shut her up, slopping a good part of the wine into the rushes. "There is no such thing as a wizard," he said when they stopped for air.

"If you say so, husband." She glanced down meekly, but a moment later her head was back up. "But I'm beginning to understand from whence there came that old Welsh saying: 'There is no rarer thing than wisdom from the mouth of a Norman.' "

He laughed and pressed the wine into her hands. "Put this in *your* mouth and quit insulting your lord and master."

She looked from his smiling, expectant face, down to the wine, then back up to his face again. She licked her lips, started to raise the cup, then shuddered and shoved it at him. "You go first."

He shrugged and downed two healthy swallows of the wine.

She watched him carefully. The effigies in the chapel bore more expression on their faces than he did on his. "Well?"

His eyes widened slightly. "I feel a sort of tingling."

"A tingling?"

His eyes grew wider. "Nay, more like a swelling and a throbbing, and a hardening. Aye, a definite hardening."

He leapt at her, and she shrieked. They fell onto the bed and their mouths came together in a kiss that started out rough and hot, and became slow and deep.

"My lord!"

Raine pulled his mouth away from hers only far enough to bellow. "Go away, Taliesin. This time the wench is willing."

An adolescent voice rose, cracked and dipped low. " 'Tis Rhodri, my lord. There is a messenger here. From the king."

Raine rolled off her, standing up, and Arianna leapt from the bed, straightening her clothing. She slanted a look at the stranger in the doorway. He was naked but for a loincloth, and sweat coated his body, which had been oiled to help him run faster. He was very thin; she could almost see his heart pumping behind his skeletal ribs.

The message was encased in a short, split cane. Raine tipped out the rolled parchment and broke the seal. Arianna watched him read, feeling proud, for she had been the one to teach him the skill. But the warm feeling vanished as she watched the change come over his face.

Saying nothing, he gave her the parchment. Though she didn't yet know what it said, still her hands shook as she unfurled the message.

The words seemed to leap at her, burning her eyes, and a low, half-worded cry escaped her. King Henry of England was once again gathering a massive army to conquer Wales and destroy the Welsh prince Owain Gwynedd. He was calling on his Black Dragon, his "best and bravest knight," to ride with him, to fight with him. To kill for him. To kill the Welsh . . . her people.

They had been so happy, she and Raine. Since the day of their babies' birth, when he had told her he loved her, she had gone through the days in a blaze of contentment. She felt, finally, secure, well loved, cherished.

But always, always, underneath her joy had lurked a fear that a day such as this one would come to pass. It was too much to hope for that the truce would last, that his people and hers could live in peace. The Normans forever dreamed of power and more power, land and more land.

And the Welsh, they dreamed of liberty. Naught else, only liberty.

But her husband was Norman, and his lord was Norman. He had taken a knightly oath of fealty—sworn to King Henry his loyalty, his pride, and his man's honor. He loved her, of this she had no doubt, and out of his love for her he would do most anything. But she could not ask him to betray his honor.

The messenger cleared his throat. "The king has started across the Berwyn range, my lord. He requests that you and your knights join him there."

"Go down to the hall, my good man," Raine said. "My servants will fill you with ale and food."

The messenger bowed. "Thank you, my lord."

Arianna let the curling parchment flutter onto the table and went over to stare unseeing out the narrow window. Damn Henry, she thought. Damn the misbegotten, greedy hellspawn. Was half of Christendom not enough for him, that he must have Wales as well? Why couldn't he have left them in peace to raise their children and grow old together?

She squeezed her lids shut and her hands fisted on the sill until her knuckles whitened. But when she opened her eyes again, nothing had changed. The sun beat down still, bright and hot on the packed earth of the bailey. She could hear the beekeeper pounding his iron drums now, simulating thunder to bring down his swarms. They made an ominous sound, like a steady barrage from a war machine. A runnel of sweat ran down between her breasts. She hadn't noticed the heat before, but now it seemed stifling.

A pair of heavy hands settled onto her shoulders. "Henry is my liege lord and my king. It is my duty to come when he summons."

He only told her what she already knew. But she felt the anger come, in spite of her acceptance of the knowledge. "I don't know if I can bear this. What if you kill my father, Raine? How will I be able to live with the man who kills my father?"

"I will not kill your father."

She whirled, knocking his hands aside. "How can you swear on an uncertainty? You could run him through on your lance or with your sword in the midst of the battle and not even know it!"

A hardness settled over his face, the old shutters fell over his eyes, turning them flat and cold. Already, she thought with a numb despair, already it is happening. And then she realized that it could be Raine who could be killed by her father.

He turned, striding away from her, toward the door. His foot struck something in the rushes and he bent to pick it up. It was one of the twins' toys—a stuffed lamb with a body made of kinky wool, a painted head, and wooden legs.

He stared at the toy, unmoving and very still. He lifted his head and looked at her and there was a bewilderment, a sort of panic in his eyes. "I cannot fight," he said.

She now stood as motionless as he, waiting . . . waiting.

His hand tightened around the toy lamb. "I will answer Henry's summons, but I'll take no army with me. Nor will I lend him my own sword for this God-cursed war of his."

"But if you arrive without your men he will be furious. He could charge you with treason, Raine. He could—"

"Nay, love, odd as it seems, he oft listens to me. Perhaps if I see him, speak reason to him, I can convince him to abandon this fool endeavor. Aye, and I will go under a flag of truce to your father as well. Perhaps I can bring about a compromise between the pair of them."

She looked from his face to the toy lamb in his hands. "You would do this for me?"

"I do it for me as well, and for our babes. But I think I do it most for Rhuddlan, because no matter who wins, be it Henry or your father, it is inevitable that this land will once again become a prize of war. It is the people who till the fields and herd the cattle, and who are even now building us a new castle to make us strong—they will be the ones to suffer. They are my people, Arianna. *Our* people, be they Welsh or English. It is my duty as their lord to protect them."

She came to stand before him. Slowly she fell to her knees, a vassal giving obeisance to her liege lord. "I love you so much."

He drew her up, brushed her cheek, then let his fingers drift down, following the curve of her throat. "And I shall always love you, sweet wife, through all your hours, all your days. Always, always . . ."

Her mouth trembled into a smile. "I didn't know there was such poetry in you, Norman."

"My lord, take me with you!"

Startled, they turned to see Rhodri hovering just inside the door. They had both forgotten him.

"I go alone, lad," Raine said, "but I thank you."

"But you'll still need a squire to carry your shield and lance. Take me in the place of Taliesin. I can speak to my father. I can convince him to trust you."

Arianna saw the yearning on Rhodri's face, the desperate hurry he was in to prove himself a man, to show himself brave enough to take a man's risks. "He speaks sense, husband," she said.

Raine, intent now on buckling his sword belt, looked up. "Very well . . . since your lady sister has given her permission."

"I'll go see to your armor and your horse, my lord," Rhodri said and ran out of the room.

And then Raine was before her, drawing her to him, and they held each other in silence, before his mouth took hers in a kiss that was filled with all the things they could not say to one another, because words were not enough.

She smoothed the front of his bliaut, which she had

twisted with her fists as she clung to him. "Promise me you won't risk your life."

His smile was wry and gentle. "No fear of that, *cariad.* I've turned into a very careful man since I wedded you."

He kissed her once more, hard and fierce and fast, and then he let her go.

But when he got to the door, she stopped him. "Raine . . ."

He turned, and she drank in the sight of his beloved face one last time just in case . . . just in case. . . . Fear clung to her, smothered her, like oily smoke, so that she couldn't breathe. *If I lose him,* she thought, *if I lose him, I will die.*

"My heart is not divided, my lord. I said once that I have chosen you. Whatever happens, that will never change. Not for all eternity."

He said nothing, he didn't smile. But she saw the love in his eyes.

"I will wait for you to come back to me, Raine. No matter how long it takes, I will wait for you."

Arianna stood on the castle ramparts as a hot dry wind blew across the empty tilting field, filling her with its restlessness.

It was from this very spot that she had seen Raine for the first time. He had looked so fierce, mounted on his enormous war-horse, his black dragon pennon snapping against a storm-tossed sky. He had stood in the middle of the field, unmoving, almost taunting them with his reckless bravery. And then a jagged lightning bolt had scarred the gray clouds, and thunder had cracked open the sky, and his charger had reared. Her heart had recognized him even then for what he was, though it had taken her thick head much longer—he was the black knight of her vision, her destiny.

She hadn't thought about the vision of Raine charging her with his lance in a long time. Or that other vision she'd had shortly afterward—of a hot, flower-carpeted hillside and a golden-headed knight awaiting her with outstretched arms. On her wedding day that vision had brought her joy and hope, but now she feared it. She didn't want to think that there would be another love in her life. She couldn't imagine that this would be so, she belonged to Raine so utterly and completely. There could never be another man for her.

Scarce an hour had passed since Raine had ridden out the gate, yet already she felt the emptiness he'd left. By this time tomorrow he would have caught up with Henry's army. In her few meetings with the English king, Henry had not struck her as a man easily led off a course once he'd set his rudder to it. But then Raine's personality was equally forceful. His whole life was a testimony to the fact that when he wanted something, he eventually got it.

A movement below caught her eye, and she leaned over the crenelated wall for a closer look. Taliesin was striding out onto the tilting field. His black mantle snapped and billowed in the wind and his helmet shone bright under the sun. She was about to call out to him, to demand to know what he was doing, when he stopped and lifted his arms to the heavens.

The wind died.

A hush fell over the earth.

It became so quiet, Arianna could hear the buzz of the flies in the moat below. And in the far, far distance, the faint wash of the surf.

For a moment he simply stood there, arms raised above his head like a chapel painting she had seen once of Moses parting the Red Sea. A blue light began to pulse around him, a shimmering light striated with bands of silver. Grass and leaves swirled around his feet, towering upward, as if he stood in the middle of a wind spout.

It began with a great rustling, like the beating wings of a thousand birds. And then she felt it—the wind had come up again. But there was a fire in this wind, it crackled and sizzled, tingling her skin, and she could taste brimstone in the air.

On the horizon, out to sea, a cloud began to form. Small at first, but then it was joined by another and then another, until the sea seemed to be spewing up clouds. The clouds became hills, then mountains, swallowing the sky and the sun as they came, rolling toward her. A darkness settled over the land, and a heaviness, and she felt the first splatters of rain.

A storm, she thought. He's making a storm!

The aura surrounding the squire was red now. His face glowed as if he stood before a great furnace. He reached higher, embracing the lowering clouds, and from the tips of his outstretched fingers spun multicolored fireballs. Lightning snaked across the sky, flash after flash, and the thunder was deafening.

Above, the skies turned so black they rivaled the pits of hell. Lightning flared again, so bright the trees stood out starkly against the dark clouds, their skeletal fingers clawing at the sky. The wind sent the rain in slashing swirls and great sheets of water that slammed against the earth with a force that drove Arianna to her knees.

She bowed before the force of the storm, awed and frightened by its power. Trees crashed and splintered and the wind screamed. The rain was like a great mouth of the sea, swallowing her.

She covered her eyes with her hands, curling into a ball on the wall-walk—and the world began to spin, turning into a sucking, whirling pool of mist and light and blue fire. . . .

Tendrils of a bloody mist rose, spread, and dissipated, became a soft white light. Images flashed, whipping in and out of the mist and light like the dots on the cubes of dice as they rolled. King Henry, his mouth twisted in rage, screaming about eyes. Rhodri, his face bled white and stark with terror, held fast by grim-visaged men. And Raine.

Raine, his lips pulled back from his teeth in a snarl, thrusting a sword through a man's hand.

And then, as if the dice had come to rest, the last image burned clearly through the mist—a man hanging on a gibbet. The rope creaked as he swayed, the still air smelled of death and rot. The ravens came. At first only one or two, then a few more, and then they descended on the hill in a cloud of black, flapping wings, loud as the wind. They landed on the barren ground and on the nearby skeletal trees and on the arms of the gibbet. One rose up and came to rest on the head of the hanging man. Slowly, the hanging man began to turn, swinging, swinging toward her.

She screamed.

The image shattered, cracking like ice beneath a mallet. A quiet whiteness came, a searing whiteness, bright and cold. Too cold to breathe. She tried to suck air into her pinched, tight chest. But the light was too cold, too bright. She began to drift, drift away into the nothingness of the cold, white light. . . .

She opened her eyes onto slick gray stones, her face in a puddle. Everything dripped, and she was soaked through her skin to her bones. Groaning, she started to push herself to her knees.

Nausea rose in her throat, and she tried to fight it off, closing her eyes. But the image of the hanging man was there, waiting. His face . . . she had screamed and shattered the image before she had seen his face.

But she knew, she knew, oh God, she knew. The visions never lied.

Fear rose up within her, burning her chest and throat. *Raine.* Her mind screamed his name. He had gone to try to bring peace between their people.

But he had ridden to his death instead.

She would go to him, warn him. She would get Taliesin. The squire was *magi,* yes, she was sure of it. He could make it storm and travel through the circle of time and be in two places at once. He could get to Raine and warn him in time.

She made it up to her knees, grabbing at the stone parapet and dragging herself to her feet. She brushed the wet hair from her eyes and looked across a field of mud and soggy grass. On the horizon the blue of the sky met the turquoise of the sea. A few fluffy clouds, like tufts of lamb's wool, drifted lazily overhead. She had to squint, for the brightness of the sun hurt her eyes. If everything weren't so dripping wet, it would have been hard to believe it had ever rained.

For the storm was gone, as if it had never been.

And so was Taliesin.

The hot August sun beat down through scraggly pines, causing Raine to itch and swelter beneath his black armor.

He was all the more uncomfortable because he had become soaked in a freakish and unseasonable storm the afternoon before, and he hadn't been able to dry out. I'll be sprouting mold like month-old cheese soon, he thought with a grim laugh. He was getting too old for this.

Rhodri rode beside him in silence, probably feeling as miserable as he looked. With his hair plastered to his head and mud streaking his face, he looked like a moat rat. "How are you holding up, boy?" Raine asked.

Rhodri straightened in his saddle. "Well, my lord. . . . My lord, do you love my sister?"

"Aye. I love her."

"Why?"

"Why?" The question took Raine by surprise.

"I mean, what makes a fellow prefer one girl over another? They all seem alike to me." He made a face. "In truth, I've little use for the lot of them. Mewling, emotional creatures. Always nattering and frittering and weeping over something."

"When the right girl comes along, you'll know it. Hell,

you won't be able to help yourself, so you might as well surrender right from the start and save yourself a lot of grief," Raine said, and then he laughed. He'd practically had to be hit over the head with a battering ram before he was man enough to accept that Arianna had conquered him. In truth, she had brought him to his knees.

Their horses' hooves made loud sucking noises as they fought through the mud. He had never known a storm like yesterday's. The wind had uprooted trees the size of keeps, and it seemed as if the heavens had emptied all the leftover rain stored up there for the last millennium.

They rode along the broken ribs of the barren hills. It was a desolate land, and soggy because of the storm. Raine saw his charger's ears prick up and then he heard the sounds himself—the wild neighing of horses, the mournful wail of a war horn, and the pitiful screams of men wounded unto death.

He spurred his horse into a gallop, shouting at Rhodri to follow. He topped a rise and looked down into the gorge below, where ran the river Ceiriog.

Rhodri reined up beside him, sucking in a sharp breath. "God's death . . ."

The Ceiriog had overflowed its banks, washing away the encampment of Henry's great army. Broken lances and riven shields lay scattered in the tough moor grass. Horses and sumpter mules floundered in the bog. What nature had not managed to destroy, the Welsh had finished off. Encumbered by heavy chain mail, the English had been no match for the fleet-footed Welsh with their deadly longbows.

The river ran red with their blood.

The royal campaign tent lay, a twisted and ripped pile of silk, in the mud. The king's fox pennon hung limply from the branch of a thick oak tree. Henry paced beneath the tree, kicking at tufts of grass and stones. They could hear his ravings long before they reached him.

Raine dismounted and walked, with Rhodri at his

heels, along the river toward the lone oak and the pacing, raging king. Here, the destruction showed worse, with the dead piled up on the bank like faggots of wood, smelling already of rot and river slime. Many, he noticed, suffered no wounds . . . they had drowned.

Raine thought with despair of Arianna's hope for peace between England and her father. Henry would never listen to reason now.

The king was surrounded by his nobles, though they all stood at a safe distance from his infamous temper. One, Raine saw, was his brother Hugh, though for once that elegant figure looked the worse for wear. His silvered mail was dull and battered like a beggar's tin cup. He had lost his helm somewhere and his golden hair had gotten matted and tangled, and lost its curl. The black mud of Wales streaked his handsome, pouting features, so that he looked more the mountebank than an earl.

Hugh spotted Raine and called out. The king froze, then swung around. He stood with his legs splayed, his fists on his hips, watching Raine approach. The hem of his ermine-trimmed purple mantle dripped muddy water into a puddle around his pointed-toed shoes. The skin above his red beard was the color of a ripe plum, and his thick chest rose and fell with his angry breaths.

He leveled a look of royal rage at Raine calculated to curdle a man's blood. "You are late, Rhuddlan."

Raine stopped before the king. "My liege," he said. He met and held the protruding gray eyes until the king was the first to blink. Then Raine looked around the savaged camp, and he allowed a slight smile to form on his lips. "Wales does not seem to agree with you, sire."

It was a calculated risk—that the king could be shocked out of his rage by Raine's impertinence. It failed. Henry flung out his arm, his voice cracking. "Seize him!"

Raine's hand fell on the hilt of his sword. Too late he realized that Henry had pointed not at himself, but at Rhodri.

Henry's men had the boy surrounded instantly. Raine had taken a step forward, his sword half out its scabbard, but he stopped when a young knight with a sharp, pointed face jerked up hard on Rhodri's arm and the boy's lips tightened with pain.

Raine spun around and confronted Henry. "Is this the mark of a king—to take his temper out on a lowly squire?" Though he kept his face impassive, there was an underlying sneer in his tone.

Henry's square jaw jutted out. "This whelp is no mere squire. He is Owain's son and my hostage, and he will pay for his father's perfidy."

"The boy had no part in this, sire." Raine put himself as close as he could between his king and Arianna's brother. "He's been with me for two years and has served me well."

"No part! No *part*. He is hostage to his father's good behavior and you see what the man has done. Gwynedd has behaved badly. Badly!" The king spat the words, his lips twisting and pulling back from his teeth. His eyes bulged obscenely, and the freckles stood out dark on his face like pox scars.

Raine stared at this man, his lord, this man who had held his loyalty and his honor for so many years. This man who claimed himself worthy to be king of all Britains. . . . This man who was frothing at the mouth like a wild boar.

"It was your choice to break the truce and invade," Raine said, his voice hard and flat. "You can't fault the man for defending his land."

Henry jerked to a stop, his massive chest heaving. His eyes remained wild, unblinking. They narrowed, turned crafty. "This land is mine by right, and I no longer suffer his presence on it."

"Nevertheless you cannot fault Owain's son. You've a son of your own—would you want him to suffer for your crimes?"

The king threw back his head and bellowed a laugh. One after another the other men joined with him, all but Raine.

But the king's laughter stopped abruptly. The laughter of the others petered out more slowly. In the ensuing silence, Henry said, his harsh voice almost conversational, "Chester, take your dagger and put out the whelp's eyes."

Earl Hugh started. He nearly laughed, thought better of it, and cleared his throat instead. It was now so quiet one could hear the water dripping off the tree. Rhodri's face had turned pale, and he stiffened against the arms that held him, but he made not a sound.

"Chester!" Henry roared.

Hugh licked his lips. "Me, sire?"

The king bent forward at the waist, pushing his face into Hugh's. "I said . . . *Put out his eyes!*"

Hugh backed up before the onslaught of Henry's bellow. "But—"

"By God's balls, if you're not man enough to do it, I am!"

The king whipped a dagger from his belt, but Raine was faster. His sword flew from the scabbard with a whistling sound, like the hiss of a wet brand . . . pinning Henry's hand to the tree at his back.

The king's fingers spasmed opened, letting go of the dagger. He gave a yell like a strangled cat, and the sound of it echoed down the gorge.

There was the hiss of more blades being drawn, but it was cut across by Raine's voice, silky and dangerous. "Put up your swords . . . or is there a man among you who wishes to be known as the one who cost his king a hand?"

Raine's sword pierced the king's hand through the web, between the thumb and forefinger—a wound that would heal in a week or two. But with a single movement of his strong wrist, he could also sever vital tendons, rendering the hand useless forever.

"Rhodri," Raine went on in that same calm, flat voice.

"Relieve these noble men of their weapons and toss them in the river. Then fetch our horses. Do it quickly, lad."

Henry's eyes bulged, shot with blood, and he snarled like a rabid cur. "You will die a traitor's death for this, Rhuddlan," he hissed, while in the background Raine could hear the splashing sounds of daggers and swords hitting the water. "I'll have you hanged and gelded and disemboweled and blinded. You will be screaming for my mercy long after you've no throat left to scream."

Raine said nothing, there was nothing to say. In the space of a heartbeat he had gone from his king's best man to his king's worst enemy, and there was no going back.

Rhodri appeared beside him, their horses' reins wrapped around his bony fist. Tiny shudders racked the boy's body and his green eyes, whole and unharmed and so like Arianna's, stared at Raine out of his pale face.

With his free hand, Raine took his horse's bit and waited for the boy to mount. "By your leave, Henry," he said, with a flash of a smile that was sheer desperate bravado.

With a single, swift movement, he pulled his blade free of the royal flesh and leapt into the saddle, spurring the charger into a gallop.

They tore down the gorge. Behind him, Raine could hear shouts. They had maybe a two-minutes' head start, he reckoned, before Henry's men would assure themselves that their king would live and collect themselves to chase after them.

A hill rose up ahead, with a copse of thick pines curling along the eastern slope. Raine veered his horse in that direction. They were perhaps a hundred yards into the trees when men and horses sprang up from the ground and rocks, surrounding them.

Two dozen longbows aimed at Raine's chest. But he was more concerned with the sword that pointed at his throat. He looked down the long blade, into familiar sea-foam eyes. Long, flowing brown mustaches lifted upward in an ironic smile.

"Welcome to Wales, Norman."

Raine sat among pine needles and cones, his back against a trunk, his arms lashed behind his back. The man who had welcomed him to Wales stood next to his drawn-up knees and looked down at him along the length of a thin, aquiline nose.

"I am Cynan ap Owain."

Raine narrowed his eyes against the sun, which shone through the tree boughs behind the man's broad back. "You look like your father."

The mustaches twitched. "Is that a compliment or an insult?" Before Raine could answer, he went on. "My brother, Rhodri, had quite a story to tell. To hear him talk you're a hero right out of a bard's tale." When Raine said nothing, he cocked a brow. "Modest, too, are you?"

He hunkered down, pulling out a dagger to cut the thongs that bound Raine's wrists. "You saved Rhodri's eyes, which is the same as saving his life. You should have called me on the insult—tying you up like this. Arianna will have my guts for lute strings. What's it like being married to my sister? I always thought the man who wed Arianna would have to be either a saint or a rogue. Which are you?"

"It varies depending on the time and the weather."

Cynan laughed. Raine rubbed the circulation back into his arms, then Cynan helped him to his feet. The two men walked toward the rest of the Welshmen, who were grouped around the horses.

Rhodri came forward, leading Raine's black charger. "My lord, what you did back there . . . I cannot thank—"

"Stuff a rag in it, Rhodri," Cynan barked. "The man doesn't want you weeping all over his hauberk. You'll give him rust spots."

Rhodri blushed, and Raine grinned at him.

But then his smile faltered. He thought of King Henry, nursing his rage and a hole in his hand, and of Arianna and their children alone at his castle and targets for revenge. He turned to Cynan, who was steadying his horse, preparing to mount. "Arianna is at Rhuddlan and Henry—"

"Isn't going anywhere fast. We saw to that." Cynan grinned, then pulled himself into his saddle with a grunt. "Still, we might as well withdraw to your castle as anywhere else. I wouldn't mind sleeping in a nice warm hall come tomorrow night."

Raine paused, his hands on the saddlebows. It occurred to him that letting the good part of a Welsh army into Rhuddlan would be like a sheep welcoming a wolf into the herd. But then, he had little choice. He was Owain of Gwynedd's man from now on, for better or worse.

He looked up and met Cynan's eyes. Green, sea-foam eyes so like Arianna's.

The man must have read his thoughts, for a smile curved the corners of his long mouth. "As I said, welcome to Wales."

They emerged from the forest onto the top of the hill. From here they could look down into the river gorge, where the English still reeled from the blow dealt by the Welsh and the storm. At the far end of it, close to them, some of the English dead lay scattered, unclaimed and unburied. One or more must be clinging still to life, Raine thought, for he picked out an occasional groan in between the trill of black birds.

A shout from one of Cynan's men brought Raine's head snapping around. A lone rider charged down the slope of the balded hill to the east of them. A red mantle billowed like a loose sail and long brown hair flapped and swirled in the wind.

Brown hair that glinted gold and red in the sun.

From out of the corner of his eye, Raine saw one of the

English wounded stagger to his feet, pulling himself up by a tree branch. The man had a loaded crossbow in his hand and he raised it level with his chest. In the instant that it took for Raine to realize what was about to happen, the Englishman fired.

The bolt shot through the air with a quick hiss, like a striking snake. The rider jerked upright, her arms flopping, and a red stain blossomed on her chest. She remained frozen in that way for one eternal moment. Then she tumbled over backward off the end of her still-galloping horse.

"Arianna!"

Cynan's hand lashed out, snagging the black charger's reins, holding Raine back. "It's too late, man. She took that bolt right in the chest."

Pain stabbed at Raine's eyes, so fierce that he gasped aloud. He pulled blindly against the man who held his horse.

"Go back down there and Henry's men will seize you," Cynan said, his voice cracking with his own pain.

"Arianna!"

Raine's raw shout of anguish echoed over the moors. He wrenched the charger's head free and drove his heels into the animal's sides.

It seemed to take forever to get to her. He kept forgetting to breathe.

He leapt from his horse without bringing it to a stop and fell to his knees beside her. She lay on her front, her face turned away from him, pressed into the ground. With trembling hands and fear screaming in his mind, he gently rolled her over. . . .

Oh, sweet Jesus.

The whole front of her chest was drenched in blood.

She looked at him with eyes dark with pain. "Raine? It hurts."

He kept it off his face—all of it, his gut-wrenching agony, the fierce, unbearable grief that even now was beginning to tear at his chest, ripping him apart, the utter certainty that his Arianna, his beautiful, sweet Arianna, was about to die. It was the hardest thing he'd ever done in his life, to look at her with that stiff, bland face he had hurt her with so often in the past.

As carefully as he could, he pulled her up so that she was lying in his lap, her back pressed against his chest. "You'll be all right, love. But we'll rest here a moment," he said, surprised he got the words out through the thickness in his throat.

She nodded, sighed. Her tunic was shiny and black with her blood. He could feel its warm stickiness on his hands. Her breath came in shallow rasps.

Raine looked across the clearing for the man who had killed her. The Englishman leaned, slumped over sideways against the tree trunk, his arms empty of the crossbow and lifeless. Crazed with pain and dying, he probably hadn't even known what he was shooting at.

Why her? Raine's mind shouted. *Oh, God, God . . . why her?*

Her hand fluttered, as if she tried to reach for him, and he wrapped his fingers around hers. They were so cold. Already she was growing cold. "Had to warn you . . ." she said, her voice so weak he barely heard. "Afraid I was too late . . ."

He gave her fingers a gentle squeeze. "You weren't too late," he said, though he had no idea what she meant. He could feel hooves thudding on the sod and angry shouts came to him on the wind. They had seen him, had Henry's men, and now they were coming for him, and they would kill him.

He looked down at her, stroked the hair from her face. Her mouth trembled into a smile. "You're safe?"

He moved his lips and prayed it came out looking like an answering smile. "Aye, I'm safe, little wife," he said, but his voice sounded rusty.

"Raine . . . I feel all cold and strange." A deep furrow creased the bridge of her nose. "Am I dying?"

He could no longer keep the pain from showing. His heart was cracking open in his chest, and he was bleeding inside. He could taste the blood in his mouth and he could feel a wetness on his face. He rubbed his cheek, surprised to see the wetness was clear, not red.

Her eyes, so dark now they were black, pooled with tears. "Oh, Raine . . . I'm so sorry."

How like her, he thought, to worry about him. But then it was easier for the ones who died. They weren't left behind to spend the endless, empty years alone.

Her lips moved and he bent closer to hear. "Kiss me."

He pressed his mouth to hers, shocked when he felt its warmth. He breathed into her, as if he could give his life for the one she was losing.

"Cariad . . . cariad . . ." He spoke into her mouth. "Will you wait for me again?"

Her lips moved against his. "Always."

Her eyes drifted closed then, as she slipped into a sleep that would ease into death. Henry's men were nearly upon them. He was glad she slept now, for they would not be gentle with him, and he wouldn't have wanted that to be the last thing she saw.

He held her in his lap until rough hands jerked him to his feet. He cried out once, when Arianna's limp body rolled off him onto the spongy ground. They dragged him by a rope back to the river, where Henry waited, his right hand wrapped in a blood-stained cloth.

"Stand him up," Henry said, when they had thrown Raine down into the mud at his feet.

Someone wrenched Raine upright by yanking on the rope that bound his arms. "Give me his sword," Henry said.

The king took Raine's sword and with a vicious slam of his wrist stabbed it deep in the ground between Raine's legs. The blade twanged in the deadly silence, then stilled.

But Raine saw neither the sword or his king. His gaze was lifted beyond, to the girl who lay alone in the grass. *What if she wakes?* he thought. *What if she wakes one last time and I'm not there?*

"Traitor," Henry spat, and swinging back his left arm, he backhanded Raine across the face. The king had on a leather gauntlet studded with mail and the sharp metal sliced through Raine's cheek, laying it open.

Raine's body shuddered from the pain of the blow, but his reason barely knew that it had happened. His gaze was on the girl who lay unmoving on the rough moorland grass.

Henry's lips peeled back from his teeth in a sneer. "Strike off the spurs of this poor knight and then he will be a knight no more."

A man stepped forward with his sword and hacked off Raine's spurs, the symbol of his knighthood. The man's sword cut through the leather of Raine's boots so close to his heels he drew blood, but Raine felt nothing. His gaze had not left the body lying in the grass.

When they dragged him away to tie him to the wheel of the cart that would carry him to prison and a traitor's death in London, he twisted his head around for one last sight of her.

Someone emerged from the woods, leading a horse. Sunlight glinted off red hair. At least, he thought, Taliesin would see that she was taken home.

27

Hamo, the rat catcher, sat at a ring-marked table in his favorite tavern, feeling good and making his third cup of ale last for a while. He liked coming to the Crooked Staff. The ale here didn't taste like cow's piss and most of the whores still had at least some of their teeth. But tonight he wasn't interested in either the whores or the ale.

He was fascinated by a girl who sat huddled on a bench in a far corner. She nursed a cup of ale in her hands, though she had yet to drink from it. Her gaze was fastened on the door and each time it opened up to the misting night, she straightened, only to sag back with disappointment when it didn't yield whoever it was she waited for.

She wasn't any whore—he had two good eyes and he could see that. Not only was the mantle she wore of good Welsh wool, but she had an air about her. It wasn't unusual for quality to wind up in a place like the Crooked Staff. Taverns here in the stews of Southwark often got those travelers who arrived after sunset and so weren't able to pass through the gate into Londontown.

Hamo had just picked up his ale and sidled over to the girl, thinking to strike up a little conversation, when again

the door opened and again she sat up . . . and stayed up
this time. Hamo turned to see just who it was that had
brought about that look of immense relief on the girl's
face. He was a young man, a boy really, with long coppery
curls and a swaggering way about him.

As the boy came up to the girl, Hamo took a step,
planting himself in the boy's way.

"Excuse me," the boy said, in a sweet, musical voice.

He was pretty as a lass and near enough to a babe to
still be pissing in his swaddling cloths. But there was
something strange about his eyes, a light glowed in them,
kind of like a candle shining through a shell. One slender,
white hand rested on the hilt of quillon dagger that just
might have seen some use here and there.

Hamo shifted aside, letting the boy pass. Hell, no
wench was worth getting his guts spilled over.

Taliesin dropped down onto the bench beside Arianna,
blowing a lock of hair out of his eyes. "Whew, what a
hellhole this place is." He looked around him, his nose
quivering at the sight of rickety benches and tables filled
with the tinkers and ditchers and scavengers that made up
the Crooked Staff's clientele. The place stank of tallow
smoke, wet wool, and human sweat. "No one bothered
you, did they? That man—"

"He was only looking." Arianna lifted the chipped clay
cup to her lips and took a swallow of the weak ale, grimacing at its bitterness. The low din was suddenly shattered by roars of laughter that came from a game of hand-
icap and cries of "Pass around the cup!"

"What did you find out?" she asked. She was glad of
the noise, for then Taliesin wouldn't be able to hear the
quiver of fear and exhaustion in her voice.

The squire rubbed his finger around a wet puddle on
the table, avoiding her eyes. "My lord hasn't come to trial
yet, and no one seems to expect it soon. Henry is afraid
he will demand a trial by combat." In such a trial a man
had the right to prove his innocence by meeting his ac-

cuser on the field of battle. Of course the accuser, King Henry, would not fight—he would have a champion take the field in his stead. But it was doubtful, so the gossip went, that there was any man in England who was a match for the Black Dragon.

"So Henry is just going to leave him shut up in the Tower until he rots," Arianna said, her voice as bitter as the ale. "May God give that whoreson of an English king a thousand cartloads of bad years."

A whore swayed past Taliesin, flashing a smile and showing off a lot of bare leg. The boy took a good long look and grinned, but then he turned his attention back to Arianna. "How are you feeling, my lady?"

"I'm fine," she said, forcing a brightness into her voice.

In truth, she felt tired and weak from the fifteen-day journey it had taken to get here. She still wasn't quite recovered yet from her wound. Her father's leech had claimed it a miracle that she lived at all. But then he hadn't known that Taliesin was *magi,* and it was a known fact that wizards were well versed in all the healing arts. For weeks, the squire had stayed by her bedside in the chamber in her father's *llys* where he had brought her, pouring concoctions down her throat the properties of which she didn't want to think about.

Taliesin leaned closer now to study her face. "If you're feeling pain, my lady, I can give you—"

"No, no. I'm all right. Well, maybe a little hungry . . ."

The squire snapped his fingers and pulled a greasy bundle from beneath his mantle. He unwrapped the cloth, giving Arianna a soggy tart filled with eggs and cheese that he'd bought from the public cookshop where he'd gone to find information as well as food.

But when he pressed the food into Arianna's hands her stomach heaved, and she had to swallow hard to keep from vomiting.

At the look on her face, Taliesin took the egg tart away

and supplanted it with another. "Here, try this instead. 'Tis eels."

She shook her head, pushing the food back at him across the table. "I guess I'm not hungry after all."

Taliesin patted her shoulder. "What you need is sleep, my lady. You will do your lord husband little good if you collapse from exhaustion or become ill because of your weakened condition."

Arianna repressed a shudder at the thought of the chamber upstairs, wedged tightly with pallets covered with flea-infested blankets. "I think I'll just sit here awhile," she said.

She leaned back against the wall and closed her eyes and immediately Raine's face filled her mind. In this memory of him he was smiling, that rare and beautiful smile. She tried not to think about where he was now, locked in a cell deep within London's infamous White Tower.

"I wonder," she said aloud. "If he even knows yet that I live."

The next day they joined the traffic of rickety carts and sumpter beasts, crossing the Thames over a wooden bridge that was falling into ruins. Rain drizzled from clouds that hugged the walls and towers of the town.

"Look there, my lady." Taliesin said, pointing to a fancy barque that bobbed alongside a rotting wharf. "That ship has come all the way from Spain. What do you guess she carries? From the smell I would say it was figs."

He shouted to her above the clamor of church bells and the clack of watermills, pointing out various other barges and ships that crammed the water. Arianna knew he was trying to distract her gaze from the traitors' heads that rotted on pikes over the gate.

She did keep her eyes averted from the gruesome sight as they paid the toll, then entered into Londontown.

From Southwark, across the river, the tall, sheer walls

and the four whitewashed turrets of the White Tower, where Raine was imprisoned, had dominated the jumble of gabled roofs, gray walls, and church spires of the city. But once through the gate they entered into a warren of narrow, twisting streets aswarm with lop-eared swine, rats as big as cats, and a multitude of people all trying to sell something. She could no longer see the Tower and Arianna was relieved that Taliesin seemed to know the way.

She followed him down a street clogged with chicken heads, feathers, and entrails from the poultry stalls that lined the way. The stink was too much for Arianna, and she covered her nose with her hand. Before long the back of her hand became splattered from the black muck being thrown up by the hooves of Taliesin's cob.

Suddenly an enormous rectangular keep loomed before her. Its walls were so tall they looked to be brushing the bottom of the sky, and the huge whitewashed expanse of stone was pierced only by narrow arrow-slits. It was easy to see how the White Tower had earned its reputation as England's most formidable prison.

They had no trouble getting inside, but once there Arianna and Taliesin were passed from one officious person to another until they were turned over to the king's gaoler.

He looked them over, a faint sneer on his steeply sloping lip. "My lady, my lord," he said, bowing in a mocking manner to each of them in turn. The ring of keys at his thick waist jangled. "You get lost? This be the White Tower ye're in. Not Saint bloody Paul Cathedral."

Arianna had to clear her tight throat. "I wish to see the Lord of Rhuddlan."

The man pursed his lips. "Can't"

"W-why not?"

"King's orders, that's why not."

Arianna pulled out the leather, silk-tasseled purse that hung from her girdle, concealed by her cloak. "I have money . . ."

The gaoler looked at the purse, licking his fat lips, but then he shook his head sadly. "Now, normally, ye see, I'm not one to say 'no, thank 'ee' to the generous offer of a little gift. But it's worth my life t' go against the king's law on this one." He leaned over, spewing garlic-scented breath in Arianna's face. "He tried to murder his royal lordship, he did. And he'll swing for it, aye. Then they'll scoop out his guts and cut off his prick an' his balls—"

"Never mind," Taliesin said. He wrapped his arm around Arianna's shoulders, supporting her sagging weight. "We'll go see the king at Winchester."

Arianna followed Taliesin numbly back down to the river, where he hired a passenger boat to take them to Winchester. *I'm going to Winchester to visit the king,* she thought. Where she would get down on her knees and beg for her husband's life. But first she would have to beg, she now knew, just for the privilege of seeing him.

The boat drifted slowly up the sluggish, muck-scummed river, past brothels with their wooden steps running down to the docks for the convenience of the boatmen and sailors.

Their pilot pointed these sights out to her, taking pride in the wonders of his city. "And there be the gallôws of Tyburn Hill, mistress," he said, his greasy finger indicating a small rise by the water's edge. Ravens wheeled and settled on wooden, cross-shaped gibbets that rose, silhouetted against the gray sky. One of them was occupied.

Arianna watched in silent horror as the hanging body began to swing in the wind. Though reason told her it could not be Raine, still she held her breath, her nails digging into her palms. Slowly the body turned . . . but the man's face was unrecognizable, picked clean by the ravens.

The stews gave way to manor houses set behind tall walls with spacious gardens. The manor houses gave way to marshlands. And then there, on a flat grassy plain, floating in the misty rain and looking like a mythical kingdom, were gabled roofs, a white palace, and the two great spires of Winchester Cathedral.

The boat pulled right up alongside the water-stained wall of the king's palace, called White Hall because it, too, was built of whitewashed stone. But as they climbed the long wooden steps that led to the entrance of the palace's great hall, a man coming down hailed them.

He was a noble, by the richness of his dress and the width of his girth, and he bowed at Arianna as she and Taliesin came abreast of him. "If you've come to see the king," the man said, "he isn't here. Gone hunting at Cumberland's estates."

Arianna's voice cracked with frustration. "When is he expected back?"

The nobleman looked around him, then leaned into her and his round, florid face creased into a wreath of smiles. "Well, he's hunting more than roe and buck, you see. 'Tis Cumberland's eldest daughter he's really after."

Amidst chuckles and more smiles, the man went on his way, leaving Arianna staring dumbly after him. Nearby, the abbey bells began to ring compline. It would be dark soon. She knew she ought to think about getting some food and finding a tavern for the night, but suddenly it all seemed such an effort just to draw breath. She felt so tired. She had concentrated all her strength on first getting into the Tower to see Raine and now on having an audience with the king.

"What do we do now?" she said, unable to keep a tremble out of her voice.

When she got no answer, she looked behind her. The wretched squire had disappeared.

"Damn you," she whispered as tears of defeat crowded her eyes. For the first time she began to doubt if she would ever win Raine's freedom, if she would even see him again. "Damn you, damn you, damn you—"

She heard a shout and whipped back around. A man stood frozen at the top of the steps, a man whose hair glinted bright gold even in the drizzle that fell on the courtyard.

"Arianna!"

Arianna turned away from the window with its view of the cathedral spires. She dropped down onto a stool before a brazier, holding her hands over the red-burning coals. Her wedding ring glinted in the firelight, and she twisted it around and around her finger.

Oh, Raine . . .

Her wound throbbed and her whole body ached with the effort it took to keep from giving way to tears and despair.

A sound at the door brought her head up. Earl Hugh of Chester entered, looking relaxed and elegant in a willow green bliaut and fur-trimmed pelisse. He seemed to have gotten over the shock he'd had on seeing her. His finely sculptured mouth was curled into one of his mocking smiles.

"Arianna . . . you make a beautiful Lazarus." He shook his head, his smile deepening. "You must have superlative leeches in Wales."

Arianna stood up, curtseying. "My lord earl—"

He waved a languid, heavily ringed hand at the table filled with platters of untouched cheese-filled wafers and tiny, crescent-shaped pork pies. "You weren't hungry?"

"Nay. Thank you . . . My lord earl—"

"Hugh, my dear. You must call me Hugh." He flashed another insouciant smile. "We're family, after all." He poured her a glass of wine, pressing it into her hands. It was verney and its sickly sweet smell caused her stomach to heave.

She set the cup back onto the table. "You have said you will help to get me an audience with the king."

He sucked on his lower lip. "Well, actually, seeing the king will do you little good, I'm afraid. He flies into a fit of temper at the mere mention of my brother's name. You haven't said what you think of my town house."

"It is very beautiful," Arianna answered, though in truth she'd paid little heed to her surroundings since he'd brought her here this evening.

"I am really a very rich man," Hugh was saying in a voice that reminded her of cod oil, smooth and slick. "And money can gratify a lot of desires. For instance, if I desired to see my brother escape from the Tower, doubtless I could arrange it."

Arianna's heart began to thump unevenly and she struggled to keep her face blank. She refused to let herself hope, for she didn't trust Earl Hugh of Chester. She could not forget that this was the same man who had shot an arrow at his brother's chest.

"You will do this for Raine?"

The earl came to stand before her and his handsome mouth curved into yet another smile. "Nay, I do it for you. And for myself, of course. I never do anything unless it is for myself." He traced the length of her collarbone where it protruded through her bliaut. "But there is a price."

The bone jumped beneath his fingers. "A price?"

"Ah, Arianna, sweet, sweet, Arianna. There is always a price."

There was a price, Hugh thought, for everything.

The price, for instance, for loving the wrong woman too much, could bring you to a cell in London's White Tower, chained to a wall.

He thought of this now as he followed the gaoler down the rotting wooden stairs that led to the subcrypt, deep in the earth below the chapel of the keep. Although the rain had stopped during the night, the walls still dripped water. Hugh suspected they probably seeped moisture even during the dry summer months. But then perhaps the dripping walls were a blessing, if that was all a man had to drink.

Arianna had warned him that the gaoler would accept no bribe, but it had been laughingly easy to get in—all he'd had to do was trot out his title. There were some benefits, he'd told her, to being the Earl of Chester.

They followed a narrow, low-ceilinged passageway that seemed to be leading into the very bowels of the earth, and stopped before an oak door with a massive iron bolt. Hugh felt Arianna shiver beside him. He wondered whether it was from the cold or the superstitious dread all humans got at the thought of being in a dark hole in the ground that was so much like the grave.

"Let me go first," he said, and his voice bounced hollowly off the stone walls. "We're not sure what we will find."

"It's worth my life to be lettin' ye in here," the gaoler whined. "The king said—"

"Shut up," Hugh growled. "Or your life won't be worth the spit it takes to say your name."

The gaoler's breath came out in another wheezing whistle, clouding around his face. But his keys clanked against the bolt of the door. A grating sound echoed, and then the door groaned open.

Hugh stepped inside the tiny cell.

It was like walking into the darkness of death. The air was fetid and damp, with a smooth feel to it, like velvet. The very walls seemed to shiver with the cold, but it was an old cold, of a place that had never known the sun. He beckoned to the gaoler to pass him the torch.

The man inside lay on a pile of filthy straw against a wall that oozed black slime. His eyes had squeezed shut at the sudden flare of light and he flung his arm over his face. Hugh stuck the torch into a bracket on the wall, then turned to study his brother.

Raine sat up and then got slowly to his feet. He moved stiffly, like an old pair of bellows, and the heavy chains that bound his ankles to the wall clanked and clattered against the stone. His eyes, glinting silver in the flickering torchlight, stared at Hugh out of a gaunt, bearded face. There was a resigned look in those familiar gray eyes, the look of a man quietly waiting to die . . . wanting to die.

"Raine . . . big brother," Hugh said, and to his shock his voice sounded unused, as if he had been the one locked in a hole for the past two months. "I've a surprise for you."

Raine stared at him, saying nothing. In the dim light it was hard to see his face, but Hugh thought it bore the look of a man for whom there were no surprises left.

Hugh motioned at the door where the gaoler still stood and the man ushered Arianna inside.

She made a tiny mewling sound when she saw him, like a lost kitten, and Raine's head snapped up. For a moment he simply stared at her—stiff, unmoving, as if he could not let himself believe. Because to believe and then to be disappointed was more than a soul could bear.

With a stifled sob, Arianna threw herself into his arms.

His head fell forward and he rubbed his face in her hair. His head fell back again, and his lids squeezed shut. Hugh, suddenly embarrassed for him, thrust the gaping gaoler from the cell, shutting the door.

Raine's fists were clenching and unclenching in her hair. His cheeks were wet with tears. She pulled his head down, and their mouths came together. He drank of her mouth the way a man dying of thirst would suck on a costrel of water.

He shuddered hard, and held her tightly against him. "Arianna . . ."

They stayed that way a long time, moving back and forth in a slow rocking motion. She leaned back within the circle of his arms and stared at his face. She ran a finger along the scar Henry had given him, now a thin red line beneath the curve of his cheekbone. "I didn't die," she said, and there were both tears and a smile in her voice. "And my scar is uglier than yours."

"Oh, God . . ."

His fingers rubbed her cheeks as if he were gathering up her tears to save them. "What a babe you are," he said, and she gave him a watery laugh that cracked on a sob.

Again she touched his face, the scar. "You have not lost your land, Raine. Father has taken back Rhuddlan, but he only keeps it for you. Do you mind this?"

Raine shook his head, but Hugh suspected he hadn't really heard, didn't really care. He was running his fingers over her face again and again, as if to assure himself that she was real. "What of—" His voice cracked and he had to start again. "What of our babes?"

"They're with my mother on the Isle of Môn. They thrive, Raine."

"This is all very touching," Hugh said suddenly. Christ, it was damn near making *him* cry. "But we have some important matters to discuss and there isn't much time. I have devised a plan, big brother, whereby tomorrow night you will escape from this tower."

The announcement hung there in the dank air of the cell. Then Raine said, "Why?" as Hugh had known he would. For his brother knew, better than anyone, to expect no charity from the Earl of Chester.

" 'Tis very simple really," Hugh drawled, lifting his elegant shoulders in a lazy shrug. "Because I want a night with your wife. She has agreed to give me the use of her delectable body for one sweet night, in return for which I will put all my considerable resources to bear on seeing that you escape. Of course, neither in nor out of the Tower are you welcome any longer in England. You'll have to spend the rest of your life in dreary little Wales, I fear, but in a manner of speaking you were near enough to done as doing that anyway . . ."

He let his voice trail off, pleased with the results of his little pronouncement.

Arianna hadn't expected him to blurt their agreement out like that—he could see by the stunned shock on her face. And Raine . . . his brother had that look he always got as a boy when he was about to be given a beating. Rigid and gathered into himself, all prepared to take something that was going to hurt, to hurt like hell.

He pushed his wife away from him, holding her at arm's length. "You have agreed to this?"

"Raine—"

He shook her slightly. *"Have* you?"

Her head bowed. Raine let go of her and Hugh began to smile. He watched the change come over his brother, saw his eyes turn empty, his face harden. He had counted on this—that Raine had always been too damn proud for his own good. How quickly, Hugh thought, we revert to what we are.

"I forbid it," Raine said to Arianna's bent head, his voice hard and flat as well.

Her head snapped back up. "You have nothing to say to it. It is my decision and I have made it."

She started to turn away from him, then she whipped back around, reaching for him. "Raine—"

He jerked out of her grasp, his chains clattering.

She stood before him, stiff as a lance, her hands fisted at her sides, and tears wet on her face. "Damn you, Raine. I want you with me again, I want you to live! I would do anything, anything—"

"Don't whore for me!"

She flinched as if he'd slapped her. Head held rigid, she turned to Hugh. "I'm ready to leave now," she said, and she started for the half-open door. Raine watched her go, a wistful yearning leaping into his eyes before he shuttered them again.

Hugh turned Arianna over to the gaoler and then came back for the torch. Raine was sagging against the wall, and Hugh realized to his shock that his brother must be weak. From hunger probably, and from being shut away from the light for so long. Hugh removed the torch from the bracket, holding it over his head. He could see more of the cell now, and he shuddered. It really was a vile place. Some unspeakable filth covered the dirt floor, and the slime on the walls was not black, it was a strange iridescent green. His skin began to itch. When he got back to Winchester, he thought, he would soak for an hour in a hot bath and throw away everything that he was wearing.

"Hugh . . ."

Hugh turned back from the door.

"Don't do this to her," Raine whispered softly.

"I'm not doing it to her, I'm doing it to you. I owe you this, Raine. I've owed this to you for years. I want you to spend every night of your marriage as I have spent mine. From now on when you lay between your wife's slender white thighs I want you knowing that another has been there before you."

Raine's head fell back against the wall, his eyes closing. "Do you want me to beg?" he asked.

Hugh laughed. "I must admit the image of you on your knees before me does have a certain appeal. But I prefer to picture you as you will be tonight, lying on your miserable pile of straw and imagining Arianna being pleasured in my bed."

Raine's eyes came slowly open. "I will kill you for this."

Hugh cocked his head, his golden curls sliding softly over his shoulder, as he thought about it. "No, you won't," he finally said. "Because I will never fight you. And you are much too honorable a knight for murder."

Hugh, Earl of Chester, paused with his hand on the latch to his bedchamber door. He thought about knocking, then didn't.

She had been standing before the window, and she

whirled, her hand going to her throat. She stared at him, her eyes wide, then she smoothed her hand down over her breasts. It was an unconsciously nervous gesture, but it caused a stirring in Hugh's groin.

She wore only a scarlet robe of soft vair. She was naked underneath.

"Take it off," Hugh said.

She undid the sash at the waist and let the robe slip back over her shoulders, to fall into a scarlet pool, like blood, at her feet. Moonbeams spilled through the window of fine translucent linen, bathing her with a silver light. It was so quiet he could hear her breathe.

She was too thin and the scar on her chest showed mean and red. Yet, still, there was a ripeness about her. She is a creature of the earth, earthy, he thought. Lusty. She would probably scream and claw a man's back when she peaked. His sex responded, swelling and hardening.

Slowly, he came to stand before her, and she watched him with eyes that were the dark green of a forest at night and just as empty. He wondered what she saw as she looked at him.

He brought his hand up to track the curve of her neck. He saw the effort it took her to keep from shuddering, and he admired her for it. She and his brother were really well suited, he thought, both so damn brave and honorable. He doubted Sybil would ever make such a sacrifice for a man, even one she claimed to love.

He let his hand drift downward, to brush across the peaks of her breasts, back and forth, back and forth, and after a moment her nipples began to harden. But he saw no pleasure on her face. "Do you think you could try to enjoy this?" he said, an edge to his voice.

Her lips curled into a sneer. "Enjoying this was no part of our bargain, my lord earl."

He turned away from her, went to the table and poured himself some wine. He studied her while he drank. Clouds had shrouded the moon and now her skin glowed golden in the soft candlelight, like honey. Only a faint band of color across her sharp cheekbones betrayed her embarrassment to be standing naked in front of him.

"You don't have to go through with it, you know," he said. "You could take your chances with King Henry—he's always had a weakness for a pretty face. Or you could try to buy your husband's freedom yourself. Raine hardly appears filled with gratitude for this grand sacrifice you're all set to make on his behalf."

"Raine is being a fool," she said, her voice low. "For it is not so unforgivable a thing, what I do. I would sleep with the devil, I would whore in the streets, I would spread my legs for every man in England, to save his life."

"And his pride would never forgive you for it."

Her head came up. "It matters not. I would do it anyway. I *am* doing it."

"No . . ." He set the wine cup on the table with a sharp click. "No, I do believe that you are not."

He picked up the discarded robe and held it out to her.

She didn't take it. Her breath rasped in her chest as she sucked it in. "Please, you cannot renege on our agreement now. Please . . . I will try to pretend that you pleasure me. I—"

He laughed. Even Sybil had never bothered to pretend. He pushed the robe into her hands. "Nay, girl, it isn't you. I've thought about it, you see, and I've discovered there are certain flaws in my logic. If you lie with me out of love for Raine, it can hardly be equated to my wife lying with me while she dreams of my brother. In both instances, I'm only getting another man's leavings."

There was another reason, too, although he would never say it aloud. Raine, with his easy courage; Raine, with his arrogant knight's code that he pretended to scoff at, but in truth would have died for; Raine, with his hopeless, naive yearning to believe that there really was truth and goodness in this God-rotted world—Raine had always been the man Hugh wished that he could be. There had been many times over the years when he had hated his brother. But there were other times when he had never loved anyone more.

Hugh shook his head, laughing at himself.

Arianna held the robe in her hands, her fingers clenched white in the deep red cloth. "Do . . . do you mean still to go through with the escape?"

Hugh poked his tongue into his cheek and cocked his head. "Well, I can hardly watch my poor brother come to a bad end on Tyburn Hill. It would be a blot on our father's good name." He picked up the cup of wine again to study it. "You know, I never understood why Raine always tried so hard to earn the old earl's respect and love." His lips curled slightly. "He was the true bastard in our family."

He looked up. Arianna still stood with the robe clutched in her hands, her eyes on his face, wide and desperate. "I do suggest you put that back on," he drawled, "before I'm moved to change my mind."

When she had covered herself he came again to stand before her. To his own surprise he bent over and dropped a brotherly-like kiss on the end of her nose. "Stay here the night. Bolt the door if you'll feel the better for it, though on my honor, miserable as it is, your virtue is safe from me."

He turned quickly away from her before he changed his mind.

At the door he paused. She stood in the middle of the room, her hands holding the edge of the robe together at her breasts, her lips parted slightly open, in surprise still, or perhaps relief. She really was quite lovely. For a moment he cursed his conscience, which had at this belated time in his life suddenly decided to make an appearance. The trouble was, lovely as she was, she wasn't Sybil. It was really ironic when you thought about it. Here he was, handsome as sin, richer than the Pope, a damned earl, for Christ's sake—he could command any woman to spread her legs for him with but a snap of his fingers. Even Sybil, the bitch, had to open her legs for him.

But she wouldn't open her heart. And that was where the irony came in. Because if she would have loved him, even just a little, he never would have had any desire to bed any others.

If she loved him, even just a little, he could have forgiven her for Raine.

He bowed farewell to his brother's wife, his mouth jerking into a mocking smile. "Behold, villainy is redeemed."

28

The king's gaoler groaned at the sight of the elegant earl sauntering toward him down the length of the White Tower's great hall. This time the man had a priest in tow instead of a woman.

What now? the gaoler thought. What bloody now?

"Ye can't see the prisoner," the gaoler said as the earl came up to him, all sleek smiles on his fair and handsome face. "It's near curfew time."

"But this was the soonest I could get the priest," the earl said, looking disappointed. "The prisoner informed me yesterday that he sought the comfort of a man of God."

"He can seek all he wants, but he won't be gettin'. It's worth my life, it is, to be lettin' all of cursed London in and out his cell like it were a bloody toll gate."

The earl leaned forward and the gaoler caught a whiff of some spicy perfume. "I spoke to the king this morning, do you understand me," the earl said, his voice low and confidential. "The king does not want his prisoner denied the absolution of God. The man is close to confessing." One of the earl's lids closed in a sly wink. "A confession might be very useful to the king when the issue comes to trial. Eh?"

The gaoler's gaze wandered over to the man in a grease-stained black cassock who stood beside the earl. The gaoler knew this priest—he was curé at All Hallow's Barking, and he was supposed to be ministering to the souls within the Tower as well, although in the gaoler's opinion he ministered more often to a bread trencher and an ale cup.

"Oh, very well," the gaoler said in a petulant whine. "Come along, come along. I'll take him his bloody priest. Christ bejesus . . ."

Raine lay on the straw in the crushing darkness, waiting. With his iron will he did not let himself think, he simply waited.

The door grated open, and the gaoler entered, holding aloft a torch. A fat man in a black cassock followed on his heels. "Here's yer priest," the gaoler said. "Take all the comfort ye want, but be quick about it."

There was a flicker of movement behind him and the gaoler half turned . . . to be struck in the back of the head by the hilt of a gem-studded dagger.

"Hullo, big brother," Hugh said, with a flash of white teeth. He bent over and fished the keys off the gaoler's inert body, tossing them at Raine.

"What are you *doing?*" the priest squealed.

"Escaping," Hugh said. "Take off your cassock, Father."

The priest thrust a dimpled chin into the air. "I will not."

Hugh jabbed the fat man in the stomach with the point of his dagger. "Take it off before I poke a hole in your belly and let out some of the hot air."

Whimpering, the priest pulled his cassock off over his head. He wore nothing underneath and his flesh looked like whale blubber in the flickering torchlight. Raine snatched the garment from the priest's hands. Christ, he felt so weak and dizzy, and even this little bit of light was stabbing at his eyes.

Hugh took Raine's chains and fastened them around the priest's plump wrists, threatening to break the man's teeth with the dagger's hilt if he didn't quit his bawling. He looked down at the gap between Raine's dirty bare feet and the hem of the cassock and his mouth curved into one of his mocking smiles. "I should have picked a taller priest. Don't you want to know how Arianna is? How we passed the night together?"

"I'm going to kill you," Raine said.

"Well, you can do that later. Right now we have to get out of here."

"You can't leave me down here like this!" the priest cried. "I'll freeze."

"Pray then for the heat of hell," Hugh said, and pushed Raine out the door, laughing.

They were crossing the Tower courtyard when the curfew bells began to ring. And then they heard the shouts of alarm.

"Hell," Hugh said, picking up his pace into a quick walk for they did not want to attract attention. "That gaoler must have a head harder than a Yule log. We're going to have to run once we get out the gate. Are you up to it?"

Raine glowered at him. "I can still beat you in a race, brother."

Hugh grinned at him. "You're on."

The guards, still confused over what the commotion was about, had started to shut the gate, but their attention was on the men spilling out the doors of the hall. Raine and Hugh slipped beneath the falling portcullis and disappeared into the dark labyrinth of London's narrow lanes and crooked alleys.

Because it was after curfew, the streets were nearly empty. The roofs of the tightly packed houses met to-

gether overhead, shutting out the night's faint bit of
moonlight. Without torches to light their way it was difficult to see where they were going, but the darkness was a
blessing as well, for pounding feet and hoarse shouts followed after them.

When Raine began to doubt if he could run much farther, they pulled up within the deep shadows cast by the
portal of a church.

"We wait here," Hugh panted into the sudden silence.
For a moment at least they had eluded pursuit. "That red-
headed squire of yours is bringing a cart. Arianna claims
he's reliable. We'd better pray that she's right."

The blood rushed in Raine's ears, and his heart
pounded. He was amazed and frightened at how much
two months in prison had weakened him. He wanted to
ask if Arianna would be with the cart, but he didn't.

But Hugh, as he so often could, read his thoughts.
"She's waiting for us in that old abandoned mill on the
road to Chester."

Us.

Hot and bitter jealousy seared the back of Raine's
throat, nearly making him choke, and his vision blurred
with rage. He squeezed his eyes shut, drawing in a deep
breath, and he saw Arianna's face—so proud, so defiant
. . . so full of love for him. He knew his wife, knew that
she would have taken no pleasure in Hugh's bed. Instead
she had allowed herself to be degraded, used, broken, and
she had done it for him.

Slowly, Raine opened his eyes and looked at his
brother and in that single moment, though Hugh didn't
know it, he was close enough to death to feel the heat of
the devil's breath.

Hugh pressed his fist against his chest. "Christ, my
heart feels like it's about to burst. I must be getting old."

Raine pulled his lips back in a sharp smile. "You always
were soft, little brother.

"And you've always been an ungrateful bastard. In

case you haven't noticed, I just saved your neck from a very nasty predicament."

"Aye, and Henry will not be pleased with you."

"Henry be buggered. He'll have to bend over and take it. The kings of England have always needed the earls of Chester much more than we have needed any cursed king. Here's the cart."

Iron wheels rattled on stones. A cart rounded the corner and pulled up to the church and Taliesin's querulous voice floated to them out of the darkness. "Couldn't you do a simple thing like escape from the Tower without rousing all of London in the process? Goddess preserve me—"

"Halt in the king's name!"

A pair of archers burst out of the alley. One carried a torch, casting a light that splashed onto the church's stone wall and bounced off Taliesin's golden helmet, blinding Raine's eyes. He heard the *whoosh* of an arrow. Then Hugh cried out, sagging against him.

Raine staggered a moment under Hugh's sudden dead weight. He still couldn't see, but he managed somehow to heave Hugh into the bed of the cart, which seemed to be filled with some kind of straw. Taliesin snapped the reins and the cart jerked forward. With a running step, Raine grabbed the tailboard and pulled himself on board.

As the cart rattled at breakneck speed through the black, deserted streets, Raine ran his hands over his brother's body, searching for the wound. He felt the wet stickiness of blood, but no arrow. Then in the intermittent flickers of moonlight, he saw that, while the shaft had been broken off, the arrowhead was still deeply imbedded in Hugh's left buttock.

It seemed Taliesin sent the cart at random down whatever street or alley looked the darkest and most impassible. Then he made a sharp turn and drove through a crumbling stone arch and into the burned-out shell of an abandoned slaughterhouse.

The place stank, of old blood and rotting entrails. The fire had destroyed the roof, so that the night sky showed dark and shadowy through the fallen timbers overhead. "We'll stop here a moment, my lord," Taliesin said. "Just till the pursuit dies off a bit."

Hugh stirred, brushing against Raine's legs. "What the hell am I lying in?"

"Rushes," Raine said.

"It smells worse than dung." Hugh took a deep, hitching breath. "No, you're right, it smells like summer. Summer grass. I used to watch you . . . you and Sybil—" He gasped in pain. "What a jest this is. I'm dying from an arrow meant for you."

"Christ, Hugh, no one ever died of an arrow in his arse."

After a short silence, Hugh said, "Is that where it is? How embarrassing."

Raine tried unsuccessfully to smother a laugh. "I'm sorry."

"Aye, you would be . . . always so damned noble." He drew in shallow, rasping breath. "I hate you. I've always hated you.

"No, you don't."

In the distance Raine heard more shouts and the patter of running feet.

Hugh groaned. "Christ . . . It hurts enough, I ought to be dying."

"Look at it this way, little brother—you'll be left with a scar that will certainly intrigue the ladies."

Hugh heaved a ragged laugh. "Still, it's a pity, mayhap, that I am not dying. Since I have no heirs, Chester would go to Sybil and the king would become her guardian. Then he could marry her off to some other poor ass who would have to share his bed with you."

"I was never in your bed, Hugh."

"You were there. You were there."

Taliesin's white face suddenly appeared before them.

"My lord, the search is coming this way. There's a boat waiting for us beneath the Southwark bridge and horses on the other side. But we'll have to make a run for the river."

"My brother can't run."

A ragged laugh came from the bed of rushes. "What did I tell you? Noble. A noble fool." Hugh's hands reached up to grab Raine's tunic. "Listen, big brother . . . about me and Arianna, we—" But whatever he was about to say remained trapped behind his lips, for in the next instant he had fainted.

"My lord," Taliesin said, grabbing Raine's arm. "Your brother the earl will be all right for the time it takes me to lead the king's men away from here. Then I'll come back for him. Even if the king's men find him, Henry can do naught but bluster against the earl for helping you to escape. Chester is too powerful an enemy to make."

Raine looked down at his unconscious brother. He hated Hugh for what he had done to Arianna, but as usual a part of him couldn't let go of the Hugh he had fought and played with, and yes, loved when they were boys.

"But you, my lord, must leave now," Taliesin was saying, beginning to sound a bit panicked. "Give me the cassock and I shall lead them off your scent. Here, you take this."

The squire pushed his golden helmet against Raine's chest. Raine took it, turning it over in his hands. The metal felt warm, hot, in truth. It felt alive. "Arianna is convinced this thing is magic and that you are a wizard."

The boy hooted. "Females! The notions they get sometimes."

A man's bull-throated shout echoed though the burntout shell. The king's men were indeed getting closer. Raine was turning the helmet over and over in his hands, thinking of Arianna. "Aye . . . the notions they get."

Taliesin tugged at the cassock, jerking it off over

Raine's head, for his master was being sluggish in getting out of it. "You are not to let your pride stop you from going to her," he said, sounding like a king issuing a command.

Raine's lips tightened, but he said nothing.

"Whatever she did, it was done for love of you." Taliesin stared at him, his eyes glittering moonsilver from out of the darkness. Raine had the oddest thought that they were no longer eyes at all, but stars. Stars shining for all eternity in a perpetual night.

Taliesin spoke to him from out of this night, nearly singing the words. "For love of her, you gave up all that you once held dearest—your title, your land, your honor embodied in the fealty you owed your king." The star-eyes shimmered, brightened. "Do you regret this sacrifice, my lord?"

"No!" Raine said on a sharp expulsion of breath.

"Then do not make her regret hers." The strange light in the squire's eyes dimmed. He turned aside, draping the cassock over his head. "This is your final trial, my lord, please do not bungle it," he said, his voice muffled by the heavy wool. "For this time I cannot be there to see you through it." He heaved a bellowy sigh. "I don't mind telling you these last few years have been very taxing on my feeble strength, what with your pride and my lady's stubbornness. It's no wonder—"

Raine grabbed the boy's shoulders and propelled him through the arch. "Taliesin, if you are going to be a diversion, for the love of Christ, quit flapping your jaws and go be it."

Taliesin started off. Then he turned back. He snatched the helmet out of his master's hands and dropped it down on top Raine's head. "On the off chance that it might indeed be magic, my lord, it would help if you were wearing it."

Again he set off. Again he turned, and running backward, he lifted a hand in farewell. "Goddess be with you, my lord," he whispered.

And Raine knew in that instant he would never see the squire again.

He took off running in the direction opposite of that Taliesin had taken. Before long he heard shouts and the pattering of running feet, but leading off away from him, and he knew the diversion was working.

He had gone about a hundred yards when a white mist began to curl up from the refuse-strewn streets. It seemed to thicken with each step he took, so that before long he was enshrouded in an impenetrable whiteness that was strangely, for mist, dry and warm.

He couldn't see a damn thing. But he could tell where he was by the smell of what coated the streets—urine and dyes in Tanners' Row, blood and entrails in Butchers' Lane, and the sharp tang of acid in Glass Workers' Street. In Goldsmiths' Lane he nearly broke his neck tripping over a heavy chain that was stretched across the street to make the escape of thieves more difficult.

The mist muffled all sounds. Occasionally he heard the rattle of a watchman's iron shaft and the creaking of signboards in the wind, but most of the time he was wrapped up in a swaddling of silence.

The slap of waves against the pier told him he had found the river. That and the smell, which was a noisome combination of night soil, rotting rushes, and fish guts. He found the boat. Across the river, the horse was there, where Taliesin had said it would be.

Raine suddenly realized that on this side of the Thames, the night was as clear and black as a Welsh lake. He looked back, expecting to see the walls and spires of London enshrouded in fog, and was shocked to see the moon hanging slender and silver as a sickle above the White Tower.

He tilted his head back and looked up at the stars. They filled the sky, shimmering and glittering like thousands of diamond flakes tossed into a well. He sucked in a deep breath. He was free, as free as the stars.

He could go south to France, sell his sword to King Louis, perhaps earn himself a new title, a new castle. Or he could go west, toward Wales, where a castle already awaited him, attached to a new liege lord, and an old dream.

Aye, he could go home, home to Wales and Arianna . . . if his pride could but live with the knowledge of the price she had paid.

She stood on top a windswept hill, a bouquet of bell heather cradled in her arms. Above her a golden sun hung suspended in a sky of so vivid a blue it made her eyes ache. Yet within her there dwelled a choking grief, suffocating her heart. She had lost him, lost him, oh God, she had lost him.

In the distance, something moved . . . a man on horseback riding toward her. Hope flared within her, sharp and hot and brilliant, like a spark off flint.

The fiery wind blew harder, searing the skin on her face. The perfume of the heather tickled her nose. Closer he came, at a slow and easy canter. Tears blurred her eyes and she stretched out her arms. The wind snatched at the flowers, blowing them away in a swirl of blue and purple petals.

He reined in halfway up the hill, dismounting, and sunlight shone bright on his golden head. For a moment her disappointment was so sharp she cried aloud with the pain of it. But then he reached up with both hands to his head and she saw that it was a helmet he wore, a golden helmet. He tossed the helmet on the ground, and this time the sunlight glinted off the blue lights in his raven-black hair.

He looked up at her, tense and hesitant as if afraid to come farther, as if unsure of her, of her love, and the thought made her smile, for he was her man and her love for him was indelible and eternal. He took a step toward her.

She laughed, hysterical with joy, and began running down the hill, running to her one true love. His arms wrapped around her, hard and strong, and she settled into his embrace as if coming home after a long, long time away.

His voice flowed over her, warm like the wind. "I love you, Arianna. God, God, I love you."

She tilted back her head to see his face, the face of her beloved.

"I told you that I would wait," she said.

"Aye."

"I will always be waiting, Raine."

"Aye," he said again.

He held her tight and spun her around and around, and the wind took with it the sound of their laughter, so that it went on and on and on, carried along the circle of time.

Epilogue

It was a perfect day for seeing the floating island. The sky overhead was the deep blue of cornflowers, but a mist hugged the marshes and blanketed the sea in a soft, thick whiteness, like fleece.

The girl sat on a boulder, her arms wrapped around her knees. The boulder had once been part of the circle of standing stones at her back, though it stood no longer, having been stricken by lightning and knocked down during some long-ago storm. The girl came here often, to this place, to think. And to look out to sea on misty days like this one, hoping for a glimpse of the floating island.

"Arianna?"

Startled, the girl spun around, dropping her knees. A frail old man stood before her, stooped and bent. His pale hands were wrapped around a shepherd's crook. His face was thin and yellow, like old parchment, and only a few white wisps of hair were left to decorate his head. She had never seen him before in her life.

"How—how did you know my name?"

He smiled. He had a nice smile. "You look like an Arianna I once knew."

"Perhaps it was my great-grandmother. I was named

for her." Excitement stirred the girl's breast, for she had always been fascinated by her great-grandparents, and here was someone, besides family, who might actually have known them.

She patted the stone beside her. "Will you take a seat, good sir? What was this Arianna like? Have you stories to tell?"

A chuckle rumbled out of the old man, strangely deep and youthful to have come from such a thin, old chest. "Oh, aye, I know stories. . . ." He settled onto the stone beside her, sighing softly. "Arianna knew a great love."

The girl sighed, too, for this fitted so exactly all the tales she had heard of her great-grandmother.

"Aye. My great-grandmother was mad with love, they say, for her husband. He was a great knight," she said with pride. "He was English, but he had a falling out with his king and so he became an honorary son of Gwynedd." She pointed to a fortress of stone that sat on a bluff above the river. "He built that castle. Do you think she might be the same Arianna, the one you knew?"

"Well, it was a very long time ago."

She searched his face. "Grandmother says they went to the floating island. Do you think this could be true? It is a magical place, the island, like the Isle of Avalon where King Arthur sleeps. Grandmother says that on the island Raine and Arianna are forever young and forever in love. And on misty days like this one, sometimes it parts, the mist does, and you can see the island floating right out there on the horizon." She pointed out to the mist-enshrouded sea. "I've never seen it, though, have you?"

"Oh, yes. Many times."

"Truly!" She squinted, trying to peer through the mist. "Well, I wish that I could see it just once."

"You only have to believe in it, and someday you will see."

The girl squeezed her eyes shut, believing, believing, and trying to will the island to appear.

The old man had a sack tied to the hook of his staff. He took it off now, opening it, and drew out a small, battered bowl. She wondered if the bowl was made of gold, for it shone brightly and its rim, she noticed, was studded with what looked to be real pearls. She thought the bowl must be very, very old. Like the man himself.

He held the bowl out to her. "This," he said, "belongs to you. I have been keeping it for you."

"Oh, I cannot accept that," the girl said, shocked. For if the bowl was gold and those *were* pearls, then it must be very valuable.

"But I told you, it is not a gift—" He stopped himself, muttered something that sounded like *Why must I always get the stubborn ones?* then said, "Please. I am a very old man with no one to give things to. And besides, it belonged for a time to your great-grandmother."

"It did? Truly?" She looked at the old, battered bowl with greater interest. Then, smiling shyly, she took it.

The old man coughed, cleared his throat. "Er . . . you don't hold any odd prejudices, do you?"

She looked up from the bowl to the old man's face. "Prejudices?"

"Aye. For instance, what would you say if your father were to tell you that you were to be wedded to a Scot?"

"A Scot!" She started to laugh and then she saw that he was serious and she shuddered. "I'd sooner marry the devil."

The old man heaved an enormous sigh and this time mumbled something that sounded oddly like *Goddess preserve me.*

He sat and ruminated in silence a moment, then asked out of nowhere, "Does your father have a bard?"

She laughed at the question. This was Wales, after all. "Yes. Of course."

"Any good, is he?"

"I suppose so. He composes beautiful love songs."

"But your father could always use another bard, couldn't he?"

"I suppose so," she said again.

Again the old man seemed to lose himself in thought. With a surprising spryness for such a very old man, he stretched to his feet. It took her a moment to realize he was leaving.

She sprang up after him. "Wait! I haven't thanked you for . . . I don't even know your name."

He turned around. A boyish smile creased his weathered face and his black eyes glittered with a white light, as if slivers of the moon had been caught within them. "My name is Taliesin," he said.

The girl watched the old man hobble down the beach. She looked down into the bowl she cradled in her hands. The metal felt warm against her palms and it seemed to surge and pulse as if alive.

As she looked down into the bowl's golden depths she thought she saw a man and a woman twirling around and around on top of a hill full of heather, their mouths open in laughter. But in the next instant they were gone.

The girl laughed at herself. It was only the sun that made the bowl feel warm and the image she had seen of the whirling couple were the clouds reflecting in the bowl's shiny bottom.

She looked down the beach again. But the old man was gone.

Then she saw it, far out to sea . . . the mist parted and there it was, the island! In the time it took her to draw breath, the mist closed up again and the island was gone.

But she was sure, oh yes, she was sure that she could hear a man and woman laughing.

AUTHOR'S NOTE

For the purposes of this novel, I have constricted the passage of time and altered a few historic events to suit my romantic inclination to make things turn out happily ever after. A *bardd teulu* would tell you that such is the right of all storytellers.

In 1157, Henry II of England did invade Wales. At the time, it was not a country so much as a collection of tiny kingdoms with a predilection for fighting more among themselves than against their common enemy. But there did emerge a strong leader in Owain, Prince of Gwynedd. And he fought Henry to a standstill.

Owain and Henry signed a truce, whereby the English king recognized the right of the Welsh to rule themselves. In return Owain swore fealty to Henry. He also gave up Rhuddlan Castle and the lands known as the Tegeingl, and he surrendered two of his sons as hostages. (Owain, the Prince of Gwynedd, had nine sons by three different women. The history books neglect to mention whether he had any daughters.)

One hot August seven years later, Henry invaded Wales again. The English were crossing the Berwyn mountain range when they were struck by a freakish rainstorm. Henry's army, already decimated by the storm, was attacked by the Welsh and destroyed. Henry flew into one of his famous rages and ordered his Welsh hostages blinded. The command was carried out, but even for that violent time many were sickened when they learned of Henry's retribution. It was an act of barbarism he never lived down.

The rainstorm that was Henry's undoing was unseasonable and violent, seeming to come out of nowhere and then disappearing just as quickly—yet the result was that once again the hated English were driven from Wales. Welsh liberty was preserved.

As for that strange and violent storm—historians have never been able to explain it. Some say it never really happened after all, but is only folklore as sung by bards. Yet this much is known: in all the Celtic tales of *magi,* the wizards all share the same powers . . . and one of those powers is the ability to conjure storms out of a clear blue sky.

Romance is part of the blood and earth of Wales. That tiny country is the birthplace of some of the most romantic tales ever recorded. Of King Arthur and the Knights of the Round Table, of Tristan and Isolde. And of that quintessential wizard, Merlin, or Myrddin as he is called in Welsh. The origins of these tales go back to the time of the Celts, and in these earlier stories there ran a common theme—that a man could be redeemed by the spiritual and physical love of a woman. Often he was sent on a quest to win the woman's love, and once won, the woman's love in turn gave him immortal life.

What stories these are, what lessons they teach us. That the redemption of mankind comes through woman, for she takes man's seed, nurtures it within her, and brings it forth into the world. That love is often a quest, to be earned and deserved before it is given. That love can be lusty and earthy, as well as emotional and spiritual. . . .

But above all that love is forever.

Starting in 1992,
there's a new place to find the hottest paperback bestsellers.